Selected Short Stories of
WILLIAM DEAN
HOWELLS

Selected Short Stories of
WILLIAM DEAN
HOWELLS

EDITED BY RUTH BARDON

OHIO UNIVERSITY PRESS

Athens, Ohio

Ohio University Press, Athens, Ohio 45701
© 1997 by Ruth Bardon
Printed in the United States of America
All rights reserved. Published 1997

Swallow Press/Ohio University Press books are printed on acid-free paper ∞ ™

01 00 99 98 97   5 4 3 2 1

Frontispiece: Engraving by W. B. Closson, from a painting by F. P. Vinton (1881).
Book design by Chiquita Babb

Library of Congress Cataloging-in-Publication Data
Howells, William Dean, 1837–1920.
 [Short stories. Selections]
 Selected short stories of William Dean Howells / edited by Ruth
Bardon.
  p. cm.
 Includes bibliographical references (p.) and index.
 ISBN 0-8214-1193-4 (cloth : alk. paper). — ISBN 0-8214-1194-2
(pbk. : alk. paper)
 1. United States—Social life and customs—19th century—Fiction.
2. United States—Social life and customs—20th century—Fiction.
3. Europe—Social life and customs—Fiction. I. Bardon, Ruth.
II. Title.
PS2022.B37H69   1997
813'.4—dc21
                                                      97-14161
                                                        CIP

in memory of my husband,
John Browning (1957–1994),
and my father,
Jack Bardon (1925–1993)

Contents

Acknowledgments

I would like to thank a number of people for their assistance: Thomas Wortham, George Hendrick, David J. Nordloh, Susan Harris, and Lewis Simpson, for their gracious replies to my inquiries; staff members of the interlibrary loan department of the University of North Carolina at Chapel Hill, for their doggedness; Richard Rust, for his encouragement; Randy Kafka, for her careful proofreading; and Christine Hait, for her support. I would like to thank William White Howells for the Estate of W. D. Howells and the Houghton Library of Harvard University for permission to use excerpts from some of Howells's unpublished materials. I would also like to thank the babysitters who made it possible for me to work: Pam Hull, Felisha McGill, Carol Mozell, Carrie Clarke, Anna Harwell and Maria Bowie; and to thank Beth and Daniel Browning, my sweet and wonderful children. My greatest appreciation is reserved for Everett Emerson, whose patience and whose real understanding of my priorities over many years enabled me to persevere.

Chronology

1875   *A Foregone Conclusion.*

1879   *The Lady of the Arastook.*

1880   *The Undiscovered Country.*

1881   *A Fearful Responsibility, Dr. Breen's Practice, A Day's Pleasure and Other Sketches.* Resigns as editor of the *Atlantic*, begins serializing stories in the *Century.* Health of Winifred, Howells's oldest child, failing. Howells has protracted illness.

1882   *A Modern Instance.*

1882–83   Travels in Europe.

1885   *The Rise of Silas Lapham.*

1886   *Indian Summer.* Begins writing regularly for *Harper's Monthly.* Haymarket Square riot.

1887   *The Minister's Charge.* Reviews Tolstoy's *Que Faire* in *Harper's.*

1888   *April Hopes.* Moves to New York.

1889   Death of Winifred Howells, aged twenty-five. *Annie Kilburn.*

1890   *A Hazard of New Fortunes, The Shadow of a Dream, A Boy's Town.*

1891   *Criticism and Fiction.*

1892   *An Imperative Duty, The Quality of Mercy.*

1893   *Christmas Every Day.*

1894   *A Traveler from Altruria.*

1895   *My Literary Passions.*

1897   *The Landlord at Lion's Head.*

1900   *Literary Friends and Acquaintance.*

1901   *A Pair of Patient Lovers.*

1902   *Literature and Life, The Flight of Pony Baker.*

1903   *Questionable Shapes.*

1904   *The Son of Royal Langbrith.*

1907   *Through the Eye of a Needle, Between the Dark and the Daylight.*

1909   Helps found NAACP.

1910   Death of Elinor Mead Howells. *My Mark Twain.*

1912   75th birthday celebration at Sherry's in New York, President Taft attending.

1916   *New Leaf Mills, Years of My Youth, The Leatherwood God, The Daughter of the Storage.*

1920   *The Vacation of the Kelwyns.*
          Dies, May 11.

Introduction

The achievement of William Dean Howells as novelist, editor, and social and literary critic is no longer in dispute. Although there will always be readers who fail to succumb to his subtle and ironic charm or who are bored by the moral complexity of his characters' lives, Howells is universally recognized as a major writer of his generation, as the leader of the late-nineteenth-century "realism war," and as a truly influential friend and mentor to a stellar list of contemporary and later writers. The Indiana University Press selected edition of his works has surely helped to secure definitively his reputation, as has a host of critical studies and biographies. Amid all this critical attention, however, Howells's importance as a short story writer has been neglected, and my purpose here is to correct this oversight.

There exists no collected edition of Howells's short fiction, and while individual short stories have received some critical treatment, I have found only the briefest critical assessment of Howells *as* a short story writer. Students of American literature who want to read a Howells short story will find one story, "Editha," in a number of readily accessible anthologies, but will have had great difficulty finding any others. They will also have been unable to find an accurate listing of Howells's short fiction. The only bibliography that separately lists Howells's short stories (Vito J. Brenni's *William Dean Howells: A Bibliography*) indiscriminately lumps together stories, travel and character sketches, and "dramatic passages" (what we would call short verse dramas). The "Chronological List of Howells' Fiction" in George C. and Ildikó de Papp Carrington's *Plots and Characters in the Fiction of William Dean Howells* (xix–xxiii) includes such "fiction" as many of the "Editor's Easy Chair" columns of *Harper's Monthly Magazine* (e.g., "The Reviewer and the Easy Chair discuss ethical values in a capitalist system"). This is fiction in the sense that Howells reports on conversations that never actually took place, but it is far from our usual understanding of the term. Finally, the excellent *Bibliography of*

William Dean Howells by William M.Gibson and George Arms lists all of Howells's works strictly chronologically; there is no special listing of "short fiction."

Furthermore, the only previous account of Howells as a short story writer, that written by Paul J. Ferlazzo as an entry in the *Dictionary of Literary Biography* (*Vol. 74: American Short-Story Writers Before 1880*), is riddled with ambiguities and outright errors. For example, Ferlazzo states: "Several stories in *A Pair of Patient Lovers* (1901) deserve mention. In the title story (*Harper's Monthly*, November 1897) Dr. Anther is surprised when, after many years, Mrs. Langbrith finally decides to refuse his proposal of marriage" (169). Any Howells scholar will recognize that Dr. Anther and Mrs. Langbrith are characters in the novel *The Son of Royal Langbrith*, written in 1904, and that these characters make no appearance at all in "A Pair of Patient Lovers." Almost every page of Ferlazzo's account of Howells as a story writer is marred by some sort of misstatement or confusion—and, as far as I know, this article provides the only distinct treatment of Howells as a short story writer. That these errors were not caught and corrected is further testimony to the need for a critical edition of Howells's short fiction.

The lack of an edition of Howells's short stories has distorted how Howells is seen by American literary specialists. Because Howells's novels and essay collections are so readily available (in the Indiana and other editions) and because his stories (and other periodical publications) are so inaccessible, we tend to think of Howells primarily as an author of books. (We also think of him as an editor, but our assessment of him as such draws our attention to the works of those writers whom he befriended and supported, rather than to Howells himself.) We overlook the fact that, in his own time, Howells was widely known as a magazine writer, and a substantial amount of what he wrote for the magazines was short fiction. In the preface to a Howells story that appears in *Current Opinion* (1916), the editor comments: "In his longer and more ambitious novels Mr. Howells sometimes grows tedious to us; in his short stories, sketches and plays, never. In his longer work, we come in contact with an uncompromising Literary Conscience, which we greatly respect but do not always enjoy. In his lighter work, a sportive Fancy is so much in evidence that we do not see the Literary Conscience unless we begin to look for it" (Wheeler 57). While I would argue that the "Literary Conscience" as well as the "sportive Fancy" is evident in most of the short fiction, the editor's words draw attention to his contemporaries' perception of Howells as, in large part, a writer of short pieces for periodicals.

Our perception of Howells is further distorted by the selective nature of the Indiana edition. Howells was an amazingly prolific writer, and the Indiana edition, as catholic as its editors try to make it, is still a selection and thus reflects some editorial bias. My strong feeling is that expanding the Howells canon can only help us to achieve a more accurate view of his total achievement. For Howells's short stories are valuable not only in themselves but as perhaps the best way to get a sense of the variety and complexity of Howells's lifetime achievement. A larger audience for Howells's short stories may lead to a rethinking of Howells's role as a writer, in terms both of his intentions and of his actual influence on the reading public. And because the avenue between writer and audience allows for movement in both directions, Howells's stories, written over a period of some sixty years, surely reflect the changes in his audience and in American literature in general as well.

Howells lived a long life and wrote a great deal, and this has been both a blessing and a curse to the scholar who wishes to know him well. As Clayton Eichelberger wrote in the introduction to his excellent research bibliography, "Where William Dean Howells is concerned, there is no end. Eventually one simply stops" (v). The magnitude of the Howells canon was recognized, of course, in his lifetime. A *Life* magazine reviewer noted in May 1887 that "Mark Twain and Mr. Howells walk around New York with their arms lovingly locked. This is probably done to keep them from writing in the streets" (quoted in Eichelberger 505). And a major part of Howells's continuous activity was the production of short stories. He wrote short stories early (as early as 1853), often (I include forty-six in my annotated story list), and late (his last story was published in 1917, just three years before his death).

Because of their quantity and because of the span of time over which they were written, the stories, taken as a whole, reflect Howells's biography and are of particular interest to those who use, as I do, a historical/biographical approach. The stories also reflect Howells's evolving literary theories: his juvenile enchantment with popular romantic literature; his rejection of this literature in favor of realism; his advances into psychological realism; and his ventures in what John W. Crowley has called the "psychic romance." Howells's stories, perhaps more than his novels, enable us to see that his biography and his ideas about literature are inseparably intertwined. This is most readily apparent in Howells's psychic romances, which clearly grew out of that period when both his life and his art reverberated from the shock of his daughter's death. But the influence of the personal on the artistic is apparent from the start.

The literary theories of writers do not necessarily reflect their lives. But this seems to be the case with Howells. One reason, perhaps, why Howells's biography and his writing seem so closely connected is the consistent morality displayed in both. Howells's personal sense of principle has been well documented and is certainly best represented by his actions in the famous Haymarket incident. A fatal explosion at a labor protest held in Haymarket Square, Chicago, in May of 1886 led to the apparently arbitrary arrests of eight anarchists, seven of whom were quickly found guilty of murder. Howells, recognizing their innocence, wrote a letter to the *New York Tribune* in which he boldly and quite independently called for the commutation of their sentences. The public reacted with anger and astonishment; in Edwin Cady's words, Howells "stood alone" (*Realist* 71), facing a barrage of vitriolic criticism. In an unpublished statement written after four of the anarchists had been hanged and one had committed suicide, Howells expanded on his ideas, writing that the anarchists "died, in the prime of the first Republic the world has ever known, for their opinions' sake." He added: "We have committed an atrocious and irreparable wrong." In his statement, significantly, he linked the gross irresponsibility of the charges with the "gifts of imagination . . . of a romantic novelist" ("A Word for the Dead"). For Howells saw literature, too, as an arena for moral choices. Howells's "open militancy" (Cady, *Realist* 11) toward romantic fiction was expressed largely in the "Editor's Study" columns of *Harper's Monthly*, which ran from 1886 to 1892.[1] And, as Cady points out, "[t]he realistic vision" championed in these columns "was of necessity a moral one" (*Realist* 13). In a sarcastic review of a contemporary novel, for example, Howells wrote: "No sordid details of verity here, if you please; no wretched being humbly and weakly struggling to do right and to be true, suffering for his foibles and his sins, tasting joy only through the mortification of self, and in the help of others; nothing of all this, but a great, whirling splendor of peril and achievement" (*Criticism and Fiction* 52).

Howells's disdain for the romantic novel and his praise for realism were demonstrated, of course, in his own writing. Henry James was speaking of Hawthorne when he said, "He combined in a singular degree the spontaneity of the imagination with a haunting care for moral problems," but the same could certainly be said of Howells (quoted in Mordell 97). The moral crises of Howells's childhood were transformed, in his art, into passion both for the small niceties of social behavior (Howells's famous "teacup realism") and for life-transforming and heart-wrenching cruxes—in Howells's notable words, "the riddle of the painful earth" ("Editor's Easy Chair" [1903] 149). Howells's life and his art moved on parallel, if not concurrent, tracks, and this is clearly related to his well-known assertion that "No man, unless he puts on the mask of fiction, can show his real face or the will behind it. For this reason the only real biographies are the novels . . . " (*YY* 110). Similarly, George Carrington speaks of Howells's "deep need to defend himself by transmuting experience into verbal art" ("Dramatic Essay" 52).

Howells's career as a short story writer falls very roughly into three overlapping phases. The first, represented by such stories as "Not a Love Story" (1859) and "A Dream" (1861), shows the juvenile and unenlightened Howells who copied his favorite writers and used the most literary style he could. The stories he produced are generally bad, but are interesting for the way the incipient realist frequently asserts himself, in a sort of reverse atavism. There are hints of the Howells to come.

The second phase begins with "Tonelli's Marriage" (1868) and continues until the end of Howells's career, demonstrating both Howells's early realism and his later psychological realism. These stories complement Howells's work as an editor and critic and mirror his novels, yet they are also departures from, and in some cases anticipations of, novels. It is highly likely that Howells felt considerable freedom in using the short story form; the brevity and relative temporality of these works allowed him to experiment while taking few risks. The stories allow us to see both emerging themes of later works and blind alleys never to be revisited.

The third phase of Howells's career begins with "A Difficult Case" in 1900 and includes many of the stories that follow, most notably the nine Turkish Room stories (see below pp. 122–24 for a fuller discussion of these stories). These "psychic romances" clearly arose from Howells's search for emotional and spiritual relief after the death of his daughter Winny in 1889. As he put it in early 1890, "And where is she, and shall I ever see her again? The world has largely resolved itself into this question for me" (*SL* 3:269). John Crowley points out the importance of these stories when he notes that "they illuminate a side of [Howells's] work unknown to most readers. That Howells should have written psychic stories at all confounds the conventional view of him as a 'realist'" (*Mask* 133). The fact that Howells, the realist, wrote romances should be less startling, in light of the fact that Howells pointedly distinguished between romance and romanticism: "Romance, as in Hawthorne, seeks the effect of reality in visionary conditions; romanticism, as in Dickens, tries for a visionary effect in actual conditions" (quoted in Cady, *Light of Common Day* 135). Howells, of course, came down on the side of the romance. (Howells's admiration for the romance is well documented by Sarah B. Daugherty in "Howells Reviews James: The Transcendence of Realism" and by Louis J. Budd in "W. D. Howells' Defense of the Romance.")

The terms "psychological realism" and "psychic romance" are useful but fuzzy, as many stories (for example, "A Sleep and a Forgetting") display hallmarks of both. "Psychological realism" is the term used by Edwin Cady and others to describe Howells's application of the realistic technique ("the truthful treatment of material" [*Criticism and Fiction* 38]) to psychological material, that is, to stories concerning people facing mental as well as moral crises. "Psychic romance" is best defined by Crowley when he says: "More intently than psychologism [psychological realism], psychic fiction would explore the mystical side of life and the conundrum of immortality" (*Mask* 135). And Crowley, of course, notes the link between Howells's interest in these areas and Winny's death, which "devastated Howells and compelled him to reconsider his religious beliefs, or, more accurately, his lack of them" (*Mask* 136).

The death of Winifred Howells has been treated at length by many critics, most notably by John Crowley in "Winifred Howells and the Economy of Pain," which was revised slightly for inclusion in *The Mask of Fiction: Essays on W. D. Howells*. Winny's problems began in her teenage years, when she was subject to unexplained spells of weakness, vertigo, and depression. Her symptoms (which closely fit our modern diagnosis of anorexia) continued for nine years, with frequent remissions and relapses, as the Howellses tried various home remedies and professional cures, culminating in their decision to entrust Winny's care to S. Weir Mitchell. She died, his patient, in 1889, when she was twenty-five. Howells's grief was compounded by his sense of guilt. We will probably never know if Winny's malady was physical, psychological, or some combination of both, but Howells clearly felt that he had unfairly dismissed Winny's pain as delusional, when it was actual. Writing soon after her death, Howells acknowledged "The torment that remains is that perhaps the poor child's pain was all along as great as she fancied" (*SL* 3:247), and at about the same time: "When I am alone I recall and reclaim all I did, and reconstruct the past from this point or that, and dramatize a different course of events in which our dearest one still lives. It is anguish, anguish that rends the heart and brain" (*SL* 3:248). That Howells's writing changed as a result of the tragedy is indisputable. His thoughts turned more and more to "the inner life" (*SL* 4:168) as he began, in the 1890s, "to delve into his past through an intense introspection equivalent to the self-analysis that Freud himself was performing during the same years" (Crowley, "Howells in the Eighties" 262). This introspection also provided the impetus for Howells's imaginative return to his childhood, in such works as *A Boy's Town* and *The Flight of Pony Baker*.

Throughout the three rough phases of Howells's career as a short story writer there appear stories that fall into clear categories. One of these, the category of the nine Turkish Room stories, I have already mentioned. Other categories are: the Dulldale stories, which are set, explicitly or by implication, in a fictional version of Jefferson, Ohio, and the other small towns in which Howells spent most of his youth; the European stories (namely, "Tonelli's Marriage," "At the Sign of the Savage," and "A Sleep and a Forgetting"); Howells's Christmas and holiday stories;[2] his stories for children (the two latter overlap considerably); the two Basil and Isabel March stories ("A Circle in the Water" and "A Pair of Patient Lovers");[3] and what might be called experimental stories, some of which, like "A Feast of Reason," can best be seen as magazine columns or essays that strayed too far and turned into fiction. There are also a number of stories that are followed by sequels, for example, "The Angel of the Lord" and "The Fulfillment of the Pact."

Howells's stories share common characteristics and are linked by a small number of related themes. In fact, it could be argued that the same theme runs through most. Though it has been identified by various labels—the "ethic/aesthetic split" (Klinkowitz), "the theme of false perception" (Carrington, *Drama*), fictionalizing (see below pp. 45–46), juxtaposition (Carrington, *Drama*), the "voltage of alienation" (Carrington, *Drama* 55), or, in Howells's own words, the "psychological juggle" (*YY* 81)—almost all of Howells's stories reflect a sort of double vision, in which the narrator or a character in the story (and so the reader) is faced with two ways of seeing the world. Most commonly, one way is the way of realism or truth or morality, and the other is the way of romanticism or literature or aesthetics. The stories are linked also by their subtlety. One critic notes a contemporary reference to "an English paper that predicted Howells's next story 'would tell how a man stepped on a girl's dress and nothing came of it'" (Eichelberger 383). What is emphasized, of course, although the English reader missed it, is the oftentimes quiet moment of mental illumination—or obfuscation. Characterizing Howells's fiction by comparing it to that of Turgenev, Edwin Cady points out that both "concentrated on character presentation and psychological development, minimizing plot and sensational incident" (*Road* 196). (Actually, the number of sensational incidents in Howells's fiction is surprisingly large.)

Howells's stories have received some critical attention. Almost all of them are listed in the Gibson and Arms bibliography, although, as I have already indicated, these listings are indiscriminate. Most of the stories are summarized in Carrington and Carrington's *Plots and Characters in the Fiction of William Dean Howells*, and these summaries are generally excellent, though again, there is little attempt to isolate the short stories. And individual stories are mentioned in passing or among discussions of other works by many of Howells's major critics, including Edwin Cady, Clara Kirk and Rudolf Kirk, Kenneth Lynn, Kermit Vanderbilt, Van Wyck Brooks and, more recently, Rodney Olsen. There are a number of excellent articles on individual stories (most notably those of Charles Crow on "A Case of Metaphantasmia"; John Crowley and Charles Crow on "A Sleep and a Forgetting"; Robert Marler on "A Dream"; Charles Feigenoff on "His Apparition"; and Myron Simon on "A Romance of Real Life") and a whole slew of criticism on "Editha." And some scholars, in concentrating on sharply defined areas of Howells's work, have paid close and careful attention to groups of stories, most notably Thomas Wortham on Howells's early career and Jerome Klinkowitz and Robert Gillespie on the Basil and Isabel March stories and novels. The most thorough treatment of Howells's short stories is that found in John Crowley's *The Mask of Fiction*, which includes thoughtful analyses of "The Angel of the Lord," "A Difficult Case," "Editha," "His Apparition," and "Though One Rose from the Dead." (I also found that the theories expressed by George Carrington in *The Immense Complex Drama: The World and Art of the Howells Novel* were especially pertinent to Howells's stories.)

Interest in Howells's shorter and more overtly psychological fictions can be seen as a natural consequence of the growing "revisionist" view of Howells. John Crowley, in his introduction to *The Mask of Fiction*, carefully delineates the "revivalist" and "revisionist" schools, explaining that the Howells revival of the 1950s, led by, among others, Edwin Cady, George Arms, Everett Carter, James Woodress, George Bennett, and Olov Fryckstedt, emphasized Howells's conscious control over his material, and his mastery; while the revisionist movement of the seventies and eighties, led by such critics as George Carrington, Kermit Vanderbilt, and Kenneth Lynn, emphasized Howells's psychological conflicts, indeed, his neuroticism (4–11). (My thumbnail summary necessarily ignores the considerable complexities of both schools.) It is easy to see why Howells's psychic romances, for example, provide grist for the revisionist mills. What is surprising is how little attention they have received.

Edwin Cady notes that "In 1884, when [Hamlin Garland] reached the East, he saw that 'all literary Boston was divided into three parts, those who liked [Howells] and read him; those who read him and hated him, and those who just plain hated him'" (*Road* 230). Howells's stories, being so much less accessible than his novels, have probably received more than their fair share of "just plain hate." As recently as 1982, Kenneth Eble wrote: "Howells' short fiction is never likely to win a place as an important contribution to literature. Few stories are anthologized and a thorough reading of his collected volumes of stories does not yield many stories that deserve to be" (170). If one is to dislike Howells, let it be on the basis of knowledge rather than prejudice. There can be little disagreement that Howells's short stories are significant for the light that they cast on his major works, and for what they reveal about contemporary magazines and the tastes of the American public. But I believe that they are valuable and significant in and of themselves, and, once rescued from obscurity and made available in a selected edition, will be well able to hold their own in the critical arena.

-2-

This edition consists of two major parts: 1) a selection of short stories preceded by critical introductions, and 2) an inclusive annotated story list. Choosing which stories to reprint was an easy and pleasant task. I was guided by my desire to choose stories that were characteristic of Howells, while at the same time revealing the variety and complexity of his work. I chose, wherever possible, to include previously uncollected works, as these have been by far the most difficult to locate. I have also applied in my selection traditional principles involving novelty, originality, and forcefulness.

It may seem that the period of time for which Howells is best known, the productive last quarter of the nineteenth century, is underrepresented in this volume. In fact, Howells wrote relatively few stories during these years, and I provide a fair representation (within the space constraints of a collection) of the types of stories he was then writing. Howells wrote four long and rather serious stories between 1894 and 1900 ("A Difficult Case," "A Parting and a Meeting," "A Circle in the Water"and "A Pair of Patient Lovers") and I chose to include only one of these, excluding the less interesting and equally or more lengthy others. My decision to include three of Howells's later Turkish Room stories, on the other hand, was based on his repeated return to this format between the years 1901 and 1913. The Turkish Room was obviously a useful tool, enabling Howells to explore the psychological issues that so occupied him in the later years of his life.

My approach to Howells's work is historical/biographical, and I chose stories that reflect Howells's development. The critical introductions to each story are meant to take advantage of existing criticism, to set forth my own critical responses, and to suggest directions for further scholarship. I have also attempted, wherever possible, to draw parallels between short stories, and to reveal connections between the stories and other aspects of Howells's life and work.

Deciding which stories to include in the annotated story list was an entirely different matter. My purpose is to provide a list that is both comprehensive and exclusive; that is, to include all of Howells's published short stories[4] and to exclude everything else. A number of problems immediately present themselves. The simplest problem is that of originality; Howells's translations from the Spanish, French, and German are usually printed as such, and Howells himself provided accounts of his translations in *Years of My Youth* (126–27). (Of course, my concern is to determine which of the short stories assigned to Howells are original and which are translations; I leave to others the much more difficult issue of deciding which translations published in such papers as the *Ashtabula Sentinel* were done by Howells and which by other writers.) Another simple problem is the question of intention: did Howells intend for the piece of work in question to stand alone or was it meant to be part of a larger work? This again is easy to answer; chapters of "The Flight of Pony Baker" or even "A Boy's Town," although they were first printed independently in magazines, clearly are meant to be part of a unified whole.

A more complicated problem is that of authorship. While I have relied heavily on both the Gibson and Arms bibliography and the "Chronological List of Howells' Fiction" provided by Carrington and Carrington, I have at times subordinated their judgement to that of Thomas Wortham, who not only has the advantage, writing more recently, of better sources, but who has focused exclusively on Howells's early fiction. Wortham, in *The Early Prose Writings of Willliam Dean Howells: 1853–1861*, reprints and discusses the bulk of Howells's early prose works, guiding his reader through those works published under Howells's pen names of "Will Narlie" and "Chispa," those published anonymously, and those published under his real name. My choices, therefore, have been heavily influenced by the expertise of one scholar.

A number of works that appear in the Gibson and Arms bibliography and in Carrington and Carrington's list are not considered by Wortham as belonging to the Howells canon. The first two items on my story list, "A Tale of Love and Politics" and "The Journeyman's Secret," fall into this category. I have erred on the side of comprehensiveness, however, and have included them in my list because Wortham says that he feels "reasonably comfortable in ascribing [them] to Howells [despite the lack of] direct or collateral proof that they are indeed his." He adds: "I should not be surprised to find out positively that [these two stories] are by Howells, but neither would I be surprised to learn that they are by someone else" (personal letter, 1991). I have followed Wortham's lead more closely in excluding from my list "The Emigrant of 1802" (1854) and "An Old-time Love-affair" (1854), which, like the two previously mentioned stories, are included in the Howells canon by both Gibson and Arms and Carrington and Carrington. The Gibson and Arms bibliography attributes the latter story to Howells on the basis of a passage in *Years of My Youth* (83–84). It seems to me, however, that the story described in the cited passage could not possibly be "An Old-time Love-affair," if only for the reason that Howells says that the "serial romance" ran through "a succession of several numbers," while "An Old-time Love-affair" was published in its entirety on a single page of a single issue. My opinion is that the work described in this passage is almost certainly "The Independent Candidate."

Other stories are reprinted and discussed by Wortham, but do not appear in Gibson and Arms or Carrington and Carrington. The third item on my list, "Dropped Dead: A Ghost Story," falls into this category. Wortham explains that this story was unknown to the earlier scholars because "no one had located a file of the weekly [in which it was published] for these years [1853–54]. Only after the Ohio Western Reserve Library moved to its new quarters" was the paper found (personal letter, 1991). "Romance of the Crossing," a later item on my list, was apparently also missed by Gibson and Arms, and another item, "The Valentine," was missed by both Gibson and Arms and Carrington and Carrington, but both are included by Wortham (and myself) in the Howells canon because of the Dulldale setting and characters.

Two other pieces deserve mention. "The Bag of Gold" (1863) is included by both Gibson and Arms and Carrington and Carrington, because of the "Italian setting and Venetian references" (Gibson and Arms 87) and "Fast and Firm—A Romance at Marseilles" (1866) is included by Gibson and Arms because of the "manner and travel itinerary closely following *Italian journeys*" (92). Wortham has serious doubts about the canonicity of these two pieces, as do I, and so I have not included them in my list. Later works of Howells (those written after 1860) provide few, if any, questions of authorship.

Another, more subjective problem, is that of fixing the determining length of a short story. When is a piece of writing a long short story and when is it a short novella? Howells himself is of some help on this issue. In "Some Anomalies of the Short Story," Howells sets out the proper lengths for various types of fiction:

First we have the short story, or novella [Howells uses these terms inter-changeably], then we have the long story, or novel, and between these we have the novelette, which is in name a smaller than the short story [*sic*], though it is in point of fact two or three times longer than a short story. We may realize them physically if we will adopt the magazine parlance and speak of the novella as a one-number story, of the novel as a serial, and of the novelette as a two-number or a three-number story; if it passes the three-number limit it seems to become a novel. (422–32)

Although I make no distinction between what Howells calls the "short story, or novella" and the "novelette," including both under the rubric of "short story," I have followed Howells's "three-number limit" with two exceptions. I include in my list "A Sleep and a Forgetting," which was printed in four sep-arate issues of *Harper's Weekly*, because Howells himself referred to it as a "long short story" (Letter of 11 March 1906). And I exclude "A Fearful Re-sponsibility," although it was originally printed in only two numbers of *Scrib-ner's* magazine, because it is simply so much longer than the other works on my list (and, to me, has the "feel" of a novella).[5]

Inevitably, the most difficult question in preparing my list was that of de-termining what exactly constitutes a short story. Howells wrote many works that were original, intended to stand alone, clearly his, and of the required length, but that are obviously far from being short stories. And although Howells wrote short stories from an early age, his major works developed as a result of the evolution of travel books into novels (as *Venetian Life*, for ex-ample, led eventually to *Their Wedding Journey*). This process of evolution created many problem items, such as "A Day's Pleasure" (which I include be-cause it has been treated as a short story by George Carrington) and "Nia-gara Revisited, Twelve Years after Their Wedding Journey" (which I do not include because Howells wrote about it: "It is not a 'story,' though it is largely fictitious" (*Life in Letters* 1:316). As Carrington and Carrington say in their preface to *Plots and Characters in the Fiction of William Dean Howells*, "How-ells' short fictions lie along a broad spectrum from obvious short stories like 'Editha' to obvious sketches like 'Doorstep Acquaintance' [*Suburban Sketches*], with many mixed works in between" (x–xi). These "mixed works," exhibiting characteristics both of the travel sketch and of the short story, are frequently of excellent quality and sometimes quite compelling (*Suburban Sketch*'s "Scene," which is almost certainly Howells's most famous sketch, is a fine example). Nevertheless, I exclude them from my list.

The difficulty of accurately singling out Howells's short stories is com-pounded by the fact that he continually wrote fictional sketches (or, as George

Arms calls them "sketches with fictional characteristics"—viii; C&C), most notably, many of the "Editor's Easy Chair" columns of *Harper's Monthly*. Howells had a fictional bent, and took naturally to the Addisonian sketch, which "develops a thesis through symbolic or allegorical fictional action or through a dialogue or a symposium of fictional characters" (ix; C&C). (Carrington and Carrington note that he wrote at least ninety-eight of these.) Again, I find some help in Howells's "Some Anomalies of the Short Story," in which he says, "The anecdote offers an illustration of character, or records a moment of action; the novella embodies a drama and develops a type" (117). A drama—a sequence of causally connected events which arrive at some sort of climax—is the defining feature, I believe, of a short story, distinguishing it from what Howells referred to as the "dramatic essay" (*LFA* 134). George Carrington discusses the two forms lucidly, noting that the dramatic essay is "analytical and didactic; the fictional and non-fictional elements are there to persuade the reader of the truth of the analyses and arguments. In contrast, the mature Howells short story is inherently symbolic, and contains no overt essay material except for occasional authorial comments (and little of that in Howells's stories from the 1890s on)" ("Dramatic Essay" 45). (I should add that Carrington goes on to argue that Howells, in "Some Anomalies of the Short Story," actually equates dramatic essays with short stories and with anecdotes, reserving the term "novella" for what we normally call a short story. This interpretation, with which I do not agree, leads of course to conclusions very different from my own, and causes Carrington to label a number of items [for example the "Easy Chair" column of October 1912] as short stories, while I maintain that they are fictional sketches. Part of the problem, as Carrington himself points out, is that Howells's "practice was varied; his definitions were allusive, partial, and implicit, and were spread over nearly fifty years"—45.)

A number of Howells's sketches are indeed storylike. Among these are "The Mouse" (from *Venetian Life*), "Mrs. Johnson" (from *Suburban Sketches*), "Buying a Horse" (from *A Day's Pleasure and Other Sketches*) and "Scene" (from *Suburban Sketches*). If I have erred in not including these in my story list, it has been through an excess of caution, perhaps in reaction to the careless way in which the term "short story" has been bandied about by some earlier Howells scholars.[6] The difficulty of easily categorizing Howells's many works of short fiction helps to explain the general unreliability of some of his bibliographies.[7]

Howells's short stories were typically printed first in a periodical and then reprinted in a collection.[8] But a few were reprinted in more than one collection; some were never reprinted at all; and some appeared originally in collections. Some of Howells's collections were made up entirely of short stories, while others included fictional sketches, poems, or dramatic passages as well. Each of the following eight collections contains at least one short story: *Suburban Sketches* (1871), *A Fearful Responsibility and Other Stories* (1881), *A Day's Pleasure and Other Sketches* (1881), *Christmas Every Day and Other Stories Told for Children* (1893), *A Pair of Patient Lovers* (1901), *Questionable Shapes* (1903), *Between the Dark and the Daylight* (1907), and *The Daughter of the Storage and Other Things in Prose and Verse* (1916).

I am glad to have had the opportunity to draw attention to Howells's valuable stories, and especially to the light that they cast on his concerns after 1890, when he moved beyond realism to the fields of psychological realism and the psychic romance. More than his novels or other writings, Howells's late stories reveal his fascination with psychology and his interest in psychic phenomena, especially those that seem to shed light on the question of immortality. Conversely, his early stories are invaluable in revealing his development as a writer and his concern, even at an early age, with the themes that permeate the entire canon: the slippery nature of perception, the variance between the ethical and the aesthetic points of view, the benefits and hazards of the creative imagination, the requirements and responsibilities of personal morality, and of course, the contrast between the false promises of romantic literature and the often ambiguous or incomprehensible nature of real life. Taken as a group, Howells's stories provide a complete and manageable overview of his artistic and moral concerns as he dealt with changes both in world literature and in his own life.

I hope that my work will be useful (and enjoyable), however, not only for Howells scholars, but for Americanists of every stripe, and indeed for anyone who appreciates the fiction of times gone by.

Notes

1. A number of these columns were later collected as *Criticism and Fiction* (1891), which was reprinted by Clara and Rudolf Kirk in *Criticism and Fiction and Other Essays* (1959). Although *Criticism and Fiction* was reprinted again in 1993 as part of the Indiana University Press *Selected Edition* of Howells, all of my references are to the Kirks' volume.

2. Howells discusses Thanksgiving and Christmas stories at some length in *Criticism and Fiction* (76–85).

3. These can obviously be connected to the other Basil and Isabel March works:

Their Wedding Journey, Niagara Revisited, Twelve Years after Their Wedding Journey, A Hazard of New Fortunes, The Shadow of a Dream, An Open-Eyed Conspiracy, Their Silver Wedding Journey, and *Hither and Thither in Germany.*

4. I am aware of at least one unpublished short story, "Luke Beazely," which is discussed by Rodney Olsen (101, 304).

5. I also include "A Parting and a Meeting" in my list, in contrast to Carrington and Carrington, who argue that since it was eventually published as a book it must be classifed as a novel (x). I think that it was a short story when it was first printed in three issues of *Cosmopolitan* and its subsequent appearance in hardback does nothing to change that.

6. I do, uncharacteristically, include as a story "Incident," which Carrington and Carrington consider to be a sketch (xii). As it is included in my text, the reader may judge.

7. It does not, however, excuse the poor scholarship exhibited by one of these, the previously mentioned *William Dean Howells: A Bibliography* by Vito J. Brenni.

8. There are occasional textual discrepancies between the two publications. I use the text found in Howells's collections, as I feel that this represents his final intentions. I have, where it was necessary, modernized Howells's punctuation. This consisted largely of changing single quotation marks to double ones. I have also corrected some minor typographical errors.

List of Abbreviations

I use the following abbreviations throughout this work. Publishing information is provided in the Works Cited list.

C&C   George and Ildikó de Papp Carrington. *Plots and Characters in the Fiction of William Dean Howells.* (1976)

LFA   William Dean Howells. *Literary Friends and Acquaintance.* (1900, Rpt. 1968)

LL   William Dean Howells. *Literature and Life, Studies.* (1902)

MLP   William Dean Howells. *My Literary Passions.* (1895)

SL   William Dean Howells. *Selected Letters of W. D. Howells.* 4 volumes. (1979–1981)

VB   Vito J. Brenni. *William Dean Howells: A Bibliography.* (1973)

W   Thomas Wortham. *The Early Prose Writings of William Dean Howells, 1853–1861.* (1990)

YY   William Dean Howells. *Years of My Youth.* (1916, Rpt. 1975)

Selected Short Stories of
WILLIAM DEAN
HOWELLS

A Dream

1 8 6 1

A DREAM" IS NOT Howells's first short story, but it is the first in which hints of the work to follow can be clearly seen. It is a transitional work: like Howells's earlier stories, it exemplifies what William C. Fischer, Jr., calls "the fiction of romantic emotion" (11), and its style is somewhat juvenile and flowery. But "A Dream" also looks to the future with its use of irony, its subversion of literary conventions, and its realistic details and believable characters. This liminal story is also notable historically, as it represents an early example of what would later become known as the theme of the village.

"A Dream" was written sometime in the late 1850s, when Howells was still in his early twenties. Because Howells submitted it to the *Knickerbocker Magazine,* a formerly influential New York literary journal, we know that "A Dream" was originally intended to stand on its own as a short story. The editors of the *Knickerbocker,* eager to encourage Western writers, to expose unknown talent, and to pull American literature away from the popular sentimentality and romance of the day, and toward what would become known as "realism," accepted the story, and filed it with stories to be published at a later time (Wortham 249–50). They did not inform Howells of their decision, however, and he assumed that his work had been rejected (*LFA* 71). It was eventually published, without Howells's knowledge, in August of 1861.

Exactly a year before "A Dream" appeared in the *Knickerbocker*, in August of 1860, Howells had visited Boston and described his "story of village life" to James T. Fields, then editor of the *Atlantic* (Wortham 249). With Fields's encouragement, Howells expanded his story into a novel, which he entitled *Geoffrey: A Study of American Life*,[1] and which he completed in the spring of 1861. "A Dream," now substantially rewritten, appeared as the first chapter of the new novel.

When Howells, in 1861, offered his novel to Fields for publication, it was rejected. As Howells recalled it in 1900, the editors wrote that they "had the less regret in returning it" because of the recent publication of "A Dream" (*LFA* 71). Olov Fryckstedt (67), Robert F. Marler, Jr. (76), and Thomas Wortham (249) all conclude from this statement that Howells believed that the previous publication was the primary grounds for rejection. Wortham, in fact, notes a letter from James R. Osgood, Fields's assistant, which indicates that the manuscript was actually rejected before the editors became aware of "A Dream," and explains that "Howells permitted his memory—in that unwitting way the ego compels one to do—to preserve ever after those hopes his youth had suffered" (249). I disagree with this reading; it seems clear to me that Howells accepted that his novel was rejected on its own merits. At any rate, *Geoffrey* remained unpublished until 1990, when it appeared in full in Thomas Wortham's *The Early Prose Writings of William Dean Howells: 1853–1861*. Howells's continuing inability to find a publisher for his novel, his awareness of the novel's faults, and his memory of what he later called the "shame and anguish" (*MLP* 87) of his first literary failure—*The Independent Candidate*[2]—combined to discourage Howells temporarily from further attempts in prose fiction. (For a fuller discussion of Howells's struggles with *Geoffrey*, see Wortham 250–54. Wortham is especially helpful in linking *Geoffrey* to other "analytical" fiction of the day.)

"A Dream," along with *Geoffrey* and "Not a Love Story," is set in the village of Dulldale, a lightly disguised rendering of Jefferson, Ohio. All of Howells's early (pre-European) fiction, in fact, is set in villages like Dulldale. Wortham, noting that none of Howells's major works uses this setting, points out that Howells "was never able to transform fully the memory of his lost Midwestern world, its shapes and scenes, into the forms of fiction. In the end even he seemed aware of the cause of his failure, aware of that profound ambivalence village life and values represented in his imagination" (235). Howells's early work, however, should not be discounted. As Wortham continues: "Long before the revolt from the village became a commonplace theme in American letters, Howells was there exploring the field for whatever fictional possibilities it possessed" (236). (Howells did, of course, return to a Midwestern village setting in his autobiographical writing, in such works for children as *A Boy's Town* (1890) and *The Flight of Pony Baker* (1902), in *The Leatherwood God*, and in two of his latest stories.)

To the reader who knows only the mature Howells, the style of "A Dream" will come as a surprise. Like most of Howells's stories and sketches from the 1850s, it is flowery and "literary," and includes some rather self-conscious authorial intrusions. It was influenced to some extent by Thackeray, who, as Howells later said, is "always holding his figures up from behind, and commenting on them, and explaining them" ("My Favorite Novelist" 283). (The influence of Thackeray is much greater, and more damaging, in *Geoffrey*.) An opposing interpretation of Howells's style in "A Dream" is that of Robert F. Marler, who argues that "the style, marked by sentence fragments, one-sentence paragraphs, commonplace diction, and abrupt transitions, is an ironic commentary on the romantic subject matter" (80).

But while "A Dream" is linked to Howells's previous stories by its setting and style, it also marks a departure from these stories and from the conventions upheld by the periodical fiction of the day. In the 1850s, according to Marler, "the composite world of fiction had rigidified into a spiritless orthodoxy of sensationalism, sentimentalism and didacticism" (76). "A Dream," through its "satiric puncture of conventional attitudes" (78) and its ironic reversals, is clearly of another order, and as clearly indicates the direction that Howells's future work was to take.

"A Dream" presents a number of conventional elements: the returning hero, his former love, the dream of romantic conquest, and the actual realization of that dream. But none of these turn out to be what the reader accustomed to sentimental fiction would expect. As Marler notes, Geoffrey's initially sentimental response to his hometown is undercut by his quick disillusionment and his feelings of isolation. Clara, the once idealized love, is, by mid-century standards, immodest and flirtatious. As Marler puts it, "her conduct insults her husband's memory and sullies her little girl's purity" (79). And the fulfillment of Geoffrey's romantic dream brings only a sense of unreality and the loss of a "beautiful illusion."

"A Dream" is thus an early example both of Howells's realism and of his satiric method. It provides the model, which Howells would use repeatedly in later years, of the sometimes violent destruction of foolish "romanticist" illusions by the sudden intrusion of reality. This pattern is discussed at length by George Carrington, who argues that Howells, "largely through his constant emphasis on perception . . . attacks efforts to deny or ignore the alien and incomprehensible nature of life" (*Drama* 53). "A Dream," immature as it may be, reveals a surprising awareness of the importance of perception, and stresses the contrast between romantic illusions and "alien and incomprehensible" real life. Carrington also points out the importance, in Howells's writing, of "juxtaposition," which "works backwards; it modifies our view of what has gone before" (167). "A Dream" essentially consists of the juxtaposition of Geoffrey's dream and its fulfillment, a fulfillment which clearly "modifies" Geoffrey's understanding of his past.

Another way in which Howells uses popular conventions for his own satirical purposes, as William Fischer points out, is through the reverie, "a well-entrenched minor convention among nineteenth-century American romantics" (4). Fischer notes that "while Hawthorne's reveries are primarily retrospective . . . and Melville's are deeply introspective, the reveries devised by Howells ordinarily look forward to some imagined event in the future" (10). Howells is clearly following the example of Ik Marvel (Donald Grant Mitchell), the author of *The Reveries of a Bachelor* (1850) and *Dream Life* (1852). (See Wortham 20–22 for a discussion of Ik Marvel's style.) But Howells is unique in emphasizing the "potential moral instability and self-deception" made possible by reverie. Geoffrey's daydreams of impressing Clara "by his superior manner and courtly reticence" are an example of what Fischer calls "anticipatory self-deception" and set "the pattern for almost all of the ensuing reveries in Howells' fiction" (11). (Fischer believes, in fact, that Howells's denigration of reverie led him to adopt a "nonsymbolic aesthetic," a distrust of the capacity of language to reveal truth, and thus a flat, nonfigurative style. Howells's use of reverie, argues Fischer, helped to create both his style and his philosophy of literature.)

Howells evinced an interest in "actual" dreams (as opposed to daydreams) throughout his career. Persis Lapham's dream-like impression of Jacob's ladder and the nightmare of *The Shadow of a Dream* come immediately to mind, as does "True, I Talk of Dreams," an article by Howells that appeared in *Harper's Monthly* in 1895.

Kenneth Lynn reads "A Dream" as an autobiographical allegory. He believes that Geoffrey's eventual escape from the attraction of his cousin is "patently a wish-fulfillment fantasy" (106), mirroring Howells's desire to escape from Jefferson—specifically, from his mother and his sister Victoria. Lynn's thesis is provocative; there is no doubt that Howells's desire to leave home to create an independent life for himself conflicted with his closeness to his mother and sister, and that he felt guilty about leaving them. Nor is Lynn alone in pointing out autobiographical elements in the story. Robert Marler compares Dulldale to Jefferson, Geoffrey to both Howells and his father, William Cooper Howells, Clara to Victoria, and Geoffrey's experience to "Howells' own neurotic forebodings" (81). And John Crowley, in an extended discussion of *Geoffrey*, mentions the novel's "autobiographical implications" (48), noting in particular Howells's need to escape from village life (51). Crowley argues, in fact, that writing *Geoffrey* helped Howells to "prepare himself psychologically for a break with Jefferson/Dulldale" (51). But Lynn misreads and oversimplifies "A Dream." His statement that Geoffrey's "determination to make a career in the city triumphs over the feminine tugs in Dulldale" (106) is not supported by the text, nor is his claim that Geoffrey has "begun to make a successful career as a lawyer in the East" (105). (In *Geoffrey*, the novel, the title character is a newspaper editor, although he "had read some books with a view to study of the law"—Wortham 201–2). More disturbing is Lynn's equation of the story with the circumstances of 1861—the year of its publication—and his disregard for the fact that the story was written, at the latest, in 1860.

"A Dream" has been undeservedly neglected by the critics. It is not mentioned in Edwin Cady's two-volume biography of Howells, and it is not included in Carrington and Carrington's *Plots and Characters in the Fiction of William Dean Howells* (1976). The latter is especially puzzling because Marler's fine discussion of the story appeared in 1974, two years before the publication of *Plots and Characters*. Other than brief mentions in Fryckstedt,[3] Lynn, and Wortham, it is ignored in all book-length studies of Howells; and it is treated in only two articles, those of Marler and Fischer.

Notes

1. The novel is apparently listed as "Geoffrey Winter" in John K. Reeves's "Manuscripts," and this is the title, as John W. Crowley explains, by which "it has become known" (*Truth* 45). Robert Marler, like Crowley, follows Reeves in referring to the novel as *Geoffrey Winter*. But Thomas Wortham notes that the title of the novel is cut away from the manuscript and that *Geoffrey: A Study of American Life* is the title used by *MacMillan's* in their rejection letter of 1862. This letter, he says, is "the only indication of the work's title we have from Howells' correspondence or memoirs" (359).

2. "The Independent Candidate," an "ambitious romance about contemporary politics" (Wortham 56) was printed in the *Ashtabula Sentinel* from November 1854 to January 1855. Unfortunately, Howells published the long story *as* he wrote it, without having any clear idea about where it was going. The result was predictably (and publicly) weak, and Howells was finally forced to finish the story by "simplifying through

death and marvelous disaster the wonderful complications into which the plot had innocently wandered" (Wortham 57). (See Cady, "Sentinel," for a full discussion of this incident.) (See Crowley, *Truth*, for a Freudian analysis of Howells's anguish over "The Independent Candidate.") (See Olsen 80–87 for the most thorough treatment of the work.)

3. Fryckstedt, in fact, states that "Dream" (*sic*) is one of a number of early stories that "portray . . . love between young people in a humorous manner" (65). This reading is difficult to reconcile with the text.

☙

A Dream

It was broad day-light when Geoffrey awoke from a dream that often haunted his sleep. There was neither order nor sequence in the dream. It was merely the presentiment of an event related to no immediate cause, and always in its result dispelling sleep. It had also this strange quality, that it referred at no time to any actual occurrence of his life, and that as often as he dreamed it, he had the consciousness that it was the reproduction of a former illusion, yet he always awoke with the sense of its actual fulfillment as near at hand.

His perfect slumber was invaded by a vague presence, which assumed the form and aspect of his cousin, whose warm, deep eyes bent looks of unutterable sadness and passion upon him. He made a movement as to embrace her, but with a quick gesture she held him away. It was a gesture which he had seen young girls use with each other—a lightning-swift action that repels but for an instant. As often as Geoffrey dreamed of this action, he commented in his dream upon its naturalness. Thus holding him away, his cousin seemed to peruse his soul with those great eyes, into which it made him wild and dizzy to look; and then, as if smitten with a sudden weakness, her resisting aspect melted away, and she fell with a sob upon his heart. That was the end of his dream.

The robins were singing in the door-yard elms, and the martens were gossiping noisily about their little house on the crest of the gable. The sun came in through the wind-shaken creeper at the window, and dappled the white floor with tremulous light and shadow. The farmer was mowing the grass in the orchard, and the hoarse *wash* of the scythe smote pleasantly upon the ear.

It was with a sweet pain that Geoffrey glanced over the room, and saw that it was almost unchanged since the time when he slept in it a child; and he puzzled himself again in a childish way, trying to give significance to the vague shapes traced by the lines in the cracked ceiling.

Breakfast awaited him when he went down, and he chatted and gossiped with the farmer's wife as he ate. She told him who were gone west, and who were married and who were dead. She had been an old playmate of his, and the one whom he most delighted to draw to school upon his sled. They laughed about that now, but it made Geoffrey's heart sad to think of it.

The farmer's wife glanced from Geoffrey's handsome, gentle face to the low front and sordid visage of her husband and sighed. Poor woman! it made her something discontented; and when the baby put its hand in the butter, she boxed its ears with energy. After that, there was not any more talk.

It is hard to tell with just what thoughts a young man goes back to the home of his childhood. With that tender sentiment and yearning for old things which he feels, is mixed a half-contempt for them. He sees nothing there but a skeleton of the past, which his own life had once animated. He comes to despise the past, and his own former self. The events of that time, like the houses and distances of the place, are all shrunken and dwarfed.

Geoffrey walked from the old farm into the village, and passed up the long street, under the dark maples. These shade-trees were the only things that had grown in the last seven years. Dulldale was scarcely larger; the buildings he had once thought great, looked mean; and the people whom he recognized had an indefinable air of having fallen away from some former grandeur. No one knew him, and he was at no pains to make himself known.

He was full of a vain and selfish melancholy, and he chose to "guard his strangeness." There is something flattering to the vanity of youth in the consciousness of one that he is greatly changed, however much the show of it in others may pain him.

Geoffrey would hardly acknowledge to himself the reason which had brought him to Dulldale. That event which he had believed to desolate his life had more than once been a theme of laughter with him. Once he had delighted to think, with the droll earnestness of youth, that the autumn of his soul was at hand; that he was a barren tree, from which the blasts of fate had stripped the leaves. Men who are not fools think such preposterous things with less cause than he. Afterward, he found that this was only a mock-autumn; that no winter, but a summer, followed it. He was a tree, from the tender blossoms of which a chill spring-breeze had merely shaken the petals.

It had not been without emotion that he received the announcement of her marriage. Though he recalled with a smile the time when he thought it must break his heart if she wedded that man, it was with a sigh of relief that he laid away the interesting paragraph in a package of her letters. He believed that a painful passage in his life was thus closed forever. Had she remained unmarried, he felt that his heart must ever have had its secret yearnings toward her. As it was, these were now impossible. The self-deception was natural.

When, afterward, her husband died, he reasoned with himself, and persuaded himself that he was really indifferent. And indeed it was true that he thought less of her than of himself in relation to the old passion. He occupied himself with affairs, and strove to forget it wholly, with tolerable success; but in his hours of solitude, some incident of those dear days would haunt him. Sometimes he awoke in the middle of the night, and thought of her. A feeling of curiosity usurped desire. The wish to see her again, and judge her by his manhood's standards, took possession of him by degrees, and by degrees he yielded to it.

He was therefore in Dulldale.

It was a day of June, and the winds came across the meadows with fragrant whispers; their voices, in gossip with the leaves of the maples, and the sweet smell of the roses and honeysuckles in the door-yards, charmed and deepened his melancholy.

He did not observe that he had walked so far, till he stood with his hand upon the well-known gate. Here, too, was little change. There had been a new lattice made for the honeysuckle to clamber upon, and the house had been re-painted. That was all. The flower-beds, on either side the walk to the door, were gay with pinks and tulips and flags, as of yore, and the old house-dog, asleep on the stone step, seemed not to have moved for seven years. His aunt sat at the window sewing, for in small places the ladies are economical of passers, and prefer to work in rooms commanding views of the street. The old lady glanced at him through her glasses, but failed to recognize him.

At the sound of his foot upon the walk, the dog sprang up with a fierce challenge, and the old lady came to the door to silence him. Scanning Geoffrey more closely, she knew him, and greeted him as kindly as she could. She was a cold woman, of few words; and after brief inquiries, she told him that she had taken him for a peddler at first.

Geoffrey smiled, remembering his aunt's virtuous loathing of peddlers, in the past.

"But you don't look like a peddler, near by," she added. "It is my eyes were at fault. Sit here, and I will call your cousin. She will be glad to see you."

The old place. The tables with their books—the Bible, Mrs. Hemans' poems,* and "The Course of Time"**—the bureau, with its glass knobs—the picture of General Washington over the chimney-piece, with vases of impossible tomatoes in plaster, on either side.

There are those who, without having mingled with the world, have that ease and self-possession which familiarity with it bestows. In certain foolish moments, Geoffrey had thought to surprise and confound his cousin, when he should meet her, by his superior manner and courtly reticence. He revelled in the anticipated enjoyment of her abasement and regret, when she should come to see what sort of man she had trifled with—a man not only of excellent mind and conversation, but of elegant presence. He invented scenes and dialogues, in which he played the forgiving but dignified and inaccessible patron, and she the frightened, fluttering, embarrassed recipient of his polite attentions.

Ah! well, are we to be judged by our foolish thoughts? Thank heaven, no! but by how much or how little restraint we put upon them.

When his cousin entered the room, it was without the least awkwardness or hesitation. Perhaps she had an intuitive perception of his feeling, and cared to defeat him a second time. Women know so many things by instinct.

Geoffrey arose with a burning face and a tumultuous heart. She gave her hand with promptness and kindness, and made him feel very boyish again, as she used to do. The victory was with her only for a moment. Geoffrey recovered himself, and while she talked, he regarded her face and her words closely.

She was very beautiful. Her ripe womanhood was lovelier than her girlish grace, which was, indeed, not lost, but was grown into that, as the tenderness and grace of the bud is glorified in the perfect flower.

She was very beautiful; and yet to her cousin's eye the old light was no longer in the comely face. Fair and blooming as ever, it was yet indescribably faded. It was as if the soul within was faded. Geoffrey could not consider then that there had never been any light such as he looked for there, but only the reflection of the glow in his own heart. Afterward he remembered this.

Clara wore her widow's weeds, and played at times with her child. She bade it go to him, and when it would not, she said daringly that the gentleman was an old flame of mamma's. "Do you know what *flame* is, darling?" Then kisses, and caresses, and baby-talk. "Come," she said, and took the little one in her arms, and went and sat beside Geoffrey: "Isn't she pretty? Do you think she has my eyes?" and she turned those eyes upon him, full.

All this, and more, displeased the old lover: why, he could not tell. He had expected to be bored by the tender reminiscences and the last dying speeches

---

* English poet Felicia Dorothea Browne Hemans (1793–1835), known universally as "Mrs. Hemans," was the most celebrated woman poet of her time, although today she is chiefly remembered as the author of "The boy stood on the burning deck."

** A poem in ten books by Scottish poet Robert Pollok (1798–1827), *The Course of Time* (1827) is a history of humankind from Adam onward.

of the dear, departed one, but his cousin said nothing of her husband, and he did not like it. "She would have forgotten me as soon," he thought.

When she turned her great eyes upon him, he met their glances unabashed. His cheek was wont to flood if she looked at him. It was pale and cool now.

They talked together of their old love-affair in a laughing way—he with that ease that the world had given him, she with the nonchalance natural to her. She was very good-natured and witty, and she made him laugh. He admired her beauty and sprightliness, and he loved her less than ever. The whole interview was of so different a nature from that he had intended, he was quite bewildered. His cousin had evoked a false and mocking spirit from him, and he answered her talk with bitter badinage, till he grew to doubt the reality of the scene. At last, baffled, disappointed, and vexed, he arose to go.

How long was he going to stay in the village? she asked.

He went away to-morrow.

Would he come and spend the evening with her?

No, he had business.

She had glided toward him, and stood looking in his face without the doubt that he would accept her invitation. Her manner till then had been of cousinly familiarity. At his harsh, curt refusal, it changed instantly. It was as if his coldness had frozen her.

"Good-by, then," she said briefly, while she watched him narrowly, but did not offer her hand.

Geoffrey exulted; but the whole scene seemed more like an illusion than ever.

"What! cousin," he cried. "You won't give me your hand, at parting? You were kinder once." He took her hand, that hung listless at her side, and drew her toward him. As in his dream, she raised her arm, and held him away, regarding him with sad, passionate eyes for an instant. Then the tears came, and she permitted and returned his embrace, clasping his neck with her arms, while her heart beat wildly against his breast. He kissed her lips; but even then a sense of unreality filled his thoughts. "Good-by," he said, and went.

That was the end of his dream.

Like one who reasons in his sleep, and struggles to be awake, he had struggled; and now he was awake, never again in any sleep to dream that dream. The golden charm was broken forever; the beautiful illusion was dispelled.

His lonely life was lonelier for the loss. It made the past hateful, and the future full of doubt.

A Romance of Real Life

1870

"ROMANCE OF REAL LIFE" seems on first encounter to be the quintessential example of Howellsian realism. It can easily be read as a didactic dramatization of the misleading lure of romance versus the clear eye of realism, and so, as a satire of contemporary literature. The story also anticipates Howells's Basil and Isabel March stories in its emphasis on the contrast between ethical and aesthetic perspectives. But it contains ambiguities as well, which become manifest in the character of the contributor, and in how he, for better or worse, parallels Howells himself.

"A Romance of Real Life," like all but one[1] of the *Suburban Sketches* (1871) was first published in Howells's own *Atlantic Monthly*.[2] These "First Studies of American Life" (Cady, *Road* 155) were clearly an Americanized version of the sort of travel sketches that constituted the earlier *Venetian Life* (1866) and *Italian Journeys* (1867). But, as Cady points out, contemporary praise of the sketches did not "recognize the experimentalism of the pieces" (*Road* 155) and modern criticism has not done much better. The most thorough discussion may be that of George Carrington (*Drama* 56–64).

Howells himself was not quite sure about the merit of his "sketches." Writing to Henry James on 2 January 1870, he commented:

> I have in type A Romance of Real Life which records a droll and curious experience of mine. In some ways these things seem rather small business to me; but I fell naturally into doing them; I persuaded myself (too fondly, perhaps) that they're a new kind of study of our life, and I have an impression that they're to lead me to some higher sort of performance. They're not easy to do, but cost me a great deal of work. (*SL* 1:352)

Later in the same letter, Howells noted again that "the whole thing was a record of actual experience" (353). Initially, a dichotomy seems to be established between 1) the story as autobiography, with the contributor filling in for Howells; and 2) the story as a piece of artistry, the precursor of "some higher sort of performance," in which the contributor must be seen as the artist's construct, created for an artistic (or didactic) purpose. By convention, Howells's earlier travel sketches have been read as the former, while "A Romance of Real Life," understandably, has been read as the latter. But neither the travel literature nor *Suburban Sketches* is served well by this either/or reading. As Crowley convincingly argues, Howells's early realistic method was inevitably tied to the therapeutic nature of his writing and this symbiosis produced "uncalculated ambiguities" (*Mask* 9). The uneasy relationship between the "I" of the story, the contributor, and Howells himself is a good example.

Writing in 1952, Louis J. Budd dismissed "A Romance of Real Life" as a sketch that "almost too neatly exemplified [Howells's] growing conviction that real everyday life should be his chief artistic subject" (39). According to this view, the contributor's romantic fantasies, nurtured by popular literature, at first lead him away from the literary possibilities of his own world. It is only after he realizes how easily he has been duped that he recognizes the charm and interest of his actual experience. Even then, it is not clear whether he abandons the "romantic" reading of his world for a more "realistic" one.

The contributor's "false reading" of Tinker is similarly emphasized by Charles L. Campbell, who uses the story to demonstrate Howells's attention to the relationship between the "real world" of his characters and their experience of literature (289). He begins his essay, in fact, by noting a whimsical passage in Howells's *Indian Summer* (1886), in which the characters wonder how they might act if they were characters in a Howells novel (173). Campbell argues that Howells subverts the contributor's attitude toward life—the belief that "life is romantic and that people one meets in life are often just like characters in fiction" (291)—not only by the events of the story, and by his ironic tone, but by the use of "fictional comparisons" (292), most notably to Richard Henry Dana's *Two Years before the Mast*. He goes on to say that Howells's discussion of "other fictional worlds . . . draws attention to the fictive nature of his own work" (292) and that Howells's work becomes, not fiction, but "a commentary upon life couched in a literary vehicle" (295).

Campbell's essay hinges on the belief that the contributor "holds a theory of life and literature which is the inverse of Howells'" (291). His interpretation of the contributor is not far from that of George Carrington, who, in a comprehensive discussion of the Howells canon, examines Howells's emphasis on perception, especially on the consequences of false perceptions (*Drama*). Carrington argues, in brief, that "in Howells, the archetypal human situation is the condition of an observer" (28). The inability to observe clearly is linked to what Carrington calls "codes"—preexisting, forced explanations of reality that cloud and distort our vision (53). In Howells's fiction, false perceptions are revealed "through the eyes of an observer who is being satirically handled" (54). In such early fiction as "A Romance of Real Life," "the author or his persona is the observed observer, himself a subject of the sketch" (954). Carrington, like Campbell, notes the irrelevance of the contributor's initial, literary approach to his actual experience.

There is much to agree with in these arguments. The ironic reversals of Tinker's encounter with Julia Hapford certainly support a literature versus life/romance versus realism reading of the story. Julia's "loud, hoarse laugh," her amusement, and her wonderfully conceived dissection of a fly irrevocably bar her from the ranks of romantic heroines, and Tinker's sordid history seems to rob him of his glamour and pathos. The "juxtaposition" (Carrington, *Drama* 167) of the imagined and the real encounter clearly ties "A Romance of Real Life" to Howells's earlier "A Dream." But the contributor's initial disappointment is quickly dispersed by the literary wanderings of his imagination. This quick retreat into aesthetic considerations demonstrates a theme which, if it is not completely new in Howells's writings,[3] is newly emphasized.

The contributor's characteristic manner of looking at the world is made clear from the start of the story. When Tinker knocks at his door, the contributor asks him in at least as much for "his pride" at the seeming correctness of his theories as for any "impulse of humanity." Tinker's story is one that "the listener exulted, while he regretted, to hear." After Tinker's departure, the contributor "recurred to his primal satisfaction in the man as calamity capable of being used for such and such literary ends, and, while he pitied him, rejoiced in him." And this satisfaction continues even after the contributor recognizes the falseness of his original reading: "The episode which had appeared so perfect in its pathetic phases did not seem less finished as a farce; and [he] could not but rejoice in these new incidents, as dramatically fashioned as the rest. It occurred to him that, wrought into a story, even better use might be made of the facts now than before." The position that a "realistic" reading of Tinker is better and truer than a "romantic" reading begs the question of whether he ought to be "read" at all. The contributor's delight in the "aesthetic value" of Tinker's story challenges and frequently supersedes his compassion for him as a fellow human being.

This split between the "aesthetic" and "ethical" points of view is dealt with by both Myron Simon and Jerome Klinkowitz. Simon, in a strongly worded argument, concentrates on the story's "essentially satiric intent" (241). He faults the contributor not only for being "an educated version of the 'fool' character who indicts himself" (241) but for his "pernicious . . . misuse of experience" (242), his cold aestheticism and self interest in the face of human tragedy. According to Simon, with each of the contributor's succeeding interpretations of Tinker (Tinker as forlorn sailor, as imaginative *naif*, and as victim of society), he "is less dependent upon and concerned with an accurate realization of Tinker's situation because his mounting preoccupation is with the literary uses that it may serve" (244). Simon emphatically contrasts Howells and the contributor, saying that while the contributor sees life "in terms of literature. . . . [Howells] would himself, of course, have chosen to reverse this formulation, and spoken of the necessity for seeing literature steadily in terms of life" (242). Similarly, he compares the egotistical responses of the contributor, "who hardly finds social reality more than a pretext for his vaporing" with "the generous humanity that motivated Howells' all-absorbing concern with reality" (245).

Jerome Klinkowitz does not deal directly with "A Romance of Real Life," but his discussion of Howells's Basil and Isabel March stories[*] suggests that Howells and the contributor do not differ nearly as much as Simon believes. He begins by demonstrating that the stories, taken individually or as a whole, are "marked by the couple's fondness for the aesthetic point of view and their eventual subordination of it to a more ethical perspective" (304). The aesthetics referred to are almost invariably literary aesthetics, as the Marches judge events by their value as fiction. Their impulse to "romanticize nearly everything in sight" (305), that is, to make up romantic stories about their casual acquaintances, is originally a harmless diversion. But in time, it becomes an automatic response that deprives them of the ability to respond ethically (307). As any reader of *A Hazard of New Fortunes* will remember, a major theme of that novel is the Marches' slow recognition of their complicity, to use Howells's term, in the life that surrounds them.

The contributor clearly has much in common with the young Basil and Isabel March. All three are unaware that the keen pleasure they take in considering fact as fiction weakens any feeling of brotherhood, of a shared fate. The primary relevance of Klinkowitz's essay to "A Romance of Real Life," however, is in the crux of his argument: "In their yearning for the picturesque rather than the actual the Marches indeed reflect Howells' early ambivalence between the romantic and the real. . . . But it is attention to the aesthetic-ethic on a thematic level that . . . presents an analogy to the author's own problems with the responsibility of the creative artist" (305).

At the end of "A Romance of Real Life," the contributor speculates about the literary value of the experience he has undergone. He considers the meaning, not of the romantic tale he originally imagined, but of the story that the reader is in fact actually reading. What happens, oddly enough, is a distorted or reversed version of the self-reflexive passage in *Indian Summer*. Rather than the characters imagining that they are characters in a Howells novel, the audience is asked to imagine that it is reading a Howells story. Our odd removal from the normal experience of reading parallels Howells's removal from the act of creative imagination. It is the contributor, not Howells, who seems to have written the story, and who therefore bears the responsibility for using his experience for literary ends.

Howells's habit of "protective narrative distancing" (Crowley, *Truth* 122) is well documented. In a famous autobiographical passage, Howells recalled how in his youth he "learnt to practice a psychological juggle; I came to deal with my own state of mind as another would deal with it, and to combat my fears as if they were alien" (*YY* 81). As George Carrington points out, Howells was thus "split from two directions at once—from the outside in, and from the inside out. He was both the material of (his own) fiction, and the artist creating fiction out of this material" ("Dramatic Essay" 52). But he juggled into literary terms not only his own life, but the lives of those around him as well. Writing in 1902, he declared: "I am never quite sure of life unless I find literature in it. Unless the thing seen reveals to me an intrinsic poetry, and puts on phrases that clothe it pleasingly to the imagination, I do not much care for it" (*LL* iii). And his preface to *A Hazard of New Fortunes* (written for the 1911 "Library edition") is disturbingly reminiscent of the contributor. Howells writes: "Opportunely for me there was a great street-car strike in New York, and the story began to find its way. . . . [The] violences . . . offered me the material of tragedy and pathos in my story. In my quality of artist I could not regret these" (4, 6). Simon's admiration of Howells blinded him to the implicit self-criticism contained in the portrait of the contributor.

If the contributor, then, speaks at least in part for Howells, it is consequently worthwhile to reconsider the degree of the contributor's romanticism. His primary theory—that the wise adventurer, rather than searching in exotic lands, "sat down beside his own register and waited for incidents to seek him out" and that all the materials of fiction can be found "within the range of one's own personal knowledge"—is surprisingly close to Howells's early theories of realism (although, of course, the "materials of fiction" the contributor seeks are "the fairies and the genii, and all the people of romance"). If the contributor speaks for Howells, then the literary musings at the story's end may constitute, not a stubborn retreat into romance, but a new approach, that of psychological realism (what Louis Budd calls "the subsurface drama"—37). Even the aesthetic approach may be vindicated, as it seems to have led the contributor to a new understanding of the place of the outcast and the former felon in American society, and thus to a greater ethical consciousness. As the narrator points out, "The contributor had either so fallen in love with the literary advantages of his forlorn deceiver that he would see no moral obliquity in him, or he had touched a subtler verity at last in pondering the affair." These two alternatives are weighed equally at the end of the story, and our respect for the contributor grows—until the "I" suddenly steps in to cut him down: "I can see clearly enough where the contributor was astray in this reasoning, but I can also understand how one accustomed to value realities only as they resembled fables should be won with such pensive sophistry."

This sharp reversal of direction is followed by a final phrase—"the mystery from which the man emerged and which swallowed him up again"—that is typically Howellsian in its helplessness at the prospect of finding solutions. (One remembers the end of *A Modern Instance*, for example: "Ah, I don't know! I don't know!"—453.) The ambiguity of this ending throws into relief the opposing stances of the "I" and the contributor, and offers no help to the reader trying to choose between them.

Carrington points out the similarities between "A Romance of Real Life" and two later sketches,[5] one of which "parallels, in fact self-plagiarizes" the earlier story ("Dramatic Essay" 59). As late as 1910, Howells was still concerned with what Carrington calls "the pitfalls lying in wait for the compulsive artist" (59). But even in stories and novels that do not deal with artists or writers directly, there are strong echoes of the conflicts explored in "A Romance of Real Life." (The Basil and Isabel March stories are a good but by no means the only example.) This neglected story provides a valuable introduction to the themes of much of Howells's later work: realism versus romance, the ethic/aesthetic split, and the complicated relationship between life and literature.

Notes

1. "Scene," in which the contributor makes his only other appearance.

2. Everett Carter mistakenly calls "A Romance of Real Life" "Howells' first prose story to achieve national publication" (62). "Tonelli's Marriage" was published in the *Atlantic Monthly* in July of 1868, and "A Dream" was published in the *Knickerbocker*, arguably a national publication, in August of 1861.

3. The opening chapter of *Venetian Life* is a good example of early attention to aesthetic considerations.

4. These are: *Their Wedding Journey* (1872), "Niagara Revisited, Twelve Years after Their Wedding Journey" (1883), *A Hazard of New Fortunes* (1890), *The Shadow of a Dream* (1890), "A Circle in the Water" (1895), "A Pair of Patient Lovers" (1897), *An Open-Eyed Conspiracy* (1897), *Their Silver Wedding Journey* (1899), and *Hither and Thither in Germany* (1920).

5. "Editor's Easy Chair" (1910), and "Worries of a Winter Walk."

ℰ

A Romance of Real Life

It was long past the twilight hour, which has been already mentioned as so oppressive in suburban places, and it was even too late for visitors, when a resident, whom I shall briefly describe as a Contributor to the magazines, was startled by a ring at his door. As any thoughtful person would have done upon the like occasion, he ran over his acquaintance in his mind, speculating whether it were such or such a one, and dismissing the whole list of improbabilities, before he laid down the book he was reading, and answered the bell. When at last he did this, he was rewarded by the apparition of an utter stranger on his threshold,—a gaunt figure of forlorn and curious smartness towering far above him, that jerked him a nod of the head and asked if Mr. Hapford lived there. The face which the lamp-light revealed was remarkable for a harsh two-days' growth of beard, and a single bloodshot eye; yet it was not otherwise a sinister countenance, and there was something in the strange presence that appealed and touched. The contributor, revolving the facts vaguely in his mind, was not sure, after all, that it was not the man's clothes rather than his expression that softened him toward the rugged visage: they were so tragically cheap, and the misery of helpless needle-women, and the poverty and ignorance of the purchaser, were so apparent in their shabby newness, of which they appeared still conscious enough to have led the way to the very window, in the Semitic quarter of the city, where they had lain ticketed, "This nobby suit for $15."

But the stranger's manner put both his face and his clothes out of his mind, and claimed a deeper interest when, being answered that the person for whom he asked did not live there, he set his bristling lips hard together, and sighed heavily.

"They told me," he said, in a hopeless way, "that he lived on this street, and I've been to every other house. I'm very anxious to find him, Cap'n,"— the contributor, of course, had no claim to the title with which he was thus decorated—"for I've a daughter living with him, and I want to see her; I've just got home from a two years voyage, and"—there was a struggle of the Adam's apple in the man's gaunt throat—"I find she's about all there is left of my family."

How complex is every human motive! This contributor had been lately thinking, whenever he turned the pages of some foolish traveller,—some empty prattler of Southern or Eastern lands, where all sensation was long ago exhausted, and the oxygen had perished from every sentiment, so has it been breathed and breathed again,—that nowadays the wise adventurer sat down beside his own register and waited for incidents to seek him out. It seemed to him that the cultivation of a patient and receptive spirit was the sole condition needed to insure the occurrence of all manner of surprising facts within the range of one's own personal knowledge; that not only the Greeks were at our doors, but the fairies and the genii, and all the people of romance, who had but to be hospitably treated in order to develop the deepest interest of fiction, and to become the characters of plots so ingenious that the most cunning invention were poor beside them. I myself am not so confident of this, and would rather trust Mr. Charles Reade,* say, for my amusement than any chance combination of events. But I should be afraid to say

---

* Charles Reade (1814–1884) was a popular and prolific English playwright and novelist. In *My Literary Passions*, Howells gently chastises Reade for being "content to use the materials of realism and produce the effect of romanticism" (193).

how much his pride in the character of the stranger's sorrows, as proof of the correctness of his theory, prevailed with the contributor to ask him to come in and sit down; though I hope that some abstract impulse of humanity, some compassionate and unselfish care for the man's misfortunes as misfortunes, was not wholly wanting. Indeed, the helpless simplicity with which he had confided his case might have touched a harder heart. "Thank you," said the poor fellow, after a moment's hesitation. "I believe I will come in. I've been on foot all day, and after such a long voyage it makes a man dreadfully sore to walk about so much. Perhaps you can think of a Mr. Hapford living somewhere in the neighborhood."

He sat down, and, after a pondering silence, in which he had remained with his head fallen upon his breast, "My name is Jonathan Tinker," he said, with the unaffected air which had already impressed the contributor, and as if he felt that some form of introduction was necessary, "and the girl that I want to find is Julia Tinker." Then he added, resuming the eventful personal history which the listener exulted, while he regretted, to hear: "You see, I shipped first to Liverpool, and there I heard from my family; and then I shipped again for Hong-Kong, and after that I never heard a word: I seemed to miss the letters everywhere. This morning, at four o'clock, I left my ship as soon as she had hauled into the dock, and hurried up home. The house was shut, and not a soul in it; and I didn't know what to do, and I sat down on the doorstep to wait till the neighbors woke up, to ask them what had become of my family. And the first one come out he told me my wife had been dead a year and a half, and the baby I'd never seen, with her; and one of my boys was dead; and he didn't know where the rest of the children was, but he'd heard two of the little ones was with a family in the city."

The man mentioned these things with the half-apologetic air observable in a certain kind of Americans when some accident obliges them to confess the infirmity of the natural feelings. They do not ask your sympathy, and you offer it quite at your own risk, with a chance of having it thrown back upon your hands. The contributor assumed the risk so far as to say, "Pretty rough!" when the stranger paused; and perhaps these homely words were best suited to reach the homely heart. The man's quivering lips closed hard again, a kind of spasm passed over his dark face, and then two very small drops of brine shone upon his weather-worn cheeks. This demonstration, into which he had been surprised, seemed to stand for the passion of tears into which the emotional races fall at such times. He opened his lips with a kind of dry click, and went on:—

"I hunted about the whole forenoon in the city, and at last I found the children. I'd been gone so long they didn't know me, and somehow I thought the people they were with weren't over-glad I'd turned up. Finally the oldest child told me that Julia was living with a Mr. Hapford on this street, and I started out here to-night to look her up. If I can find her, I'm all right. I can get the family together, then, and start new."

"It seems rather odd," mused the listener aloud, "that the neighbors let them break up so, and that they should all scatter as they did."

"Well, it ain't so curious as it seems, Cap'n. There was money for them at the owners', all the time; I'd left part of my wages when I sailed; but they didn't know how to get at it, and what could a parcel of children do? Julia's a good girl, and when I find her I'm all right."

The writer could only repeat that there was no Mr. Hapford living on that street, and never had been, as far as he knew. Yet there might be such a person in the neighborhood; and they would go out together, and ask at some of the houses about. But the stranger must first take a glass of wine; for he looked used up.

The sailor awkwardly but civilly enough protested that he did not want to give so much trouble, but took the glass, and, as he put it to his lips, said formally, as if it were a toast or some form of grace, "I hope that I may have the opportunity of returning the compliment." The contributor thanked him; though, as he thought of all the circumstances of the case, and considered the cost at which the stranger had come to enjoy his politeness, he felt little eagerness to secure the return of the compliment at the same price, and added, with the consequence of another set phrase, "Not at all." But the thought had made him the more anxious to befriend the luckless soul fortune had cast in his way; and so the two sallied out together, and asked the astonished people who answered their summons whether any Mr. Hapford were known to live in the neighborhood.

And although the search for this gentleman proved vain, the contributor could not feel that an expedition which set familiar objects in such novel lights was altogether a failure. He entered so intimately into the cares and anxieties of his *protégé*, that at times he felt himself in some inexplicable sort a shipmate of Jonathan Tinker, and almost personally a partner of his calamities. The estrangement of all things which takes place, within doors and without, about midnight may have helped to cast this doubt upon his identity; —he seemed to be visiting now for the first time the streets and neighborhoods nearest his own, and his feet stumbled over the accustomed walks. In his quality of houseless wanderer, and—so far as he appeared to others— possibly worthless vagabond, he also got a new and instructive effect upon

the faces which, in his real character, he knew so well by their looks of neigh-
borly greeting; and it is his belief that the first hospitable prompting of the
human heart is to shut the door in the eyes of homeless strangers who present themselves after eleven o'clock. By that time the servants were all abed,
and the gentleman of the house answers the bell, and looks out with a loath
and bewildered face, which gradually changes to one of suspicion, and of
wonder as to what those fellows can possibly want of him, till at last the prevailing expression is one of contrite desire to atone for the first reluctance by
any sort of service. The contributor professes to have observed these changing phases in the visages of those whom he that night called from their
dreams, or arrested in the act of going to bed; and he drew the conclusion—
very proper for his imaginable connection with the garroting and other ad-
venturous brotherhoods—that the most flattering moment for knocking on
the head people who answer a late ring at night is either in their first selfish
bewilderment, or their final self-abandonment to their better impulses. It
does not seem to have occurred to him that he would himself have been a
much more favorable subject for the predatory arts than any of his neighbors,
if his shipmate, the unknown companion of his researches for Mr. Hapford,
had been at all so minded. But the faith of the gaunt giant upon which he re-
posed was good, and the contributor continued to wander about with him
in perfect safety. Not a soul among those they asked had ever heard of a
Mr. Hapford,—far less of a Julia Tinker living with him. But they all listened
to the contributor's explanation with interest and eventual sympathy; and
in truth,—briefly told, with a word now and then thrown in by Jonathan
Tinker, who kept at the bottom of the steps, showing like a gloomy spectre
in the night, or, in his grotesque length and gauntness, like the other's
shadow cast there by the lamplight,—it was a story which could hardly fail
to awaken pity.

At last, after ringing several bells where there were no lights, in the mere
wantonness of good-will, and going away before they could be answered (it
would be entertaining to know what dreams they caused the sleepers within),
there seemed to be nothing for it but to give up the search till morning, and
go to the main street and wait for the last horse-car to the city.

There, seated upon the curbstone, Jonathan Tinker, being plied with a few
leading questions, told in hints and scraps the story of his hard life, which
was at present that of a second mate, and had been that of a cabin-boy and of
a seaman before the mast. The second mate's place he held to be the hardest
aboard ship. You got only a few dollars more than the men, and you did not
rank with the officers; you took your meals alone, and in everything you be-

longed by yourself. The men did not respect you, and sometimes the captain abused you awfully before the passengers. The hardest captain that Jonathan Tinker ever sailed with was Captain Gooding of the Cape. It had got to be so that no man would ship second mate under Captain Gooding; and Jonathan Tinker was with him only one voyage. When he had been home awhile, he saw an advertisement for a second mate, and he went round to the owners'. They had kept it secret who the captain was; but there was Captain Gooding in the owners' office. "Why, here's the man, now, that I want for a second mate," said he, when Jonathan Tinker entered; "he knows me."—"Captain Gooding, I know you 'most too well to want to sail under you," answered Jonathan. "I might go if I hadn't already been with you one voyage too many already."

"And then the men!" said Jonathan, "the men coming aboard drunk, and having to be pounded sober! And the hardest of the fight falls on the second mate! Why, there isn't an inch of me that hasn't been cut over or smashed into a jell. I've had three ribs broken; I've got a scar from a knife on my cheek; and I've been stabbed bad enough, half a dozen times, to lay me up."

Here he gave sort of a desperate laugh, as if the notion of so much misery and such various mutilation were too grotesque not to be amusing. "Well, what can you do?" he went on. "If you don't strike, the men think you're afraid of them; and so you have to begin hard and go on hard. I always tell a man, 'Now, my man, I always begin with a man the way I mean to keep on. You do your duty and you're all right. But if you don't'—Well, the men ain't Americans any more,—Dutch, Spaniards, Chinese, Portuguee,—and it ain't like abusing a white man."

Jonathan Tinker was plainly part of the horrible tyranny which we all know exists on shipboard; and his listener respected him the more that, though he had heart enough to be ashamed of it, he was too honest not to own it.

Why did he still follow the sea? Because he did not know what else to do. When he was younger, he used to love it, but now he hated it. Yet there was not a prettier life in the world if you got to be a captain. He used to hope for that once, but not now; though he thought he could navigate a ship. Only let him get his family together again, and he would—yes, he would—try to do something ashore.

No car had yet come in sight, and so the contributor suggested that they should walk to the car-office, and look in the "Directory," which is kept there, for the name of Hapford, in search of whom it had already been arranged that they should renew their acquaintance on the morrow. Jonathan Tinker, when they had reached the office, heard with constitutional phlegm that the name of Hapford, for whom he inquired was not in the "Directory." "Never mind," said the other; "come round to my house in the morning. We'll find him yet." So they parted with a shake of the hand, the second mate saying that he believed he should go down to the vessel and sleep aboard,—if he could sleep,— and murmuring at the last moment the hope of returning the compliment, while the other walked homeward, weary as to the flesh, but, in spite of his sympathy for Jonathan Tinker, very elate in spirit. The truth is,—and however disgraceful to human nature, let the truth still be told,—he had recurred to his primal satisfaction in the man as calamity capable of being used for such and such literary ends, and, while he pitied him, rejoiced in him as an episode of real life quite as striking and complete as anything in fiction. It was literature made to his hand. Nothing could be better, he mused; and once more he passed the details of the story in review, and beheld all those pictures which the poor fellow's artless words had so vividly conjured up: he saw him leaping ashore in the gray summer dawn as soon as the ship hauled into the dock, and making his way, with his vague sea-legs unaccustomed to the pavements, up through the silent and empty city streets; he imagined the tumult of fear and hope which the sight of the man's home must have caused in him, and the benumbing shock of finding it blind and deaf to all his appeals; he saw him sitting down upon what had been his own threshold, and waiting in a sort of bewildered patience till the neighbors should be awake, while the noises of the streets gradually arose, and the wheels began to rattle over the stones, and the milk-man and the ice-man came and went, and the waiting figure began to be stared at, and to challenge the curiosity of the passing policeman; he fancied the opening of the neighbor's door, and the slow, cold understanding of the case; the manner, whatever it was, in which the sailor was told that one year before his wife had died, with her babe, and that his children were scattered, none knew where. As the contributor dwelt pityingly upon these things, but at the same time estimated their æsthetic value one by one, he drew near the head of his street, and found himself a few paces behind a boy slouching onward through the night, to whom he called out, adventurously, and with no real hope of information—

"Do you happen to know anybody on this street by the name of Hapford?"

"Why, no, not in this town," said the boy; but he added that there was a street of the same name in a neighboring suburb, and that there was a Hapford living on it.

"By Jove!" thought the contributor, "this is more like literature than ever"; and he hardly knew whether to be more provoked at his own stupidity in not thinking of a street of the same name in the next village, or delighted at the element of fatality which the fact introduced into the story; for Tinker, according to his own account, must have landed from the cars a few rods from the very door he was seeking, and so walked farther and farther from it every moment. He thought the case so curious, that he laid it briefly before the boy, who, however he might have been inwardly affected, was sufficiently true to the national traditions not to make the smallest conceivable outward sign of concern in it.

At home, however, the contributor related his adventures and the story of Tinker's life, adding the fact that he had just found out where Mr. Hapford lived. "It was the only touch wanting," said he; "the whole thing is now perfect."

"It's too perfect," was answered from a sad enthusiasm. "Don't speak of it! I can't take it in."

"But the question is," said the contributor, penitently taking himself to task for forgetting the hero of those excellent misfortunes in his delight at their perfection, "how am I supposed to sleep to-night, thinking of that poor soul's suspense and uncertainty? Never mind,—I'll be up early, and run over and make sure that it is Tinker's Hapford, before he gets out here, and have a pleasant surprise for him. Would it not be a justifiable coup de théâtre to fetch his daughter here, and let her answer the ring at the door when he comes in the morning?"

This plan was discouraged. "No, no; let them meet in their own way. Just take him to Hapford's house and leave him."

"Very well. But he's too good a character to lose sight of. He's got to come back here and tell us what he intends to do."

The birds, the next morning, not having had the second mate on their minds either as an unhappy man or a most fortunate episode, but having slept long and soundly, were singing in a very sprightly way in the way-side trees; and the sweetness of their notes made the contributor's heart light as he climbed the hill and rang at Mr. Hapford's door.

The door was opened by a young girl of fifteen or sixteen, whom he knew at a glance for the second mate's daughter, but of whom, for form's sake, he asked if there was a girl named Julia Tinker living there.

"My name is Julia Tinker," answered the maid, who had rather a disappointing face.

"Well," said the contributor, "your father's got back from his Hong-Kong voyage."

"Hong-Kong voyage?" echoed the girl, with a stare of helpless inquiry, but of no other visible emotion.

"Yes. He had never heard of your mother's death. He came home yesterday morning, and was looking for you all day."

Julia Tinker remained open-mouthed but mute; and the other was puzzled at the want of feeling shown, which he could not account for even as a national trait. "Perhaps there's some mistake," he said.

"There must be," answered Julia: "my father hasn't been to sea for a good many years. My father," she added, with a diffidence indescribably mingled with a state of distinction,—"my father's in State's Prison. What kind of looking man was this?"

The contributor mechanically described him.

Julia Tinker broke into a loud, hoarse laugh. "Yes, it's him, sure enough." And then, as if the joke were too good to keep: "Miss Hapford, Miss Hapford, father's got out. Do come here!" she called into a back room.

When Mrs. Hapford appeared, Julia fell back, and, having deftly caught a fly on the door-post, occupied herself in plucking it to pieces, while she listened to the conversation of the others.

"It's all true enough," said Mrs. Hapford, when the writer had recounted the moving story of Jonathan Tinker, "so far as the death of his wife and baby goes. But he hasn't been to sea for a good many years, and he must have just come out of State's Prison, where he was put for bigamy. There's always two sides to a story, you know; but they say it broke his first wife's heart, and she died. His friends don't want him to find his children, and this girl especially."

"He's found his children in the city," said the contributor gloomily, being at a loss what to do or say, in view of the wreck of his romance.

"O, he's found 'em has he?" cried Julia, with heightened amusement. "Then he'll have me next, if I don't pack and go."

"I'm very, very sorry," said the contributor, secretly resolved never to do another good deed, no matter how temptingly the opportunity presented itself. "But you may depend he won't find out from me where you are. Of course I had no earthly reason for supposing his story was not true."

"Of course," said kind-hearted Mrs. Hapford, mingling a drop of honey with the gall in the contributor's soul, "you only did your duty."

And indeed, as he turned away he did not feel altogether without compensation. However Jonathan Tinker had fallen in his esteem as a man, he had ever risen in literature. The episode which had appeared so perfect in its pathetic phases did not seem less finished as a farce; and this person, to whom all things of every-day life presented themselves in periods more or less rounded, and capable of use as facts or illustrations, could not but rejoice in these new incidents, as dramatically fashioned as the rest. It occurred to him that, wrought into a story, even better use might be made of the facts now than before, for they had developed questions of character and of human nature which could not fail to interest. The more he pondered upon his acquaintance with Jonathan Tinker, the more fascinating the erring mariner became, in his complex truth and falsehood, his delicately blending shades of artifice and *naïveté*. He must, it was felt, have believed to a certain point his own inventions; nay, starting with that groundwork of truth,—the fact that his wife was really dead, and that he had not seen his family for two years,— why should he not place implicit faith in all the fictions reared upon it? It was probable that he felt a real sorrow for her loss, and that he found a fantastic consolation in depicting the circumstances of her death so that they should look like his inevitable misfortunes rather than his faults. He might well have repented his offense during those two years of prison; and why should he not now cast their dreariness and shame out of his memory, and replace them with the freedom and adventure of a two years' voyage to China,—so probable, in all respects, that the fact should appear an impossible nightmare? In the experiences of his life he had abundant material to furnish forth the facts of such a voyage, and in the weariness and lassitude that should follow a day's walking equally as after a two years' voyage and two years' imprisonment, he had as much physical proof in favor of one hypothesis as the other. It was doubtless true, also, as he said, that he had gone to his house at dawn, and sat down on the threshold of his ruined home; and perhaps he felt the desire he had expressed to see his daughter, with a purpose of beginning life anew; and it may have cost him a veritable pang when he found that his little ones did not know him. All the sentiments of the situation were such as might persuade a lively fancy of the truth of its own inventions; and as he heard these continually repeated by the contributor in their search for Mr. Hapford, they must have acquired an objective force and repute scarcely to be resisted. At the same time, there were touches of nature throughout Jonathan Tinker's narrative which could not fail to take the faith of another. The contributor, in reviewing it, thought it particularly charming that his mariner had not overdrawn himself, or attempted to paint his character otherwise than as it probably was; that he had shown his ideas and practices of life to be those of a second mate; nor more or less, without the gloss of regret or the pretenses to refinement that might be pleasing to the supposed philanthropist with whom he had fallen in. Captain Gooding was of course a true portrait; and there was nothing in Jonathan Tinker's statement of the relations of a second mate to his superiors and his inferiors which did not agree perfectly with what the contributor had just read in "Two Years before the Mast,"—a book which had possibly cast its glamour upon the adventure. He admired also the just and perfectly characteristic air of grief in the bereaved husband and father,—those occasional escapes from the sense of loss into a brief hilarity and forgetfulness, and those relapses into the hovering gloom, which every one has observed in this poor, crazy human nature when oppressed by sorrow, and which it would have been hard to simulate. But, above all, he exulted in that supreme stroke of the imagination given by the second mate when, at parting, he said he believed he would go down and sleep on board the vessel. In view of this, the State's Prison theory almost appeared a malign and foolish scandal.

Yet even if this theory were correct, was the second mate wholly answerable for beginning his life again with the imposture he had practiced? The contributor had either so fallen in love with the literary advantages of his forlorn deceiver that he would see no moral obliquity in him, or he had touched a subtler verity at last in pondering the affair. It seemed now no longer a farce, but had a pathos which, though very different from that of its first aspect, was hardly less tragical. Knowing with what coldness or, at the best, uncandor, he (representing Society in its attitude towards convicted Error) would have met the fact had it been owned to him at first, he had not virtue enough to condemn the illusory stranger, who must have been helpless to make at once evident any repentance he felt or good purpose he cherished. Was it not one of the saddest consequences of the man's past,—a dark necessity of misdoing,—that, even with the best will in the world to retrieve himself, his first endeavor must involve a wrong? Might he not, indeed, be considered a martyr, in some sort, to his own admirable impulses? I can see clearly enough where the contributor was astray in this reasoning, but I can also understand how one accustomed to value realities only as they resembled fables should be won with such pensive sophistry; and I can certainly sympathize with his feeling that the mariner's failure to reappear according to appointment added its final and most agreeable charm to the whole affair, and completed the mystery from which the man emerged and which swallowed him up again.

Incident

1 8 7 2

"I NCIDENT"[1] APPEARED IN THE *Pellet*, "an occasional newspaper published in Boston by the Massachusetts Homeopathic Hospital Fair" (Brenni 23). It was forgotten until the 1970s, when it was "unearthed" by George Hendrick (Carrington & Carrington, xii). Despite its brevity, "Incident" effectively demonstrates some of Howells's major themes and methods.

"Incident" is an early example of what Jerome Klinkowitz has defined as the "aesthetic-ethic split" (304). Like Basil and Isabel March on their wedding journey (and in many other circumstances as well), the nameless couple of "Incident" are "alone together" in a crowd of strangers—emotionally distancing themselves from any larger group. And, like Basil and Isabel March, or the contributor of "Scene" and "A Romance of Real Life," they see the world they travel through as a spectacle designed for their amusement and its people as charming players upon a separate stage, rather than recognizing the common bonds connecting them to those they observe. But the aesthetic distance of the characters in "Incident," unlike that of the others, is both less and more than that described by Klinkowitz, as the young couple's imaginative re-creation of the anonymous painter's life has ambiguous results. It seems simultaneously to promote a sense of brotherhood and community and therefore an ethical "bondage" (to use a Howellsian term),[2] and, conversely, to reduce the painter to a charming fictional character in a story they are creating. (For a more thorough discussion of this process of "fictionalizing," see pp. 45–46 of this book.)

The ambiguity of the couple's response to the painter is amplified by the social distinctions that separate them. "In his quality of husband and father," they find him attractive; "in his character of house-painter" he is "somewhat disagreeable." Either way, he is pigeonholed, narrowly categorized. The couple cannot, or will not, see past the labels that they use, despite the fact that their "fictionalizing" would seem to provide an avenue toward greater understanding and empathy.

The young man and young woman of "Incident," like so many of Howells's other fictional characters, feel no connection or complicity with their companions. In this, they demonstrate the alienation that George Carrington sees as a defining feature of Howells's fictional universe (*Drama* 28). But the story is typical in other ways as well. It clearly reveals Howells's sense of life's capriciousness, of the sudden and seemingly arbitrary reversals that punctuate human existence. The concealment of violent events in neutral language (what Carrington calls, unforgettably, Howells's "deadening, anaesthetic style" —*Drama* 204) is also characteristic. And the fact that the main characters are distanced from the climactic action of the story, so that the violence occurs only offstage, demonstrates Howells's initial squeamishness (which became less pronounced as the years went on).[3]

Perhaps the aspect of "Incident" most interesting to the modern reader is its ending. The young man's answer can of course be read quite flatly—the couple has physically come "very near" an accident. But the reader accustomed to Howells's habitual use of irony and to his typically ambiguous endings is apt to consider how near the couple has actually come. It may be that their "fictionalizing" has brought them imaginatively close to the painter, and the "very near" is meant to describe both physical and emotional proximity. But it is more likely that the couple is not even aware of their social and emotional isolation, and the "very near" ironically comments on the ethical distance that they were unable to bridge. The ending thus brings us back to the theme of alienation, which is central not only to "Incident," but to the entire Howells canon.

Notes

1. This story should not be confused with "An Incident," published in the *Ohio State Journal* on 28 December 1858. According to Rodney Olsen, "An Incident" is a parody of the sentimental sketches then appearing in the New York *Ledger*, "a popular story weekly" with "an extraordinary following" (152, 158).

2. See Carrington, *Drama* 39 for a discussion of Howellsian bondage.

3. Consider, for instance, the violence of *The Landlord at Lion's Head* (1897).

౽

Incident

In spite of her being a young lady and his being a young gentleman delightfully alone together in a whole car full of strangers, they had begun to find the ride tiresome. It was a hot day, the dust descended upon them in a cloud, the cinders from the locomotive ticked like a small, bitter rain against their closed windows, through which they no longer cared to look at the landscape—at its darkling or glistening river, its dusty-bladed fields of corn, its half-mown meadows, its line of distant hills against a horizon piled or strewn with sultry clouds dry as ash-heaps.

They had almost ceased to care for the country-stations when they came to Ulyssesville, but the absurdity of the name amused them; and so they looked for the twentieth time at the bustle and the business of such stations; the girl-operator within bending over her telegraph ribbon, the station master coming out of the door with a despatch in his hand; the recumbent dog with his tongue out; the man in his shirt-sleeves getting a drink of water at the bucket in the waiting room. Then they saw, hurrying around the corner, a man in white linen overalls, who had a paint-pot in one hand, and must be a house painter. With the other hand he led a pretty boy of six years, whom he left there by the corner to stare wide-eyed at the cars, and came aboard, turning first for a pleasant glance back at the little one. "Run home now, Willy," he said, "and tell mother I'll be back on the six o'clock train to supper"; and as the boy unheedful of his voice stood still, rapt in admiration of the train, he called out again, "Run, Willy!" and Willy, wheeling swiftly about, ran off as hard as he could.

"How cunning!" cried the young lady, who interpreted the drama at once, and perceived that Willy, as a signal favor, had been allowed to come to the station with his father, having promised that he would go straight home again as soon as his father left him. "Wouldn't you like to know what kind of home he is running too, and what sort of woman mother is? She must be very nice; Willy looked so well kept, and his father is as neat as a pin in those white linen overalls. I wonder if she made them? I wonder if Willy will forget his message? I wonder what kind of home it is."

"O," said the young gentleman, humoring her fancy, "it is a house of four rooms, and it has a little garden that the painter tends himself. They eat in the kitchen in winter, but the supper is going to be in the sitting-room to-night, because it is so hot. Willy has a sister four years old, and a little brother of six months. The mother has the baby on her arm while she pours out the tea."

He spoke, with his eye on the painter, who had now come inside, and with a glance at his paint-bucket, had taken a seat in the corner of the car, as if he were afraid the smell of paint might be offensive. There was nothing else noticeable about the man, and his face was as common and as good a kind face as one could anywhere see. A pleasant glow was in it, as if his heart had reflected its tenderness there, and his recent thoughts of his wife and children were made visible. So the young gentleman fancied, and saw no shadow descending.

He has no shadow, the terrible, the inexorable, the inevitable! He moves unseen among us, and his touch falls upon one and another, who vanish swiftly or fade slowly away, and leave a vacant name and a passing memory. It seems as if his approach, from far or near, should be deeply and unmistakably figured in those doomed suddenly to die, as if some awful distinction must invest them, hallowing them from the friendly or unfriendly slight with which we treat each other, and making them august and dear to us. They are to go on that long, strange journey, but no token of departure is in them; they stand at the borders of another world, but it is only the light of our own that illumines them; and we cannot know them for souls hovering upon eternity, but must forever mistake them for men like others, full of time's uses, and cares and stains.

Presently our friends, having paid their homage to the painter in his quality of husband and father, began to think him somewhat disagreeable in his character of house-painter, and to fancy that the pungent odors of his turpentine were helping to make the atmosphere of the car more oppressive. The conductor half-paused, and looked doubtfully at him as he passed, and after a little while, the painter rose, and stepped out of the car. The young gentleman, going to get a drink at the water jar in the corner, saw him sitting on the steps, and taking in great comfort the draft of air made by the train. He was holding fast by the iron railing, and the young gentleman was sensible of a vague feeling of envy for him as he turned to resume his own seat in the sultry car. But he talked to the young lady of other things, and had forgotten the painter, when the train came rather abruptly to a stand-still, and he noticed that it had stopped in the open country, among fields where mowers were clattering up and down the broad meadows. With two or three others, he quitted the car for a breath of the open air, and walked mechanically to the rear of the train. Two brakemen were running down the track; one of the men in the meadows had left his mower, and was leaping through the tall grass to the same point. At that point between the tracks lay a little white heap, very still.

A train came roaring up out of the west, and being signalled, stopped, and sent out other brakemen, and there was a little parley. Then what was there was lifted aboard that train. He had promised to come home on it.

When the young gentleman returned to his place, "Aren't you looking rather pale?" asked the young lady. "What did we stop for? Ought we to have met that train there? Have we come near an accident?"

"Very near," he answered.

Christmas Every Day

1886

I F, AS EDWIN CADY ARGUES, the late psychological fiction reveals "the Howells nobody knows" (*Light* 138), then "Christmas Every Day" reveals the Howells nobody knows today.[1] For in his lifetime, Howells was popularly known as a humorist, and, to a lesser extent, as a writer of Christmas fiction and of children's stories. As Don Cook explains, "it was humor, his amusing and genial wit, that first earned [Howells] a national audience. . . . Indeed the gradual revelation of his serious interests and intentions was taken by much of his audience as a betrayal of trust, a treason against the genial and genteel bond he had established with his readers" (69). "Christmas Every Day" is perhaps the most purely appealing of Howells's lighter fictions, yet it has biographical and psychological significance as well; and this "moral tale" is linked thematically to Howells's practice of realism.

Howells, of course, was a father, and his letters demonstrate his deep involvement in the lives of his three children.[2] Perhaps the most pertinent to "Christmas Every Day" is his letter of 31 October 1868, to his father, William C. Howells:

Tell Aurelia [Howells's sister] that the poem she gave me [Clement C. Moore's "A Visit from St. Nicholas"] has been read ragged already. Winny knew the piece before, but having it in a little book by itself seems to give it a new zest. Every night after dinner I have to come down the parlor chimney "with a bound"—the idea being represented by rattling on the screen and then jumping out into the middle of the floor. Then I am Winifred Howells, and lie asleep on the sofa while she brings me a Christmas Tree. (*SL* 1:304)

It is only natural that Howells would turn, at some point, to children's literature. What may at first seem odd is his timing. "Christmas Every Day," Howells's first work intended specifically for children, appeared in *St. Nicholas*, a children's magazine, in January of 1886, when Winny, John, and Mildred were respectively twenty-two, seventeen, and thirteen—undoubtedly older than the intended audience. The four other stories included in the volume *Christmas Every Day and Other Stories Told for Children* did not appear in print before the book publication in 1893. *A Boy's Town* was serially published in *Harper's Young People* from April to August of 1890, and appeared as a book later that year. Four of the Pony Baker stories were published between 1898 and 1902 (in *Youth's Companion* and *Harper's Weekly*) and *The Flight of Pony Baker* itself appeared in 1902.

There are a number of explanations for Howells's seemingly delayed decision to write for children. When his children were young, he was struggling to establish himself as a serious novelist and was furthermore tied down by his obligations to the *Atlantic Monthly*. Any desire to indulge himself by writing for his, or other, children had to make way before the overwhelming need to prove himself as a marketable writer and successful editor. *A Boy's Town* and later *The Flight of Pony Baker* were clearly linked to the autobiographical impulse that so influenced Howells's writings from the nineties on. The publication of *Christmas Every Day*, on the other hand, may have been prompted by the desire to return to and expand upon the material of "Christmas Every Day." All five of the *Christmas* stories are told by "the papa," "Turkeys Turning the Tables" on Christmas morning and "The Pony Engine and the Pacific Express" on Christmas Eve; and "Butterflyflutterby and Flutterbybutterfly," told by the papa to his niece and nephew, hearkens back to the papa's preoccupation with pigs: "The nephew hemmed twice in his throat, and asked, drowsily, 'Is it a little-pig story, or a fairy-prince story?' for he had heard from his cousins that their papa would tell you a little-pig story if he got the chance; and you had to look out and ask him which it was going to be beforehand" (112–13). The remaining story, "The Pumpkin-Glory," has a Thanksgiving theme (and also manages to work in a pig).

This leaves the question of why, in 1886, Howells turned for the first time to children's literature. Speculation is always risky, but I suggest that in the mid eighties, as Winny's health waxed and waned, Howells's thoughts increasingly returned to the happy days of her childhood. That the story is told by a father to a single daughter (unlike three out of the four 1893 stories) seems to recall the years 1863–68, when Winny was an only child. John Crowley points out that the period just before the publication of "Christmas Every Day" was an unusually good one for Winny, who was even planning to make her social debut in the fall of 1885. But by October, she was once again lapsing into invalidism (*Mask* 91). It is not clear whether "Christmas Every Day" was composed during one of Winny's highs or lows, but either condition could have prompted Howells to remember fondly the days when she was "beaming and blooming" (*SL* 1:250). There is no proof, as far as I know, that the story was composed with Winny in mind, but Howells's anguish over her state of health in the eighties and the loving companionship between father and daughter in the story make it seem likely.

"Christmas Every Day" was by no means Howells's only foray into literature specifically designed for the holiday season. As George Carrington points out, "December issues of periodicals were saturated with Christmas features throughout Howells' life" ("Sketches" 243), and Howells contributed his share. He was best known for a series of twelve domestic farces commonly called the Roberts-Campbell plays[3] (after their principal characters). A number of these were set specifically at Christmas time, and the first seven appeared in the Christmas issue of *Harper's*.[4] Howells's plays quickly became a seasonal institution. Booth Tarkington, in his memorial tribute to Howells, remembered that "a college boy of the late 'eighties and 'golden 'nineties' came home at Christmas to be either in the audience at a Howells farce or in the cast that gave it. Few things were surer" (348).

Howells's contributions to Christmas issues of periodicals continued into the twentieth century with six allegorical Christmas sketches in *Harper's Monthly* (both in the "Editor's Study" and in the later "Editor's Easy Chair") and in *Harper's Weekly* (in "Life and Letters"). Unlike the Roberts-Campbell plays, these sketches dealt directly with the season, as Howells "turned the occasion and the Christmas-allegory form to his own uses" (Carrington, "Sketches" 243). But Howells's real interest, according to Carrington, was in the freedom offered him by the convention of the Christmas vision: "At any other time of publication allegory would have drawn attention to itself by its very mode of being, but at Christmas readers of Howells' time were ready to swallow any amount of allegorical form and whimsical tone; in fact, once

Irving and Dickens had set the style, they demanded it" ("Sketches" 252). (Howells wrote allegorical sketches at other times of year as well, about eighty in all, and the Altrurian works are of course allegorical, but Carrington implies that the Christmas sketches allowed Howells an outlet for "uncertainties, anxieties, guilt, and other painful feelings" ["Sketches" 252] that the other works could not supply.)

Howells dealt with the holiday most directly in *The Night before Christmas* (1910), a play that was first published in *Harper's Monthly* and was later included in *The Daughter of the Storage* (1916). The play concerns Christmas as a secular holiday, an occasion for excessive and ultimately numbing shopping and gift giving—and it dramatizes the fatigue and disgust that accompany this emphasis on materialism. Meserve suggests that the play is "close in spirit to 'Christmas Every Day' and other Howells stories in which the materialistic view, the attitude toward gifts, the wish to do away with Christmas, and the tiredness and the hypocrisy are clearly shown" (602). This equation renders a disservice to "Christmas Every Day," which, although gently criticizing materialism and greed, has a markedly different tone. While *The Night before Christmas* concludes by affirming that the joy of Christmas is renewed by the innocence of children, this "sentimentalized" (Meserve 602) ending by no means erases the harsh criticism that preceded it. "Christmas Every Day," on the other hand, suggests that Christmas as it is is perfect and delightful, and that it is only when one tampers with the holiday that it becomes tainted and hypocritical.

Howells's skill as a humorist, although obvious to his readers, generally has been passed over by critics. Perhaps this is because of the subtlety of his humor, that is, the way in which it is usually inseparable from plot and character. In "Christmas Every Day," the humor lies both in character—the teasing interplay between father and daughter—and in plot—the narrated story itself. But it appears also, quite broadly, in the quality that William Gibson calls "Howells' love of the ridiculous" ("Heart" 32) and Don Cook calls "his fondness for *reductio ad absurdum*" (79). Cook, writing of Howells's serious fiction, notes the importance of parody in his work and argues that Howells's frequent method was to "render . . . the clichés of romance untenable by subjecting them to the test of pragmatism—that is by looking to their results" (72). There, in a nutshell, is the situation of the tale within a tale of "Christmas Every Day." The fictional little girl's "romantic" ideal is tested against its inevitable results—and these are seen to be completely undesirable. This paradigm appears in such novels as *A Modern Instance* (1882) and *April Hopes* (1888), in which "the characters [are allowed] to act out their foolish clichés and thus bring upon themselves the logically resulting miseries" (Cook 75). As Cook points out, however, "to contemporary readers, the element of parody in Howells' fiction was frequently invisible" (76). Howells's method followed his belief that "it should . . . be the novelist's business to keep out of the way" and his work, subtle, ironic, and relatively free of didacticism, had to "take its [often poor] chances with readers" (*SL* 3:220). But "Christmas Every Day," as a comic tale, allowed Howells to indulge his parodic instincts and to carry the little girl's desire to its simultaneously logical and absurd end. Parody, here, is absorbed into our understanding of a child's point of view and in the loving affection that infuses the story.

Notes

1. This may be changing, as there has been a relative surge of popular interest in "Christmas Every Day." It was included in 1992 in *A Christmas Sampler: Classic Stories of the Season, from Twain to Cheever,* an anthology edited by E. A. Crawford and Teresa Kennedy. Inexplicably, these editors include only half of Howells's story, letting it end abruptly and quite inconclusively on April Fools' Day. The story made a more satisfactory appearance in *The Christmas Box* (1993), written by Richard Paul Evans. A small excerpt from Howells's story is included in Evans's book, in which "Christmas Every Day" is read by a father to his young daughter. The success of *The Christmas Box* prompted its publishers to reissue separately a lavishly illustrated gift edition of "Christmas Every Day" in 1996. Finally, "Christmas Every Day" seems to have been the (unacknowledged) inspiration for a current children's video. "Elmo Saves Christmas," broadcast and released as a home video by the Children's Television Workshop in 1996, uses the characters of "Sesame Street" to tell a story that echoes Howells's both in plot and in a number of details.

2. Howells's involvement may have been too deep. Crowley, among other critics, argues that Winifred Howells's mysterious illness was at least in part neurotic, and that her psychological problems stemmed from her father's confused ambitions for her. See *Mask*, especially 98–105.

3. These were "The Sleeping Car" (1882), "The Elevator" (1884), "The Garroters" (1885), "The Mouse Trap" (1886), "Five O'Clock Tea" (1887), "A Likely Story" (1888), "The Albany Depot" (1889), "A Letter of Introduction" (1892), "Evening Dress" (1892), "The Unexpected Guests" (1893), "A Masterpiece of Diplomacy" (1894), and "The Smoking Car" (1898). They are all included in Meserve's *Complete Plays*.

4. "Evening Dress" appeared in a May issue of *Cosmopolitan*. "A Letter of Introduction," "The Unexpected Guests," and "A Masterpiece of Diplomacy" appeared in January and February issues of *Harper's Monthly*. "The Smoking Car" appeared in the Christmas issue of *Frank Leslie's*. All of the rest appeared in Christmas issues of *Harper's Monthly* or *Harper's Weekly*. Brenda Murphy oversimplifies, therefore, when she says that "each . . . appeared in the Christmas issue of *Harper's*" (122).

ℭ

Christmas Every Day

The little girl came into her papa's study, as she always did Saturday morning before breakfast, and asked for a story. He tried to beg off that morning, for he was very busy, but she would not let him. So he began:

"Well, once there was a little pig—"

She put her hand over his mouth and stopped him at the word. She said she had heard little pig-stories till she was perfectly sick of them.

"Well, what kind of story *shall* I tell then?"

"About Christmas. It's getting to be the season. It's past Thanksgiving already."

"It seems to me," her papa argued, "that I've told as often about Christmas as I have about little pigs."

"No difference! Christmas is more interesting."

"Well!" Her papa roused himself from his writing by a great effort. "Well, then, I'll tell you about the little girl that wanted it Christmas every day in the year. How would you like that?"

"First-rate!" said the little girl; and she nestled into comfortable shape in his lap, ready for listening.

"Very well, then, this little pig—Oh, what are you pounding me for?"

"Because you said little pig instead of little girl."

"I should like to know the difference between a little pig and a little girl that wanted it Christmas every day!"

"Papa," said the little girl, warningly, "if you don't go on, I'll give it to you!" And at this her papa darted off like lightning, and began to tell the story as fast as he could.

Well, once there was a little girl who liked Christmas so much that she wanted it to be Christmas every day in the year; and as soon as Thanksgiving was over she began to send postal-cards to the old Christmas Fairy to ask if she mightn't have it. But the old fairy never answered any of the postals; and after a while the little girl found out that the Fairy was pretty particular, and wouldn't notice anything but letters—not even correspondence cards in envelopes; but real letters on sheets of paper, and sealed outside with a monogram—or your initial, anyway. So, then, she began to send her letters; and in about three weeks—or just the day before Christmas it was—she got a letter from the Fairy, saying she might have it Christmas every day for a year, and then they would see about having it longer.

The little girl was a good deal excited already, preparing for the old-fashioned, once-a-year Christmas that was coming the next day, and perhaps the Fairy's promise didn't make such an impression on her as it would have made at some other time. She just resolved to keep it to herself, and surprise everybody with it as it kept coming true; and then it slipped out of her mind altogether.

She had a splendid Christmas. She went to bed early, so as to let Santa have a chance at the stockings, and in the morning she was up the first of anybody and went and felt them, and found hers all lumpy with packages of candy, and oranges and grapes, and pocket-books and rubber balls, and all kinds of small presents, and her big brother's with nothing but the tongs in them, and her young lady sister's with a new silk umbrella, and her papa's and mamma's with potatoes and pieces of coal wrapped up in tissue-paper, just as they always had every Christmas. Then she waited around till the rest of the family were up, and she was the first to burst into the library, where the doors were opened, and look at the large presents laid out on the library-table—books, and portfolios, and boxes of stationery, and breastpins, and dolls, and little stoves, and dozens of handkerchiefs, and inkstands, and skates, and snow-shovels, and photograph-frames, and little easels, and boxes of water-colors, and Turkish paste, and nougat, and candied cherries, and dolls' houses, and waterproofs—and the big Christmas tree, lighted and standing in a waste-basket in the middle.

She had a splendid Christmas all day. She ate so much candy that she did not want any breakfast; and the whole fore-noon the presents kept pouring in that the expressman had not had time to deliver the night before; and she went round giving the presents she had got for other people, and came home and ate turkey and cranberry for dinner, and plum-pudding and nuts and raisins and oranges and more candy, and then went out and coasted, and came in with a stomach-ache, crying; and her papa said he would see if his house was turned into that sort of fool's paradise another year; and they had a light supper, and pretty early everybody went to bed cross.

Here the little girl pounded her papa in the back, again.

"Well, what now? Did I say pigs?"

"You made them *act* like pigs."

"Well, didn't they?"

"No matter; you oughtn't to put it into a story."

"Very well, then, I'll take it out."

Her father went on:

The little girl slept very heavily, and she slept very late, but she was wakened at last by the other children dancing round her bed with their stockings full of presents in their hands.

"What is it?" said the little girl, and she rubbed her eyes and tried to rise up in bed.

"Christmas! Christmas! Christmas!" they all shouted, and waved their stockings.

"Nonsense! It was Christmas yesterday."

Her brothers and sisters just laughed. "We don't know about that. It's Christmas to-day, anyway. You come into the library and see."

Then all at once it flashed on the little girl that the fairy was keeping her promise, and her year of Christmases was beginning. She was dreadfully sleepy, but she sprang up like a lark—a lark that had overeaten itself and had gone to bed cross—and darted into the library. There it was again! Books, and portfolios, and boxes of stationery, and breastpins—

"You needn't go over it all, papa; I guess I can remember just what was there," said the little girl.

Well, there was the Christmas tree blazing away, and the family picking out their presents, but looking pretty sleepy, and her father perfectly puzzled, and her mother ready to cry. "I'm sure I don't see how I'm to dispose of all these things," said her mother, and her father said it seemed to him they had had something just like it the day before, but he supposed he must have dreamed it. This struck the little girl as the best kind of a joke; and so she ate so much candy she didn't want any breakfast, and went round carrying presents, and had turkey and cranberry for dinner, and then went out and coasted, and came in with a—

"Papa!"

"Well, what now?"

"What did you promise, forgetful thing?"

"Oh! oh yes!"

Well, the next day, it was just the same, but everybody getting crosser; and at the end of a week's time so many people had lost their tempers that you could pick up lost tempers anywhere; they perfectly strewed the ground. Even when people tried to recover their tempers they usually got somebody else's, and it made the most dreadful mix.

The little girl began to get frightened, keeping the secret all to herself; she wanted to tell her mother, but she didn't dare to; and she was ashamed to ask the Fairy to take back her gift, it seemed ungrateful and ill-bred, and she thought she would try to stand it, but she hardly knew how she could, for a whole year. So it went on and on, and it was Christmas on St. Valentine's Day and Washington's Birthday, just the same as any day, and it didn't even skip the First of April, though everything was counterfeit that day, and that was some *little* relief.

After a while coal and potatoes began to be awfully scarce, so many had been wrapped up in tissue-paper to fool papas and mammas with. Turkeys got to be about a thousand dollars apiece—

"Papa!"
"Well, what?"
"You're beginning to fib!"
"Well, *two* thousand, then."

And they got to passing off almost anything for turkeys—half-grown humming-birds, and even rocs out of the Arabian Nights—the real turkeys were so scarce. And cranberries—well, they asked a diamond apiece for cranberries. All the woods and orchards were cut down for Christmas-trees, and where the woods and orchards used to be it looked just like a stubble-field, with the stumps. After a while they had to make Christmas-trees out of rags, and stuff them with bran, like old-fashioned dolls; but there were plenty of rags, because people got so poor, buying presents for one another, that they couldn't get any new clothes, and they just wore their old ones to tatters. They got so poor that everybody had to go to the poor-house, except the confectioners, and the fancy-store keepers, and the picture book sellers, and the expressmen; and *they* all got so rich and proud that they would hardly wait upon a person when he came to buy. It was perfectly shameful!

Well, after it had gone on about three or four months, the little girl, whenever she came into the room in the morning and saw those great ugly, lumpy stockings dangling at the fire-place, and the disgusting presents around everywhere, used to just sit down and burst out crying. In six months she was perfectly exhausted; she couldn't even cry anymore; she just lay on the lounge and rolled her eyes and panted. About the beginning of October she took to sitting down on dolls whenever she found them—French dolls, or any kind—she hated the sight of them so; and by Thanksgiving she was crazy, and just slammed her presents across the room.

By that time people didn't carry presents around nicely anymore. They flung them over the fence, or through the window, or anything; and, instead of running their tongues out and taking great pains to write "For dear Papa," or "Mamma," or "Brother," or "Sister," or "Susie," or "Sammie," or "Billie," or "Bobbie," or "Jimmie," or "Jennie," or whoever it was, and troubling to get the spelling right, and then signing their names, and "Xmas, 18—," they use to write in the gift-books, "Take it, you horrid old thing!" and then go and bang it against the front door. Nearly everybody had built barns to hold their presents, but pretty soon the barns overflowed, and then they used to let them lie out in the rain, or anywhere. Sometimes the police used to come and tell them to shovel their presents off the sidewalk, or they would arrest them.

"I thought you said everybody had gone to the poor-house," interrupted the little girl.

"They did go, at first," said her papa; "but after a while the poor-houses got so full that they had to send the people back to their own houses. They tried to cry, when they got back, but they couldn't make the least sound."

"Why couldn't they?"

"Because they had lost their voices, saying 'Merry Christmas' so much. Did I tell you how it was on the Fourth of July?"

"No; how was it?" And the little girl nestled closer, in expectation of something uncommon.

Well, the night before, the boys stayed up to celebrate, as they always do, and fell asleep before twelve o'clock, as usual, expecting to be wakened by the bells and cannon. But it was nearly eight o'clock before the first boy in the United States woke up, and then he found out what the trouble was. As soon as he could get his clothes on he ran out of the house and smashed a big cannon-torpedo down on the pavement; but it didn't make any more noise than a damp wad of paper; and after he tried about twenty or thirty more, he began to pick them up and look at them. Every single torpedo was a big raisin! Then he just streaked it up-stairs, and examined his fire-crackers and toy-pistol and two-dollar collection of fireworks, and found that they were nothing but sugar and candy painted up to look like fire-works! Before ten o'-clock every boy in the United States found out that his Fourth of July things had turned into Christmas things; and then they just sat down and cried—

they were so mad. There are about twenty million boys in the United States, and so you can imagine what a noise they made. Some men got together before night, with a little powder that hadn't turned into purple sugar yet, and they said they would fire off one cannon, anyway. But the cannon burst into a thousand pieces, for it was nothing but rock-candy, and some of the men nearly got killed. The Fourth of July orations all turned into Christmas carols, and when anybody tried to read the Declaration, instead of saying, "When in the course of human events it becomes necessary," he was sure to sing, "God rest you, merry gentlemen." It was perfectly awful.

The little girl drew a deep sigh of satisfaction.

"And how was it at Thanksgiving?"

Her papa hesitated. "Well, I'm almost afraid to tell you. I'm afraid you'll think it's wicked."

"Well, tell anyway," said the little girl.

Well, before it came Thanksgiving it had leaked out who had caused all these Christmases. The little girl had suffered so much that she had talked about it in her sleep; and after that hardly anybody would play with her. People just perfectly despised her, because if it had not been for her greediness it wouldn't have happened; and now, when it came Thanksgiving, and she wanted them to go to church, and have squash-pie and turkey, and show their gratitude, they said all the turkeys had been eaten up for her old Christmas dinners, and if she would stop the Christmases, they would see about the gratitude. Wasn't it dreadful? And the very next day the little girl began to send letters to the Christmas Fairy, and then telegrams, to stop it. But it didn't do any good; and then she got to calling at the Fairy's house, but the girl that came to the door always said, "Not at home," or "Engaged," or "At dinner," or something like that; and so it went on till it came to the old once-a-year Christmas Eve. The little girl fell asleep, and when she woke up in the morning—

"She found it was all nothing but a dream," suggested the girl.

"No, indeed!" said her papa. "It was all every bit true!"

"Well, what *did* she find out, then?"

"Why, that it wasn't Christmas at last, and wasn't ever going to be, any more. Now it's time for breakfast."

The little girl held her papa fast around the neck.

"You sha'n't go if you're going to leave it *so!*"

"How do you want it left?"

"Christmas once a year."

"All right," said her papa; and he went on again.

Well, there was the greatest rejoicing all over the country, and it extended clear up to Canada. The people met together everywhere, and kissed and cried for joy. The city carts went around and gathered up all the candy and raisins and nuts, and dumped them into the river; and it made the fish perfectly sick; and the whole United States, as far out as Alaska, was one blaze of bonfires, where the children were burning up their gift-books and presents of all kinds. They had the greatest *time!*

The little girl went to thank the old Fairy because she had stopped its being Christmas, and she said she hoped she would keep her promise that Christmas never, never came again. Then the Fairy frowned, and asked her if she was sure she knew what she meant; and the little girl asked her, Why not? and the old Fairy said that now she was behaving just as greedily as ever, and she'd better look out. This made the little girl think it all over carefully again, and she said she would be willing to have it Christmas about once in a thousand years; and then she said a hundred, and then she said ten, and at last she got down to one. Then the Fairy said that was the good old way that had pleased people ever since Christmas began, and she was agreed. Then the little girl said, "What're your shoes made of?" And the Fairy said, "Leather." And the little girl said, "Bargain's done forever," and skipped off, and hippity-hopped the whole way home, she was so glad.

"How will that do?" asked the papa.

"First-rate!" said the little girl; but she hated to have the story stop, and was rather sober. However, her mamma put her head in at the door, and asked her papa:

"Are you never coming to breakfast? What have you been telling that child?"

"Oh, just a moral tale."

The little girl caught him around the neck again.

"*We* know! Don't you tell *what* papa! Don't you tell *what!*"

The Magic of a Voice

1899

B ECAUSE IT DEALS WITH social conventions and manners, "The Magic of a Voice" confirms to an extent Frank Norris's characterization of Howellsian realism as "the drama of a broken teacup, the tragedy of a walk down the block" (164–65). But the story is also a subtle study in the psychology of perception and imagination. "The Magic of a Voice," in a variation of the theme of realism versus romance, pits reality against a Howellsian device that might be called "fictionalizing."

Fictionalizing is a literary action in which fictional characters are made to consider themselves, or more frequently, their acquaintances, as characters in a contemplated piece of fiction. (It is treated in a very general way by Charles Campbell, who notes examples of "a technique shared by Howells with many other novelists of the realistic movement, that of relating their story to other fictional worlds"—289.) Fictionalizing is central to Howells's writing, especially to the Basil and Isabel March stories. In "A Pair of Patient Lovers" (1897), for example, Basil and Isabel March regularly embroider the facts about their companions to make reality more "complete" and "dramatic" (73). They invent imaginary conversations and scenerios that are more satisfying (because they are more like literature) than "poor real life" (*Their Wedding Journey* 42). At one point, Basil March discusses his fictionalizing: "My wife and I talked the affair over far into the night, and in the paucity of particulars I was almost driven to their invention. But I managed to keep a good conscience, and at the same time to satisfy the demand for facts in a measure by the indulgence of conjectures which Mrs. March continually took for them" (73). Such "indulgence of conjectures" appears also in "A Circle in the Water" (1895), another Basil and Isabel March story. Again, Basil and Isabel make up alternatives to reality, explaining that the facts, as they exist, are "so graceless, so tasteless!" and lamenting the absence of "anything dramatic, anything artistic" in the plights of their neighbors (341).

The Marches consistently consider, not their responsibility to their friends, but the neatness or symmetry of their friends' circumstances. In doing so, they are clearly taking what Jerome Klinkowitz calls the aesthetic, as opposed to the ethical, approach (304). But by creating imaginary scripts for their friends to follow, and by inventing scenes and conversations that only might have taken place, the Marches move beyond the relative passivity of making aesthetic judgments. Instead, they treat their acquaintances as elements to be manipulated in order to achieve a desired aesthetic result (a result, by the way, that clearly reflects the romantic conventions of popular nineteenth-century literature). Fictionalizing is the aesthetic reaction turned into action. (Howells's most extreme example of fictionalizing can be found in "Braybridge's Offer.")

The fictionalizing in "Magic" differs from that of the two earlier stories in an important respect: it moves the plot forward. It is no longer a tool for understanding reality, but a replacement for reality. In this way, and in other ways as well, "Magic" is remarkably similar to "The Pursuit of the Piano," its contemporary,[1] and it is worthwhile to consider the conflict between reality and romantic fictionalizing that these stories explore.

The two stories begin the same way: an unaccompanied male character is suddenly and unexpectedly attracted by a single isolated aspect of an unknown woman. Both men construct around this single aspect an imagined whole.[2] In "Magic," Stephen Langbourne, having heard only a woman's voice, imaginatively fills in the missing elements to create an entire person: "The owner of that voice had imagination and humor. . . . [She was] tall and pale, with full, blue eyes and a regular face. . . . She dressed simply in dark blue, and her hair was of a dark mahogany color." In "Pursuit," Hamilton Gaites, having seen a name and address on the side of a packing case for a piano, similarly imagines a personality, a home, and a family for their owner. He assumes that "the young lady was seventeen, or would be when the piano reached Lower Merritt, for it was clearly meant to arrive on her birthday; it was a birthday-present and a surprise" (83). And the imaginative creations of both Langbourne and Gaites become in each story an impetus to action, become in fact the prime motivating force in the plot.

In each story, too, the imaginer learns more about the real object of his speculation—and eventually finds that, in a way, he was wrong about the right person and right about the wrong person. Faced with these facts, each hero quickly modifies his ideal creation to correspond more closely with reality. The following passage from "The Pursuit of the Piano," although it occurs before Hamilton Gaites has learned the full truth about Phyllis Desmond, illustrates the process:

> [The piano] had now a pathos for him which had been wanting earlier in his romance. It was no longer a gay surprise for a young girl's birthday; it was the sober means of living to a woman who must work for her living. But he found it not the less charming for that; he had even a more romantic interest in it, mingled with the sense of patronage, of protection, which is so agreeable to a successful man. (113)

And each character ends by concluding that the reality is in fact better than the imagined ideal.

In both "Magic" and "Pursuit," the hazards of fictionalizing are mitigated by its advantages, as the imaginative act leads each protagonist to new ventures and to boldness in courtship, and as each is able to discard the false images he has formed. Howells's attitude toward the romantic imagination is comparatively indulgent in these stories; "romanticism" invariably leads to error, but it is at least a driving force that can propel otherwise stagnant characters into action.

Although the two stories resemble each other in plot and theme, they differ in tone. "Pursuit" is consistently comic; Hamilton Gaites falls in love gradually and reluctantly, and the worst that he has to suffer is some social awkwardness. Stephen Langbourne, on the other hand, is instantly in love and suffers one disappointment after another. Disappointment gives way to humiliation, and then to rejection, before the finally happy ending. Langbourne, in fact, approaches the typical hero of Howells's mature period, described by George Carrington as "isolated and humiliated" (*Drama* 4). This isolation, Carrington explains, is linked to the false expectations created by the imagination: "the mere perception of exterior reality [here opposed to the "fictionalizing" imagination] carries for Howells a voltage of alienation . . .

based on the contrast between the expected qualities of reality and perception and the actual qualities, which are always different" (*Drama* 55).

What is interesting about "Magic" (and to a lesser extent, about "Pursuit")
is that the "voltage of alienation," while it is clearly present, is downplayed
in favor of the love story. Both the expectations created by the imagination
and the perception of reality are less important than the "magic" of attraction
and are in fact controlled by it. Langbourne's creation of an ideal Barbara
Simpson is obviously controlled by the "magic" of love, but so too is his actual
perception. Just as, after hearing Juliet Bingham being bossy and cold, "he
perceived that Miss Bingham had not such a good figure as he had fancied the
night before, and that her eyes were set rather too near together," so too does
Barbara grow more and more physically attractive to him. Howells's emphasis is on the flexibility and resilience of both the romantic imagination and
human consciousness of perception.

Carrington's discussion of the nature of perception is pertinent to this
story. He argues that true perception, when it occurs in Howells, is fleeting:
"perception occurs for Howells only through change in the perceiver or the
thing perceived, and the perception itself is only a momentary condition. The
perceiver remains, and may be permanently changed by his perception, but
the perception dies" (*Drama* 41). Thus, Langbourne sees Barbara clearly for
only a moment, after which he sees her with the eyes of love (for which, of
course, her physical qualities are unimportant).

"The Magic of a Voice," then, examines the complicated relationship between love and perception. The romantic formula of "love at first sight" is
simultaneously satirized and demonstrated by this subtle story. "Magic" also
reveals the shift in Howells's attention from social and political issues to a
more fully conscious exploration of psychology. (All of the stories in *A Pair of
Patient Lovers*, in fact, can be seen as part of Howells's transition from realism
to psychological realism.) Barbara's move to the piano at the end of the story
is especially striking, as it reveals her repressed desire to accept Langbourne's
proposal. Her performance of the music that would signal her acceptance of
Langbourne amounts, in fact, to a physical version of a Freudian slip:

[S]he rose nervously, as if she could not sit still, and went to the piano. The
Spanish song he had given her was lying open upon it, and she struck some of
the chords absently, and then let her fingers rest on the keys.

"Miss Simpson," he said, coming stiffly forward, "I should like to hear you
sing that song once more before I—Won't you sing it?"

"Why, yes," she said, and she slipped laterally into the piano-seat.

By her actions, Barbara "speaks" the acceptance that she verbally represses, and Langbourne, as soon as he learns the significance of the song, understands this.

"Magic" has received almost no critical attention. Its most notable treatment is that by Oscar Firkins, who dismisses the story in a single sentence: "'The Spell of a Voice' [*sic*] is dim—not obscure but simply dim" (208). While "Magic" may not be a great story, it is certainly a good story, and one that extends our understanding of Howells's concerns and his methods.

Notes

1. "The Pursuit of the Piano" was first published in April of 1900, only four months after "Magic" appeared in *Lippincott's*.

2. G. Ferris Cronkhite compares "Magic" to Chekhov's "The Kiss," noting that in both the "hero is in love with an illusory image of a woman," but, oddly, he dismisses "Piano" as "fail[ing] to focus on the inner life" (477).

᷂

The Magic of a Voice

I.

There was a full moon, and Langbourne walked about the town, unable to come into the hotel and go to bed. The deep yards of the houses gave out the scent of syringas and June roses; the light of lamps came through the fragrant bushes from the open doors and windows, with the sound of playing and singing and bursts of young laughter. Where the houses stood near the street, he could see people lounging on the thresholds, and their heads silhouetted against the luminous interiors. Other houses, both those which stood further back and those that stood nearer, were dark and still, and to those he attributed the happiness of love in fruition, safe from unrest and longing.

His own heart was tenderly oppressed, not with desire, but with the memory of desire. It was almost as if in his faded melancholy he were sorry for the disappointment of someone else.

At last he turned and walked back through the streets of dwellings to the business centre of the town, where a gush of light came from the veranda of his hotel, and the druggist's window cast purple and yellow blurs out upon the footway. The other stores were shut, and he alone seemed to be abroad. The church clock struck ten as he mounted the steps of his hotel and dropped the remnants of his cigar over the side.

He had slept badly on the train the night before, and he had promised himself to make up his lost sleep in the good conditions that seemed to offer themselves. But when he sat down in the hotel office he was more wakeful than he had been when he started to walk himself drowsy.

The clerk gave him the New York paper which had come by the evening train, and he thanked him, but remained musing in his chair. At times he thought he would light another cigar, but the hand that he carried to his breast pocket dropped nervelessly to his knee again, and he did not smoke. Through his memories of disappointment pierced a self-reproach which did not permit him the perfect self-complacency of regret; and yet he could not have been sure, if he had asked himself, that this pang did not heighten the luxury of his psychological experience.

He rose and asked the clerk for a lamp, but he turned back from the stairs to inquire when there would be another New York mail. The clerk said there was a train from the south due at eleven-forty, but it seldom brought any mail; the principal mail was at seven. Langbourne thanked him, and came back to beg the clerk to be careful and not have him called in the morning, for he wished to sleep. Then he went up to his room, where he opened his window to let in the night air. He heard a dog barking, a cow lowed; from a stable somewhere the soft thumping of horses' feet came at intervals lullingly.

II.

Langbourne fell asleep so quickly that he was aware of no moment of waking after his head touched the fragrant pillow. He woke so much refreshed by his first sound, soft sleep that he thought it must be nearly morning. He got his watch into a ray of the moonlight and made out that it was only a little after midnight, and he perceived that it must have been the sound of low murmuring voices and broken laughter in the next room which had wakened him. But he was rather glad to have been roused to a sense of his absolute comfort, and he turned unresentfully to sleep again. All the heaviness of his heart was gone; he felt curiously glad and young; he had somehow forgiven the wrong he had suffered and the wrong he had done. The subdued murmuring went on in the next room, and he kept himself awake to enjoy it for a while. Then he let himself go, and drifted away into gulfs of slumber, where, suddenly, he seemed to strike against something, and started up in bed.

A laugh came from the next room. It was not muffled, as before, but frank and clear. It was woman's laughter, and Langbourne easily inferred girlhood as well as womanhood from it. His neighbors must have come by the late train, and they had probably begun to talk as soon as they got into their room. He imagined their having spoken low at first for fear of disturbing some one, and then, in their forgetfulness, or their belief that there was no one near, allowed themselves greater freedom. There were survivals of their earlier caution at times, when their voices sank so low as scarcely to be heard; then there was a break in it when they rose clearly distinguishable from each other. They were never so distinct that he could make out what was said; but each voice unmistakably conveyed character.

Friendship between girls is never equal; they may equally love each other, but one must worship and one must suffer worship. Langbourne read the differing temperaments necessary to this relation in the differing voices. That which bore mastery was a low, thick murmur, coming from deep in the throat, and flowing out in a steady stream of indescribable coaxing and drolling. The owner of that voice had imagination and humor which could charm with absolute control her companion's lighter nature, as it betrayed itself in a gay tinkle of amusement and a succession of nervous whispers. Langbourne did not wonder at her subjection; with the first sounds of that rich, tender voice, he had fallen under its spell too; and he listened intensely, trying to make out some phrase, some word, some syllable. But the talk kept its subaudible flow, and he had to content himself as he could with the sound of the voice.

As he lay eavesdropping with all his might he tried to construct an image of the two girls from their voices. The one with the crystalline laugh was little and lithe, quick in movement, of a mobile face, with gray eyes and fair hair; the other was tall and pale, with full, blue eyes and a regular face, and lips that trembled with humor; very demure and yet very honest; very shy and yet very frank; there was something almost mannish in her essential honesty; there was nothing of feminine coquetry in her, though everything of feminine charm. She was a girl who looked like her father, Langbourne perceived with a flash of divination. She dressed simply in dark blue, and her hair was of a dark mahogany color. The smaller girl wore light gray checks or stripes, and the shades of silver.

The talk began to be less continuous in the next room, from which there came the sound of sighs and yawns, and then of mingled laughter at these. Then the talk ran unbrokenly for a while, and again dropped into laughs that recognized the drowse creeping upon the talkers. Suddenly it stopped altogether, and left Langbourne, as he felt, definitively awake for the rest of the night.

He had received an impression which he could not fully analyze. With some inner sense he kept hearing that voice, low and deep, and rich with whimsical suggestion. Its owner must have a strange, complex nature, which would perpetually provoke and satisfy. Her companionship would be as easy and reasonable as a man's, while it had the charm of a woman's. At the moment it seemed to him that life without this companionship would be something poorer and thinner than he had yet known, and that he could not endure to forego it. Somehow he must manage to see the girl and make her acquaintance. He did not know how it could be contrived, but it could certainly be contrived, and he began to dramatize their meeting on these various terms. It was interesting and it was delightful, and it always came, in its safe impossibility, to his telling her that he loved her, and to her consenting to be his wife. He resolved to take no chance of losing her, but to remain awake, and somehow see her before she could leave the hotel in the morning. The resolution gave him calm; he felt that the affair was so far settled.

Suddenly he started from his pillow; and again he heard that mellow laugh, warm and rich as the cooing of doves on sunlit eaves. The sun was shining through the crevices of his window-blinds; he looked at his watch; it was half-past eight. The sound of fluttering skirts and flying feet in the corridor shook his heart. A voice, the voice of the mellow laugh, called as if to someone on the stairs, "I must have put it in my bag. It doesn't matter, anyway."

He hurried on his clothes, in the vain hope of finding his neighbors before breakfast; but before he had finished dressing he heard wheels before the veranda below, and he saw the hotel barge* drive away as if to the station. There were two passengers in it; two women, whose faces were hidden by the fringe of the barge-roof, but whose slender figures showed themselves from their necks down. It seemed to him that one was tall and slight, the other slight and little.

---

* According to *Webster's*, "a large horse-drawn omnibus usually used for excursions or the transportation of groups (as from a railroad station to a hotel)"; the term was chiefly of New England usage.

III.

He stopped in the hall, and then, tempted by his despair, he stepped within the open door of the next room and looked vaguely over it, with shame at being there. What was it that the girl had missed, and had come back to look for? Some trifle, no doubt, which she had not cared to lose, and yet had not wished to leave behind. He failed to find anything in the search, which he could not make very thorough, and he was going guiltily out when his eye fell upon an envelope, perversely fallen beside the door and almost indiscernible against the white paint, with the addressed surface inward.

This must be the object of her search, and he could understand why she was not very anxious when he found it a circular from a nursery-man, containing nothing more than a list of flowering shrubs. He satisfied himself that this was all without satisfying himself that he had quite a right to do so; and he stood abashed in the presence of the superscription on the envelope somewhat as if Miss Barbara F. Simpson, Upper Ashton Falls, N.H., were there to see him tampering with her correspondence. It was indelicate, and he felt that his whole behavior had been indelicate, from the moment that her laugh had wakened him in the night till now, when he had invaded her room. He had no more doubt that she was the taller of the two girls than that this was her name on the envelope. He liked Barbara; and Simpson could be changed. He seemed to hear her soft throaty laugh in response to the suggestion, and with a leap of the heart he slipped the circular into his breast pocket.

After breakfast he went to the hotel office, and stood leaning on the long counter and talking with the clerk till he could gather courage to look at the register, where he knew the names of the girls must be written. He asked where Upper Ashton Falls was, and whether it would be a good place to spend a week.

The clerk said that it was about thirty miles up the road, and was one of the nicest places in the mountains; Langbourne could not go to a nicer; and there was a very good little hotel. "Why," he said, "there were two ladies here overnight that just left for there, on the seven-forty. Odd you should ask about it."

Langbourne owned that it was odd, and then he asked if the ladies lived at Upper Ashton Falls, or were merely summer folks.

"Well, a little of both," said the clerk. "They're cousins, and they've got an aunt living there that they stay with. They used to go away winters,—teaching, I guess,—but this last year they stayed right through. Been down to Springfield, they said, and just stopped the night because the accommodation don't go any farther. Wake you up last night? I had to put 'em into the room next to yours, and girls usually talk."

Langbourne answered that it would have taken a good deal of talking to wake him the night before, and then he lounged across to the time-table hanging on the wall, and began to look up the trains for Ashton Falls.

"If you want to go to the Falls," said the clerk, "there's a through train at four, with a drawing-room on it, that will get you there by five."

"Oh, I fancy I was looking up the New York trains," Langbourne returned. He did not like these evasions, but in his consciousness of Miss Simpson he seemed unable to avoid them. The clerk went out on the veranda to talk with a farmer bringing supplies, and Langbourne ran to the register, and read there the names of Barbara F. Simpson and Juliet D. Bingham. It was Miss Simpson who had registered for both, since her name came first, and the entry was in a good, simple hand, which was like a man's in its firmness and clearness. He turned from the register decided to take the four-o'clock train for Upper Ashton Falls, and met a messenger with a telegram which he knew was for himself before the boy could ask his name. His partner had suddenly fallen sick; his recall was absolute, his vacation was at an end; nothing re-mained for him but to take the first train back to New York. He thought how little prescient he had been in his pretence that he was looking the New York trains up; but the need of one had come already, and apparently he should never have any use for a train to Upper Ashton Falls.

IV.

All the way back to New York Langbourne was oppressed by a sense of loss such as his old disappointment in love now seemed never to have inflicted. He found that his whole being had set toward the unseen owner of the voice which had charmed him, and it was like a stretching and tearing of the nerves to be going from her instead of going toward her. He was as much under duress as if he were bound by a hypnotic spell. The voice continually sounded, not in his ears, which were filled with the noises of the train, as usual, but in the inmost of his spirit, where it was a low, cooing coaxing murmur. He real-ized now how intensely he must have listened for it in the night, how every tone of it must have pervaded him and possessed him. He was in love with it, he was as entirely fascinated by it as if it were the girl's whole presence, her looks, her qualities.

The remnant of the summer passed in the fret of business which was doubly irksome through his feeling of being kept from the girl whose personality he constructed from the sound of her voice, and set over his fancy in an absolute sovereignty. The image he had created of her remained a dim and blurred vision through the day, but by night it became distinct and compelling. One evening, late in the fall, he could endure the stress no longer, and he yielded to the temptation which had beset him from the first moment he renounced his purpose of returning in person the circular addressed to her as a means of her acquaintance. He wrote to her, and in terms as dignified as he could contrive, and as free from any ulterior import, he told her he had found it in the hotel hallway and had meant to send it to her at once, thinking it might be of some slight use to her. He had failed to do this, and now, having come upon it among some other papers, he sent it with an explanation which he hoped she would excuse him for troubling her with.

This was not true, but he did not see how he could begin with her by saying that he had found the circular in her room, and had kept it by him ever since, looking at it every day, and leaving it where he could see it last thing before he slept every night and the first thing after he woke in the morning. As to her reception of the story, he had to trust his knowledge that she was, like himself, of country birth and breeding, and to his belief that she would not take alarm at his overture. He did not go much into the world and was little acquainted with its usages, yet he knew enough to suspect that a woman of the world would either ignore his letter, or would return a cold and snubbing expression of Miss Simpson's thanks for Mr. Stephen M. Langbourne's kindness.

He had not only signed his name and given his address carefully in hopes of a reply, but he had enclosed the business card of his firm as a token of his responsibility. The partner in a wholesale stationery house ought to be an impressive figure in the imagination of a village girl; but it was some weeks before any answer came to Langbourne's letter. The reply began with an apology for the delay, and Langbourne perceived that he had gained rather than lost by the writer's hesitation; clearly she believed that she had put herself in the wrong, and that she owed him a certain reparation. For the rest, her letter was discreetly confined to an acknowledgement of the trouble he had taken.

But this spare return was richly enough for Langbourne; it would have sufficed, if there had been nothing in the letter, that the handwriting proved Miss Simpson to have been the one who had made the entry of her name and her friend's in the hotel register. This was most important as one step in corroboration of the fact that he had rightly divined her; that the rest should come true was almost a logical necessity. Still, he was puzzled to contrive a pretext for writing again, and he remained without one for a fortnight. Then, in passing a seedsman's store which he used to pass every day without thinking, he one day suddenly perceived his opportunity. He went in and got a number of the catalogues and other advertisements, and addressed them then and there, in a wrapper the seedsman gave him, to Miss Barbara F. Simpson, Upper Ashton Falls, N.H.

Now the response came with a promptness which at least testified of the lingering compunction of Miss Simpson. She asked if she were right in supposing that the seedsman's catalogues and folders had come to her from Langbourne and whether the seedsman in question was reliable; it was so difficult to get garden seeds that one could trust.

The correspondence now established itself, and with one excuse or another it prospered throughout the winter. Langbourne was not only willing, he was most eager, to give her proof of his reliability; he spoke of stationers in Springfield and Greenfield to whom he was personally known; and he secretly hoped she would satisfy herself through friends in those places that he was an upright and trustworthy person.

Miss Simpson wrote delightful letters, with that whimsical quality which had enchanted him in her voice. The coaxing and caressing was not there, and could not be expected to impart itself, unless in those refuges of deep feeling supposed to lurk between the lines. But he hoped to provoke it from these in time, and his own letters grew the more earnest the more ironical hers became. He wrote to her about a book he was reading, and when she said she had not seen it, he sent it her; in one of her letters she casually betrayed that she sang contralto in the choir, and then he sent her some new songs, which he had heard in the theatre, and which he had informed himself from a friend were contralto. He was always tending to the expression of the feeling which swayed him; but on her part there was no sentiment. Only in the fact that she was willing to continue this exchange of letters with a man personally unknown to her did she betray that romantic tradition which underlies all our young life, and in those unused to the world tempts to things blameless in themselves, but of the sort shunned by the worldlier wise. There was no great wisdom in Miss Simpson's letters, but Langbourne did not miss it; he was content with her mere words, as they related the little events of her simple daily life. These repeated themselves from the page in the tones of her voice and filled him with a passionate intoxication.

Towards spring he had his photograph taken, for no reason that he could have given; but since it was done he sent one to his mother in Vermont, and then he wrote his name on another, and sent it to Miss Simpson in New Hampshire. He hoped, of course, that she would return a photograph of herself; but she merely acknowledged his with some dry playfulness. Then, after disappointing him so long that he had ceased to expect anything, she enclosed a picture. The face was so far averted that Langbourne could get nothing but the curve of a longish cheek, the point of a nose, the segment of a crescent eyebrow. The girl said that as they should probably never meet, it was not necessary that he should know her when he saw her; she explained that she was looking away because she had been attracted by something on the other side of the photograph gallery just at the moment the artist took the cap off the tube of his camera, and she could not turn back without breaking the plate.

Langbourne replied that he was going up to Springfield on business the first week in May, and that he thought he might push on as far north as Upper Ashton Falls. To this there came no rejoinder whatever, but he did not lose courage. It was now the end of April, and he could not bear to wait for a further verification of his ideal; the photograph had confirmed him in its evasive fashion at every point of his conjecture concerning her. It was the face he had imagined her having, or so he now imagined, and it was just such a long oval face as would go with the figure he attributed to her. She must have the healthy pallor of skin which associates itself with masses of dark, mahogany-colored hair.

V.

It was so long since he had known a Northern spring that he had forgotten how much later the beginning of May was in New Hampshire; but as his train ran up from Springfield he realized the difference of the season from that which he had left in New York. The meadows were green only in the damp hollows; most of the trees were as bare as in midwinter; the willows in the swamplands hung out their catkins, and the white birches showed faint signs of returning life. In the woods were long drifts of snow, though he knew that in the brown leaves along the edges the pale pink flowers of the trailing arbutus were hiding their wet faces. A vernal mildness overhung the landscape. A blue haze filled the distances and veiled the hills; from the farm door-yards the smell of burning leaf-heaps and garden-stalks came through the window which he lifted to let in the dull, warm air. The sun shone down from a pale sky, in which the crows called to one another.

By the time he arrived in Upper Ashton Falls the afternoon had waned so far towards evening that the first robins were singing their vespers from the leafless choirs of the maples before the hotel. He indulged the landlord in his natural supposition that he had come up to make a timely engagement for summer board; after supper he even asked what the price of such rooms as his would be by the week in July, while he tried to lead the talk round to the fact which he wished to learn.

He did not know where Miss Simpson lived; and the courage with which he set out on his adventure totally lapsed, leaving in its place an accusing sense of silliness. He was where he was without reason, and in defiance of the tacit unwillingness of the person he had come to see; she certainly had given him no invitation, she had given him no permission to come. For the moment, in his shame, it seemed to him that the only thing for him was to go back to New York by the first train in the morning. But then what would the girl think of him? Such an act must forever end the intercourse which had now become an essential part of his life. That voice which had haunted him for so long, was he never to hear it again? Was he willing to renounce forever the hope of hearing it?

He sat at his supper so long, nervelessly turning his doubts over in his mind, that the waitress came out of the kitchen and drove him from the table with her severe, impatient stare.

He put on his hat, and with his overcoat on his arm he started out for a walk which was hopeless, but not so aimless as he feigned to himself. The air was lullingly warm still as he followed the long village street down the hill toward the river, where the lunge of rapids filled the dusk with a sort of humid uproar; then he turned and followed it back past the hotel as far as it led towards the open country. At the edge of the village he came to a large, old-fashioned house, which struck him as typical, with its outward swaying fence of the Greek border pattern, and its gate-posts topped by tilting urns of painted wood. The house itself stood rather far back from the street, and as he passed it he saw that it was approached by a pathway of brick which was bordered with box. Stalks of last year's hollyhocks and lilacs from garden beds on either hand lifted their sharp points, here and there broken and hanging down. It was curious how these details insisted through the twilight.

He walked on until the wooden village pathway ended in the country mud, and then again he returned up upon his steps. As he reapproached the house he saw lights. A brighter radiance streamed from the hall door, which was apparently open, and a softer glow flushed the windows of one of the rooms that flanked the hall.

As Langbourne came abreast of the gate the tinkle of a gay laugh rang out to him; then ensued a murmur of girls' voices in the room, and suddenly this stopped, and the voice that he knew, the voice that seemed never to have ceased to sound in his nerves and pulses, rose in singing words set to the Spanish air of *La Paloma*.

It was one of the songs he had sent to Miss Simpson, but he did not need this material proof that it was she whom he now heard. There was no question of what he should do. All doubt, all fear, had vanished; he had again but one impulse, one desire, one purpose. But he lingered at the gate till the song ended, and then he unlatched it and started up the walk towards the door. It seemed to him a long way; he almost reeled as he went; he fumbled tremulously for the bell-pull beside the door, while a confusion of voices in the adjoining room—the voices which had waked him from his sleep, and which now sounded like voices in a dream—came out to him.

The light from the lamp hanging in the hall shone full in his face, and the girl who came from that room beside it to answer his ring gave a sort of conscious jump at sight of him as he uncovered and stood bareheaded before her.

VI.

She must have recognized him from the photograph he had sent, and in stature and figure he recognized her as the ideal he had cherished, though her head was gilded with the light from the lamp, and he could not make out whether her hair was dark or fair; her face was, of course, a mere outline, without color or detail against the luminous interior.

He managed to ask, dry-tongued and with a heart that beat into his throat, "Is Miss Simpson at home?" and the girl answered, with a high, gay tinkle:

"Yes, she's at home. Won't you walk in?"

He obeyed, but at the sound of her silvery voice his heart dropped back into his breast. He put his hat and coat on an entry chair, and prepared to follow her into the room she had come out of. The door stood ajar, and he said, as she put out her hand to push it open, "I am Mr. Langbourne."

"Oh, yes," she answered in the same high, gay tinkle, which he fancied had now a note of laughter in it.

An elderly woman of a ladylike village type was sitting with some needlework beside a little table, and a young girl turned on the piano-stool and rose to receive him. "My aunt, Mrs. Simpson, Mr. Langbourne," said the girl who introduced him to these presences, and she added, indicating the girl at the piano, "Miss Simpson."

They all three bowed silently, and in the hush the sheet on the music frame slid from the piano with a sharp clash, and skated across the floor to Langbourne's feet. It was the song of *La Paloma* which she had been singing; he picked it up, and she received it with a drooping head, and an effect of guilty embarrassment.

She was short and of rather a full figure, though not too full. She was not plain, but she was by no means the sort of beauty who had lived in Langbourne's fancy for the year past. The oval of her face was squared; her nose was arched; she had a pretty, pouting mouth, and below it a deep dimple in her chin; her eyes were large and dark, and they had the questioning look of near-sighted eyes; her hair was brown. There was a humorous tremor in her lips, even with the prim stress she put upon them in saying, "Oh, thank you," in a thick whisper of the voice he knew.

"And I," said the other girl, "am Juliet Bingham. Won't you sit down, Mr. Langbourne?" She pushed towards him the arm-chair before her, and he dropped into it. She took her place on the hair-cloth sofa, and Miss Simpson sank back upon the piano stool with a painful provisionality, while her eyes sought Miss Bingham's in a sort of admiring terror.

Miss Bingham was easily mistress of the situation; she did not try to bring Miss Simpson into the conversation, but she contrived to make Mrs. Simpson ask Langbourne when he arrived at Upper Ashton Falls; and she herself asked him when he had left New York, with many apposite suppositions concerning the difference in the season in the two latitudes. She presumed he was staying at the Falls house, and she said, always in her high, gay tinkle, that it was very pleasant there in the summer time. He did not know what he answered. He was aware that from time to time Miss Simpson said something in a frightened undertone. He did not know how long it was before Mrs. Simpson made an errand out of the room, in the abeyance which age practices before youthful society in this country; he did not know how much longer it was before Miss Bingham herself jumped actively up, and said, Now she would run over to Jenny's, if Mr. Langbourne would excuse her, and tell her that they could not go the next day.

"It will do just as well in the morning," Miss Simpson pitifully entreated.

"No, she's got to know tonight," said Miss Bingham, and she said she should find Mr. Langbourne there when she got back. He knew that in compliance with simple village tradition he was being purposely left alone with

Miss Simpson, as rightfully belonging to her. Miss Bingham betrayed no in-
tentionality to him, but he caught a glimpse of mocking consciousness in the
sidelong look she gave Miss Simpson as she went out; and if he had not
known before he perceived then, in the vanishing oval of her cheek, the corner of her arched eyebrow, the point of her classic nose, the original of the
photograph he had been treasuring as Miss Simpson's.

VII.

"It was *her* picture I sent you," said Miss Simpson. She was the first to break
the silence to which Miss Bingham abandoned them, but she did not speak till
her friend had closed the outer door behind her and was tripping down the
brick wall to the gate.

"Yes," said Langbourne, in a dryness which he could not keep himself from
using.

The girl must have felt it, and her voice faltered a very little as she continued. "We—I—did it for fun. I meant to tell you. I—"

"Oh, that's all right," said Langbourne. "I had no business to expect yours,
or to send you mine." But he believed that he had; that his faithful infatuation
had somehow earned him the right to do what he had done, and to hope for
what he had not got; without formulating the fact, he divined that she believed it too. Between the man-soul and the woman-soul it can never go so far
as it had done in their case without giving them claims upon each other
which neither of them can justly deny.

She did not attempt to deny it. "I oughtn't to have done it, and I ought to
have told you at once—the next letter—but I—you said you were coming,
and I thought if you did come—I didn't really expect you to; and it was all a
joke,—off-hand."

It was very lame, but it was true, and it was piteous; yet Langbourne could
not relent. His grievance was not with what she had done, but what she was;
not what she really was, but what she materially was; her looks, her figure,
her stature, her whole presence, so different from that which he had been carrying in his mind, and adoring for a year past.

If it was ridiculous, and if with her sense of the ridiculous she felt it so, she
was unable to take it lightly, or to make him take it lightly. At some faint
gleams which passed over her face he felt himself invited to regard it less seriously; but he did not try, even provisionally, and they fell into a silence that
neither seemed to have the power of breaking.

It must be broken, however; something must be done; they could not sit there dumb forever. He looked at the sheet of music on the piano and said, "I see you've been trying that song. Do you like it?"

"Yes, very much," and now for the first time she got her voice fairly above a whisper. She took the sheet down from the music-rest and looked at the picture of the lithographed title. It was of a tiled roof lifted among cypresses and laurels with pigeons strutting on it and sailing over it.

"It was that picture," said Langbourne, since he must say something, "that I believe I got the song for; it made me think of the roof of an old Spanish house I saw in Southern California."

"It must be nice, out there," said Miss Simpson, absently staring at the picture. She gathered herself together to add, pointlessly, "Juliet says she's going to Europe. Have you ever been?"

"Not to Europe, no. I always feel as if I wanted to see my own country first. Is she going soon?"

"Who? Juliet? Oh, no! She was just saying so. I don't believe she's engaged her passage yet."

There was invitation to greater ease in this, and her voice began to have the tender, coaxing quality which had thrilled his heart when he heard it first. But the space of her variance from his ideal was between them, and the voice reached him faintly across it.

The situation grew more and more painful for her, he could see, as well as for him. She too was feeling the anomaly of their having been intimates without having been acquaintances. They necessarily met as strangers after the exchange of letters in which they had spoken with the confidence of friends.

Langbourne cast about in his mind for some middle ground where they could come together without that effect of chance encounter which had reduced them to silence. He could not recur to any of the things they had written about; so far from wishing to do this, he almost had a terror of touching upon them by accident, and he felt that she shrank from them too, as if they involved a painful misunderstanding which could not be put straight.

He asked questions about Upper Ashton Falls, but these led up to what she had said of it in her letters; he tried to speak of the winter in New York, and he remembered that every week he had given her a full account of his life there. They must go beyond their letters or they must fall far back of them.

VIII.

In their attempts to talk he was aware that she was seconding all his endeavors with intelligence, and with a humorous subtlety to which he could not pretend. She was suffering from their anomalous position as much as he, but she had the means of enjoying it while he had not. After half an hour of these defeats Mrs. Simpson operated a diversion by coming in with two glasses of lemonade on a tray and some slices of sponge-cake. She offered this refreshment first to Langbourne and then to her niece, and they both obediently took a glass, and put a slice of cake in the saucer which supported the glass. She said to each in turn, "Won't you take some lemonade? Won't you have a piece of cake?" and then went out with her empty tray, and the air of having fulfilled the duties of hospitality to her niece's company.

"I don't know," said Miss Simpson, "but it's rather early in the season for *cold* lemonade," and Langbourne, instead of laughing, as her tone invited him to do, said:

"It's very good, I'm sure." But this seemed too stiffly ungracious, and he added: "What delicious sponge-cake! You never get this out of New England."

"We have to do something to make up for our doughnuts," Miss Simpson suggested.

"Oh, I like doughnuts, too" said Langbourne. "But you can't get the right kind of doughnuts, either, in New York."

They began to talk about cooking. He told her of the tamales which he had first tasted in San Francisco, and afterward found superabundantly in New York; they both made a great deal of the topic; Miss Simpson had never heard of tamales. He became solemnly animated in their exegesis, and she showed a resolute interest in them.

They were in the midst of the forced discussion when they heard a quick foot on the brick walk, but they had both fallen silent when Miss Bingham flounced elastically in upon them. She seemed to take in with a keen glance which swept them from her lively eyes that they had not been getting on, and she had the air of taking them at once in hand.

"Well, it's all right about Jenny," she said to Miss Simpson. "She'd a good deal rather go day after to-morrow, anyway. What have you been talking about? I don't want to make you go over the same ground. Have you got through with the weather? The moon's out, and it feels more like the beginning of June than the last of April. I shut the front door against dor-bugs; I couldn't help it, though they won't be here for another six weeks yet. Do you have dor-bugs in New York, Mr. Langbourne?"

"I don't know. There may be some in the Park," he answered.

"We think a great deal of our dor-bugs in Upper Ashton," said Miss Simpson demurely, looking down. "We don't know what we should do without them."

"Lemonade!" exclaimed Miss Bingham, catching sight of the glasses and saucers on the corner of the piano, where Miss Simpson had allowed Langbourne to put them. "Has Aunt Elmira been giving you lemonade while I was gone? I will just see about that!" She whipped out of the room, and was back in a minute with a glass in one hand and a bit of sponge-cake between the fingers of the other. "She had kept some for me! Have you sung *Paloma* for Mr. Langbourne, Barbara?"

"No," said Barbara, "We hadn't gone around to it, quite."

"Oh, do!" Langbourne entreated, and he wondered that he had not asked her before; it would have saved them from each other.

"Wait a moment," cried Juliet Bingham, and she gulped the last draught of her lemonade upon a final morsel of sponge-cake, and was down at the piano while still dusting the crumbs from her fingers. She struck the refractory sheet of music flat upon the rack with her palm, and then tilted her head over her shoulder towards Langbourne, who had risen with some vague notion of turning the sheets of the song. "Do you sing?"

"Oh, no. But I like—"

"Are you ready, Bab?" she asked, ignoring him; and she dashed into the accompaniment.

He sat down in his chair behind the two girls, where they could not see his face.

Barbara began rather weakly, but her voice gathered strength, and then poured full volume to the end, where it weakened again. He knew that she was taking refuge from him in the song, and in the magic of her voice he escaped from the disappointment he had been suffering. He let his head drop and his eyelids fall, and in the rapture of her singing he got back what he had lost; or rather, he lost himself again to the illusion which had grown so precious to him.

Juliet Bingham sounded the last note almost as she rose from the piano; Barbara passed her handkerchief over her forehead, as if to wipe the heat from it, but he believed that this was a ruse to dry her eyes in it: they shone with a moist brightness in the glimpse he caught of them. He had risen, and they all stood talking; or they all stood, and Juliet talked. She did not offer to sit down again, and after stiffly thanking them both, he said he must be going, and took leave of them. Juliet gave his hand a nervous grip; Barbara's hand was lax and cold; the parting with her was painful; he believed that she felt it so much as he.

The girls' voices followed him down the walk,—Juliet's treble, and Barbara's contralto,—and he believed that they were making talk purposely against a pressure of silence, and did not know what they were saying. It occurred to him that they had not asked how long he was staying, or invited him to come again: he had not thought to ask if he might; and in the intolerable inconclusiveness of this ending he faltered at the gate till the lights in the window of the parlor disappeared, as if carried into the hall, and then they twinkled into darkness. From an upper entry window, which reddened with a momentary flush and was then darkened, a burst of mingled laughter came. The girls must have thought him beyond hearing, and he fancied the laugh a burst of hysterical feeling in them both.

IX.

Langbourne went to bed as soon as he reached his hotel because he found himself spent with the experience of the evening; but as he rested from his fatigue he grew wakeful, and he tried to get its whole measure and meaning before him. He had a methodical nature, and he now balanced one fact against another none the less passionately because the process was a series of careful recognitions. He perceived that the dream in which he had lived for the year past was not wholly an illusion. One of the girls whom he had heard but not seen was what he had divined her to be: a dominant influence, a control to which the other was passively obedient. He had not erred greatly as to the face or figure of the superior, but he had given all the advantages to the wrong person. The voice, indeed, the spell which had bound him, belonged with the one to whom he had attributed it, and the qualities with which it was inextricably blended in his fancy were hers; she was more like his ideal than the other, though he owned that the other was a charming girl too, and that in the thin treble of her voice lurked a potential fascination which might have made itself ascendently felt if he had happened to feel it first.

There was a dangerous instant in which he had a perverse question of changing his allegiance. This passed into another moment, almost as perilous, of confusion through a primal instinct of the man's by which he yields a double or divided allegiance and simultaneously worships at two shrines; in still another breath he was aware that this was madness.

If he had been younger, he would have had no doubt as to his right in the circumstances. He had simply corresponded all winter with Miss Simpson; but though he opened his heart freely and had invited her to the same confidence with him, he had not committed himself, and he had a right to drop the whole affair. She would have no right to complain; she had not committed herself either: they could both come off unscathed. But he was now thirty-five, and life had taught him something concerning the rights of others which he could not ignore. By seeking her confidence and by offering her his, he had given her a claim which was none the less binding because it was wholly tacit. There had been a time when he might have justified himself in dropping the affair; that was when she had failed to answer his letter; but he had come to see her in defiance of her silence, and now he could not withdraw, simply because he was disappointed, without cruelty, without atrocity.

This was what the girl's wistful eyes said to him; this was the reproach of her trembling lips; this was the accusation of her dejected figure, as she drooped in vision before him on the piano-stool and passed her hand soundlessly over the key-board. He tried to own to her that he was disappointed, but he could not get the words out of his throat; and now in her presence, as it were, he was not sure that he was disappointed.

X.

He woke late, with a longing to put his two senses of her to the proof of the day; and as early in the fore-noon as he could hope to see her, he walked out towards her aunt's house. It was a mild, dull morning, with a misted sunshine; in the little crimson tassels of the budded maples overhead the bees were droning.

The street was straight, and while he was yet a good way off he saw the gate open before the house, and a girl whom he recognized as Miss Bingham close it behind her. She then came down under the maples towards him, at first swiftly, and then more and more slowly, until finally she faltered to a stop. He quickened his own pace and came up to her with a "Good-morning" called to her and a lift of his hat. She returned neither salutation, and said, "I was coming to see you, Mr. Langbourne." Her voice was still a silver bell, but it was not gay, and her face was severely unsmiling.

"To see *me*?" he returned. "Has anything—"

"No, there's nothing the matter. But—I should like to talk with you." She held a little packet, tied with blue ribbon, in her intertwined hands, and she looked urgently at him.

"I shall be very glad," Langbourne began, but she interrupted,—

"Should you mind walking down to the Falls?"

He understood that for some reason she did not wish him to pass the house, and he bowed. "Wherever you like. I hope Mrs. Simpson is well. And Miss Simpson?"

"Oh, perfectly," said Miss Bingham, and they fenced with some questions and answers of no interest till they had walked back through the village to the Falls at the other end of it, where the saw in a mill was whirring through a long pine log, and the water, streaked with sawdust, was spreading over the rocks below and flowing away with a smooth swiftness. The ground near the mill was piled with fresh-sawed, fragrant lumber and strewn with logs.

Miss Bingham found a comfortable place on one of the logs, and began abruptly:

"You may think it's pretty strange, Mr. Langbourne, but I want to talk to you about Miss Simpson." She seemed to satisfy a duty of convention by saying Miss Simpson at the outset, and after that she called her friend Barbara. "I've brought you your letters to her," and she handed him the packet she had been holding. "Have you got hers with you?"

"They are at the hotel," answered Langbourne.

"Well, that's right, then. I thought perhaps you had brought them. You see," Miss Bingham continued, much more cold-bloodedly than Langbourne thought she need, "we talked it over last night, and it's too silly. That's the way Barbara feels herself. The fact is," she went on confidingly, and with the air of saying something that he might appreciate, "I always thought it was some *young* man, and so did Barbara; or I don't believe she would ever have answered your first letter."

Langbourne knew he was not a young man in a young girl's sense; but no man likes to have it said that he is old. Besides, Miss Bingham herself was not apparently in her first quarter of a century, and probably Miss Simpson would not see the earliest twenties again. He thought none the worse of her for that; but he felt that he was not so unequally matched in time with her that she need take the attitude with regard to him which Miss Bingham indicated. He was not in the least gray nor the least bald, and his tall figure kept his youthful lines.

Perhaps his face manifested something of his suppressed resentment. At any rate, Miss Bingham said apologetically, "I mean that if we had known that it was a *serious* person we should have acted differently. I oughtn't to have let her thank you for those seedsman's catalogues; but I thought it couldn't do any harm. And then, after your letters had begun to come, we didn't know just when to stop them. To tell you the truth, Mr. Langbourne, we got so interested we couldn't *bear to* stop them. You wrote so much about your life in New York, that it was like a visit there every week; and it's pretty quiet at Upper Ashton in the winter time."

She seemed to refer this fact to Langbourne for sympathetic appreciation; he said mechanically, "Yes."

She resumed: "But when your picture came, I said it had *got* to stop; and so we just sent back my picture,—or I don't know but what Barbara did it without asking me,— and we did suppose that would be the last of it; when you wrote back that you were coming here, we didn't believe you really would unless we said so. That's all there is about it; and if there is anybody to blame, I am the one. Barbara would never have done it in the world if I hadn't put her up to it."

In these words the implication that Miss Bingham had operated the whole affair finally unfolded itself. But distasteful as the fact was to Langbourne, and wounding as was the realization that he had been led on by this witness of his infatuation for the sake of the entertainment which his letters gave two girls in the dull winter of a mountain village, there was still greater pain, with an additional embarrassment, in the regret which his words conveyed. It appeared that it was not he who had done the wrong; he had suffered it, and so far from having to offer reparation to a young girl for having unwarrantably wrought her up to expect of him a step from which he afterwards recoiled, he had a duty of forgiving her a trespass on his own invaded sensibilities. It was humiliating to his vanity; it inflicted a hurt to something better than his vanity. He began very uncomfortably: "It's all right, as far as I'm concerned. I had no business to address Miss Simpson in the first place—"

"Well," Miss Bingham interrupted, "That's what I told Barbara; but she got to feeling badly about it; she thought if you had taken the trouble to send back the circular that she dropped in the hotel, she couldn't do less than acknowledge it, and she kept on so about it that I had to let her. That was the first false step."

These words, while they showed Miss Simpson in a more amiable light, did not enable Langbourne to see Miss Bingham's merit so clearly. In the methodical and consecutive working of his emotions, he was aware that it was no longer a question of divided allegiance, and that there could never be any such question again. He perceived that Miss Bingham had not such a good figure as he had fancied the night before, and that her eyes were set rather too near together. While he dropped his own eyes, and stood trying to think what he should say in answer to her last speech, her high, sweet voice tinkled out in gay challenge, "How do, John?"

He looked up and saw a square-set, brown-faced young man advancing towards them in his shirt-sleeves; he came deliberately, finding his way in and out among the logs, till he stood smiling down, through a heavy moustache and thick black lashes, into the face of the girl, as if she were some sort of joke. The sun struck into her face as she looked up at him, and made her frown with a knot between her brows that pulled her eyes still closer together, and she asked, with no direct reference to his shirt-sleeves,—"A'n't you forcing the season?"

"Don't want to let the summer get the start of you," the young man generalized, and Miss Bingham said,—

"Mr. Langbourne, Mr. Dickery." The young man silently shook hands with Langbourne, whom he took into the joke of Miss Bingham with another smile; and she went on: "Say, John, I wish you'd tell Jenny I don't see why we shouldn't go this afternoon, after all."

"All right," said the young man.

"I suppose you're coming too?" she suggested.

"Hadn't heard of it," he returned.

"Well, you have now. You've got to be ready at two o'clock."

"That so?" the young fellow inquired. Then he walked away among the logs, as casually as he had arrived, and Miss Bingham rose and shook some bits of bark from her skirt.

"Mr. Dickery is the owner of the mills," she explained, as she explored Langbourne's face for an intelligence which she did not seem to find there. He thought, indifferently enough, that this young man had heard the two girls speak of him, and had satisfied a natural curiosity in coming to look him over; it did not occur to him that he had any especial relationship to Miss Bingham.

She walked up into the village with Langbourne, and he did not know whether he was to accompany her home or not. But she gave him no sign of dismissal till she put her hand upon her gate to pull it open without asking him to come in. Then he said, "I will send Miss Simpson's letters to her at once."

"Oh, any time will do, Mr. Langbourne," she returned sweetly. Then, as if it had just occurred to her, she added, "We're going after May-flowers this afternoon. Wouldn't you like to come too?"

"I don't know, " he began, "whether I shall have the time—"

"Why, you're not going away to-day!"

"I expected—I— But if you don't think I shall be intruding—"

"Why, *I* should be delighted to have you. Mr. Dickery's going, and Jenny Dickery, and Barbara. I don't *believe* it will rain."

"Then, if I may," said Langbourne.

"Why, certainly, Mr. Langbourne!" she cried, and he started away. But he had gone only a few rods away when he wheeled about and hurried back. The girl was going up the walk to the house, looking over after her shoulder after him; at his hurried return she stopped and came back to the gate again.

"Miss Bingham, I think—I think I had better not go."

"Why, just as you feel about it, Mr. Langbourne," she assented.

"I will bring the letters this evening, if you will let me—if Miss Simpson— if you will be at home."

"We shall be very happy to see you, Mr. Langbourne," said the girl formally, and then he went back to his hotel.

XI.

Langbourne could not have told just why he had withdrawn his acceptance of Miss Bingham's invitation. If at the moment it was the effect of a quite reasonless panic, he decided later that it was because he wished to think. It could not be said, however, that he did think, unless thinking consists of a series of dramatic representations which the mind makes to itself from a given impulse, and which it is quite powerless to end. All the afternoon, which Langbourne spent in his room, his mind was the theatre of scenes with Miss Simpson, in which he perpetually evolved the motives governing him from the beginning, and triumphed out of his difficulties and embarrassments. Her voice, as it acquiesced in all, no longer related itself to that imaginary personality which had inhabited his fancy. That was gone irrevocably; and the voice belonged to the likeness of Barbara, and no other; from her similitude, little, quaint, with her hair of cloudy red and her large, dim-sighted eyes, it played upon the spiritual sense within him with the coaxing, drolling, mocking charm which he had felt from the first. It blessed him with intelligent and joyous forgiveness. But as he stood at her gate that evening this unmerited felicity fell from him. He now really heard her voice, through the open doorway, but perhaps because it was mixed with other voices—the treble of Miss Bingham, and the bass of a man who must be the Mr. Dickery he had seen at the saw mills—he turned and hurried back to his hotel, where he wrote a short letter saying that he had decided to take the express for New York that night. With an instinctive recognition of her authority in the affair, or with a cowardly shrinking from direct dealing with Barbara, he wrote to Juliet Bingham, and he addressed to her the packet of letters which he sent for Barbara. Superficially, he had done what he had no choice but to do. He had been asked to return her letters, and he returned them, and brought the affair to an end.

In his long ride to the city he assured himself in vain that he was doing right if he was not sure of his feelings towards the girl. It was quite because he was not sure of his feeling that he could not be sure he was not acting falsely and cruelly.

The fear grew upon him through the summer, which he spent in the heat and stress of the town. In his work he could forget a little the despair in which he lived; but in a double consciousness like that of a hypochondriac, the girl whom it seemed to him he had deserted was visibly and audibly present with him. Her voice was always in his inner ear, and it visualized her looks and movements to his inner eye.

Now he saw and understood at last that what his heart had more than once misgiven him might be the truth, and that though she had sent back his letters, and asked her own in return, it was not necessarily her wish that he should obey her request. It might very well have been an experiment of his feeling towards her, a mute quest of the impression she had made upon him, a test of his will and purpose, an overture to a clearer and truer understanding between them. This misgiving became a conviction from which he could not escape.

He believed too late that he had made a mistake, that he had thrown away the supreme chance of his life. But was it too late? When he could bear it no longer, he began to deny that it was too late. He denied it even to the pathetic presence which haunted him, and in which the magic of her voice itself was merged at last, so that he saw her more than he heard her. He overbore her weak will with his stronger will, and set himself strenuously to protest to her real presence what now he always said to her phantom. When his partner came back from vacation, Langbourne told him that he was going to take a day or two off.

XII.

He arrived at Upper Ashton Falls long enough before the early autumnal dusk to note that the crimson buds of the maples were now their crimson leaves, but he kept as close to the past as he could by not going to find Barbara before the hour of the evening when he had turned from her gate without daring to see her. It was a soft October evening now, as it was a soft May evening then; and there was a mystical hint of unity in the like feel of the dull, mild air. Again voices were coming out of the open doors and windows of the house, and they were the same voices that he had last heard there.

He knocked, and after a moment of startled hush within Juliet Bingham came to the door. "Why, Mr. Langbourne!" she screamed.

"I—I should like to come in, if you will let me," he gasped out.

"Why, certainly, Mr. Langbourne," she returned.

He had not dwelt so long and so intently on the meeting at hand without considering how he should account for his coming, and he had formulated a confession of his motives. But he had never meant to make it to Juliet Bingham, and now he found himself unable to allege a word in explanation of his presence. He followed her into the parlor. Barbara silently gave him her hand and then remained passive in the background, where Dickery held aloof, smiling in what seemed his perpetual enjoyment of the Juliet Bingham joke. She at once put herself in authority of the situation; she made Langbourne let her have his hat; she seated him when and where she chose; she removed and put back the lampshades; she pulled up and pulled down the window blinds; she shut the outer door because of the night air, and opened it because of the unreasonable warmth within. She excused Mrs. Simpson's absence on account of a headache, and asked him if he would have a fan; when he refused it she made him take it, and while he sat helplessly dangling it from his hand, she asked him about the summer he had had, and whether he had passed it in New York. She was very intelligent about the heat in New York, and tactful in keeping the one-sided talk from falling. Barbara said nothing after a few faint attempts to take part in it, and Langbourne made briefer and briefer answers. His reticence seemed only to heighten Juliet Bingham's satisfaction, as she said, with a final supremacy, that she had been intending to go out with Mr. Dickery to a business meeting of the book club, but they would be back before Langbourne could get away; she made him promise to wait for them. He did not know if Barbara looked any protest,—at least she spoke none,— and Juliet went out with Dickery. She turned at the door to bid Barbara say, if anyone called, that she was at the book-club meeting. Then she disappeared, but reappeared and called, "See here, a minute, Bab!" and at the outer threshold she detained Barbara in vivid whisper, ending aloud, "Now you be sure to do both, Bab! Aunt Elmira will tell you where the things are." Again she vanished, and was gone long enough to have reached the gate and come back from it. She was renewing all her whispered and out-spoken charges when Dickery showed himself at her side, put his hand under her elbow, and wheeled her about, and while she called gayly over her shoulder to the others, "Did you ever?" walked her definitively out of the house.

Langbourne did not suffer the silence which followed her going to possess him. What he had to do he must do quickly, and he said, "Miss Simpson, may I ask you one question."

"Why, if you won't expect me to answer it," she suggested quaintly.

"You must do as you please about that. It has to come before I try to excuse myself for being here; it's the only excuse I can offer. It's this: Did you send Miss Bingham to get back your letters from me last spring?"

"Why, of course!"

"I mean, was it your idea?"

"We thought it would be better."

The evasion satisfied Langbourne, but he asked, "Had I given you some cause to distrust me at that time?"

"Oh, no," she protested. "We got to talking it over, and—and we thought we had better."

"Because I had come here without being asked?"

"No, no; it wasn't that," the girl protested.

"I know I oughtn't to have come. I know I oughtn't to have written to you in the beginning, but you had let me write, and I thought you would let me come. I always tried to be sincere with you; to make you feel that you could trust me. I believe that I am an honest man; I thought I was a better man for having known you through the letters. I couldn't tell you how much they had been to me. You seemed to think, because I lived in a large place, that I had a great many friends; but I have very few; I might say I hadn't any—such as I thought I had when I was writing to you. Most of the men I know belong to some sort of clubs; but I don't. I went to New York when I was feeling alone in the world,—it was from something that had happened to me partly through my own fault,—and I've never got over being alone there. I've never gone into society; I don't know what society is, and I suppose that's why I'm acting differently than a society man now. The only change I ever had from business was reading at night: I've got a pretty good library. After I began to get your letters, I went out more—to the theatre, and lectures, and concerts, and all sorts of things—so that I could have something interesting to write about; I thought you'd get tired of always hearing about me. And your letters filled up my life, so that I didn't seem alone anymore. I read them all hundreds of times; I should have said that I knew them by heart, if they had not been as fresh at last as they were at first. I seemed to hear you talking in them." He stopped as if withholding himself from what he had nearly said without intending, and resumed: "It's some comfort to know that you didn't want them back because you doubted me, or my good faith."

"Oh, no, indeed," said Barbara compassionately.

"Then why did you?"

"I don't know. We—"

"No; *not* 'we.' *You!*"

She did not answer for so long that he believed she resented his speaking so peremptorily and was not going to answer him at all. At last she said, "I thought you would rather give them back." She turned and looked at him, with the eyes which he knew saw his face dimly, but saw his thought clearly.

"What made you think that?"

"Oh, I don't know. Didn't you want to?"

He knew that the fact which their words veiled was now in their mutual consciousness. He spoke the truth in saying, "No, I never wanted to," but this was only a mechanical truth, and he knew it. He had an impulse to put the burden of the situation on her, and press her to say why she thought he wished to do so; but his next emotion was shame for this impulse. A thousand times, in these reveries in which he had imagined meeting her, he had told her first of all how he had overheard her talking in the room next to his own in the hotel, and of the power her voice had instantly and lastingly had upon him. But now, with a sense spiritualized by her presence, he perceived that this, if it was not unworthy, was secondary, and that the right to say it was not yet established. There was something that must come before this,—something that could alone justify him in any further step. If she could answer him first as he wished, then he might open his whole heart out, at whatever cost; he was not greatly to blame, if he did not realize that the cost could not be wholly his, as he asked, remotely enough from her question, "After I wrote that I was coming up here, and you did not answer me, did you think I was coming?"

She did not answer, and he felt that he had been seeking a mean advantage. He went on: "If you didn't expect it, if you never thought I was coming, there's no need for me to tell you anything else."

Her face turned towards him a very little, but not so much as even to get a sidelong glimpse at him; it was as if it were drawn by a magnetic attraction; and she said, "I didn't know but you would come."

"Then I will tell you why I came—the only thing that gave me the right to come against your will, if it *was* against it. I came to ask you to marry me. Will you?"

She now turned to look fully at him, though he was aware of being a mere blur in her near-sighted vision.

"Do you mean to ask it now?"

"Yes."

"And have you wished to ask it ever since you first saw me?"

He tried to say that he had, but he could not; he could only say, "I wish to ask it now more than ever."

She shook her head slowly. "I'm not sure how you want me to answer you."

"Not sure?"

"No. I'm afraid I might disappoint you again."

He could not make out whether she was laughing at him. He sat, not knowing what to say, and he blurted out, "Do you mean that you won't?"

"I shouldn't want you to make another mistake."

"I don't know what you"—he was going to say "mean," but he substituted "wish. If you wish for more time, I can wait as long as you choose."

"No, I might wish for time, if there was anything more. But if there's nothing else you have to tell me—then no, I cannot marry you."

Langbourne rose, feeling justly punished, somehow, but bewildered as much as humbled, and he stood stupidly unable to go. "I don't know what you could expect me to say after you've refused me—"

"Oh, I don't expect anything."

"But there *is* something I should like to tell you. I know that I behaved that night as if—as if I hadn't come to ask you—what I have; I don't blame you for not trusting me now. But it is no use to tell you what I intended if it is all over."

He looked down into his hat, and she said in a low voice, "I think I ought to know. Won't you—sit down?"

He sat down again. "Then I will tell you at the risk of—But there's nothing left to lose! You know how it is, when we think about a person or a place before we see them: we make some sort of picture of them, and expect them to be like it. I don't know how to say it; you do look more like what I thought than you did at first. I suppose I must seem a fool to say it; but I thought you were tall, and that you were—well!—rather masterful—"

"Like Juliet Bingham?" she suggested, with a gleam in the eye next him.

"Yes, like Juliet Bingham. It was your voice made me think—it was your voice that first made me want to see you, that made me write to you, in the beginning. I heard you talking that night in the hotel, where you left that circular; you were in the room next to mine; and I wanted to come right up here then; but I had to go back to New York, and so I wrote to you. When your letters came, I always seemed to hear you speaking in them."

"And when you saw me you were disappointed. I knew it."

"No; not disappointed—"

"Why not? My voice didn't go with my looks; it belonged to a tall, strong-willed girl."

"No," he protested. "As soon as I got away it was just as it always had been. I mean that your voice and looks went together again."

"As soon as you got away?" the girl questioned.

"I mean—What do you care for it, anyway!" he cried, in self-scornful exasperation.

"I know," she said thoughtfully, "that my voice isn't like me; I'm not good enough for it. It ought to be Juliet Bingham's—"

"No, no!" he interrupted, with a sort of disgust that seemed not to displease her, "I can't imagine it!"

"But we can't any of us have everything, and she's got enough as it is. She's a head higher than I am, and she wants to have her way ten times as bad."

"I didn't mean that," Langbourne began. "I—but you must think me enough of a simpleton already."

"Oh, no, not near," she declared. "I'm a good deal of a simpleton myself at times."

"It doesn't matter," he said desperately; "I love you."

"Ah, that belongs to the time when you thought I looked differently."

"I don't want you to look differently. I—"

"You can't expect me to believe that now. It will take time for me to do that."

"I will give you time," he said, so simply that she smiled.

"If it was my voice you cared for I should have to live up to it, somehow, before you cared for me. I'm not certain that I ever could. And if I couldn't? You see, don't you?"

"I see that I was a fool to tell you what I have," he so far asserted himself. "But I thought I ought to be *honest.*"

"Oh, you've been honest!" she said.

"You have a right to think that I am a flighty, romantic person," he resumed, "and I don't blame you. But if I could explain, it has been a very real experience for me. It was your nature that I cared for in your voice. I can't tell you just how it was; it seemed to me that unless I could hear it again, and always, my life would not be worth much. This was something deeper and better than I could make you understand. It wasn't merely a fancy; I do not want you to believe that."

"I don't know whether fancies are such very bad things. I've had some of my own," Barbara suggested.

He sat still with his hat between his hands, as if he could not find a chance of dismissing himself, and she remained looking down at her skirt where it tented itself over the toe of her shoe. The tall clock in the hall ticked second after second. It counted thirty of them at least before he spoke, after a preliminary noise in his throat.

"There is one thing I should like to ask: If you had cared for me, would you have been offended at my having thought you looked differently?"

She took some time to consider this. "I might have been vexed, or hurt, I suppose, but I don't see how I could really have been offended."

"Then I understand," he began, in one of his inductive emotions; but she rose nervously, as if she could not sit still, and went to the piano. The Spanish song he had given her was lying open upon it, and she struck some of the chords absently, and then let her fingers rest on the keys.

"Miss Simpson," he said, coming stiffly forward, "I should like to hear you sing that song once more before I—Won't you sing it?"

"Why, yes," she said, and she slipped laterally into the piano-seat.

At the end of the first stanza he gave a long sigh, and then he was silent to the close.

As she sounded the last notes of the accompaniment Juliet Bingham burst into the room with somehow the effect to Langbourne of having lain in wait outside for that moment.

"Oh, I just *knew* it!" she shouted, running upon them. "I bet John anything! Oh, I'm so happy it's come out all right; and now I'm going to have the first—"

She lifted her arms as if to put them round his neck; he stood dazed, and Barbara rose from the piano-stool and confronted her with nothing less than horror in her face.

Juliet Bingham was beginning again, "Why, haven't you—"

"*No!*" cried Barbara. "I forgot all about what you said! I just happened to sing it because he asked me," and she ran from the room.

"Well, if I ever!" said Juliet Bingham, following her with astonished eyes. Then she turned to Langbourne. "It's perfectly ridiculous, and I don't see how I can ever explain it. I don't think Barbara has shown a great deal of tact," and Juliet Bingham was evidently prepared to make up the defect by a diplomacy which she enjoyed. "I don't know where to begin exactly; but you must certainly excuse my—manner, when I came in."

"Oh, certainly," said Langbourne in polite mystification.

"It was all through a misunderstanding that I don't think *I* was to blame for, to say the least; but I can't explain it without making Barbara appear perfectly—Mr. Langbourne, *will* you tell me whether you are engaged?"

"No! Miss Simpson has declined my offer," he answered.

"Oh, then it's all right," said Juliet Bingham, but Langbourne looked as if he did not see why she should say that. "Then I can understand; I see the whole thing now; and I didn't want to make *another* mistake. Ah—won't you —sit down?"

"Thank you. I believe I will go."

"But you have a right to know—"

"Would my knowing alter the main facts?" he asked dryly.

"Well, no, I can't say it would," Juliet Bingham replied with an air of candor. "And, as you *say*, perhaps it's just as well," she added with an air of relief.

Langbourne had not said it, but he acquiesced with a faint sigh, and absently took the hand of farewell which Juliet Bingham gave him. "I know Barbara will be very sorry not to see you; but I guess it's better."

In spite of the supremacy which the turn of affairs had given her, Juliet Bingham looked far from satisfied, and she let Langbourne know with a sense of inconclusiveness which showed in the parting inclination towards him; she kept the effect of this after he turned from her.

He crept light-headedly down the brick walk with a feeling that the darkness was not half thick enough, though it was so thick that it hid a figure that leaned upon the gate and held it shut, as if forcibly to interrupt his going.

"Mr. Langbourne," said the voice of this figure, which, though so unnaturally strained, he knew for Barbara's voice, "you have got to *know!* I'm ashamed to tell you, but I should be more ashamed not to, after what's happened. Juliet made me promise when she went out to the book-club meeting that if I—if you—if it turned out as *you* wanted, I would sing that song as a sign—It was just a joke—like my sending her picture. It was my mistake and I am sorry, and I beg your pardon—I—"

She stopped with a quick catch in her breath, and the darkness round them seemed to become luminous with the light of hope that broke upon him within.

"But if there really was no mistake," he began. He could not get further.

She did not answer, and for the first time her silence was sweeter than her voice. He lifted her tip-toe in his embrace, but he did not wish her taller; her yielding spirit lost itself in his own, and he did not regret the absence of the strong will which he had once imagined hers.

A Difficult Case

1900

A DIFFICULT CASE," one of Howells's best stories, deserves a much wider audience than it has received. It is a wonderfully integrated work of fiction; the relationships between husband and wife and minister and parishioner mirror and comment on the arguments that make up the core of the story. These arguments—about the possibility of immortality and the essential contradictions of human nature—in turn find their parallel in the plot. And the questions raised are further represented by the conflict within the main character's mind. The story is interesting not only in itself, but as a reflection of Howells's struggle to make sense of his daughter's death and to rationalize his seemingly futile hope that she might live on in another world.

"A Difficult Case" began as an idea for a short story to be called "Transfusion." Writing in his *Indian Summer* notebook, Howells imagined an "Old fellow who goes to a young friend for cheer when he is gloomy, and impoverishes his spirit. Friend expostulates with him; he stops coming; or on the way commits suicide. Perhaps young man's wife interferes." Cady remarks on the Hawthornian quality of this simple outline, and he is echoed by John

Crowley, who notes that the story "might well have been titled 'The Minister in a Maze,' since it was undoubtedly inspired by that chapter in *The Scarlet Letter*" (*Mask* 138). (Crowley, of course, is thinking of the passage in "A Difficult Case" in which Ewbert finds himself "beset by a strange temptation,—by the wish to take up these notions [of the qualities of a life after death] and expose their fallacy." Hawthorne's influence on Howells, in fact, was major. In *My Literary Passions* (1895), Howells wrote: "[Hawthorne has] held me by his potent spell, and for a time he dominated me as completely as any author I have read. More truly than any other American author he has been a passion with me" (187). Howells was particularly impressed by *The Scarlet Letter*, which he called Hawthorne's "supreme romance,—the great wonder-book . . . destined by the perfection of its form to endure with our language" ("Recent Literature"). (It is possible that the episode of Ewbert's temptation was also influenced by Poe, whose "Imp of the Perverse" [1845] most obviously sounds the theme of the temptation to do evil at one's own expense.)[1]

Hawthorne's influence, of course, extended beyond the simple idea of the minister struggling with temptation. It was Hawthorne, according to Louis J. Budd, who "helped to teach Howells that the best subject for fiction was the subsurface drama" (37), and who demonstrated that authenticity and fidelity to experience were not inconsistent with romance, that romantic fiction, in fact, could be just as "true" as realistic fiction.

It is important to stress that the realism war, of which Howells was the undisputed leader, did not see as its enemy romance, but "romanticism"—that is, sensational writing "which asks to be accepted with all its fantasticality on the ground of reality" (*MLP* 217). Howells always held in esteem the pure romance, which did not pretend to mimic reality. Writing in 1895, he said: "I have always had a great love for the absolutely unreal, the purely fanciful in all the arts, as well as of the absolutely real" (*MLP* 216). And he consistently praised the Hawthornian or Jamesian romance, which "attempted to distill and analyze inner human experience, to study with poetic liberty and insight the mental drama, and to allegorize the laws of man's psychological or moral make-up" (Budd 34). Sarah Daugherty asserts, in fact, that Howells's "Henry James, Jr." which is sometimes treated as the Declaration of Independence of the Realism War, actually "confirms Howells's penchant for romance" (154). In his essays on James, Daugherty argues, Howells "was less concerned with psychological or social realism than with an ideal of human character, an ideal that James dramatized through his use of romantic fable and the melodramatic mode" (150). And in *Criticism and Fiction*, which even the Kirks treat as a blanket condemnation of romantic writing (xiii–xiv), Howells actually encourages the writing of romances, albeit a bit guardedly (56).

"A Difficult Case" is significant in revealing the beginning of Howells's movement, not only toward romance, but toward the psychic. It is generally conceded by those critics who have looked at Howells's later writings that as Howells grew older, he moved away from psychological realism and toward a different genre, the psychic romance. "A Difficult Case" represents Howells's first fictional attempt to grapple with the question of immortality,[2] a question that had preoccupied him since the death of his daughter Winny in 1889. As such, it is representative of the direction Howells's work was taking at the turn of the century. In a letter written to his sister Aurelia in March of 1898, Howells wrote: "I am an elderly man, and I ought to deal more with things of spiritual significance. . . . I believe I can find a new audience for my studies of the inner life" (*SL* 4:168). And in 1908, he argued that "the new realism must concern itself with the *in*spects—with the psychical physiognomies which our earlier, our Hawthornian magic unveiled" ("Easy Chair" [1908] 798). In the explicit discussions of religion and of the possibility of immortality; in the implicit portrayal of the inefficacy of religion (reminiscent of *A Modern Instance*) and of the limitations of what is often called Christian love; and in the acute depiction of complicated psychological states, "A Difficult Case" is a thorough and meticulous study of the inner life.

The story consists largely of an alternating series of dialogues. Clarence Ewbert, the minister of a "Rixonite" church (a fictional denomination), discusses the question of immortality with old Ransom Hilbrook, and then discusses Hilbrook with Emily Ewbert, his wife. The dialogues culminate in Emily Ewbert's confrontation with Hilbrook—which, in Howells's typically understated way, provides the climax of the action. John Crowley, in his excellent (and uncontested) analysis of the story, points out that its action demonstrates the efficacy of love: "What had made belief in immortality possible for Hilbrook was the personification in Ewbert of that perfect love that the minister speculated would exist in afterlife" (*Mask* 145). It also reveals the limitations of that love, bound as it must be on earth to such human qualities as greed and fear. Crowley notes: "As Mrs. Ewbert's love for her husband is compromised by her greed for social status, so Ewbert's love for Hilbrook is limited by his psychological and physical need to survive" (*Mask* 144). The alternating dialogues serve to demonstrate the two poles between which the story oscillates: the selflessly spiritual ideal and the selfishly human reality.

The dichotomy demonstrated by the story's narrative structure is mirrored by the conflict within the main character's mind. As Ewbert wavers between his spiritual and his human responsibilities, he grows more and more emotionally distanced from the arguments that he makes. Although his faith is apparently unshaken, he is deeply disturbed by his ability to see both sides of the arguments he pursues. He becomes aware of the "intellectual juggles" he relies on, and even as he is "urging some reason upon Hilbrook . . . [he] recognize[s] with dismay a quality of question in his own mind." His intellectual discomfort becomes acute in the Hawthornian scene noted by Crowley:

> he figured the old man's helpless amaze at the demoniacal gayety with which he should mock his own seriousness in the past, the cynical ease with which he should show the vanity of the hopes he had been so fervent in awakening. He had throughout recognized the claim that all the counter-doubts had upon the reason, and he saw how effective he could make these if he were now to become their advocate.

Finally, he becomes psychologically split: "He was aware of talking rationally and forcibly; but in the subjective undercurrent paralleling his objective thought he was holding discourse with himself to an effect wholly different from that produced in Hilbrook."

The story's ambivalence reflects Howells's own uncertainties on a number of levels. Most simply, it is "an expression of Howells's own uncertain opinions on the subject" of immortality, as Howells uses "the device of dramatizing in the persons of several characters various points of view" (Blackstock 207). But more importantly, the story seems to dramatize "a dialogue between [Howells's] best and worse attitudes toward Winifred, who had died, he guiltily imagined, feeling as abandoned as old Hilbrook" (Crowley, *Mask* 144). There is no doubt that Howells was a loving father who tried with every available means to help his daughter. But her death left him wracked with self-blame. Writing to his father a few weeks after Winny's death in March 1889, Howells said: "When I am alone I recall and reclaim all I did, and reconstruct the past from this point or that, and dramatize a different course of events in which our dearest one still lives. It is anguish, anguish that rends the heart and brain; but you can understand how inevitable it is" (*SL* 3:248).

Howells felt responsible, if not for his daughter's death, then at least for the circumstances under which it occurred.[3] Winny died far from home, and it was Howells who, overcoming his wife's objections, had decided to send her away. Crowley points out that Howells was influenced by the failure of at-home care to help his brain-damaged brother Henry. It was the decision to keep Henry at home, Howells believed, that "made him the horrible burden" that he was (*SL* 3:178). But Winny's death changed Howells's opinion. In the letter to his father quoted above, Howells continues: "Elinor and I now feel, as we never did before, the comfort you must have in having still kept your afflicted child with you" (*SL* 3:248). Furthermore, Winny died under the care of S. Weir Mitchell, the doctor of Howells's (and not Elinor Howells's) choice. Howells's guilt was compounded by the fact that his frustration over the mysterious nature of Winny's disease and its resistance to years of cures could manifest itself in anger at his daughter and in skepticism about her symptoms. In a letter to his father in November 1888, Howells had written:

> [W]e have come to this [sending Winny to Dr. Weir Mitchell] only thro' the entire failure of our experiment. She has fairly baffled us, and has almost worn her mother out. There are some proofs that she suffers little or no pain, but she manages to work upon our sympathy so that we are powerless to carry out our plans for her good. (*SL* 3:235)

Crowley is quick to point out that "given the prevailing attitude, even in medical circles, toward the female neurotic . . . Howells had shown a commendable generosity of spirit (*Mask* 95). And in fact Howells continues in this letter by saying "It will be a fearfully costly experiment,—perhaps $2000 in all—but we *must* make it or else let her slide into dementia and death." Finally, Mitchell's apparent discovery at the postmortem of an actual physical disease (although this supposition is controversial) may have added immeasurably to Howells's sense of guilt.[4]

Ewbert's failure to save Hilbrook is clearly suggestive of Howells's failure to save his daughter. Both tried valiantly, but were finally disabled by human weaknesses—fatigue, uncertainty, selfishness, and the demands of other loved ones. Neither, being human, could give himself solely and entirely to the needy one. Perhaps Ewbert's brief success—"the miracle of [Hilbrook's] resuscitation"—is a manifestation of Howells's desire to have cured his daughter, if only temporarily. But even this success is qualified. Ewbert's temporary revival of Hilbrook's dead spirit is made possible "upon terms which, until he was himself much older, he could not question as to their beneficence, and in fact it never came to his being quite frank with himself concerning them. He kept his thoughts on this point in that state of solution which holds so many conjectures from precipitation in actual conviction." In other words, Ewbert keeps himself from the realization that what effected the miracle was not his "intellectual juggles" or skilled argument, but his love and commitment—and his failure to sustain these was a failure of personality and will.

Ewbert's sense of failure is challenged by the words of his wife: "What did it matter whether such a man believed that there was another world or not?" And the answer that Ewbert implicitly finds is not a Rixonite one, referring "this world's mysteries and problems to the world to come," but an earthly one. It is, in fact, a variation of what Arnold Fox has called Howells's doctrine of complicity (and what George Carrington calls "bondage"—*Drama* 39), first expressed in Mr. Sewall's sermon in *The Minister's Charge*. Sewall) preaches that:

> no man . . . sinned or suffered to himself alone. . . . only those who had had the care of others laid upon them, lived usefully, fruitfully. Let no one shrink from such a burden, or seek to rid himself of it. Rather let him bind it fast upon his neck, and rejoice in it. The wretched, the foolish, the ignorant whom we found at every turn, were something more; they were the messenger of God. (341–42)

The action of the story reveals Ewbert's sense of complicity with Hilbrook, and contrasts it to his wife's lack of compassion. This contrast is ironically presented at the story's end. In his sermon, Ewbert stresses the importance of earthly ties—in other words, of complicity. What he has learned from Hilbrook is the necessity of human love, if not towards all, than at least towards one. As Crowley points out, Ewbert's stance affirms "a willed belief in the ideal of love and a commitment to life itself, whatever its mysteries and imperfections" (*Mask* 144). But Mrs. Ewbert considers the sermon primarily as a means to future prestige and success. The story thus ends "in an ironic balance, a calculated irresolution that was expressive of Howells's persistent agnosticism" (Crowley, *Mask* 145).

Mrs. Ewbert's closing comments echo the attitudes that she has voiced throughout the story. And her narrowminded ambitions are matched by her apparent lack of self-awareness. For example, her belief that "the Rixonites were cold; and if there was anything Emily Ewbert had always detested, it was coldness" is eventually followed by her frigid treatment of Ransom Hilbrook. Clarence Ewbert, on the other hand, is aware of his wife's weaknesses: when he is dissatisfied with his own treatment of Hilbrook, "his wife's applause . . . set the seal to his displeasure with it." At one point he even considers that his wife's possessive attitudes might provide "a potent argument for sacerdotal celibacy." Yet (as is typical in Howells's fictional marriages) he is swayed by her, and relies heavily on her. Baffled by Hilbrook's recalcitrance, he "had an aimless wish for his wife, as if she would have known what to do." It is the narrator, and not Ewbert, as Crowley points out (*Mask* 141–43), who subtly undercuts Mrs. Ewbert.

"A Difficult Case" was apparently well received by its first audience. Henry James, writing to Howells in August 1901, said: "The thing that most took me [in "your elegant volume of short tales"] was that entitled A Difficult Case, which I found beautiful and admirable, ever so true and ever so *done*" (Lubbock 375).[5] And Samuel Clemens, "who evidently identified himself with Hilbrook" (Crowley, *Mask* 246), wrote: "I read the Difficult Situation [*sic*] night before last, & got a world of evil joy out of it" (Smith 719). The story has been mentioned briefly, and favorably, by a number of modern-day critics, including Kermit Vanderbilt (197), Rudolf and Clara Kirk (145), Edward Wagenknecht (212, 253), and Louis Budd (40). It is discussed at some length by Lawrence Berkove, who, in "'A Difficult Case': W. D. Howells's Impression of Mark Twain," examines the similarities between Ransom Hilbrook and Mark Twain, emphasizing especially their shared lack of a belief in the immortality of the soul. Berkove concludes that while Howells's influence on Twain is well established, "A Difficult Case" suggests that Howells, rather than imitating Twain, or simply creating a Twain-like character, "assimilated" him, adopting to a considerable degree "Twain's values, ideas, and ways of thinking" (613).

This critical attention makes "A Difficult Case" one of Howells's better-known short stories. (It can be said to hold a very distant second place to Howells's only well-known story, "Editha.") But its reputation has been oddly directed by a single comment of Edwin Cady's. Writing in *The Realist at War* (1958), Cady asserted that "the final implication of the story is that the minister has received a divine sign" (201). Cady's comment, taken in its context, clearly means that Ewbert has learned a lesson about the efficacy of love from the example of Hilbrook's life. But the suggestion of "a divine sign" is misleading, especially in the context of such later works as "An Angel of the Lord" and "Though One Rose from the Dead," in which characters believe that they receive explicitly supernatural messages from another world. Cady's unfortunate choice of phrasing has been repeated by a number of apparently complaisant critics (Paul Ferlazzo, for example, writes, "in the end the minister seems to receive a divine sign"—169) and thus the impression that "A Difficult Case" is one of Howells's occult tales persists.

Notes

1. Hawthorne's influence on Howells is treated explicitly by Richard H. Brodhead in "Hawthorne Among the Realists: The Case of Howells."

2. I am ignoring *The Undiscovered Country* (1880), as its attention to the question of immortality is limited to the phenomenon of spiritualism, i.e., the manifestation of spirits in séances conducted by mediums.

3. Crowley posits another factor in Howells's feelings of blame: "the guilt he felt after Winifred's death sprang not only from bitterly conscious regret that he had not been more devoted, but also from a subliminal sense of deeper selfishness. His parental love and his yearning to see her well again had coexisted with an unconscious—and, when he became aware of it, what could only have seemed an unnatural—hope that she would not recover. This was the psychic revelation that Howells would face squarely in 'A Sleep and a Forgetting' (1906), his last fictional transformation of Winifred's tragedy" (*Mask* 113). Crowley's suggestion is rooted in his belief that Winny's apparent neuroticism was caused largely by Howells's confused ambitions for her: his hope that she become "a *great* (i.e. masculine) writer" while remaining "a sainted girl, [preserving] her delicate 'feminine' perfection of being." Crowley concludes: "'Nervous prostration' was an expression of Winifred's refusal to become an adult" (*Mask* 103–5).

4. The best treatment of this controversy is Crowley's "Winifred Howells and the Economy of Pain"(*Mask* 83–114).

5. An interesting sidelight is that this letter also includes James's remarks about an as-yet-unpublished novel which "had its earliest origin in a circumstance mentioned to me—years ago—in respect to no less a person than yourself." The incident is of course Howells's meeting with a friend of James's (Jonathan Sturges) in Whistler's garden, which was transformed into Strethers's famous advice to Little Bilham in *The Ambassadors* (1903).

A Difficult Case

I.

It was in the fervor of their first married years that the Ewberts came to live in the little town of Hilbrook, shortly after Hilbrook University had been established there under the name of its founder, Josiah Hilbrook. The town itself had just changed its name, in compliance with the conditions of his public benefactions, and in recognition of the honor he had done it in making it a seat of learning. Up to a certain day it had been called West Mallow, ever since it was set off from the original town of Mallow; but after a hundred and seventy years of this custom it began on that day to call itself Hilbrook, and thenceforward, with the curious American acquiescence in the accomplished fact, no one within or without its limits called it West Mallow again.

The memory of Josiah Hilbrook himself began to be lost in the name he had given the place; and except for the perfunctory mention of its founder in the ceremonies of Commencement Day, the university hardly remembered him as a man, but rather regarded him as a locality. He had, in fact, never been an important man in West Mallow, up to the time he had left it to seek his fortune in New York; and when he died, somewhat abruptly, and left his money, as it were, out of a clear sky, to his native place in the form of a university, a town hall, a soldier's monument, a drinking-fountain, and a public library, his fellow-townsmen, in making the due civic acknowledgement and acceptance of his gifts, recalled with effort the obscure family to which he belonged.

He had not tried to characterize the university by his peculiar religious faith, but he had given a church building, a parsonage, and a fund in support of preaching among them at Hilbrook to the small body of believers to which his people adhered. This sect had a name by which it was officially known to itself; but, like the Shakers, the Quakers, the Moravians, it early received a nickname, which it passively adopted, and even among its own members the body was rarely spoken of or thought of except as the Rixonites.

Mrs. Ewbert fretted under the nickname, with an impatience perhaps the greater because she had merely married into the Rixonite church, and had accepted its doctrine because she loved her husband rather than because she had been convinced of its truth. From the first she complained that the Rixonites were cold; and if there was anything Emily Ewbert had always detested, it was coldness. No one, she once testified, need talk of their passive waiting for a sign, as a religious life; if there were not some strong, central belief, some rigorously formulated creed, some—

"Good old root and herb theology," her husband interrupted.

"Yes!" she heedlessly acquiesced. "Unless there is something like *that*, all the waiting in the world won't"—she cast about for some powerful image—"won't keep the cold chills from running down my back when I think of my duty as a Christian."

"Then don't think of your duty as a Christian, my dear," he pleaded, with the caressing languor which sometimes made her say, in reprobation of her own pleasure in it, that *he* was a Rixonite, if there ever *was* one. "Think of your duty as a woman, or even as a mortal."

"I believe you're thinking of making a sermon on that," she retorted; and he gave a sad, consenting laugh, as if it were quite true, though in fact he never really preached a sermon on mere femininity or mere mortality. His sermons were all very good, however; and that was another thing that put her out of patience with his Rixonite parishioners—that they should sit there Sunday after Sunday, year in and year out, and listen to his beautiful sermons, which ought to melt their hearts and bring tears into their eyes, and not seem influenced by them any more than if they were so many dry chips.

"But think how long they've had the gospel," he suggested, in pensive self-derision which she would not share.

"Well, one thing, Clarence," she summed up, "I'm not going to let you throw yourself away on them; and unless you see some of the university people in the congregation, I want you to use your old sermons from this out. They'll never know the difference; and I'm going to make you take one of the old sermons along every Sunday, so as to be prepared."

II.

One good trait of Mrs. Ewbert was that she never meant half she said—she could not; but in this case there was more meaning than usual in her saying. It really vexed her that the university families, who had all received them so nicely, and who appreciated her husband's spiritual and intellectual quality as fully as even she could wish, came some of them so seldom, and some of them never, to hear him at the Rixonite church. They ought, she said, to have been just suited by his preaching, which inculcated with the peculiar grace of his gentle, poetic nature a refinement of the mystical theology of the founder. The Rev. Adoniram Rixon, who had seventy years before formulated his conception of the religious life as a patient waiting upon the divine will, with a constant reference of this world's mysteries and problems to the world to come, had doubtless meant a more strenuous abeyance than Clarence Ewbert was now preaching to a third generation of his followers. He had doubtless meant them to be eager and alert in this patience, but the version of his gospel which his latest apostle gave taught a species of acquiescence which was foreign to the thoughts of the founder. He put as great stress as could be asked upon the importance of a realizing faith in the life to come, and an implicit trust in it for the solution of the problems and complexities of life; but so far from wishing his hearers to be constantly taking stock, as it were, of their spiritual condition, and interrogating Providence as to its will concerning them, he besought them to rest in confidence of the divine mindfulness, secure that while they fulfilled all their plain, simple duties toward one another, God would inspire them to act according to his purposes in the more psychological crises and emergencies, if these should ever be part of their experience.

In maintaining, on a certain Sunday evening, that his ideas were much more adapted to the spiritual nourishment of the president, the dean, and the several professors of Hilbrook University than to that of the hereditary Rixonites who nodded in a slumbrous acceptance of them, Mrs. Ewbert failed as usual to rouse her husband to a due sense of grievance with the university people.

"Well," he said, "you know I can't *make* them come, my dear."

"Of course not. And I would be the last to have you lift a finger. But I know that you feel about it just as I do."

"Perhaps; but I hope not so much as you *think* you feel. Of course, I'm very grateful for your indignation. But I know you don't undervalue the good I may do to my poor sheep—they're *not* an intellectual flock—in trying to lead them in the ways of spiritual modesty and unconsciousness. How do we know but they profit more by my preaching than the faculty would? Perhaps our university friends are spiritually unconscious enough already, if not modest."

"I see what you mean," said Mrs. Ewbert, provisionally suspending her sense of the whimsical quality in his suggestion. "But you need never tell me that they wouldn't appreciate you more."

"More than old Ransom Hilbrook?" he asked.

"Oh, I hope *he* isn't coming here tonight, again!" she implored, with a nervous leap in the point of the question. "If he's coming here *every* Sunday night"—

As he knew she wished, her husband represented that Hilbrook's having come the last Sunday night was no proof that he was going to make a habit of it.

"But he *stayed* so late!" she insisted from the safety of her real belief that he was not coming.

"He came very early, though," said Ewbert, with a gentle sigh, in which her sympathetic penetration detected a retrospective exhaustion.

"I shall tell him you're not well," she went on: "I shall tell him you are lying down. You ought to be, now. You're perfectly worn out with that long walk you took." She rose, and beat up the sofa pillows with a menacing eye upon him.

"Oh, I'm very comfortable here," he said from the depths of his easy-chair. "Hilbrook won't come tonight. It's past the time."

She glanced at the clock with him, and then desisted. "If he does, I'm determined to excuse you somehow. You ought never to have gone near him, Clarence. You've brought it upon yourself."

Ewbert could not deny this, though he did not feel himself so much to blame for it as she would have liked to make out in her pity of him. He owned that if he had never gone to see Hilbrook the old man would probably never have come near them, and that if he had not tried so much to interest him when he did come Hilbrook would not have stayed so long; and even in this contrite mind he would not allow that he ought not to have visited him and ought not to have welcomed him.

III.

The minister had found his parishioner in the old Hilbrook homestead, which Josiah Hilbrook, while he lived, suffered Ransom Hilbrook to occupy, and when he died bequeathed to him, with a sufficient income for all his simple wants. They were cousins, and they had both gone out into the world about the same time: one had made a success of it and remained; and the other had made a failure of it, and come back. They were both Rixonites, as the families of both had been in the generation before them. It could be supposed that Josiah Hilbrook, since he had given the money for a Rixonite church and the perpetual pay of a Rixonite minister in his native place, had died in the faith; and it might have been supposed that Ransom Hilbrook, from his constant attendance upon its services, was living in the same faith. What was certain was that the survivor lived alone in the family homestead on the slope of the stony hill overlooking the village. The house was gray with age, and it crouched low on the ground where it had been built a century before, and anchored fast by the great central chimney characteristic of the early New England farmhouse. Below it staggered the trees of an apple orchard belted in with a stone wall, and beside it sagged the sheds whose stretch united the gray old house to the gray old barn, and made it possible for Hilbrook to do his chores in rain or snow without leaving cover. There was a door-yard defined by a picket fence, and near the kitchen door was a well with a high pent roof, where there had once been a long sweep.

These simple features showed to the village on the opposite slope with a distinctness that made the place seem much lonelier that if it had been much more remote. It gained no cheerfulness from its proximity, and when the windows of the house lighted up with the pale gleam of the sunset, they imparted to the village a sense of dreary solitude which its own lamps could do nothing to relieve.

Ransom Hilbrook came and went among the villagers in the same sort of inaccessible contiguity. He did not shun passing the time of day with people he met; he was in and out at the grocer's, the meat man's, the baker's, upon the ordinary domestic occasions; but he never darkened any other doors, except on his visits to the bank where he cashed his check for his quarterly allowance. There had been a proposition to use him representatively in the ceremonies celebrating the acceptance of the various gifts of Josiah Hilbrook; but he had not lent himself to this, and upon experiment the authorities found that he was right in his guess that they could get along without him.

He had not said it surlily, but sadly, and with a gentle deprecation of their insistence. While the several monuments that testified to his cousin's wealth and munificence rose in the village beyond the brook, he continued in the old homestead without change, except that when his housekeeper died he began to do for himself the few things that the ailing and aged woman had done for him. How he did them was not known, for he invited no intimacy from his neighbors. But from the extent of his dealings with the grocer it was imagined that he lived mainly upon canned goods. The fish man paid him a weekly visit, and once a week he got from the meat man a piece of salt pork, which it was obvious to the meanest intelligence was for his Sunday baked beans. From his purchase of flour and baking powder it was reasonably inferred that he now and then made himself hot biscuit. Beyond these meagre facts everything was conjecture, in which the local curiosity played somewhat actively, but, for the most part, with a growing acquiescence in the general ignorance none felt authorized to dispel. There had been a time when some fulfilled a fancied duty to the solitary in trying to see him. But the visitors who found him out of doors were not asked within, and were obliged to dismiss themselves, after an interview across the pickets of the dooryard fence or from the trestles or inverted feed pails on which they were invited to seats in the barn or shed. Those who happened to find their host more ceremoniously at home were allowed to come in, but were received in rooms so comfortless from the drawn blinds or fireless hearths that they had not the spirits for the task of cheering him up which they had set themselves, and departed in greater depression than that they left him to.

IV.

Ewbert felt all the more compelled to his own first visit by the fame of these failures, but he was not hastened in it. He thought best to wait for some sign or leading from Hilbrook; but when none came, except the apparent attention with which Hilbrook listened to his preaching and the sympathy which he believed he detected at times in the old eyes blinking upon him through his sermons, he felt urged to the visit which he vainly delayed.

Hilbrook's reception was wary and non-committal, but it was by no means so grudging as Ewbert had been led to expect. After some ceremonious moments in the cold parlor Hilbrook asked him into the warm kitchen, where apparently he passed most of his own time. There was something cooking in a pot on the stove, and a small room opened out of the kitchen, with a bed in it, which looked as if it were going to be made, as Ewbert handsomely maintained. There was an old dog stretched on the hearth behind the stove, who whimpered with rheumatic apprehension when his master went to put the lamp on the mantel above him.

In describing the incident to his wife Ewbert stopped at this point, and then passed on to say that after they got to talking Hilbrook seemed more and more gratified, and even glad, to see him.

"Everybody's glad to see *you*, Clarence," she broke out, with tender pride. "But why do you say, 'After we got to talking'? Didn't you go to talking at once?"

"Well, no," he answered, with a vague smile; "we did a good deal of listening at first, both of us. I didn't know just where to begin, after I got through my excuses for coming, and Mr. Hilbrook didn't offer any opening. Don't you think he's a very handsome old man?"

"He has a pretty head, and his close-cut white hair gives it a neat effect, like a nice child's. He has a refined face; such a straight nose and a delicate chin. Yes, he is certainly good-looking. But what"—

"Oh, nothing. Only, all at once I realized that he had a sensitive nature. I don't know why I shouldn't have realized it before. I had somehow taken it for granted that he was a self-conscious hermit, who lived in a squalid seclusion because he liked being wondered at. But he did not seem to be anything of the kind. I don't know whether he's a good cook, for he didn't ask me to eat anything; but I don't think he's a bad housekeeper."

"With his bed unmade at eight o'clock in the evening!"

"He may have got up late," said Ewbert. "The house seemed very orderly, otherwise; and what is really the use of making up a bed till you need it?"

Mrs. Ewbert passed the point, and asked, "What did you talk about when you got started?"

"I found that he was a reader, or had been. There was a case of good books in the parlor, and I began by talking with him about them."

"Well, what did he say about them?"

"That he wasn't interested in them. He had been once, but he was not now."

"I can understand that," said Mrs. Ewbert philosophically. "Books *are* crowded out after your life fills up with other interests."

"Yes."

"Yes, what?" Mrs. Ewbert followed him up.

"So far as I could make out, Mr. Hilbrook's life hadn't filled up with other interests. He did not care for the events of the day, as far as I tried him on them, and he did not care for the past. I tempted him with autobiography; but he seemed quite indifferent to his own history, though he was not reticent about it. I proposed the history of his cousin in the boyish days which he had said they spent together; but he seemed no more interested in his cousin than in himself. Then I tried his dog and his pathetic sufferings, and I said something about the pity of the poor old fellow's last days being so miserable. That seemed to strike a gleam of interest from him, and he asked me if I thought animals might live again. And I found—I don't know just how to put it so as to give you the right sense of his psychological attitude."

"No matter! Put it any way, and I will take care of the right sense. Go on!" said Mrs. Ewbert.

"I found that his question led up to the question whether men lived again, and to a confession that he didn't or couldn't believe they did."

"Well, upon my word!" Mrs. Ewbert exclaimed. "I don't see the business he has coming to church, then. Doesn't he understand that the idea of immortality is the very essence of Rixonitism? I think it was personally insulting to *you*, Clarence. What did you say?"

"I didn't take a very high hand with him. You know I don't embody the idea of immortality, and the church is no bad place even for unbelievers. The fact is, it struck me as profoundly pathetic. He wasn't arrogant about it, as people sometimes are,—they seem proud of not believing; but he was sufficiently ignorant in his premises. He said he had seen too many dead people. You know he was in the civil war."

"No!"

"Yes,—through it all. It came out on my asking him if he were going to the Decoration Day services. He said that the sight of the first great battlefield

deprived him of the power of believing in a life hereafter. He was not very ex-
planatory, but as I understood it the overwhelming presence of death had ex-
tinguished his faith in immortality; the dead riders were just like their dead
horses"—

"Shocking!" Mrs. Ewbert broke in.

"He said something went out of him." Ewbert waited a moment before
adding: "It was very affecting, though Hilbrook himself was as apathetic
about it as he was about everything else. He was not interested in not believing, even, but I could see that it had taken the heart out of life for him. If our
life here does not mean life elsewhere, the interest of it must end with our ac-
tivities. When it comes to old age, as it has with old Hilbrook, it has no meaning at all, unless it has the hope of more life in it. I felt his forlornness, and I
strongly wished to help him. I stayed a long time talking; I tried to interest
him in the fact that he was not interested, and"—

"Well, what?"

"If I didn't fatigue Hilbrook, I came away feeling perfectly exhausted myself. Were you uneasy at my being out so late?"

V.

It was some time after the Ewberts had given up expecting him that old
Hilbrook came to return the minister's visit. Then, as if some excuse were
necessary, he brought a dozen eggs in a paper bag, which he said he hoped
Mrs. Ewbert could use, because his hens were giving him more than he knew
what to do with. He came to the back door with them; but Mrs. Ewbert always let her maid of all work go out Sunday evening, and she could receive
him in the kitchen himself. She felt obliged to make him the more welcome on
account of his humility, and she showed him into the library with perhaps ex-
aggerated hospitality.

It was a chilly evening of April, and so early that the lamp was not yet
lighted; but there was a pleasant glow from the fire on the hearth, and
Ewbert made his guest sit down before it. As he lay back in the easy-chair,
stretching his thin old hands toward the blaze, the delicacy of his profile was
charming, and that senile parting of the lips with which he listened reminded
Ewbert of his own father's looks in his last years; so that it was with an affectionate eagerness he set about making Hilbrook feel his presence acceptable,
when Mrs. Ewbert left them to finish up the work she had promised herself
not to leave for the maid. It was much that Hilbrook had come at all, and he

ought to be made to realize that Ewbert appreciated his coming. But Hilbrook seemed indifferent to his efforts, or rather, insensible to them, in the several topics that Ewbert advanced; and there began to be pauses, in which the minister racked his brain for some new thing to say, or found himself saying something he cared nothing for in a voice of hollow resolution, or falling into commonplaces which he tried to give vitality by strenuousness of expression. He heard his wife moving about in the kitchen and dining room, with a clicking of spoons and knives and a faint clash of china, as she put the supper things away, and he wished that she would come in and help him with old Hilbrook; but he could not very well call her, and she kept at her work, with no apparent purpose of leaving it.

Hilbrook was a farmer, so far as he was anything industrially, and Ewbert tried him with questions of crops, soils, and fertilizers; but he tried him in vain. The old man said he had never cared much for those things, and now it was too late for him to begin. He generally sold his grass standing, and his apples on the trees; and he had no animals about the place except his chickens,—they took care of themselves. Ewbert urged, for the sake of conversation, even of a disputative character, that poultry were liable to disease, if they were not looked after; but Hilbrook said, Not if there were not too many of them, and so made an end of that subject. Ewbert desperately suggested that he must find them company,—they seemed sociable creatures; and then, in his utter dearth, he asked how the old dog was getting on.

"Oh, he's dead," said Hilbrook, and the minister's heart smote him with a pity for the survivor's forlornness which the old man's apathetic tone had hardly invited. He inquired how and when the dog had died, and said how much Hilbrook must miss him.

"Well, I don't know," Hilbrook returned. "He wa'n't much comfort, and he's out of his misery, anyway." After a moment he added, with a gleam of interest: "I've been thinkin', since he went, of what we talked about the other night,—I don't mean animals, but men. I tried to go over what you said, in my own mind, but I couldn't seem to make it."

He lifted his face, sculptured so fine by age, and blinked at Ewbert, who was glad to fancy something appealing in his words and manner.

"You mean as to a life beyond this?"

"Ah!"

"Well, let us see if we can't go over it together."

Ewbert had forgotten the points he had made before, and he had to take up the whole subject anew. He did so at first in an involuntary patronizing confidence that Hilbrook was ignorant of the ground; but from time to time the old man let drop a hint of knowledge that surprised the minister. Before they had done, it appeared that Hilbrook was acquainted with the literature of immortality from Plato to Swedenborg, and even to Mr. John Fiske. How well he was acquainted with it Ewbert could not quite make out; but he had recurrently a misgiving, as if he were in the presence of a doubter whose doubt was hopeless through his knowledge. In this bleak air it seemed to him that he at last detected the one thing in which the old man felt an interest: his sole tie with the earth was the belief that when he left it he should cease to be. This affected Ewbert as most interesting, and he set himself, with all his heart and soul, to dislodge Hilbrook from his deplorable conviction. He would not perhaps have found it easy to overcome at once that repugnance which Hilbrook's doubt provoked in him, if it had been less gently, less simply owned. As it was, it was not possible to deal with it in any spirit of mere authority. He must meet it and overcome it in terms of affectionate persuasion.

It should not seem difficult to overcome it; but Ewbert still had not yet succeeded in arraying his reasons satisfactorily against it when his wife returned from her work in the kitchen, and sat down beside the library table. Her coming operated a total diversion, in whch Hilbrook lapsed into his apathy, and was not to be roused from it by the overtures to conversation which she made. He presently got to his feet and said he must be going, against all her protests that it was very early. Ewbert wished to walk home with him but Hilbrook would not suffer this, and the minister had to come back from following him to the gate, and watching his figure lose itself in the dark, with a pang in his heart for the solitude which awaited the old man under his own roof. He ran swiftly over their argument in his mind, and questioned himself whether he had used him with unfailing tenderness, whether he had let him think that he regarded him as at all reprobate and culpable. He gave up the quest as he rejoined his wife with a long, unconscious sigh that made her lift her head.

"What is it, Clarence?"

"Nothing"—

"You look perfectly exhausted. You look worried. Was it something you were talking about?"

Then he told her, and he had trouble to keep her resentment in bounds. She held that, as a minister, he ought to have rebuked the wretched creature; that it was nothing short of offensive to him for Hilbrook to take such a position. She said his face was all flushed, and that she knew he would not sleep, and she should get him a glass of warm milk; the fire was out in the stove, but she could heat it over the lamp in a tin cup.

VI.

Hilbrook did not come again till Ewbert had been to see him; and in the meantime the minister suffered from the fear that the old man was staying away because of some hurt which he had received in their controversy. Hilbrook came to church as before, and blinked at him through the two sermons which Ewbert preached on significant texts, and the minister hoped he was listening with a sense of personal appeal in them. He had not only sought to make them convincing as to the doctrine of another life, but he had dealt in terms of loving entreaty with those who had not the precious faith of this in their hearts, and he had wished to convey to Hilbrook an assurance of peculiar sympathy.

The day following the last of his sermons, Ewbert had to officiate at the funeral of a little child whose mother had been stricken to the earth by her bereavement. The hapless creature had sent for him again and again, and had clung about his very soul, beseeching him for assurance that she should see her child hereafter, and have it hers, just as it was, forever. He had not the heart to refuse her this consolation, and he pushed himself, in giving it, beyond the bounds of imagination. When she confessed her own inability to see how it could be, and yet demanded of him that it should be, he answered that our inability to realize the fact had nothing to do with its reality. In the few words he said over the little one, at the last, he recurred to this position, and urged it upon all his hearers; but in the moment of doing so a point that old Hilbrook had made in their talk suddenly presented itself. He experienced inwardly such a collapse that he could not be sure that he had spoken, and he repeated his declaration in a voice of such harsh defiance that he could scarcely afterwards bring himself down to the meek level of a closing prayer.

As they walked home together, his wife asked, "Why did you repeat yourself in that passage, Clarence, and why did you lift your voice so? It sounded like contradicting some one. I hope you were not thinking of anything that wretched old man said?"

With the mystical sympathy by which the wife divines what is in her husband's mind she had touched the truth, and he could not deny it. "Yes, yes, I was," he owned in a sort of anguish, and she said:—

"Well, then, I wish he wouldn't come about anymore. He has perfectly obsessed you. I could see that the last two Sundays you were preaching right at him." He had vainly hoped she had not noticed this, though he had not concealed from her that his talk with Hilbrook had suggested his theme. "What are you going to do about him?" she pursued relentlessly.

"I don't know,—I don't know, indeed," said Ewbert; and perhaps he did not know, he felt that he must do something, that he must at least not leave him to himself. He hoped that Hilbrook would come to him, and so put him under the necessity of doing something; but Hilbrook did not come, and after waiting a fortnight Ewbert went to him, as was his duty.

VII.

The spring had advanced so far that there were now days when it was pleasant to be out in the soft warmth of the afternoons. The day when Ewbert climbed to the Hilbrook homestead it was even a little hot, and he came up to the dooryard mopping his forehead with his handkerchief, and glad of the southwestern breeze which he caught at this point over the shoulder of the hill. He had expected to go round to the side door of the house, where he had parted with Hilbrook on his former visit, but he stopped on seeing the old man at his front door, where he was looking vaguely at a mass of Spanish willow fallen dishevelled beside it, as if he had some thought of lifting its tangled spray. The sun shone on his bare head, and struck silvery gleams from his close-cropped white hair; there was something uncommon in his air, though his dress was plain and old-fashioned; and Ewbert wished that his wife were there to share his impression of distinction in Hilbrook's presence.

He turned at Ewbert's cheerful hail, and after a moment of apparent uncertainty as to who he was, he came down the walk of broken brick and opened the gate to his visitor.

"I was just out, looking round at the old things," he said, with an effort at apology. "This sort of weather is apt to make fools of us. It gets into our heads, and before we know we feel as if we had something to do with the season."

"Perhaps we have," said the minister. "The spring is in us, too."

The old man shook his head. "It was once, when we were children; now there's what we remember of it. We like to make believe about it,—that's natural; and it's natural we should make believe that there is going to be a spring for us somewhere else like what we see for the grass and bushes, here, every year; but I guess not. A tree puts out its leaves every spring; but by and by the tree dies, and then it doesn't put out its leaves any more."

"I see what you mean," said Ewbert, "and I allow that there is no real analogy between our life and that of the grass and bushes; yet somehow I feel strengthened in my belief in the hereafter by each renewal of the earth's life. It isn't a proof, it isn't a promise; but it's a suggestion, an intimation."

They were in the midst of a great question, and they sat down on the decaying doorstep to have it out; Hilbrook having gone in for his hat and come out again, with its soft wide brim shading his thin face, frosted with half a week's beard.

"But character," the minister urged at a certain point,—"what becomes of character? You may suppose that life can be lavished by its Origin in the immeasurable superabundance which we see in nature. But character,—that is a different thing; that cannot die."

"The beasts that perish have character; my old dog had. Some are good and some bad; they're kind and they're ugly."

"Ah, excuse me! That isn't character; that's temperament. Men have temperament, too; but the beasts haven't character. Doesn't that fact prove something,—or no, not prove, but give us some reasonable expectation of a hereafter?"

Hilbrook did not say anything for a moment. He broke a bit of fragrant spray from the flowering currant—which guarded the doorway on his side of the steps; Ewbert sat next the Spanish willow—and softly twisted the stem between his thumb and finger.

"Ever hear how I came to leave Hilbrook,—West Mallow, as it was then?" he asked at last.

Ewbert was forced to own that he had heard a story, but he said, mainly in Hilbrook's interest, that he had not paid much attention to it.

"Thought there wa'n't much in it? Well, that's right, generally speakin'. Folks like to make up stories about a man that lives alone like me, here; and they usually get in a disappointment. I ain't goin' to go over it. I don't care any more about it now than if it had happened to someone else: but it did happen. Josiah got the girl, and I didn't. I presume they like to make out that I've grieved over it ever since. Sho! It's forty years since I gave it a thought, that way." A certain contemptuous indignation supplanted the wonted gentleness of the old man, as if he spurned the notion of such sentimental folly. "I've read of folks mournin' all their lives through, and in their old age goin' back to a thing like that, as if it still meant somethin'. But it ain't true; I don't suppose I care any more for losin' her now than Josiah would for gettin' her if he were alive. It did make a difference for a while; I ain't goin' to deny that. It lasted me four or five years, in all, I guess; but I was married to somebody else when I went to the war,"—Ewbert controlled a start of surprise; he had always taken it for granted that Hilbrook was a bachelor—"and we had one child. So you may say that I was well over that first thing. *It wore out*; and if it wa'n't that it makes me mad to have folks believin' that I'm sufferin' from it yet, I presume I shouldn't think of it from one year's end to another. My wife and I always got along well together; she was a good woman. She died when I was away at the war, and the little boy died after I got back. I was sorry to lose her, and I thought losin' *him* would kill me. It didn't. It appeared one while as if I couldn't live without him, and I was always contrivin' how I should meet up with him somewhere else. I couldn't figure it out."

Hilbrook stopped, and swallowed dryly. Ewbert noticed how he had dropped more and more into the vernacular, in these reminiscences; in their controversies he had used the language of books and had spoken like a cultivated man, but now he was simply and touchingly rustic.

"Well," he resumed, "that wore out, too. I went into business, and I made money and I lost it. I went through all that experience, and I got enough of it, just as I got enough of fightin'. I guess I was no worse scared than the rest of 'em, but when it came to the end I'd 'bout made up my mind that if there was another war I'd go to Canady; I was sick of it, and I was sick of business even before I lost money. I lost pretty much everything. Josiah—he was always a good enough friend of mine—wanted me to start in again, and he offered to back me, but I said no. I said if he wanted to do something for me, he could let me come home and live on the old place, here; it wouldn't cost him anything like so much, and it would be a safer investment. He agreed, and here I be, to make a long story short."

Hilbrook had stiffened more and more, as he went on, in the sort of defiance he had put on when he first began to speak of himself, and at the end of his confidence Ewbert did not venture any comment. His forbearance seemed to leave the old man freer to resume at the point where he had broken off, and he did so with something of lingering challenge.

"You asked me just now why I didn't think character, as we call it, gave us some right to expect a life after this. Well, I'll try to tell you. I consider that I've been the rounds, as you may say, and that I've got as much character as most men. I've had about everything in my life that most have, a good deal more than some. I've seen that everything wears out, and that when a thing's worn out it's for good and all. I think it's reasonable to suppose that when I wear out it will be for good and all, too. There isn't anything of us, as I look at it, except the potentiality of experiences. The experiences come through the passions that you can tell on the fingers of one hand; love, hate, hope, grief and you may say greed for the thumb. When you've had them, that's the end of it; you've exhausted your capacity; you're used up, and so's your character,—that often dies before the body does."

"No, no!" Ewbert protested. "Human capacity is infinite;" but even while he spoke this seemed to him a contradiction in terms. "I mean that the passions renew themselves with new occasions, new opportunities, and character grows continually. You have loved twice, you have grieved twice; in battle you hated more than once; in business you must have coveted many times. Under different conditions, the passions, the potentiality of experiences, will have a pristine strength. Can't you see it in that light? Can't you draw some hope from that?"

"Hope!" cried Ransom Hilbrook, lifting his fallen head and staring at the minister. "Why, man, you don't suppose I *want* to live hereafter? Do you think I'm anxious to have it all over again, or *any* of it? Is that why you've been trying to convince me of immortality? I know there's something in what you say,—more than what you realize. I've argued annihilation up to this point and that, and almost proved it to my own mind; but there's always some point that I can't quite get over. If I had the certainty, the absolute certainty, that this was all there was to be of it, I wouldn't want to live an hour longer, not a minute! But it's the uncertainty that keeps me. What I'm afraid of is, that if I get out of it here, I might wake up in my old identity, with the potentiality of new experiences in new conditions. That's it. I'm tired. I've had enough. I want to be let alone. I don't want to do anything more, or have anything more done to me. I want to *stop*."

Ewbert's first impression was that he was shocked, but he was too honest to remain in this conventional assumption. He was profoundly moved, however, and intensely interested. He realized that Hilbrook was perfectly sincere, and he could put himself in the old man's place, and imagine why he should feel as he did. Ewbert blamed himself for not having conceived of such a case before; and he saw that if he were to do anything for this lonely soul, he must begin far back to the point from which he had started with him. The old man's position had a kind of dignity which did not admit the sort of pity Ewbert had been feeling for him, and the minister had before him the difficult and delicate task of persuading Hilbrook, not that a man, if he died, should live again, but that he should live upon terms so kind and just that none of the fortuities of mortal life should be repeated in that immortality. He must show the immortal man to be a creature so happily conditioned that he would be in effect newly created, before Hilbrook would consent to accept the idea of living again. He might say to him that he would probably not be consulted in the matter, since he had not been consulted as to his existence here; but such an answer would brutally ignore the claim that such a man's developed consciousness could justly urge to some share in the counsels of omnipotence. Ewbert did not know where to begin, and in his despair he began with a laugh.

"Upon my word," he said, "you've presented a problem that would give any casuist pause, and it's beyond my powers without some further thought. Your doubt, as I now understand it, is not of immortality, but of mortality; and there I can't meet you in argument without entirely forsaking my own ground. If it will not seem harsh, I will confess that your doubt is rather consoling to me; for I have so much faith in the Love which rules the world that I am perfectly willing to accept reexistence on any terms that Love may offer. You may say that this is because I have not yet exhausted the potentialities of experience, and am still interested in my own identity; and one half of this, at least, I can't deny. But even if it were otherwise, I should trust to find among those Many Mansions which we are told of some chamber where I should be at rest without being annihilated; and I can even imagine my being glad to do any sort of work about the House, when I was tired of resting."

VIII.

"I am *glad* you said that to him!" cried Ewbert's wife, when he told her of his interview with old Hilbrook. "That will give him something to think about. What did he say?"

Ewbert had been less and less satisfied with his reply to Hilbrook, in which it seemed to him that he had passed from mockery to reproof, with no great credit to himself; and his wife's applause now set the seal to his displeasure with it.

"Oh, he said simply that he could understand a younger person feeling differently, and that he did not wish to set himself up as a censor. But he could not pretend that he was glad to have been called out of nonentity into being, and that he could imagine nothing better than eternal unconsciousness."

"Well?"

"I told him that his very words implied the refusal of his being to accept nonentity again; that they expressed, or adumbrated, the conception of an eternal consciousness of the eternal unconsciousness he imagined himself longing for. I'm not so sure they did, now."

"Of *course* they did. And *then* what did he say?"

"He said nothing in direct reply; he sighed, and dropped his poor head on his breast, and seemed very tired; so that I tried talking of other things for a while, and then I came away. Emily, I'm afraid I wasn't perfectly candid, perfectly kind, with him."

"I don't see how you could have been more so!" she retorted, in tender indignation with him against himself. "And I think what he said was terrible. It was bad enough for him to pretend to believe that he was not going to live again, but for him to tell you that he was *afraid* he was!" An image sufficiently monstrous to typify Hilbrook's wickedness failed to present itself to Mrs. Ewbert, and she went out to give the maid instructions for something unusually nourishing for Ewbert at their midday dinner. "You look fairly fagged out, Clarence," she said, when she came back; "and I insist upon your not going up to that dreadful old man's again,—at least, not till you've got over this shock."

"Oh, I don't think it has affected me seriously," he returned lightly.

"Yes, it has! yes, it has!" she declared. "It's just like your thinking you hadn't taken cold, the other day when you were caught in the rain; and the next morning you got up with a sore throat, and it was Sunday morning, too."

Ewbert could not deny this, and he had no great wish to see Hilbrook soon again. He consented to wait for Hilbrook to come to him, before trying to satisfy these scruples of conscience which he had hinted at; and he reasonably hoped that the painful points would cease to rankle with the lapse of time, if there should be a long interval before they met.

That night, before the Ewberts had finished their tea, there came a ring at the door, from which Mrs. Ewbert disconsolately foreboded a premature evening call. "And just when I was counting on a long, quiet, restful time for you, and getting you to bed early!" she lamented in undertone to her husband; to the maid who passed through the room with an inquring glance, to the front door, she sighed, still in undertone, "Oh yes, of course we're at *home.*"

They both listened for the voice at the door, to make out who was there; but the voice was so low that they were still in ignorance while the maid was showing the visitor into the library, and until she came back to them.

"It's that old gentleman who lives all alone by himself on the hill over the brook," she explained; and Mrs. Ewbert rose with an air of authority, waving her husband to keep his seat.

"Now, Clarence, I am simply not going to *let* you go in. You are sick enough as it is, and if you are going to let that *awful* old man spend the whole evening here, and drain the life out of you! *I* will see him, and tell him"—

"No, no, Emily! It won't do. I *must* see him. It isn't true that I'm sick. He's old, and he has a right to the best we can do for him. Think of his loneliness! I shall certainly not let you send him away." Ewbert was excitedly gulping his second cup of tea; he pushed his chair back, and flung his napkin down as he added, "You can come in, too, and see that I get off alive."

"I shall not come near you," she answered resentfully; but Ewbert had not closed the door behind him, and she felt it her duty to listen.

IX.

Mrs. Ewbert heard old Hilbrook begin at once in a high senile key without any form of response to her husband's greeting: "There was one thing you said to-day that I've been thinkin' over, and I've come down to talk with you about it."

"Yes?" Ewbert queried submissively, though he was aware of being quite as fagged as his wife accused him of being, after he spoke.

"Yes," Hilbrook returned. "I guess I ha'n't been exactly up and down with with myself. I guess I've been playing fast and loose with myself. I guess you're right about my wantin' to have enough consciousness to enjoy my un-consciousness," and the old gentleman gave a laugh of rather weird enjoyment. "There are things," he resumed seriously, "that are deeper in us than anything we call ourselves. I supposed I had gone to the bottom, but I guess I hadn't. All the while there was something down there that I hadn't got at; but you reached it and touched it, and now I know it's there. I don't know but it's my Soul that's been havin' its say all the time, and me not listenin'. I guess you made your point."

Ewbert was still not so sure of that. He had thrown out that hasty suggestion without much faith in it at the time, and his faith in it had not grown since.

"I'm glad," he began, but Hilbrook pressed on as if he had not spoken.

"I guess we're built like an onion," he said, with a severity that forbade Ewbert to feel anything undignified in the homely illustration. "You can strip away layer after layer till you seem to get to nothing at all; but when you've got to that nothing you've got to the very thing that had the life in it, and that would have grown again if you had put it in the ground."

"Exactly!" said Ewbert.

"You made a point that I can't get round," Hilbrook continued, and it was here that Ewbert enjoyed a little instant of triumph. "But that ain't the point with me. I see that I can't prove that we shan't live again any more than you can prove that we shall. What I want you to do *now* is convince me, or to give me the least reason to believe, that we shan't live exactly on the same terms that we live now. I don't want to argue immortality any more; we'll take that for granted. But how is it going to be any different from mortality with the hope of death taken away?"

Hilbrook's apathy was gone, and his gentleness; he had suddenly an air and tone of fierce challenge. As he spoke he brought a clenched fist down on the arm of his chair; he pushed his face forward and fixed Ewbert with the vitreous glitter of his old eyes. Ewbert found him terrible, and he had a confused sense of responsibilty for him, as if he had spiritually constituted him, in the charnel of unbelief, out of the spoil of death, like some new and fearfuler figment of Frankenstein's. But if he had fortuitously reached him, through the one insincerity of his being, and bidden him live again forever, he must not forsake him or deny him.

"I don't know how far you accept or reject the teachings of Scripture on this matter," he began rather vaguely, but Hilbrook stopped him.

"You didn't go to the Book for the point you made *against* me. But if you go to it now for the point I want you to make *for* me, what are you going to find? Are you going to find the promise of a life any different from the life here? I accept it all,—all that the Old Testament says, and all that the New Testament says; and what does it amount to on this point?"

"Nothing but the assurance that if we live rightly here we shall be happy in the keeping of the divine Love there. That assurance is everything to me."

"It isn't to me!" cried the old man. "We are in the keeping of divine Love here, too, and are we happy? Are those who love rightly happy? It's because we're not conditioned for happiness here; and how are we going to be conditioned differently there? We are going to suffer to all eternity through our passions, our potentialities of experience, there just as we do here."

"There may be other passions, other potentialities of experience," Ewbert suggested, casting about in the void.

"Like what?" Hilbrook demanded. "I've been trying to figure it out, and I can't. I should like you to try it. You can't imagine a new passion in the soul any more than you can imagine a new feature in the face. There they are: eyes, ears, nose, mouth, chin; love, hate, greed, hope, fear! You can't add to them or take away from them." The old man dropped from his defiance in an entreaty that was even more terrible to Ewbert. "I wish you could. I should like to have you try. Maybe I haven't been over the whole ground. Maybe there's some principle I've missed." He hitched his chair closer to Ewbert's, and laid some tremulous fingers on the minister's sleeve. "If I've got to live forever, what have I got to live for?"

"Well," said Ewbert, meeting him fully in his humility, "Let us try to think. Apparently, our way has brought us to a dead wall; but I believe there's light beyond it, if we can only break through. Is it really necessary that we should discover some new principle? Do we know all that love can do from our experience of it here?"

"Have you seen a mother with her child?" Hilbrook retorted.

"Yes, I know. But even that had some alloy of selfishness. Can't we imagine love in which there is no greed,—for greed, and not hate, is the true antithesis of love which is all giving, while greed is all getting,—a love that is absolutely pure?"

"*I* can't," said the old man. "All the love I ever felt had greed in it; I wanted to keep the thing I loved for myself."

"Yes, because you were afraid in the midst of your love. It was fear that alloyed it, not greed. And in easily imaginable conditions in which there is no fear of want, or harm, or death, love would be pure; for it is these things that greed itself wants to save us from. You can imagine conditions in which there shall be no fear, in which love casteth out fear?"

"Well," said Hilbrook provisionally.

Ewbert had not thought of these points himself before, and he was pleased with his discovery though afterwards he was aware that it was something like an intellectual juggle. "You see," he temporized, "We have got rid of two of the passions already, fear and greed, which are the potentialities of our unhappiest experience in this life. In fact, we have got rid of three, for without fear and greed men cannot hate."

"But how can we exist without them?" Hilbrook urged. "Shall we be made up of two passions,—of love, and hope alone?"

"Why not?" Ewbert returned, with what he felt a specious brightness.

"Because we should not be complete beings with these two elements alone."

"Ah, as we know ourselves here, I grant you," said the minister. "But why should we not be far more simply constituted somewhere else? Have you ever read Isaac Taylor's Physical Theory of Another Life?* He argues that the immortal body would be a far less complex mechanism than the mortal body. Why should not the immortal soul be simple, too? In fact, it would necessarily be so, being one with the body. I think I can put my hand on that book, and if I can I must make you take it with you."

He rose briskly from his chair, and went to the shelves, running his fingers along the books with that subtlety of touch by which the student knows a given book in the dark. He heard Mrs. Ewbert stirring about in the rooms beyond with an activity in which he divined a menacing impatience; and he would have been glad to get rid of old Hilbrook before her impatience burst in an irruption upon them. Perhaps because of this distraction he could not

---

*Isaac Taylor. *The Physical Theory of Another Life.* London, 1858. Samuel Clemens mentioned this book in a letter written to Howells in July of 1889 (Smith II, 606).

find the book, but he remained on foot, talking with an implication in his tone that they were both preparing to part, and were now merely finishing off some odds and ends of discourse before they said good-night.

Old Hilbrook did not stir. He was far too sincere a nature, Ewbert saw, to conceive of such inhospitality as a hint for his departure, or he was too deeply interested to be aware of it. The minister was obliged to sit down again, and it was eleven o'clock before Hilbrook rose to go.

X.

Ewbert went out to the gate with the old man, and when he came back to his study, he found his wife there looking strangely tall and monumental in her reproach. "I supposed you were in bed long ago, my dear," he attempted lightly.

"You *don't* mean that you've been out in the night air without your hat on!" she returned. "Well, this is too *much!*" Her long-pent-up impatience broke in tears, and he strove in vain to comfort her with caresses. "Oh what a fatal day it was when you stirred that wretched old creature up! *Why* couldn't you leave him alone!"

"To his apathy? To his despair? Emily!" Ewbert dropped his arms from the embrace in which he had folded her woodenly unresponsive frame, and regarded her sadly.

"Oh yes, of course," she answered, rubbing her handkerchief into her eyes. "But you don't know that it was despair; and he was quite happy in his apathy; and as it is, you've got him on your hands; and if he's going to come here every night and stay till morning, it will kill you. You know you're not strong; and you get so excited when you sit up talking. Look how flushed you are, now, and your eyes—as big! You won't sleep a wink to-night,—I know you won't."

"Oh yes, I shall, " he answered bravely. "I believe I've done some good work with poor old Hilbrook; and you mustn't think he's tired me. I feel fresher than I did when he came."

"It's because you're excited," she persisted. "I know you won't sleep."

"Yes, I shall. I shall just stay here, and read my nerves down a little. Then I'll come."

"Oh yes!" Mrs. Ewbert exulted disconsolately, and she left him to his book. She returned to say: "If you *must* take anything to make you sleepy, I've left some warm milk on the back of the stove. Promise me you won't take any sulphonal!* You know how you feel the next day!"

"No, no, I won't," said Ewbert; and he kept his word, wiith the effect of remaining awake all night. Toward morning he did not know but he had drowsed; he was not aware of losing consciousness, and he started from his drowse with the word "consciousness" in his mind, as he heard Hilbrook speaking it.

XI.

Throughout the day, under his wife's watchful eye, he failed of the naps he tried for, and he had to own himself as haggard, when night came again, as the fondest anxiety of a wife could pronounce a husband. He could not think of his talk with old Hilbrook without an anguish of brain exhaustion; and yet he could not help thinking of it. He realized what the misery of mere weakness must be, and the horror of not having the power to rest. He wished to go to bed before the hour when Hilbrook commonly appeared, but this was so early that Ewbert knew he should merely toss about and grow more and more wakeful from his premature effort to sleep. He trembled at every step outside, and at the sound of feet approaching the door on the short brick walk from the gate, he and his wife arrested themselves with their teacups poised in the air. Ewbert was aware of feebly hoping the feet might go away again; but the bell rang, and then he could not meet his wife's eyes.

"If it's that old Mr. Hilbrook," she said to the maid in transit through the room, "Tell him that Mr. Ewbert is not well, but *I* shall be glad to see him," and now Ewbert did not dare to protest. His forebodings were verified when he heard Hilbrook asking for him, but though he knew the voice, he detected a difference in the tone that puzzled him.

His wife did not give Hilbrook time to get away, if he had wished, without seeing her; she rose at once and went out to him. Ewbert heard her asking him into the library, and then he heard them in parley there; and presently they came out into the hall again, and went to the front door together. Ewbert's heart misgave him of something summary on her part, and he did not know what to make of the cheerful parting between them. "Well, I bid you good-evening, ma'am," he heard old Hilbrook say briskly, and his wife return sweetly, "Good-night, Mr. Hilbrook. You must come again soon."

---

* A tradename for sulfonmethane, apparently a mild tranquilizer which, if used habitually, leads to addiction.

"You may put your mind at rest, Clarence," she said, as she reentered the dining room and met his face of surprise. "He didn't come to make a call; he just wanted to borrow a book,—Physical Theory of Another Life."

"How did you find it?" asked Ewbert, with relief.

"It was where it always was," she returned indifferently. "Mr. Hilbrook seemed to be very much interested in something you said about it. I do believe you *have* done him good, Clarence; and now, if you can only get a full night's rest, I shall forgive him. But I hope he won't come *very* soon again, and will never stay so late when he does come. Promise me you won't go near him till he's brought the book back!"

XII.

Hilbrook came the night after he had borrowed the book, full of talk about it, to ask if he might keep it a little longer. Ewbert had slept well the intervening night, and had been suffered to see Hilbrook upon promising his wife that he would not encourage the old man to stay; but Hilbrook stayed without encouragment. An interest had come into his apathetic life which renewed it, and gave vitality to a whole dead world of things. He wished to talk, and he wished even more to listen, that he might confirm himself from Ewbert's faith and reason in the conjectures with which his mind was filled. His eagerness as to the conditions of a future life, now that he had begun to imagine them, was insatiable, and Ewbert, who met it with glad sympathy, felt drained of his own spiritual forces by the strength which he supplied the old man. But the case was so strange, so absorbing, so important, that he could not refuse himself to it. He could not deny Hilbrook's claim to all that he could give him in this sort; he was as helpless to withold the succor he supplied as he was to hide from Mrs. Ewbert's censoriously anxious eye the nervous exhaustion to which it left him after each visit that Hilbrook paid him. But there was a drain from another sourse of which he could not speak to her till he could make sure that the effect was not some trick of his own imagination.

He had been aware, in twice urging some reason upon Hilbrook, of a certain perfunctory quality in his performance. It was as if the truth, so vital at first, had perished in its formulation, and in the repetition he was sensible, or he was fearful, of an insincerity, a hollowness in the arguments he had originally employed so earnestly against the old man's doubt. He recognized with dismay a quality of question in his own mind, and he fancied that as Hilbrook waxed in belief he himself waned. The conviction of a life hereafter was not something which he was *sharing* with Hillbrook; he was *giving* it absolutely, and with such entire unreserve that he was impoverishing his own soul of its most precious possession.

So it seemed to him in those flaccid moods to which Hilbrook's visits left him, when mind and body were both spent in the effort he had been making. In the intervals in which his strength renewed itself, he put this fear from him as a hypochondriacal fancy, and he summoned a cheerfulness which he felt less and less to meet the hopeful face of the old man. Hilbrook had renewed himself, apparently, in the measure that the minister had aged and waned. He looked, to Ewbert, younger and stronger. To the conventional question how he did, he one night answered that he never felt better in his life. "But you," he said, casting an eye over the face and figure of the minister, who lay back in his easy-chair, with his hands stretched nerveless on the arms, "*you* look rather peaked. I don't know as I noticed it before, but come to think, I seemed to feel the same way about it when I saw you in the pulpit yesterday."

"It was a very close day," said Ewbert. "I don't know why I shouldn't be about as well as usual."

"Well, that's right," said Hilbrook, in willing dismissal of the trifle which had delayed him from the great matter in his mind.

Some new thought had occurred to him in corroboration of the notions they had agreed upon in their last meeting. But in response Ewbert found himself beset by a strange temptation,—by the wish to take up these notions and expose their fallacy. They were indeed mere toys of their common fancy which they had constructed together in mutual supposition, but Ewbert felt a sacredness in them, while he longed so strangely to break them one by one and cast them in the old man's face. Like all imaginative people, he was at times the prey of morbid self-suggestions, whose nature can scarcely be stated without excess. The more monstrous the thing appeared to his mind and conscience, the more fascinating it became. Once the mere horror of such a conception as catching a comely parishoner about the waist and kissing her, when she had come to him with a case of conscience, had so confused him in her presence as to make him answer her wildly, not because he was really tempted to the wickedness, but because he realized so vividly the hideousness of the impossible temptation. In some such sort he now trembled before old Hilbrook, thinking how dreadful it would be if he were suddenly to begin undoing the work of faith in him, and putting back in its place the doubts which he had uprooted before. In a swift series of dramatic representations he figured the old man's helpless amaze at the demoniacal gayety with which he should mock his own seriousness in the past, the cynical ease with which he should show the vanity of the hopes he had been so fervent in awakening. He had throughout recognized the claim that all the counter-doubts had upon the reason, and he saw how effective he could make these if he were now to become their advocate. He pictured the despair in which he could send his proselyte tottering home to his lonely house through the dark.

He rent himself from the spell, but the last picture remained so real with him that he went to the window and looked out, saying, "Is there a moon?"

"It ain't up yet, I guess," said old Hilbrook, and from something in his manner, rather than from anything he recollected of their talk, Ewbert fancied him to have asked a question, and to be now waiting for an answer. He had not the least notion what the question could have been, and he began to walk up and down, trying to think of something to say, but feeling his legs weak under him and the sweat cold on his forehead. All the time he was aware of Hilbrook following him with an air of cheerful interest, and patiently waiting till he should take up the thread of their discourse again.

He controlled himself at last, and sank into his chair. "Where were we?" he asked. "I had gone off on a train of associations, and I don't just recall our last point."

Hilbrook stated it, and Ewbert said, "Oh, yes," as if he recognized it, and went on from it upon the line of thought which it suggested. He was aware of talking rationally and forcibly; but in the subjective undercurrent paralleling his objective thought he was holding discourse with himself to an effect wholly different from that produced in Hilbrook.

"Well, sir," said the old man when he rose to go at last, "I guess you've settled it for me. You've made me see that there can be an immortal life that's worth living; and I was afraid there wa'n't! I shouldn't care, now, if I woke up any morning in the other world. I guess it would be all right; and that there would be new conditions every way, so that a man could go on and be himself, without feelin' that he was in any danger of being' wasted. You've made me want to meet my boy again; and I used to dread it; I didn't think I was fit for it. I don't know whether you expect me to thank you; I presume you don't; but I"—he faltered, and his voice shook in sympathy with the old hand that he put trembling into Ewbert's—"I *bless* you!"

XIII.

The time had come when the minister must seek refuge and counsel with his wife. He went to her as a troubled child goes to its mother, and she heard the confession of his strange experience with the motherly sympathy which performs the comforting office of perfect intelligence. If she did not grasp its whole significance, she seized what was perhaps the main point, and she put herself in antagonism to the cause of his morbid condition, while administering an inevitable chastisement for the neglect of her own prevision.

"That terrible old man," she said, "has simply been draining the life out of you, Clarence. I saw it from the beginning, and I warned you against it; but you wouldn't listen to me. *Now* I suppose you *will* listen, after the doctor tells you you're in danger of nervous prostration, and that you've got to give up everything and rest. *I* think you've been in danger of losing your reason, you've overworked it so; and I sha'nt be easy till I've got you safely away at the seaside, and out of the reach of that—that *vampire.*"

"Emily!" the minister protested. "I can't allow you to use such language. At the worst, and supposing that he had really been that drain upon me which you say (though I don't admit it), what is my life for but to give to others?"

"But *my* life isn't for you to give to others, and *your* life *is* mine, and I think I have some right to say what shall be done with it, and I don't choose to have used it up on old Hilbrook." It passed through Ewbert's languid thought, which it stirred to a vague amusement, that the son of an older church than the Rixonite might have found in this thoroughly terrestrial attitude of his wife a potent argument for sacerdotal celibacy; but he did not attempt to formulate it, and he listened submissively while she went on:

"*One* thing: I am certainly not going to let you see him again till you've seen the doctor, and I hope he won't come about. If he does, *I* shall see him."

The menace in this declaration moved Ewbert to another protest, which he worded conciliatingly: "I shall have to let you. But I know you won't say anything to convey a sense of responsibility to him. I couldn't forgive myself if he were allowed to feel that he had been preying on me. The fact is, I've been overdoing in every way, and nobody is to blame for my morbid fancies but myself. I *should* blame myself very severely if you based any sort of superstition on them, and acted from that superstition."

"Oh, you needn't be afraid!" said Mrs. Ewbert. "I shall take care of his feelings, but I shall have my own opinions, all the same, Clarence."

Whether a woman with opinions so strong as Mrs. Ewbert's, and so indistinguishable from her prejudices, could be trusted to keep them to herself, in dealing with the matter in hand, was a question which her husband felt must largely be left to her goodness of heart for its right solution.

When Hilbrook came that night, as usual, she had already had it out with him in several strenuous reveries before they met, and she was able to welcome him gently to the interview which she made very brief. His face fell in visible disappointment when she said that Mr. Ewbert would not be able to see him, and perhaps there was nothing to uplift him in the reasons she gave, though she obscurely resented his continued dejection as a kind of ingratitude. She explained that poor Mr. Ewbert was quite broken down, and that the doctor had advised his going to the seaside for the whole of August, where he promised everything from the air and the bathing. Mr. Ewbert merely needed toning up, she said; but to correct the impression she might be giving that his breakdown was a trifling matter, she added that she felt very anxious about it, and she wanted him to get away as soon as possible. She said with a confidential effect, as of something in which Hilbrook could sympathize with her: "You know it isn't merely his church work proper; it's his giving himself spiritually to all sorts of people so indiscriminately. He can't deny himself to any one; and sometimes he's perfectly exhausted by it. You must come and see him as soon as he gets back, Mr. Hilbrook. He will count upon it, I know; he's so much interested in the discussions he has been having with you."

She gave the old man her hand for good-by, after she had artfully stood him up, in a double hope,—a hope that he would understand that there was some limit to her husband's nervous strength, and a hope that her closing invitation would keep him from feeling anything personal in her hints.

Hilbrook took his leave in the dreamy fashion age has with so many things, as if there were a veil between him and experience which kept him from the full realization of what had happened; and as she watched his bent shoulders down the garden walk, carrying his forward-drooping head at a slant that scarcely left the crown of his hat visible, a fear came upon her which made it impossible for her to recount all the facts of her interview to her husband. It became her duty, rather, to conceal what was painful to herself in it, and she merely told him that Mr. Hilbrook had taken it all in the right way, and she had made him promise to come and see them as soon as they got back.

XIV.

Events approved the wisdom of Mrs. Ewbert's course in so many respects that she confidently trusted them for the rest. Ewbert picked up wonderfully at the seaside, and she said to him again and again that it was not merely those interviews with old Hilbrook which had drained his vitality, but it was the whole social and religious keeping of the place. Everybody, she said, had thrown themselves upon his sympathies, and he was carrying a load that no-body could bear up under. She addressed these declarations to her lingering consciousness of Ransom Hilbrook, and confirmed herself, by their repetition, in the belief that he had not taken her generalizations personally. She now extended these so as to inculpate the faculty of the university, who ought to have felt it their duty not to let a man of Ewbert's intellectual quality stagger on alone among them, with no sign of appreciation or recognition in the work he was doing, not so much for the Rixonite church as for the whole community. She took several ladies at the hotel into her confidence on this point, and upon study of the situation they said it was a shame. After that she felt more bitter about it, and attributed her husband's collapse to a concealed sense of the indifference of the university people, so galling to a sensitive nature.

She suggested this theory to Ewbert, and he denied it with blithe derision, but she said that he need not tell *her*, and confirming herself in it she began to relax her belief that old Ransom Hilbrook had preyed upon him. She even went so far as to say that the only intellectual companionship he had ever had in the place was that which he found in the old man's society. When she discovered, after the fact, that Ewbert had written to him since they came away, she was not so severe with him as she might have expected herself to be in view of an act which, if not quite clandestine, was certainly without her privity. She would have considered him fitly punished by Hilbrook's failure to reply, if she had not shared his uneasiness at the old man's silence. But she did not allow this to affect her good spirits, which were essential to her husband's comfort as well as her own. She redoubled her care of him in every sort, and among all the ladies who admired her devotion to him there was none who enjoyed it as much as herself. There was none who believed more implicitly that it was owing to her foresight and oversight that his health mended so rapidly, and that at the end of the bathing season she was, as she said, taking him home quite another man. In her perfect satisfaction she suffered him his small joke about not feeling it quite right to go with her if that were so; and though a woman of little humor, she even professed to find pleasure in his joke after she fully understood it.

"All that I ask," she said, as if it followed, "is that you won't spoil everything by letting old Hilbrook come every night and drain the life out of you again."

"I won't," he retorted, "if you'll promise to make the university people come regularly to my sermons."

He treated the notion of Hilbrook's visits lightly; but with his return to the familiar environment he felt a shrinking from them in an experience which was like something physical. Yet when he sat down the first night in his study, with his lamp in its wonted place, it was with an expectation of old Hilbrook in his usual seat so vivid that its defeat was more a shock than its fulfilment upon supernatural terms would have been. In fact, the absence of the old man was spectral; and though Ewbert employed himself fully the first night in answering an accumulation of letters that required immediate reply, it was with nervous starts from time to time, which he could trace to no other cause. His wife came in and out, with what he knew to be an accusing eye, as she brought up those arrears of housekeeping which always await the house-wife on the return from any vacation; and he knew that he did not conceal his guilt from her.

They both ignored the stress which had fallen back upon him, and which accumulated, as the days of the week went by, until the first Sunday came.

Ewbert dreaded to look in the direction of Hilbrook's pew, lest he should find it empty; but the old man was there, and he sat blinking at the minister, as his custom was, through the sermon, and thoughtfully passing the tip of his tongue over the inner edge of his lower lip.

Many came up to shake hands with the minister after church, and to tell him how well he was looking, but Hilbrook was not among them. Some of the university people who had made a point of being there that morning, out of a personal regard for Ewbert, were grouped about his wife, in the church vestibule, where she stood answering their questions about his health. He glimpsed between the heads and shoulders of this gratifying group the figure of Hilbrook dropping from grade to grade on the steps outside, till it ceased to be visible, and he fancied, with a pang, that the old man had lingered to speak with him, and had then given up and started home.

The cordial interest of the university people was hardly a compensation for the disappointment he shared with Hilbrook; but his wife was so happy in it that he could not say anything to damp her joy. "Now," she declared, on their way home, "I am perfectly satisfied that they will keep coming. You never preached so well, Clarence, and if they have any appreciation at all, they simply won't be able to keep away. I wish you could have heard all the nice things they said about you. I guess they've waked up to you, at last, and I do believe that the idea of losing you has had a great deal to do with it. And *that* is something we owe to old Ransom Hilbrook more than to anything else. I saw the poor old fellow hanging about, and I couldn't help feeling for him. I knew he wanted to speak with you, and I'm not afraid that he will be a burden again. It will be such an inspiration, the prospect of having the university people come every Sunday, now, that you can afford to give a little of it to him, and I want you to go and see him soon; he evidently isn't coming till you do."

XV.

Ewbert had learned not to inquire too critically for a logical process in his wife's changes of attitude toward any fact. In her present mood he recognized an effect of the exuberant good-will awakened by the handsome behavior of the university people, and he agreed with her that he must go to see old Hilbrook at once. In this good intention his painful feeling concerning him was soothed, and Ewbert did not get up to the Hilbrook place till well into the week. It was Thursday afternoon when he climbed through the orchard, under the yellowing leaves which dappled the green masses of the trees like intenser spots of the September sunshine. He came round by the well to the side door of the house, which stood open, and he did not hesitate to enter when he saw how freely the hens were coming and going through it. They scuttled out around him and between his legs, with guilty screeches, and left him standing alone in the middle of the wide, low kitchen. A certain discomfort of the nerves which their flight gave him was heightened by some details quite insignificant in themselves. There was no fire in the stove, and the wooden clock on the mantel behind it was stopped; the wind had carried in some red leaves from the maple near the door, and these were swept against the farther wall, where they lay palpitating in the draft.

The neglect in all was evidently too recent to suggest any supposition but that of the master's temporary absence, and Ewbert went to the threshold to look for his coming from the sheds or the barn. But these were all fast shut, and there was no sign of Hilbrook anywhere. Ewbert turned back into the room again, and saw the door of the old man's little bedroom standing slightly ajar. With a chill of apprehension he pushed it open, and he could not have experienced a more disagreeable effect if the dark fear in his mind had been realized than he did to see Hilbrook lying in his bed alive and awake. His face showed like a fine mask above the sheet, and his long, narrow hands rested on the covering across his breast. His eyes met those of Ewbert not only without surprise, but without any apparent emotion.

"Why, Mr. Hilbrook," said the minister, "are you sick?"

"No, I am first-rate," the old man anwered.

It was on the point of the minister's tongue to ask him, "Then what in the world are you doing in bed?" but he substituted the less authoritative suggestion, "I am afraid I disturbed you—that I woke you out of a nap. But I found the door open and the hens inside, and I ventured to come in"—

Hilbrook replied calmly, "I heard you; I wa'n't asleep."

"Oh," said Ewbert, apologetically, and he did not quite know what to do; he had an aimless wish for his wife, as if she would have known what to do. In her absence he decided to shut the door against the hens, who were returning adventurously to the threshold, and then he asked, "Is there something I can do for you? Make a fire for you to get up by"—

"I ha'n't got any call to get up," said Hilbrook; and, after giving Ewbert time to make the best of this declaration, he asked abruptly, "What was that you said about my wantin' to be alive enough to know I was dead?"

"The consciousness of unconsciousness?"

"Ah!" the old man assented, as with satisfaction in having got the notion right; and then he added, with a certain defiance: "There ain't anything *in* that. I got to thinking it over, when you was gone, and the whole thing went to pieces. That idea don't prove anything at all, and all that we worked out of it had to go with it."

"Well," the minister returned, with an assumption of cosiness in his tone which he did not feel, and feigning to make himself easy in the hard kitchen chair which he pulled up to the door of Hilbrook's room, "let's see if we can't put that notion together again."

"*You* can, if you want to," said the old man, dryly "I got no interest in it any more; 'twa'n't nothing but a metaphysical toy, anyway." He turned his head apathetically on the pillow, and no longer faced his visitor, who found it impossible in the conditions of tacit dismissal to philosophize further.

"I was sorry," Ewbert began, "not to be able to speak with you after church, the other day. There were so many people"—

"That's all right,' said Hilbrook unresentfully. "I hadn't anything to say, in particular."

"But *I* had," the minister persisted. "I thought a great deal about you when I was away, and I went over our talks in my own mind a great many times. The more I thought about them, the more I believed that we had felt our way to some important truth in the matter. I don't say final truth, for I don't suppose that we shall ever reach that in this life."

"Very likely," Hilbrook returned, with his face to the wall. "I don't see as it makes any difference; or if it does, I don't care for it."

Something occurred to Ewbert which seemed to him of more immediate usefulness than the psychological question. "Couldn't I get you something to eat, Mr. Hilbrook? If you haven't had any breakfast today, you must be hungry."

"Yes, I'm hungry," the old man assented, "but I don't want to eat anything."

Ewbert had risen hopefully in making his suggestion, but now his heart sank. Here, it seemed to him, a physician rather than a philosopher was needed, and at the sound of wheels on the wagon track to the door his imagination leaped to the miracle of the doctor's providential advent. He hurried to the threshold and met the fish-man, who was about to announce himself with the handle of his whip on the clapboarding. He grasped the situation from the minister's brief statement, and confessed that he had expected to find the old gentleman *dead* in his bed some day, and he volunteered to send some of the women folks from the farm up the road. When these came, concentrated in the person of the farmer's bustling wife, who had a fire kindled in the stove and the kettle on before Ewbert could get away, he went for the doctor, and returned with him to find her in possession of everything in the house except the owner's interest. Her usefulness had been arrested by an invisible but impassable barrier, although she had passed and repassed the threshold of Hilbrook's chamber with tea and milk toast. He said simply that he saw no object in eating; and he had not been sufficiently interested to turn his head and look at her in speaking to her.

With the doctor's science he was as indifferent as with the farm-wife's service. He submitted to have his pulse felt, and he could not help being prescribed for, but he would have no agency in taking his medicine. He said, as he had said to Mrs. Stephson about eating, that he saw no object in it.

The doctor retorted, with the temper of a man not used to having his will crossed, that he had better take it, if he had any object in living, and Hilbrook answered that he had none. In his absolute apathy he did not even ask to be let alone.

"You see," the baffled doctor fumed in the conference that he had with Ewbert apart, "he doesn't really need any medicine. There's nothing the matter with him, and I only wanted to give him something to put an edge to his appetite. He's got cranky living here alone; but there *is* such a thing as starving to death, and that's the only thing Hilbrook's in danger of. If you're going to stay with him—he oughtn't to be left alone"—

"I can come up, yes, certainly, after supper," said Ewbert, and he fortified himself inwardly for the question this would raise with his wife.

"Then you must try to interest him in something. Get him to talking, and then let Mrs. Stephson come in with a good bowl of broth, and I guess we may trust Nature to do the rest."

XVI.

When we speak of Nature, we figure her as one thing, with a fixed purpose and office in the universal economy; but she is an immense number of things, and her functions are inexpressibly varied. She includes decay as well as growth; she compasses death as well as birth. We call certain phenomena unnatural; but in a natural world how can anything be unnatural, except the supernatural? These facts gave Ewbert pause in view of the obstinate behavior of Ransom Hilbrook in dying for no obvious reason, and kept him from pronouncing it unnatural. The old man, he reflected, had really less reason to live than to die, if it came to reasons; for everything that had made the world home to him had gone out of it, and left him in exile here. The motives had ceased; the interests had perished; the strong personality that had persisted was solitary amid the familiar environment grown alien.

The wonder was that he should ever have been roused from his apathetic unfaith to inquiry concerning the world beyond this, and to a certain degree of belief in possibilities long abandoned by his imagination. Ewbert had assisted at the miracle of this resuscitation upon terms which, until he was himself much older, he could not question as to their beneficence, and in fact it never came to his being quite frank with himself concerning them. He kept his thoughts on this point in that state of solution which holds so many conjectures from precipitation in actual conviction.

But his wife had no misgivings. Her dread was that in his devotion to that miserable old man (as she called him, not always in compassion) he should again contribute to Hilbrook's vitality at the expense, if not the danger, of his own. She of course expressed her joy that Ewbert had at last prevailed upon him to eat something, when the entreaty of his nurse and the authority of his doctor availed nothing; and of course she felt the pathos of his doing it out of affection for Ewbert, and merely to please him, as Hilbrook declared. It did not surprise her that any one should do anything for the love of Ewbert, but it is doubtful if she fully recognized the beauty of this last efflorescence of the aged life; and she perceived it her duty not to sympathize entirely with Ewbert's morbid regret that it came too late. She was much more resigned than he to the will of Providence, and she urged a like submissiveness upon him.

"Don't talk so!" he burst out. "It's horrible!" It was in the first hours after Ewbert's return from Hilbrook's death-bed, and his spent nerves gave way in a gush of tears.

"I see what you mean," she said, after a pause in which he controlled his sobs. "And I suppose," she added, with a touch of bitterness, "that you blame *me* for taking you away from him here when he was coming every night and sapping your very life. You were very glad to have me do it at the time! And what use would there have been in your killing yourself, anyway? It wasn't as if he were a young man with a career of usefulness before him, that might have been marred by his not believing this or that. He had been a complete failure every way, and the end of the world had come for him. What did it matter whether such a man believed that there was another world or not?"

"Emily! Emily!" the minister cried out. "What are you saying?"

Mrs. Ewbert broke down in her turn. "I don't know *what* I'm saying!" she retorted from behind her handkerchief. "I'm trying to show you that it's your duty to yourself—and to me—and to people who can know how to profit by your teaching and your example, not to give way as you're doing, simply because a worn-out old agnostic couldn't keep his hold on the truth. I don't know what your Rixonitism is for if it won't let you wait upon the divine will in such a thing, *too*. You're more conscientious than the worst kind of Congregationalist. And now for you to blame me"—

"Emily, I don't blame *you*," said her husband. "I blame myself."

"And you see that that's the same thing! You ought to thank me for saving your life; for it was just as if you were pouring your heart's blood into him, and I could see you getting more anæmic every day. Even now you're not half as well as when you got home! And yet I do believe that if you could bring old Hilbrook back into a world that he was sick and tired of, you'd give your own life to do it."

XVII.

There was reason and there was justice in what she said, though they were so chaotic in form, and Ewbert could not refuse to acquiesce.

After all, he had done what he could, and he would not abandon himself to a useless remorse. He rather set himself to study the lesson of old Hilbrook's life, and in the funeral sermon that he preached he urged upon his hearers the necessity of keeping themselves alive through some relation to the undying frame of things, which they could do only by cherishing earthly ties; and when these were snapped in the removal of objects, by attaching the threads through an effort of the will to yet other objects: the world could furnish these inexhaustibly. He touched delicately upon the peculiarities, the eccentrities of the deceased, and he did cordial justice to his gentleness, his blameless, harmless life, his heroism on the battlefields of his country. He declared that he would not be the one to deny an inner piety, and certainly not a steadfast courage, in Hilbrook's acceptance of whatever his sincere doubts implied.

The sermon apparently made a strong impression on all who heard it. Mrs. Ewbert was afraid that it was rather abstruse in passages, but she felt sure that all the university people would appreciate these. The university people, to testify their respect for their founder, had come in a body to the obsequies of his kinsman; and Mrs. Ewbert augured the best things for her husband's future usefulness from their presence.

The Angel of the Lord

1901

"THE ANGEL OF THE LORD" was first printed in the *Century* magazine as "At Third Hand, a Psychological Inquiry." It was later included, along with "His Apparition" and "Though One Rose from the Dead," in *Questionable Shapes* (1903). The three stories that make up this volume are linked by their supernatural theme, specifically, the theme of communications from the spirit world. "Though One Rose" and "Angel" are further linked by being "Turkish Room" stories; that is, they are told by or to the members of a small community of friends who gather in the "Turkish Room" of a fictional club each afternoon.

"The Angel of the Lord" was the first of Howells's nine Turkish Room stories. The others are "Though One Rose from the Dead," also in *Questionable Shapes*; "A Case of Metaphantasmia," "Braybridge's Offer," "The Chick of the Easter Egg," "The Eidolons of Brooks Alford," and "A Memory That Worked Overtime," all in *Between the Dark and the Daylight*; "A Presentiment," in *The Daughter of the Storage*; and "The Fulfillment of the Pact," published in *Harper's Weekly*. ("His Apparition," the third story in *Questionable Shapes*, is linked to the Turkish Room stories by the presence of Wanhope, one of the Turkish Room habitués, but it is not written in the Turkish Room "style.")

The Turkish Room stories are characterized by multiple layers of narration. All but one of them are narrated by Acton, a novelist, but Acton merely recreates conversations that were dominated by other speakers.[1] He establishes the setting (the Turkish Room) and then repeats the stories as they were told to him by other characters, along with the questions, digressions, and arguments that interrupted the storytelling. These interruptions serve to distance the reader from the content of the stories, and to focus attention instead on questions of interpretation. Thus the stories are linked thematically as well as by their common setting and narrative structure.

The Turkish Room, "as it was called from its cushions and hangings of Indian and Egyptian stuffs," is part of a New York men's club. The room and its usual occupants are briefly introduced in each of the stories, but the fullest description is found in the opening paragraphs of "Braybridge's Offer":

> We had ordered our dinners and were sitting in the Turkish room at the club, waiting to be called, each in his turn, to the dining-room. It was always a cosey [*sic*] place, whether you found yourself in it with cigars and coffee after dinner, or with whatever liquid or solid appetizer you preferred in the half-hour or more that must pass before dinner after you had made out your menu. It intimated an exclusive possession in the three or four who happened first to find themselves together in it, and it invited the philosophic mind to contemplation more than any other spot in the club.
>
> Our rather limited little down-town dining-club was almost a celibate community at most times. A few husbands and fathers joined us at lunch; but at dinner we were nearly always a company of bachelors, dropping in an hour or so before we wished to dine, and ordering from a bill of fare what we liked. Some dozed away in the intervening time; some read the evening papers or played chess; I preferred the chance society of the Turkish room. I could be pretty sure of finding Wanhope there in these sympathetic moments, and where Wanhope was there would probably be Rulledge, passively willing to listen and agree, and Minver ready to interrupt and dispute. I myself like to look in and linger for either the reasoning or the bickering, at it happened . . . (147)

Acton, the narrator, is a novelist, and as such, he is frequently teased about his quiet attention to the stories being told. For example, the following passage occurs in "The Chick of the Easter Egg":

> "Fine?" I couldn't help bursting out; "it's a stroke of poetry."

Minver cut in: "The thrifty Acton making a note of it for future use in literature."

"Eh!" Newton queried. "Oh! I don't mind. You're welcome to it, Mr. Acton. It's a pity somebody shouldn't use it, and of course *I* can't."

"Acton will send you a copy with the usual forty-per-cent. discount and ten off for cash," the painter said. (178)

This quiet undercutting of the novelist's transformation of life into literature links Acton to the much darker character of "the contributor," who appears without a name in Howells's *Suburban Sketches* (see "A Romance of Real Life"). Minver, another artist, is a painter. He is critical and questioning, "usually a censor of our several foibles rather than a sharer in our philosophic speculations and metaphysical conjectures" ("A Presentiment" 45). Rulledge, "being of no employ whatever, and spending his whole life at the club in an extraordinary idleness," serves as a foil to Minver and also provides the stories with some comic relief. He is characterized by his eager credulity, his sentimentality, and his easy sympathy, and is called "at once romantic and literal" ("Eidolons"). And Wanhope, the psychologist, is cerebral and intellectual, slow to commit himself to any belief, a caricature of the detached scientist. (Carrington and Carrington call Wanhope "an alienist" [psychiatrist] but I do not find evidence for this—*Plots and Characters* 302.)

"The Angel of the Lord" is also significant in that it is Howells's first mature treatment of the "psychic" material that was to form an important part of his later fiction. He had used similar material in *The Undiscovered Country* (1880), but the emphasis in that novel is strictly on the phenomenon of spiritualism, i.e., the manifestation of spirits in seances conducted by mediums. And, as one writer explains, Howells was "interested not so much in the truth behind the claims of the spiritualists as in their motivations, and not so much in the phenomena themselves as in the reactions of people to them" (Fox, "Spiritualism" 123). While Howells never lost interest in the psychology of spiritualism and psychic phenomena, by 1901, he was fully engaged with the mysteries of the phenomena themselves.

It is important to point out that Howells did not carefully distinguish between what we would call the psychological and the psychic. In his "Easy Chair" column of June, 1903, for example, he discusses the rise of "a whole order of literature . . . calling itself psychological, as realism called itself scientific, and dealing with life on its mystical side" (149). Similarly, Howells declared that his "passion for the psychological" led him to admire a contemporary play dealing with mental telepathy (quoted in Fox, "Spiritualism" 122), and he has Wanhope, a psychologist, declare that "all psychology is in a manner dealing with the occult" ("Though One Rose from the Dead" 215). Howells's seemingly careless use of the word "psychological" may have been based on his unwillingness or inability to take a stand on the origin of subjective phenomena. In 1909, speaking of visions, he said: "Whether they are natural or supernatural, they are precious: whether they are the effect of causes quite within ourselves, or are intimations to us from the source of all life that death too shall have an end somewhere, somehow, they are to be cherished and kept in the heart, and not cast out of it as idle and futile" (*In After Days* 5).

Psychology and the psychic are linked in other ways as well. As Howard Kerr points out, "during the last two decades of the century, the spiritualistic medium played a significant role in the field of psychology by providing such pioneer investigators as Pierre Janet, Theodore Flourney, William James and F. W. H. Myers with data for their theories of multiple personality, hysteria, and the unconscious" (117). The transatlantic Society for Psychical Research included both skeptics and believers, and its members, according to Kerr, "were applying sophisticated theories of trance, hysteria, alternate personality, and hallucinations to the *perception* of spirits by the living" (208). Howells's failure to distinguish carefully between the psychological and the psychic is understandable.

Furthermore, Howells's treatment of supernatural themes was, as I've implied, grounded in psychological realism. While his curiosity about psychic phenomena was genuine, he never let the "ghost story" dominate. This was noted as early as 1924, when Oscar Firkins asserted that Howells "proved impervious to those temptations to which the uprightness of other realists has succumbed" (64). "Angel" is a good example of how Howells carefully balances between the psychological and psychic, between explanations based on idiosyncrasies of character and those based on supernatural causes.

Howells's interest in the psychic and psychological sprang originally from a number of personal and biographical sources. His youthful morbidity and hypochondria (his well-documented fear of hydrophobia, for example) is thoroughly treated in the Cady and Lynn biographies, as well as in Howells's own *Years of My Youth* (91–94). His interest in ghosts was well nourished by the interest in supernatural phenomena which swept the country after the "Rochester Rappings" of 1848 (Kerr 4–5) and which was, according to *Years of My Youth*, to be found in the village of Howells's childhood (88, 91). The Swedenborgianism of Howells's father no doubt contributed, as did the popularity of supernatural themes in the literature of the period. (An extended treatment of this topic can be found in Howard Kerr's *Mediums, and Spirit-*

Rappers, and Roaring Radicals.) And Howells's friendship with the psychologist William James, who founded the American branch of the British Society for Psychical Research and eventually became president of the combined British and American group (Kerr 207) almost certainly brought the *Proceedings* of that group to his attention (Fox, "Spiritualism" 124).

James, in fact, had a profound influence on Howells. Like Howells, he combined his interest in psychology with serious speculation about the supernatural. A recent biography of James notes his belief in immortality, mental telepathy, and communication from the dead (Leahey 201). Charles Crow, in fact, identifies James as "the most distinguished and credible investigator of psychic phenomena in the United States" (171). In his *Principles of Psychology* (1891) and other works, James "addressed himself to the questions disturbing Howells: the crisis of faith, the workings of the mind and strange and terrifying psychic phenomena" (Crow 170).

Howells's interests were further encouraged by some new elements in his intellectual life. Through his book reviewing and editorship, Howells became acquainted with the ideas of Jean-Martin Charcot, Pierre Janet, T. A. Ribot, Josiah Royce, and Nathaniel Shaler (Crowley and Crow 42–43, Fox, "Spiritualism" 127). He became personally involved with one of the greatest frauds in American spiritualism when in 1875 he published Robert Dale Owens Jr.'s ingenuous account of the infamous "Katie King" (Kerr 111–16, 122).[2] Howells was also closely following the development of "psychological" fiction, most notably the works of Ibsen, Hauptmann, Maeterlinck, and of course Henry James ("Editor's Easy Chair" [1903] 149). At the end of the century, according to Van Wyck Brooks, Howells "took to studying psychology and medical books and magazines, reading case-histories, recording his own dreams, and this led to his writing two volumes of short stories about the 'filmy shapes that haunt the dusk.' These were *Between the Dark and the Daylight* and *Questionable Shapes*, and he told Dr. Weir Mitchell that they were all psychic stories out of his own life" (223).

But psychic and supernatural issues, specifically, belief in an afterlife, did not become a pressing—indeed a passionate—issue for Howells until after the death of his daughter Winny in 1889. As John Crowley puts it, "That no afterlife would exist to compensate Winifred for her suffering was an almost unbearable thought" (*Mask* 136). Howells's futile attempts "to imagine her well and happy somewhere" (*SL* 3:249) are movingly chronicled in the letters he wrote during this "black time" (Cady, *Realist* 58) and for all the years to follow (Vanderbilt 197–98). For Howells's personal beliefs about immortality, like practically all of his religious beliefs, were tenuous at best. Throughout his life, he was a hopeful agnostic, waiting to be convinced of the truth of any religious doctrine. Howells's persistent agnosticism meant, for him, perpetual engagement with religious questions, and an unending interest in and respect for the ramifications of these questions. And his years as a realist provided him with the method to probe these issues. Howells's much maligned "teacup" realism, to use Frank Norris's famous phrase, consisting as it did of close attention to the quiet but profound subtleties of thought and behavior in everyday life, grew out of his ideas about the proper role of literature, but could just as well have developed from his rejection of formal religion, and the resulting need to learn about life empirically. Arnold Fox argues, in fact, that "Howells' interest in the paranormal surprises the reader . . . because it is alien to the spirit which dominates his work, a spirit which is clearly speculative rather than dogmatic, naturalistic rather than supernaturalistic" ("Spiritualism" 130).

Howells's ambivalence about immortality found an appropriate literary medium in the fictional frame of the Turkish Room. As Charles Crow explains, Howells's explorations of "the shadowy territory of dreams, subconscious motive and parapsychological experience . . . stimulated [him] to bold technical innovations, especially in the use of unreliable and multiple narrators" (169). The specific connection between the content of "Angel" and its form is well explicated by John Crowley in *The Mask of Fiction*. According to Crowley, "Howells's problem was how to 'speak to' questionable shapes without committing himself to a belief in their reality" (147). Howells was also bound by his respect for the theories of F. W. H. Myers, who argued that traditional ghost stories, by providing a tidy frame for the events they describe, inevitably distort and misrepresent "the intractable disorder of an actual psychic event" (Crowley 148). By using a fictional frame, Howells could, in Crowley's words, "at once leave the psychic phenomenon apparently 'inviolate' and establish the aesthetic distance that his agnosticism demanded between himself and it" (148).

The fact that "Angel" is actually thrice framed, with Acton reporting on Wanhope's retelling of Mrs. Ormond's story, causes the reader to focus on the interpretation of events. As Crowley points out, the fictional frame not only "enclose[s] the psychic case history . . . but break[s] its narrative continuity" (149) and the triple distancing further prevents the reader from being immersed in the events themselves. The reader, removed in time and place, is asked to evaluate witnesses, and is presented with varying points of view. At the same time, the inability to reach definite conclusions is quietly criticized, as Howells uses Wanhope to gently mock his own agnosticism.

"The Angel of the Lord" was followed in 1912 by a sequel, "The Fulfillment of the Pact."

Notes

1. In "A Case of Metaphantasmia," Acton narrates, but the main speaker is a stranger named Newton, who is introduced by a club member named Halson. In "Braybridge's Offer," Acton repeats a conversation led by two storytellers, Wanhope and Halson. In "The Chick of the Easter Egg" Acton reports on a story told by Newton. "The Eidolons of Brooks Alford" is presented in part as it was told by Wanhope, in the usual setting of the Turkish Room, and in part is told directly by Acton. "A Memory That Worked Overtime" differs slightly from the other stories in that it is set in Minver's house, and the main speaker is Minver's brother. While it is therefore not precisely a Turkish Room story, it is told in the Turkish Room "style." "A Presentiment" focuses on a story told by Minver. In "The Fulfillment of the Pact" the storyteller is Wanhope. "Though One Rose from the Dead" is the only story not narrated by Acton. It is told by Wanhope to Acton, presumably in a letter. It is not really in the Turkish Room "style," but since it contains direct references to the club, I am including it in this list.

2. Katie King, the "most famous single spirit of the century" (Kerr 111–12) was a "materialized spirit" who appeared in 1874 to a British medium named Florence Cook. Her endorsement as actual by William Crookes, "a rising young physicist later to be knighted for his contributions to science" (Kerr 112) led many to believe that she represented the first scientific proof of spiritualism. She reappeared in Philadelphia later that year, asked for Robert Dale Owens, and met with him during forty seances. Owens, convinced that he was talking to a spirit, arranged for the publication of "Touching Spiritual Visitants from a Higher Life" in the *Atlantic Monthly* of January, 1875. Owens's discovery that Katie was actually a flesh-and-blood assistant to the mediums came too late for him to withdraw his article from publication. His prompt retraction of his claims, appearing in a letter to the *New York Tribune*, shortly preceded the appearance of his article and ensured his public humiliation.

ℰ

The Angel of the Lord

A ll that sort of personification," said Wanhope, "is far less remarkable than the depersonification which has now taken place so thoroughly that we no longer think in the old terms at all. It was natural that the primitive peoples should figure the passions, conditions, virtues, vices, forces, qualities, in some sort of corporal shape, with each a propensity or impulse of its own, but it does not seem to me so natural that the derivative peoples should cease to do so. It is rational that they should do so, and I don't know that any stronger proof of our intellectual advance could be alleged than the fact that the old personifications survive in the parlance while they are quite extinct in the consciousness. We still talk of death at times as if it were an embodied force of some kind, and of love in the same way; but I don't believe that any man of the commonest common-school education thinks of them so. If you try to do it yourself, you are rather ashamed of the puerility, and when a painter or a sculptor puts them in an objective shape, you follow him with impatience, almost with contempt."

"How about the poets?" asked Minver, less with the notion, perhaps, of refuting the psychologist than of bringing the literary member of our little group under the disgrace that had fallen upon him as an artist.

"The poets," said I, "are as extinct as the personifications."

"That's very handsome of you, Acton," said the artist. "But go on, Wanhope."

"Yes, get down to business," said Rulledge. Being of no employ whatever, and spending his whole life at the club in an extraordinary idleness, Rulledge was always using the most strenuous expressions, and requiring everybody to be practical. He leaned directly forward with the difficulty that a man of his girth has in such movement, and vigorously broke off the ash of his cigar against the edge of his saucer. We had been dining together, and had been served with coffee in the Turkish room, as it was called from its cushions and hangings of Indian and Egyptian stuffs. "What is the instance you've got up your sleeve?" He smoked with great energy, and cast his eyes alertly about as if to make sure that there was no chance of Wanhope's physically escaping him, from the corner of the divan, where he sat pretty well hemmed in by the rest of us, spreading in an irregular circle before him.

"You unscientific people are always wanting an instance, as if an instance were convincing. An instance is only suggestive; a thousand instances, if you please, are convincing," said the psychologist. "But I don't know that I wish to be convincing. I would rather be enquiring. That is much more interesting, and, perhaps, profitable."

"All the same," Minver persisted, apparently in behalf of Rulledge, but with an after-grudge of his own, "you'll allow that you were thinking of something in particular when you began with that generalization about the lost art of personifying?"

"Oh, that is very curious," said the psychologist. "We talk of generalizing, but is there any such thing? Aren't we always striving from one concrete to another, and isn't what we call generalizing merely a process of finding our way?"

"I see what you mean," said the artist, expressing in that familiar formula the state of the man who hopes to know what the other man means.

"That's what I say," Rulledge put in. "You've got something up your sleeve. What is it?"

Wanhope struck the little bell on the table before him, but, without waiting for a response, he intercepted a waiter who was passing with a coffee-pot, and asked, "Oh, couldn't you give me some of that?"

The man filled his cup for him, and after Wanhope put in the sugar and lifted it to his lips, Rulledge said, with his impetuous business air, "It's easy to see what Wanhope does his high thinking on."

"Yes," the psychologist admitted, "coffee is an inspiration. But you can overdo an inspiration. It would be interesting to know whether there hasn't been a change in the quality of thought since the use of such stimulants came in—whether it hasn't been subtilized—"

"Was that what you were going to say?" demanded Rulledge, relentlessly. "Come, we've got no time to throw away!"

Everybody laughed.

"You haven't, anyway," said I.

"Well, none of his own," Minver admitted for the idler.

"I suppose you mean I have thrown it all away. Well, I don't want to throw away other peoples'. Go on, Wanhope."

II.

The psychologist set his cup down and resumed his cigar, which he had to pull at pretty strongly before it revived. "I should not be surprised," he began, "if a good deal of the fear of death had arisen, and perpetuated itself in the race, from the early personification of dissolution as an enemy of a certain dreadful aspect, armed and threatening. That conception wouldn't have been found in men's minds at first; it would have been the result of later crude meditation upon the fact. But it would have remained through all the imaginative ages, and the notion might have been intensified in the more delicate temperaments as time went on, and by the play of heredity it might come down to our own day in certain instances with a force scarcely impaired by the lapse of incalculable time."

"You said just now," said Rulledge, in rueful reproach, "that personification had gone out."

"Yes, it has. I did say that, and yet I suppose that though such a notion of death, say, no longer survives in the consciousness, it does survive in the unconsciousness, and that any vivid accident or illusory suggestion would have force to bring it to the surface."

"I wish I knew what you were driving at," said Rulledge.

"You remember Ormond, don't you?" asked Wanhope, turning suddenly to me.

"Perfectly," I said. "I—he isn't living, is he?"

"No; he died two years ago."

"I thought so," I said, with the relief that one feels in not having put a fellow-creature out of life, even conditionally.

"You knew Mrs. Ormond, too, I believe," the psychologist pursued.

I owned that I used to go to the Ormonds' house.

"Then you know what a type she was, I suppose," he turned to the others, "and as they're both dead it's no contravention of the club etiquette against talking of women, to speak of her. I can't very well give the instance—the sign—that Rulledge is seeking without speaking of her, unless I use a great deal of circumlocution." We all urged him to go on, and he went on. "I had the facts I'm going to give, from Mrs. Ormond. You know that the Ormonds left New York a couple of years ago?"

He happened to look at Minver as he spoke, and Minver answered: "No; I must confess that I didn't even know they had left the planet."

Wanhope ignored his irrelevant ignorance. "They went to live provisionally at a place up the Housatonic road, somewhere—perhaps Canaan; but it doesn't matter. Ormond had been suffering some time with an obscure affection of the heart—"

"Oh, come now!" said Rulledge. "You're not going to spring anything so pat as heart-disease on us?"

The psychologist smiled. "I'm afraid you're not interested. I'm not much interested myself in these unrelated instances."

"Oh, no!" "Don't!" "Do go on!" the different entreaties came, and after a little time taken to recover his lost equanimity, Wanhope went on: "I don't know whether you knew that Ormond had rather a peculiar dread of death." We none of us could affirm that we did, and again Wanhope resumed: "I shouldn't say that he was a coward above other men. I believe he was rather below the average in cowardice. But the thought of death weighed upon him. You find this much more commonly among the Russians, if we are to believe their novelists, than among Americans. He might have been a character out of one of Tourguénief's books, the idea of death was so constantly present with him. He once told me that the fear of it was a part of his earliest consciousness, before the time when he could have had any intellectual conception of it. It seemed to be something like the projection of an alien horror into his life—a prenatal influence—"

"Jove!" Rulledge broke in. "I don't see how the women stand it. To look forward nearly a whole year to death as the possible end of all they're hoping for and suffering for! Talk of men's courage after that! I wonder we're not all marked."

"I never heard of anything of the kind in Ormond's history," said Wanhope, tolerant of the incursion.

Minver took his cigar out to ask, the more impressively, perhaps, "What do you fellows make of the terror that a two months' babe starts in its sleep with before it can have any notion of what fear is on its own hook?"

"We don't make anything of it," the psychologist answered. "Perhaps the pathologists do."

"Oh, it's easy enough to say wind," Rulledge indignantly protested.

"Too easy, I agree with you," Wanhope consented.

"We cannot tell what influences reach us from our environment, or what our environment really is, or how much or little we mean by the word. The sense of danger seems to be inborn, and possibly it is a survival of our race life when it was wholly animal and took care of itself through what we used to call the instincts. But, as I was saying, it was not danger that Ormond seemed to be afraid of, if it came short of death. He was almost abnormally indifferent to pain. I knew of his undergoing an operation that most people would take ether for, and not wincing, because it was not supposed to involve a fatal result."

"Perhaps he carried his own anodyne with him," said Minver, "like the Chinese."

"You mean a sort of self-anaesthesia?" Wanhope asked. "That is very interesting. How far such a principle, if there is one, can be carried in practice. The hypnotists—"

"I'm afraid I didn't mean anything so serious or scientific," said the painter.

"Then don't switch Wanhope off on a side track," Rulledge implored. "You know how hard it is to keep him on the main line. He's got a mind that splays all over the place if you give him the least chance. Now, Wanhope, come down to business."

Wanhope laughed amiably. "Why, there's so very little of business. I'm not sure it wasn't Mrs. Ormond's attitude toward the fact that interested me most. It was nothing short of devout. She was a convert. She believed he really saw—I suppose," he turned to me, "there's no harm in our recognizing now that they didn't always get on smoothly together?"

"Did they ever?" I asked.

"Oh, yes—oh, yes," said the psychologist, kindly. "They were very fond of each other, and often very peaceful."

"I never happened to be by," I said.

"Used to fight like cats and dogs," said Minver. "And they didn't seem to mind people. It was very swell, in a way, their indifference, and it did help to take away a fellow's embarrassment."

"That seemed to come mostly to an end that summer," said Wanhope, "if you could believe Mrs. Ormond."

"You probably couldn't," the painter put in.

"At any rate she seemed to worship his memory."

"Oh, yes; she hadn't him there to claw."

"Well, she was quite frank about it with me," the psychologist pursued. "She admitted that they had always quarreled a good deal. She seemed to think it was a token of their perfect unity. It was as if they were each quarreling with themselves, she said. I'm not sure that there wasn't something in the notion. There is no doubt but that they were tremendously in love with each other, and there is something curious in the bickerings of married people if they are in love. It's one way of having no concealments; it's perfect confidence of a kind—"

"Or unkind," Minver suggested.

"What has all that got to do with it?" Rulledge demanded.

"Nothing directly," Wanhope confessed, "and I'm not sure that it has much to do indirectly. Still, it has a certain atmospheric relation. It is very remarkable how thoughts connect themselves with one another. It's a sort of wireless telegraphy. They do not touch at all; there is apparently no manner of tie between them, but they communicate—"

"Oh, Lord!" Rulledge fumed.

Wanhope looked at him with a smiling concern, such as a physician might feel in the symptoms of a peculiar case. "I wonder," he said absently, "how much of our impatience with a fact delayed is a survival of the childhood of the race, and how far it is the effect of conditions in which possession is the ideal?"

Rulledge pushed back his chair, and walked away in dudgeon. "I'm not a busy man myself. When you've got anything to say you can send for me."

Minver ran after him, as no doubt he meant some one should. "Oh, come back! He's just going to begin;" and when Rulledge, after some pouting, had been pushed down into his chair again, Wanhope went on, with a glance of scientific pleasure at him.

III.

"The house they had taken was rather a lonely place, out of sight of neighbors, which they had got cheap because it was so isolated and inconvenient, I fancy. Of course Mrs. Ormond, with her exaggeration, represented it as a sort of solitude which nobody but tramps of the most dangerous description ever visited. As she said, she never went to sleep without expecting to wake up murdered in her bed."

"Like her," said Minver, with a glance at me full of relish for the touch of character which I would feel with him.

"She said," Wanhope went on, "that she was anxious from the first for the effect upon Ormond. In the stress of any danger, she gave me to understand, he always behaved very well, but out of its immediate presence he was full of all sorts of gloomy apprehensions, unless the surroundings were cheerful. She could not imagine how he came to take the place, but when she told him so—"

"I've no doubt she told him so pretty promptly," the painter grinned.

"—he explained that he had seen it on a brilliant day in spring, when all the trees were in bloom, and the bees humming in the blossoms, and the orioles singing, and the outlook from the lawn down over the river valley was at its best. He had fallen in love with the place, that was the truth, and he was so wildly in love with it all through that he could not feel the defect she did in it. He used to go gaily about the wide, harking old house at night, shutting it up, and singing or whistling while she sat quaking at the notion of their loneliness and their absolute helplessness—an invalid and a little woman—in case anything happened. She wanted him to get the man who did the odd jobs about the house, to sleep there, but he laughed at her, and they kept on with their usual town equipment of two serving-women. She could not account for his spirits, which were usually so low when they were alone—"

"And not fighting," Minver suggested to me.

"—and when she asked him what the matter was he could not account for them, either. But he said one day, that the fear of death seemed to be lifted from his soul, and that made her shudder."

Rulledge fetched a long sigh and Minver interpreted, "Beginning to feel that it's something like now."

"He said that for the first time within his memory he was rid of that nether consciousness of mortality which had haunted his whole life, and poisoned, more or less, all his pleasure in living. He had got a reprieve, or a respite, and he felt like a boy—another kind of boy from what he had ever been. He was full of all sorts of brilliant hopes and plans. He had visions of success in business beyond anything he had known, and talked of buying the place he had taken, and getting a summer colony of friends about them. He meant to cut the property up, and make the right kind of people inducements. His world seemed to have been emptied of all trouble as well as all mortal danger."

"Haven't you psychologists some message about a condition like that?" I asked.

"Perhaps it's only the pathologists again," said Minver.

"The alienists, rather more specifically," said Wanhope. "They recognize it as one of the beginnings of insanity—*folie des grandeurs* as the French call the stage."

"Is it necessarily that?" Rulledge demanded, with a resentment which we felt so droll in him that we laughed.

"I don't know that it is," said Wanhope. "I don't know why we shouldn't sometimes, in the absence of proofs to the contrary, give such a fact the chance to evince a spiritual import. Of course it had no other import to poor Mrs. Ormond, and of course I didn't dream of suggesting a scientific significance."

"I should think not!" Rulledge puffed.

Wanhope went on: "I don't think I should have dared to do so to a woman in her exaltation concerning it. I could see that however his state had affected her with dread or discomfort in the first place, it had since come to be her supreme hope and consolation. In view of what afterward happened, she regarded it as the effect of a mystical intimation from another world that was sacred, and could not be considered like an ordinary fact without sacrilege. There was something very pathetic in her absolute conviction that Ormond's happiness was an emanation from the source of all happiness, such as sometimes, where the consciousness persists, comes to a deathbed. That the dying are not afraid of dying is a fact of such common, such almost invariable observation—"

"You mean," I interposed, "when the vital forces are beaten so low that the natural dread of ceasing to be, has no play? It has less play, I've noticed, in age than in youth, but for the same reason that it has when people are weakened by sickness."

"Ah," said Wanhope, "that comparative indifference to death in the old, to whom it is so much nearer than it is to the young, is very suggestive. There may be something in what you say; they may not care so much because they have no longer the strength—the muscular strength—for caring. They are too tired to care as they used. There is a whole region of most important inquiry in that direction—"

"Did you mean to have him take that direction?" Rulledge asked, sulkily.

"He can take any direction for me," I said. "He is always delightful."

"Ah, thank you!" said Wanhope.

"But I confess," I went on, "that I was wondering whether the fact that the dying are indifferent to death could be established in the case of those who die in the flush of health and strength, like, for instance, people who are put to death."

Wanhope smiled. "I think it can—measurably. Most murderers make a good end, as the saying used to be, when they end on the scaffold, though they are not supported by religious fervor of any kind, or the exaltation of a high ideal. They go meekly and even cheerfully to their death, without rebellion or even objection. It is most exceptional that they make a fight for their lives, as that woman did a few years ago at Dannemora, and disgusted all refined people with capital punishment."

"I wish they would make a fight always," said Rulledge, with unexpected feeling. "It would do more than anything to put an end to that barbarity."

"It would be very interesting, as Wanhope says," Minver remarked. "But aren't we getting rather far away? From the Ormonds, I mean."

"We are, rather," said Wanhope. "Though I agree that it would be interesting. I should rather like to have it tried. You know Frederick Douglass acted upon such principle when his master attempted to whip him. He fought, and he had a theory that if the slave had always fought there would soon have been an end of whipping, and so an end of slavery. But probably it will be a good while before criminals are—"

"Educated up to the idea," Minver proposed.

"Yes," Wanhope absently acquiesced. "There seems to be a resignation intimated to the parting soul, whether in sickness or in health, by the mere proximity of death. In Ormond's case there seems to have been something more positive. His wife says that in the beginning of those days he used to come to her and wonder what could be the matter with him. He had a joy he could not account for by anything in their lives, and it made her tremble."

"Probably it didn't. I don't think there was anything that could make Mrs. Ormond tremble, unless it was the chance that Ormond would get the last word," said Minver.

No one minded him, and Wanhope continued: "Of course she thought he must be going to have a fit of sickness, as the people say in the country, or used to say. Those expressions often survive in the common parlance long after the peculiar mental and moral conditions in which they originated have passed away. They must once have been more accurate than they are now. When one said 'fit of sickness' one must have meant something specific; it would be interesting to know what. Women use those expressions longer than men; they seem to be inveterate in their nerves; and women apparently do their thinking in their nerves rather than their brains."

IV.

Wanhope had that distant look in his eyes which warned his familiars of a possible excursion, and I said, in the hope of keeping him from it, "Then isn't there a turn of phrase somewhat analogous to that in a personification?"

"Ah, yes—a personification," he repeated with a freshness of interest, which he presently accounted for. "The place they had taken was very completely furnished. They got it fully equipped, even to linen and silver; but what was more important to poor Ormond was the library, very rich in English classics, which appeared to go with the house. The owner was a girl who married and lived abroad, and these were her father's books. Mrs. Ormond said that her husband had the greatest pleasure in them: their print, which was good and black, and their paper, which was thin and yellowish, and their binding, which was tree calf* in the poets, he specially liked. They were English editions as well as English classics, and she said he caressed the

---

* According to *Webster's*, "a calfskin leather chemically treated so as to change its color and produce on it a treelike design."

books, as he read them, with that touch which the book-lover has; he put his face into them, and inhaled their odor as if it were the bouquet of wine; he wanted her to like it, too."

"Then she hated it," Minver said, unrelentingly.

"Perhaps not, if there was nobody else there," I urged.

For once, Wanhope was not to be tempted off on another scent. "There was a good deal of old-fashioned fiction of the suspiratory and exclamatory sort, like Mackenzie's, and Sterne's and his followers, full of feeling, as people understood feeling a hundred years ago. But what Ormond rejoiced in most were the poets, good and bad, like Gray and Collins and Young, and their contemporaries, who personified nearly everything from Contemplation to Indigestion, through the whole range of the Vices, Virtues, Passions, Propensities, Attributes, and Qualities, and gave them each a dignified capital letter to wear. She said he used to come roaring to her with the passages in which these personifications flourished, and read them off with mock admiration, and then shriek and sputter with laughter. You know the way he had when a thing pleased him, especially a thing that had some relish of the quaint or rococo. As nearly as she would admit, in view of his loss, he bored her with these things. He was always hunting down some new personification, and when he had got it, adding it to the list he kept. She said he had thousands of them, but I suppose he had not so many. He had enough, though, to keep him amused, and she said he talked of writing something for the magazines about them, but probably he never would have done it. He never wrote anything, did he?" Wanhope asked of me.

"Oh, no. He was far too literary for that," I answered. "He had a reputation to lose."

"Pretty good," said Minver, "even if Ormond is dead."

Wanhope ignored us both. "After a while, his wife said, she began to notice a certain change in his attitude toward the personifications. She noticed this, always expecting that fit of sickness for him; but she was not so much troubled by his returning seriousness. Oh, I ought to tell you that when she first began to be anxious for him she privately wrote home to their family doctor, telling him how strangely happy Ormond was, and asking him if he could advise anything. He wrote back that if Ormond was so very happy they had better not do anything to cure him; that the disease was not infectious, and was seldom fatal."

"What an ass!" said Rulledge.

"Yes, I think he was, in this instance. But probably he had been consulted a good deal by Mrs. Ormond," said Wanhope. "The change that began to set her mind at rest about Ormond was his taking the personifications more seriously. Why, he began to ask, but always with a certain measure of joke in it, why shouldn't there be something in the personifications? Why shouldn't Morn and Eve come corporeally walking up their lawn, with little or no clothes on, or Despair be sitting in their woods with her hair over her face, or Famine coming gauntly up to their back door for a hand-out? Why shouldn't they any day see pop-eyed Rapture passing on the trolley, or Meditation letting the car she intended to take go by without stepping lively enough to get on board? He pretended that we could have the personifications back again, if we were not so conventional in our conceptions of them. He wanted to know what reason there was for representing Life as a very radiant and bounding party, when Life usually neither shone nor bounded; and why Death should be figured as an enemy with a dart, when it was so often the only friend a man had left, and had the habit of binding up wounds rather than inflicting them. The personifications were all right, he said, but the poets and painters did not know how they really looked. By the way," Wanhope broke off, "did you happen to see Hauptmann's* 'Hännele' when it was here?"

None of us had, and we waited rather restively for the passing of the musing fit which he fell into. After a while he resumed at a point whose relation to the matter in hand we could trace:

"It was extremely interesting for all reasons, by its absolute fearlessness and freshness in regions where there has been nothing but timid convention for a long time; but what I was thinking of was the personification of Death as it appears there. The poor little dying pauper, lying in her dream at the almshouse, sees the figure of Death. It is not the skeleton with the dart, or the phantom with the shrouded face, but a tall, beautiful young man,—as beautiful as they could get into the cast, at any rate,—clothed in simple black, and standing with his back against the mantlepiece, with his hands resting on the hilt of a long, two-handed sword. He is so quiet that you do not see him until some time after the child has seen him. When she begins to question him whether she may not somehow get to heaven without dying, he answers with a sort of sorrowful tenderness, a very sweet and noble compassion, but unsparingly as to his mission. It is a singular moment of pure poetry that makes the heart ache, but does not crush or terrify the spirit."

"And what has it got to do with Ormond?" asked Rulledge, but with less impatience than usual.

"Why, nothing, I'm afraid, that I can make out very clearly. And yet there

---

* Gerhart Hauptmann (1862–1946), German playwright, novelist, and poet. His *The Assumption of Hannele* (*Hannele's Himmelfahrt*, 1893) includes both realistic scenes in prose and neoromantic scenes in verse.

is an obscure connection with Ormond, or his vision, if it was a vision. Mrs. Ormond could not be very definite about what he saw, perhaps because even at the last moment he was not definite himself. What she was clear about, was the fact that his mood, though it became more serious, by no means became sadder. It became a sort of solemn joy instead of the light gaiety it had begun by being. She was no sort of scientific observer, and yet the keenness of her affection made her as closely observant of Ormond as if she had been studying him psychologically. Sometimes the light in his room would wake her at night, and she would go to him, and find him lying with a book faced down on his breast, as if he had been reading, and his fingers interlaced under his head, and a kind of radiant peace in his face. The poor thing said that when she would ask him what the matter was, he would say, 'Nothing; just happiness,' and when she would ask him if he did not think he ought to do something, he would laugh, and say perhaps it would go off of itself. But it did not go off; the unnatural buoyancy continued after he became perfectly tranquil. 'I don't know,' he would say. 'I seem to have got to the end of my troubles. I haven't a care in the world, Jenny. I don't believe you could get a rise out of me if you said the nastiest thing you could think of. It sounds like nonsense, of course, but it seems to me that I have found out the reason of things, though I don't know what it is. Maybe I've only found out that there is a reason of things. That would be enough, wouldn't it?'"

V.

At this point Wanhope hesitated with a kind of diffidence that was rather charming in him. "I don't see," he said, "just how I can keep the facts from this on out of the line of facts which we are not in the habit of respecting very much, or that we relegate to the company of things that are not facts at all. I suppose that in stating them I shall somehow make myself responsible for them, but that is just what I don't want to do. I don't want to do anything more than give them as they were given to me."

"You won't be able to give them half as fully," said Minver, "if Mrs. Ormond gave them to you."

"No," Wanhope said gravely, "and that's the pity of it; for they ought to be given as fully as possible."

"Go ahead," Rulledge commanded, "and do the best you can."

"I'm not sure," the psychologist thoughtfully said, "that I am quite satisfied to call Ormond's experiences hallucinations. There ought to be some other word that doesn't accuse his sanity in that degree. For he apparently didn't show any other signs of an unsound mind."

"None that Mrs. Ormond would call so," Minver suggested.

"Well, in his case, I don't think she was such a bad judge," Wanhope returned. "She was a tolerably unbalanced person herself, but she wasn't altogether disqualified for observing him, as I've said before. They had a pretty hot summer, as the summer is apt to be in the Housatonic valley, but when it got along into September the weather was divine, and they spent nearly the whole time out of doors, driving over the hills. They got an old horse from a native, and they hunted out a rickety buggy from the carriage-house, and they went wherever the road led. They went mostly at a walk, and that suited the horse exactly, as well as Mrs. Ormond, who had no faith in Ormond's driving, and wanted to go at a pace that would give her a chance to jump out safely if anything happened. They put their hats in the front of the buggy, and went about in their bare heads. The country people got used to them, and were not scandalized by their appearance, though they were both getting a little gray, and must have looked as if they were old enough to know better.

"They were not really old, as age goes nowadays: he was not more than forty-two or -three, and she was still in the late thirties. In fact, they were

Nel mezzo del cammin di nostra vita—

in that hour when life, and the conceit of life, is strongest, and when it feels as if it might go on forever. Women are not very articulate about such things, and it was probably Ormond who put their feeling into words though she recognized at once that it was her feeling, and shrank from it as if it were something wicked, that they would be punished for; so that one day, when he said suddenly, 'Jenny, I don't feel as if I could ever die,' she scolded him for it. Poor women!" said Wanhope, musingly, "they are not always cross when they scold. It is often the expression of their anxieties, their forebodings, their sex-timidities. They are always in double the danger that men are, and their nerves double that danger again. Who was that famous *salonnière*—Mme. Geoffrin, was it?—that Marmontel says always scolded her friends when they were in trouble, and came and scolded him when he was put into the Bastille? I suppose Mrs. Ormond was never so tender of Ormond as she was when she took it out of him for suggesting what she wildly felt herself, and felt she should pay for feeling."

Wanhope had the effect of appealing to Minver, but the painter would not relent. "I don't know. I've seen her—or heard her—in very devoted moments."

"At any rate," Wanhope resumed, "she says she scolded him, and it did not do the least good. She could not scold him out of that feeling, which was all mixed up in her retrospect with the sense of the weather and the season, the leaves just beginning to show the autumn, the wild asters coming to crowd the goldenrod, the crickets shrill in the grass, and the birds silent in the trees, the smell of the rowan in the meadows, and the odor of the old logs and fresh chips in the woods. She was not a woman to notice such things much, but he talked of them all and made her notice them. His nature took hold upon what we call nature, and clung fondly to the lowly and familiar aspects of it. Once she said to him, trembling for him, 'I should think you would be afraid to take such a pleasure in those things,' and when he asked her why, she couldn't or wouldn't tell him; but he understood, and he said: 'I've never realized before that I was so much a part of them. Either I am going to have them forever, or they are going to have me. We shall not part, for we are all members of the same body. If it is the body of death, we are members of that. If it is the body of life, we are members of that. Either I have never lived, or else I am never going to die.' She said: 'Of course you are never going to die; a spirit can't die.' But he told her he didn't mean that. He was just as radiantly happy when they would get home from one of their drives, and sit down to their supper, which they had country-fashion instead of dinner, and then when they would turn into their big, lamplit parlor, and sit down for a long evening with his books. Sometimes he read to her as she sewed, but he read mostly to himself, and he said he hadn't had such a bath of poetry since he was a boy. Sometimes in the splendid nights, which were so clear that you could catch the silver glint of the gossamers in the thin air, he would go out and walk up and down the long veranda. Once, when he coaxed her out with him, he took her under the arm and walked her up and down, and he said: 'Isn't it like a ship? The earth is like a ship, and we're sailing, sailing! Oh, I wonder where!' Then he stopped with a sob, and she was startled, and asked him what the matter was, but he couldn't tell her. She was more frightened than ever at what seemed a break in his happiness. She was troubled about his reading the Bible so much, especially the Old Testament; but he told her he had never known before what majestic literature it was. There were some turns or phrases in it that peculiarly took his fancy and seemed to feed it with inexhaustible suggestion. 'The Angel of the Lord' was one of these. The idea of a divine messenger, embodied and commissioned to intimate the creative will to the creature: it was sublime, it was ineffable. He wondered that men had ever come to think in any other terms of the living law that we were under, and that could much less conceivably operate like an insensate mechanism than it could reveal itself as a constant purpose. He said he believed that in every great moral crisis, in every ordeal of conscience, a man was aware of standing in the presence of something sent to try him and test him, and that this something was the Angel of the Lord.

"He went off that night, saying to himself, 'The Angel of the Lord, the Angel of the Lord!' and when she lay a long time awake, waiting for him to go to sleep, she heard him saying it again in his room. She thought he might be dreaming, but when she went to him, he had his lamp lighted, and was lying with that rapt smile on his face which she was so afraid of. She told him she was afraid and she wished he would not say such things; and that made him laugh, and he put his arms around her, and laughed and laughed, and said it was only a kind of swearing, and she must cheer up. He let her give him some trional to make him sleep, and then she went off to her bed again. But when they both woke late, she heard him, as he dressed, repeating fragments of verse, quoting quite without order, as the poem drifted through his memory. He told her at breakfast that it was a poem which Longfellow had written to Lowell upon the occasion of his wife's death, and he wanted to get it and read it to her. She said she did not see how he could let his mind run on such gloomy things. But he protested he was not the least gloomy, and that he supposed his recollection of the poem was a continuation of his thinking about the Angel of the Lord.

"While they were at table a tramp came up the drive under the window, and looked in at them hungrily. He was a very offensive tramp, and quite took Mrs. Ormond's appetite away: but Ormond would not send him round to the kitchen, as she wanted; he insisted upon taking him a plate and a cup of coffee out on the veranda himself. When she expostulated with him, he answered fantastically that the fellow might be an angel of the Lord, and he asked her if she remembered Parnell's poem of 'The Hermit.' Of course she didn't, but he needn't get it, for she didn't want to hear it, and if he kept making her so nervous, she should be sick herself. He insisted upon telling her what the poem was, and how the angel in it had made himself abhorrent to the hermit by throttling the babe of the good man who had housed and fed them, and committing other atrocities, till the hermit couldn't stand it any longer, and the angel explained that he had done it all to prevent the greater harm that would have come if he had not killed and stolen in season. Ormond laughed at her disgust, and said he was curious to see what a tramp would do that was treated with real hospitality. He thought they had made a mistake in not asking this tramp in to breakfast with them; then they might have stood a chance of being murdered in their beds to save them from mischief."

VI.

"Mrs. Ormond really lost her patience with him, and felt better than she had for a long time by scolding him in good earnest. She told him he was talking very blasphemously, and when he urged that his morality was directly in line with Parnell's, and Parnell was an archbishop, she was so vexed that she would not go to drive with him that morning, though he apologized and humbled himself in every way. He pleaded that it was such a beautiful day, it must be the last they were going to have; it was getting near the equinox, and this must be a weather-breeder. She let him go off alone, for he would not lose the drive, and she watched him out of sight from her upper window with a heavy heart. As soon as he was fairly gone, she wanted to go after him, and she was wild all the forenoon. She could not stay indoors, but kept walking up and down the piazza and looking for him, and at times she went a bit up the road he had taken, to meet him. She had got to thinking of the tramp, though the man had gone directly off down another road after he had his breakfast. At last she heard the old creaking, rattling buggy, and as soon as she saw Ormond's bare head, and knew he was all right, she ran up to her room and shut herself in. But she couldn't hold out against him when he came to her door with an armful of wild flowers that he had gathered for her, and boughs from some young maples that he had found all red in a swamp. She showed herself so interested that he asked her to come with him after their midday dinner and see them, and she said perhaps she would, if he would promise not to keep talking about things that made her so miserable. He asked her, 'What things?' and she answered that he knew well enough, and he laughed and promised.

"She didn't believe he would keep his word, but he did at first, and he tried not to tease her in any way. He tried to please her in the whims and fancies she had about going this way or that, and when she decided not to look up his young maples with him, because the first autumn leaves made her melancholy, he submitted. He put his arms across her shoulder as they drove through the woods, and pulled her to him, and called her 'poor old thing,' and accused her of being morbid. He wanted her to tell him all there was in her mind, but she could not; she could only cry on his arm. He asked her if it was something about him that troubled her, and she could only say that she hated to see people so cheerful without reason. That made him laugh, and they were very gay after she had got her cry out; but he grew serious again. Then her temper rose, and she asked, 'Well, what is it?' and he said at first, 'Oh, nothing,' as people do when there is really something, and presently he confessed that he was thinking about what she had said of his being cheerful without reason. Then, as she said, he talked so beautifully that she had to keep her patience with him, though he was not keeping his word to her. His talk, as far as she was able to report it, didn't amount to much more than this: that in a world where death was, people never could be cheerful with reason unless death was something altogether different from what people imagined. After people came to their intellectual consciousness, death was never wholly out of it, and if they could be joyful with that black drop at the bottom of every cup, it was proof that death was not what it seemed. Otherwise there was no logic in the scheme of being, but it was a cruel fraud by the Creator upon the creature; a poor practical joke, with the laugh all on one side. He had got rid of his fear of it in that light, which seemed to have come to him before the fear left him, and he wanted her to see it in the same light, and if he died before her—. But there she stopped him and protested it would kill her if she did not die first, with no apparent sense, even when she told me, of her fatuity, which must have amused poor Ormond. He said what he wanted to ask was that she would believe he had not been the least afraid to die, and he wished her to remember this always, because she knew how he always used to be afraid of dying. Then he really began to talk of other things, and he led the way back to the times of their courtship and their early married days, and their first journeys together, and all their young-people friends, and the simple-hearted pleasure they used to take in society, in teas and dinners, and going to the theater. He did not like to think how that pleasure had dropped out of their life, and he did not know why they had let it, and he was going to have it again when they went to town.

"They had thought of staying a long time in the country, perhaps till after Thanksgiving, for they had become attached to their place; but now they suddenly agreed to go back to New York at once. She told me that as soon as they agreed she felt a tremendous longing to be gone that instant, as if she must go to escape from something, some calamity, and she felt, looking back, that there was a prophetic quality in her eagerness."

"Oh, she was always so," said Minver. "When a thing was to be done, she wanted it done like lightning, no matter what the thing was."

"Well, very likely," Wanhope consented. "I never make much account of those retroactive forebodings. At any rate, she says she wanted him to turn about and drive home so they could begin packing, and when he demurred, and began to tease, as she called it, she felt as if she should scream, till he turned the old horse and took the back track. She was wild to get home, and kept hurrying him, and wanting to whip the horse; but the old horse merely wagged his tail, and declined to go faster than a walk, and this was the only thing that enabled her to forgive herself afterward."

"Why, what had she done?" Rulledge asked.

"She would have been responsible for what happened, according to her notion, if she had had her way with the horse; she would have felt that she had driven Ormond to his doom."

"Of course!" said Minver. "She always found a hole to creep out of. Why couldn't she go back a little further, and hold herself responsible through having made him turn around?"

"Poor woman!" said Rulledge, with a tenderness that made Minver smile. "What was it that did happen?"

Wanhope examined his cup for some dregs of coffee, and then put it down with an air of resignation. I offered to touch the bell, but "No, don't," he said. "I'm better without it." And he went on: "There was a lonely piece of woods that they had to drive through before they struck the avenue leading to their house, which was on a cheerful upland overlooking the river, and when they had got about half-way through this woods, the tramp whom Ormond had fed in the morning, slipped out of a thicket on the hillside above them, and crossed the road in front of them, and slipped out of sight among the trees on the slope below. Ormond stopped the horse, and turned to his wife with a strange kind of whisper. 'Did you see it?' he asked, and she answered yes, and bade him drive on. He did so, slowly looking back round the side of the buggy till a turn of the road hid the place where the tramp had crossed their track. She could not speak, she says, till they came in sight of their house. Then her heart gave a great bound, and she broke out on him, blaming him for having encouraged the tramp to lurk about, as he must have done, all day, by his foolish sentimentality in taking his breakfast out to him. 'He saw that you were a delicate person, and now to-night he will be coming round, and—' She says Ormond kept looking at her, while she talked, as if he did not know what she was saying, and all at once she glanced down at her feet, and discovered that her hat was gone.

"That, she owned, made her frantic, and she blazed out at him again, and accused him of having lost her hat by stopping to look at that worthless fellow, and then starting up the horse so suddenly that it had rolled out. He usually gave her as good as she sent when she let herself go in that way, and she told me she would have been glad if he had done it now, but he only looked at her in a kind of daze, and when he understood, at last, he bade her get out and go into the house—they were almost at the door,—and he would go back and find her hat himself. 'Indeed, you'll do nothing of the kind,' she said she told him. 'I shall go back with you, or you'll be hunting up that precious vagabond and bringing him home to supper.' Ormond said, 'All right,' with a kind of dreamy passivity, and he turned the old horse again, and they drove slowly back, looking for the hat in the road, right and left. She had not noticed before it was getting late, and perhaps it was not so late as it seemed when they got into that lonely piece of woods again, and the veils of shadow began to drop round them, as if they were something falling from the trees, she said. They found the hat easily enough at the point where it must have rolled out of the buggy, and he got down and picked it up. She kept scolding him, but he did not seem to hear it. He stood dangling the hat by its ribbons from his right hand, while he rested his left on the dashboard, and looking—looking down into the wooded slope where the tramp had disappeared. A cold chill swept over her, and she stopped her scolding. 'Oh, Jim,' she said, 'do you see something? What do you see?' He flung the hat from him, and ran plunging down the hillside—she covered up her face when she told me, and said she should always see him running—till the dusk among the trees hid him. She ran after him, and she heard him calling, calling joyfully, 'Yes, I'm coming!' and she thought he was calling back to her, but the rush of his feet kept getting farther, and then he seemed to stop with a sound like falling. He couldn't have been much ahead of her, for it was only a moment till she stood on the edge of a boulder in the woods, looking over, and there at the bottom Ormond was lying with his face turned under him, as she expressed it; and the tramp, with a heavy stick in his hand, was standing by him, stooping over him, and staring at him. She began to scream, and it seemed to her that she flew down from the brink of the rock, and caught the tramp and clung to him, while she kept screaming 'Murder!' The man didn't try to get away; he only said, over and over, 'I didn't touch him, lady; I didn't touch him.' It all happened simultaneously, like events in a dream, and while there was nobody there but herself and the tramp, and Ormond lying between them, there were some people that must have heard her from the road and come down to her. They were neighbor-folk that knew her and Ormond, and they naturally laid hold of the tramp; but he didn't try to escape. He helped them gather poor Ormond up, and he went back to the house with them, and staid while one of them ran for the doctor. The doctor could only tell them that Ormond was dead, and that his neck must have been broken by his fall over the rock. One of the neighbors went to look at the place the next morning, and found one of the roots of a young tree growing on the rock, torn out, as if Ormond had caught his foot in it; and that had probably made his fall a headlong dive. The tramp knew nothing but that he heard shouting and running, and got up from the foot of the rock, where he was going to pass the night, when something came flying through the air, and struck at his feet. Then it scarcely stirred, and the next thing, he said, the lady was onto him, screeching and tearing. He piteously protested his innocence, which was apparent enough, at the inquest, and before, for that matter. He said Ormond was about the only man that ever treated him white, and Mrs. Ormond was remorseful for having let him get away before she could tell him that she didn't blame him, and ask him to forgive her."

VII.

Wanhope desisted with a provisional air, and Rulledge went and got himself a sandwich from the lunch-table.

"Well, upon my word!" said Minver. "I thought you had dined, Rulledge."

Rulledge came back munching, and said to Wanhope, as he settled himself in his chair again: "Well, go on."

"Why, that's all."

The psychologist was silent, with Rulledge staring indignantly at him.

"I suppose Mrs. Ormond had her theory?" I ventured.

"Oh, yes—such as it was," said Wanhope. "It was her belief—her religion —that Ormond had seen Death, in person or personified, or the angel of it; and that the sight was something beautiful, and not terrible. She thought that she should see Death, too in the same way, as a messenger. I don't know that it was such a bad theory," he added impartially.

"Not," said Minver, "if you suppose that Ormond was off his nut. But, in regard to the whole matter, there is always a question of how much truth there was in what she said about it."

"Of course," the psychologist admitted, "that is a question which must be considered. The question of testimony in such matters is the difficult thing. You might often believe in supernatural occurrences if it were not for the witnesses. It is very interesting," he pursued, with his scientific smile, "to note how corrupting anything supernatural or mystical is. Such things seem mostly to happen either in the privity of people who are born liars, or else they deprave the spectator so, through his spiritual vanity or his love of the marvelous, that you can't believe a word he says."

"They are as bad as horses on human morals," said Minver. "Not that I think it ever needed the coming of a ghost to invalidate any statement of Mrs.

Ormond's." Rulledge rose and went away growling something, partially audible, to the disadvantage of Minver's wit, and the painter laughed after him: "He really believes it."

Wanhope's mind seemed to be shifted from Mrs. Ormond to her convert, whom he followed with his tolerant eyes. "Nothing in all this sort of inquiry is so impossible to predicate as the effect of any given instance upon a given mind. It would be very interesting—"

"Excuse me!" said Minver. "There's Whitley. I must speak to him."

He went away, leaving me alone with the psychologist.

"And what is your own conclusion in this instance?" I asked.

"Why, I haven't formulated it yet."

Editha

1905

E DITHA" IS WITHOUT DOUBT Howells's best-known story, for it is included in a number of anthologies, including *The American Tradition
in Literature* (ed. Perkins and Perkins), *The Heath Anthology of American Literature* (ed. Lauter), *The Norton Anthology of American Literature* (ed.
Baym), *American Literature: A Prentice Hall Anthology* (ed. Elliott), and *The
Harper American Literature* (ed. McQuade). "Editha" is particularly interesting as a reflection of contemporary concerns; critics have approached it as
an indictment of American imperialism, first in Cuba and the Philippines
and later, by extension, in Southeast Asia, and as a statement of feminism.
Howells the ever unfashionable and hopelessly dated has, at least in this story,
been relevant to major debates of the late twentieth century.

"Editha" was known to Howells scholars, of course, long before its inclusion in college textbooks and anthologies. The story first appeared in the
January 1905, issue of *Harper's Monthly* and was reprinted first in *Different
Girls* (1906)[1] and then in *Between the Dark and the Daylight* (1907). But except
for Oscar Firkins's capsule commentary in 1924 ("'Editha,' a tale whose careless brevity belies its weight and saps its power, impales the young woman

who drives her reluctant lover to premature death in a questionable war"—210), no specific critical reference was apparently made to the story until Everett Carter briefly discussed it in 1954. Citing the revival of the historical romance at the turn of the nineteenth century, Carter notes Howells's theory that "America's unconscious revulsion from the shameful imperialism of the Spanish-American War" made the escapism offered by historical romance both a pleasure and a relief. "Editha" is then described as an attack on "all the nonsense about the heroic romanticism of war" and on the sentimentalism embodied in the period's popular literature (231).[2]

Carter was thus the first to voice explicitly what became the standard reading of "Editha" and to point out the story's equation of jingoism and war fever with the false ideals presented in "romanticist" literature. (Howells had of course expressed both his anti-romanticism and his anti-imperialism in many columns over the years, most notably in *Harper's Weekly* from 1901 to 1902.) And this is the view shared by the first sustained treatment of "Editha," Harold Kehler's two-page "item" in the 1961 *Explicator*. Citing Carter directly, Kehler notes that "it is a well-known commonplace that the tragic outcome of the clash between the opposing values held by Editha and George represents a bitter indictment, not only of our country's role in the war, but also of the romantic world view itself" (item 41). Kehler then focuses on the symbolic function of "liquid refreshment" in the story, making a convincing argument that images of lemonade, liquor, and water are used to suggest, respectively, the "veil of sugar-coated romanticism," the "'hellfire' of irrational excitement," and clarity and true vision (item 41).

Carter's reading is echoed, too, by William J. Free, who in 1966 wrote a full-length article on "Editha"'s exemplification of the ideas of C. S. Peirce, Howells's friend and, according to William James, the true founder of American pragmatism (Free 285). Free argues that Howells's "best novels and stories resemble laboratory experiments in pragmatic ethics, in which he exposes the beliefs of his characters to the test of experience" (285). (Free's ideas closely parallel those of Don L. Cook, who argues that Howells explodes "the clichés of romance . . . by subjecting them to the test of pragmatism—that is by looking to their results"—72.) Editha, in Free's view, represents a "mistaken method" of fixing belief, a method that Peirce labeled "tenacity" (286). When her false belief is tested by reality and found to be lacking, Editha finds a way to tenaciously maintain her illusions by "submerging reality into her belief" (289).

Editha's mental maneuverings create a structure that is, Free argues, typical of Howells's fiction: "The progressive contrast of true and false belief culminating in a crisis of doubt and a subsequent adjustment of belief to reality forms a structural principle visible . . . in most of Howells' novels" (291). "Editha" is therefore a useful model for the study of the more complex novels. (Free, in fact, provides a thumbnail analysis of *The Rise of Silas Lapham* for the purpose of showing the similarities between the structures of each of that novel's three subplots—"the business story, the love story, and the social story"—and that of "Editha"—n. 292.) Free's structural analysis can be profitably compared to the thematic analysis of George Carrington, who states that "the typical Howells action" consists of "an explosive intrusion of reality, a violent period of conflict and confusion, a simmering-down period characterized by much discussion and readjustment, and then a renewal of the surface, leading, by and by, to the next explosion" (*Drama* 67). And, like Free, Carrington sees the major conflicts of Howells's novels as the results of the clash between reality and false preconceptions (*Drama* 53–54, 141).

Free, like Kehler, cites Carter directly, noting that "'Editha' shows how closely Howells' moral and political ideas became united in his mind with his war against romantic and sentimental fiction" (291). What Free, Kehler, and Carter share, of course, is the understandable assumption that the story's primary concerns are anti-imperialism and anti-romanticism, and it is the former, I assume, that brought "Editha" into the undergraduate canon in the 1960s.[3] Although "Editha" has been in print on and off since 1905, its earliest publication in a college textbook was apparently in *The American Tradition in Literature*, which first appeared in 1956, and which was republished a number of times in the 1960s —when the story could be included in the incipient debate about American involvement in Southeast Asia. (The fact that one editor of the anthology was a Quaker may have contributed to the story's continuing inclusion, but this is purely speculative.) But assumptions about the story's major focus changed dramatically in the mid to late 1970s.

The transition apparently began with the analysis of John Crowley,[4] who, after concurring that Howells's anti-imperialism contributed to "Editha," goes on to examine the psychology of war "frenzy" (31) in general and the unconscious motivations of the women—both Editha and Mrs. Gearson— who stay behind. Crowley bases his analysis in part on Howells's biography, noting that Howells's guilt about sitting out the Civil War motivated considerable parts of his fiction (notably *A Fearful Responsibility* and the discussions of the practice of buying military substitutes in *The Rise of Silas Lapham* and *A Hazard of New Fortunes*).[5] Crowley suggests that the war in "Editha," never specifically named, symbolically recalls the Civil War and points out that "the scene in which the men of Balcolm Works clamor to enlist closely resembles Howells' account in *Years of My Youth* of the atmosphere in Columbus in 1861" (231). This substitution—Spanish-American War for Civil War and George for Howells—implies, in Crowley's words, Howells's concern that "his decision not to enlist may have been as passive and cowardly an evasion as Gearson's 'decision' *to* enlist" (31). Thus the focus of criticism shifts from anti-imperialism and anti-romanticism to the psychology of an individual faced with the prospect of volunteering.

Crowley concludes that George "invites [Editha] to manipulate him" into enlisting (31), and notes that his habitual irony is actually his "defense against debilitating uncertainty" (32). In his need to be delivered from doubt, George welcomes Editha's decisiveness, his friends' adoration and the further encouragement of alcohol. He not only shares responsibility for his own death, but seems "almost eager to die" (32), since death will relieve him of the burden of integrity, the obligation to match his actions to his beliefs and his beliefs to his actions.

Crowley points out, however, that "George's complicity in his own death is overshadowed by the narrative focus on Editha" (33), and in this way Crowley rejoins the company of Carter, Kehler, and Free. But Crowley stresses Editha's "villainy," noting that her obsessive worry that George will lose an arm in combat hides her unconscious wish to see him symbolically castrated, and thus kept in subjection to her (33).[6] And he suggests that "a subtle affinity" (33) exists between Editha and Mrs. Gearson, in that both desire power over George. As he puts it, "George Gearson is depicted as the prey of two women . . . sisters under the skin; they represent two faces of a single imago, the castrating mother" (39). The story again has biographical implications: Crowley argues that "Howells's imaginative act of killing off Gearson in "Editha" expressed a nexus of unconscious desires: of escape from women's power, of revenge on women for having that power, of self-punishment for wanting such revenge" (40).

Crowley's analysis opens the door to feminist interpretations of "Editha," and at least three have appeared. Philip Furia, in "'Editha': The Feminine View," asserts that the story is "a subtle, psychological study that has very little to do with war or patriotism and far more with a woman's struggle for sexual independence and domination" (278). Like Crowley, Furia emphasizes the image of the lost arm. But while Crowley emphasized the lost arm as a symbol of castration, Furia examines it as a more general image of weakness and subordination, literally, disarmament.[7] Far from ignoring sexual imagery, however, Furia argues that Editha "displac[es] all of her sexual energy onto the war" (279), finally making the war "a substitute for the sexual consummation" of her love for George (280). Therefore George and Editha's concerns about the war comment metaphorically on their love affair. The war itself "becomes a metaphor for women's struggle to resist male domination" (280); Mrs. Balcolm's terse criticism of Editha is stated "in the language appropriate to the discovery of a sexual indiscretion" (281); Editha's obsession with George's arm reveals her desire to gain control over him; her letter to George is "a thinly-disguised proposition with Editha's virginity [in the words of the letter, her "honor"] proffered as bait" (280); and Mrs. Gearson's discovery of the letter is "a grotesque parody of the cliché scene of a mother opening one of her daughter's love letters" (281). The core of the story, in Furia's eyes, is the fact that "Editha manipulates her sexuality to overpower and dominate her lover" (278).

Furia, like Crowley, argues that Mrs. Gearson joins Editha in desiring power over George. He summarily dismisses her claim that she's glad that George did not live long enough to kill anyone, commenting that "that bit of idealism is as false as Editha's patriotism" (281) and concluding that she took a perverse pleasure in George's death, since it kept her from losing him to another woman. Both Editha and Mrs. Gearson, Furia states, "prefer to have George dead rather than lose their control over him" (281).

Furia's ideas, while provocative, seem long on theory and short on support, and they are matched in this respect by those of Michael Bellamy. Bellamy, like Furia, notes that Editha has a "tendency to divert sexual feelings to other enterprises" (283), and that she makes "the consummation [of her relationship to George] contingent upon his enlistment" (283). Like Crowley, he notes George's "death wish" (283) and comments that the "empty pantaloon" or sleeve is a symbol of castration (285). (In fact, Bellamy precedes Crowley with this observation.) And like both, he argues for an identification of Editha with Mrs. Gearson. But Bellamy's major premise (based on the psychoanalytical theories of Norman O. Brown) is that George's enlistment is a "surrender of his individuality" (284), a denial of death that implies a denial of selfhood. And George's wish that Editha visit Mrs. Gearson becomes, in Bellamy's scheme, a desire to return to the womb by proxy, and thus to experience vicariously a "second death" (285).

A third feminist critique of "Editha" is provided by Susan K. Harris, who focuses attention on Editha's aggressive use of language in a culture where women's words are divorced from action. Harris to some degree defends Editha, arguing that "her grave faults include possession of language, will, and energy" (74), and concludes that she is at least in part a "victim [as well as an] avenger of her culture's gender restrictions" (76).

It's clear that the feminist approach to "Editha" has by no means been exhausted; the field is open to further exploration. Equally interesting is the place the story occupies in the development of Howells's fiction as he moved from the type of realism expounded in his early criticism to the psychological explorations of his mature years. "Editha," first labeled as a prototype of the realistic method, belongs as much to Howells's "studies of the inner life" (*SL* 4:168). The story's depiction of mob psychology and of the influence of the media (here, yellow journalism), and the almost Jamesian (for Howells) tracing of thought and emotion, further tie it to the twentieth rather than the nineteenth century. On the other hand, the story repeats and reworks a number of Howells's early themes. The contrast of realism and romanticism is central, of course, but so is the ethic/aesthetic split (see above pp. 14–15), which clearly plays a role in Editha's "duplex emotioning" and her detachment from the reality of George's enlistment. Before George volunteers, the narrator notes that "it all interested [Editha] intensely; she was undergoing a tremendous experience, and she was being equal to it." Similarly, when George departs for the war, Editha "felt a sort of noble distinction in the abstraction, the almost unconsciousness, with which they parted." Like Basil and Isabel March and like the "contributor" of *Suburban Sketches*, Editha filters her experience through a romantic aestheticism that conceals her moral responsibility.

"Editha," rather than signaling a departure from Howells's earlier concerns, is an enlargement of those concerns. The story represents a successful blending of Howells's literary past and future, and its continuing popularity is no surprise.

Notes

1. *Different Girls* was a collection of short stories about young women, edited by Howells and Henry Mills Alden.

2. Howells was not alone in using a literary pulpit to denounce American imperialism. He was joined in the Anti-Imperialist League by a number of writers, including Mark Twain, whose "To the Person Sitting in Darkness" (1901) provoked both violent criticism and praise (Cleanth Brooks 1335).

3. This assumption is shared also by John B. Humma, who considers the story to be "an allegorical fable of American moral degeneration" (77).

4. Crowley first discussed "Editha" in "Howells's Obscure Hurt," which appeared in the *Journal of American Studies* in August 1975. His article was revised for inclusion in *The Mask of Fiction* (1989). All citations to Crowley in this introduction refer to this later revision.

5. It should be noted that Henry James, Samuel Clemens, and Henry Adams joined Howells in avoiding military service.

6. It is only in Crowley's later revision that he connects losing an arm with castration. In the 1975 version, George's empty sleeve is figured only as "a badge of courage" (209).

7. Edward Piacentino, in "Arms in Love and War in Howells' 'Editha,'" exhaustively examines arms imagery in this story.

ᷡᷡ

Editha

T he air was thick with the war feeling, like the electricity of a storm which has not yet burst. Editha sat looking out into the hot spring afternoon, with her lips parted, and panting with the intensity of the question whether she could let him go. She had decided that she could not let him stay, when she saw him at the end of the still leafless avenue, making slowly up towards the house, with his head down and his figure relaxed. She ran impatiently out on the veranda, to the edge of the steps, and imperatively demanded greater haste of him with her will before she called aloud to him: "George!"

He had quickened his pace in mystical response to her mystical urgence, before he could have heard her; now he looked up and answered, "Well?"

"Oh, how united we are!" she exulted, and then she swooped down the steps to him. "What is it?" she cried.

"It's war," he said, and he pulled her up to him and kissed her.

She kissed him back intensely, but irrelevantly, as to their passion, and uttered from deep in her throat, "How glorious!"

"It's war," he repeated, without consenting to her sense of it; and she did not know just what to think at first. She never knew what to think of him; that made his mystery, his charm. All through their courtship, which was contemporaneous with the growth of the war feeling, she had been puzzled by his want of seriousness about it. He seemed to despise it even more than he abhorred it. She could have understood his abhorring any sort of bloodshed; that would have been a survival of his old life when he thought he would be a minister, and before he changed and took up the law. But making light of a cause so high and noble seemed to show a want of earnestness at the core of his being. Not but that she felt herself able to cope with a congenital defect of that sort, and make his love for her save him from himself. Now perhaps the miracle was already wrought in him. In the presence of the tremendous fact that he announced, all triviality seemed to have gone out of him; she began to feel that. He sank down on the top step, and wiped his forehead with a handkerchief, while she poured out upon him her question of the origin and authenticity of his news.

All the while, in her duplex emotioning, she was aware that now at the very beginning she must put a guard upon herself against urging him, by any word or act, to take the part that her whole soul willed him to take, for the completion of her ideal of him. He was very nearly perfect as he was, and he must be allowed to perfect himself. But he was peculiar, and he might very well be reasoned out of his peculiarity. Before her reasoning went her emotioning: her nature pulling on his nature, her womanhood upon his manhood, without her knowing the means she was using to the end she was willing. She had always supposed that the man who won her would have done something to win her; she did not know what, but something. George Gearson had simply asked for her love, on the way home from a concert, and she gave her love to him without, as it were, thinking. But now, it flashed upon her, if he could do something worthy to have won her—be a hero, *her* hero—it would be even better than if he had done it before asking her; it would be grander. Besides, she had believed in the war from the beginning.

"But don't you see, dearest," she said, "that it wouldn't have come to this if it hadn't been the order of Providence? And I call any war glorious that is for the liberation of people who have been struggling for years against the cruelest oppression. Don't you think so, too?"

"I suppose so," he returned, languidly. "But war! Is it glorious to break the peace of the world?"

"That ignoble peace! It was no peace at all, with that crime and shame at our very gates." She was conscious of parroting the current phrases of the newspapers, but it was no time to pick and choose her words. She must sacrifice anything to the high ideal she had for him, and after a good deal of rapid argument she ended with the climax: "But now it doesn't matter about the how or why. Since the war has come, all that is gone. There are no two sides any more. There is nothing now but our country."

He sat with his eyes closed and his head leant back against the veranda, and he remarked, with a vague smile, as if musing aloud, "Our country— right or wrong."

"Yes, right or wrong!" she returned, fervidly. "I'll go and get you some lemonade." She rose rustling, and whisked away; when she came back with two tall glasses of clouded liquid on a tray, and the ice clucking in them, he still sat as she had left him, and she said, as if there had been no interruption: "But there is no question of wrong in this case. I call it a sacred war. A war for liberty and humanity, if ever there was one. And I know you will see it just as I do, yet."

He took half the lemonade at a gulp, and he answered as he set the glass down: "I know you always have the highest ideal. When I differ from you I ought to doubt myself."

A generous sob rose in Editha's throat for the humility of a man, so very nearly perfect, who was willing to put himself below her.

Besides, she felt, more subliminally, that he was never so near slipping through her fingers as when he took that meek way.

"You shall not say that! Only, for once I happen to be right." She seized his hand in her two hands, and poured her soul from her eyes into his. "Don't you think so?" she entreated him.

He released his hand and drank the rest of his lemonade, and she added, "Have mine, too," but he shook his head in answering, "I've no business to think so, unless I act so, too."

Her heart stopped a beat before it pulsed on with leaps that she felt in her neck. She had noticed that strange thing in men: they seemed to feel bound to do what they believed, and not think a thing was finished when they said it, as girls did. She knew what was in his mind, but she pretended not, and she said, "Oh, I am not sure," and then faltered.

He went on as if to himself, without apparently heeding her: "There's only one way of proving one's faith in a thing like this."

She could not say she understood, but she did understand.

He went on again. "If I believed—if I felt as you do about this war—Do you wish me to feel as you do?"

Now she was really not sure; so she said: "George, I don't know what you mean."

He seemed to muse away from her as before. "There is a sort of fascination in it. I suppose that at the bottom of his heart every man would like at times to have his courage tested, to see how he would act."

"How can you talk in that ghastly way?"

"It *is* rather morbid. Still, that's what it comes to, unless you're swept away by ambition or driven by conviction. I haven't the conviction or the ambition, and the other thing is what it comes to with me. I ought to have been a preacher, after all; then I couldn't have asked it of myself, as I must, now I'm a lawyer. And you believe that it's a holy war, Editha?" he suddenly addressed her. "Oh, I know you do! But you wish me to believe so, too?"

She hardly knew whether he was mocking or not, in the ironical way he always had with her plainer mind. But the only thing was to be outspoken with him.

"George, I wish you to believe whatever you think is true, at any and every cost. If I've ever tried to talk you into anything, I take it all back."

"Oh, I know that, Editha. I know how sincere you are and how—I wish I had your undoubting spirit! I'll think it over; I'd like to believe as you do. But I don't, now; I don't, indeed. It isn't this war alone; though this seems particularly wanton and needless; but it's every war—so stupid; it makes me sick. Why shouldn't this thing have been settled reasonably?"

"Because," she said, very throatily again, "God meant it to be war."

"You think it was God? Yes, I suppose that is what people will say."

"Do you suppose it would have been war if God hadn't meant it?"

"I don't know. Sometimes it seems as if God had put this world into men's keeping to work it as they pleased."

"Now, George, that is blasphemy."

"Well, I won't blaspheme. I'll try to believe in your pocket Providence," he said, and then he rose to go.

"Why don't you stay to dinner?" Dinner at Balcom's Works was at one o'-clock.

"I'll come back to supper, if you'll let me. Perhaps I shall bring you a convert."

"Well, you may come back, on that condition."

"All right. If I don't come, you'll understand."

He went away without kissing her, and she felt it a suspension of their engagement. It all interested her intensely; she was undergoing a tremendous experience, and she was being equal to it. While she stood looking after him, her mother came out through one of the long windows onto the veranda, with a catlike softness and vagueness.

"Why didn't he stay to dinner?"

"Because—because—war has been declared," Editha pronounced, without turning.

Her mother said, "Oh, my!" and then said nothing more until she had sat down in one of the large Shaker chairs and rocked herself for some time. Then she closed whatever tacit passage of thought there had been in her mind with the spoken words: "Well, I hope *he* won't go."

"And *I* hope he *will*," the girl said, and confronted her mother with a stormy exultation that would have frightened any creature less unimpressionable than a cat.

Her mother rocked herself again for an interval of cogitation. What she arrived at in speech was: "Well, I guess you've done a wicked thing, Editha Balcom."

The girl said, as she passed indoors through the same window her mother had come out by: "I haven't done anything—yet."

In her room, she put together all her letters and gifts from Gearson, down to the withered petals of the first flower he had offered, with that timidity of his veiled in that irony of his. In the heart of the packet she enshrined her engagement ring which she had restored to the pretty box he had brought it her in. The she sat down, if not calmly yet strongly, and wrote:

> "GEORGE:—I understood when you left me. But I think we had better emphasize your meaning that if we cannot be one in everything we had better be one in nothing. So I am sending these things for your keeping till you have made up your mind.
>
> "I shall always love you, and therefore I shall never marry any one else. But the man I marry must love his country first of all, and be able to say to me,
>
> > "'I could not love thee, dear, so much,
> > Loved I not honor more.'
>
> "There is no honor above America with me. In this great hour there is no other honor.
>
> "Your heart will make my words clear to you. I had never expected to say so much, but it has come upon me that I must say the utmost.
>
> > EDITHA"

She thought she had worded her letter well, worded it in a way that could not be bettered; all had been implied and nothing expressed.

She had it ready to send with the packet she had tied with red, white, and blue ribbon, when it occurred to her that she was not just to him, that she was not giving him a fair chance. He said he would go and think it over, and she was not waiting. She was pushing, threatening, compelling. That was not a woman's part. She must leave him free, free, free. She could not accept for her country or herself a forced sacrifice.

In writing her letter she had satisfied the impulse from which it sprang; she could well afford to wait till he had thought it over. She put the packet and the letter by, and rested serene in her consciousness of having done what was laid upon her by her love itself to do, and yet used patience, mercy, justice.

She had her reward. Gearson did not come to tea, but she had given him till morning, when, late at night there came up from the village the sound of fife and drum, with a tumult of voices, in shouting, singing, and laughing. The noise drew nearer and nearer; it reached the street end of the avenue; there it silenced itself, and one voice, the voice she knew best, rose over the silence. It fell; the air was filled with cheers; the fife and drum struck up, with the shouting, singing, and laughing again, but now retreating; and a single figure came hurrying up the avenue.

She ran down to meet her lover and clung to him. He was very gay, and he put his arm around her with a boisterous laugh. "Well, you must call me Captain now; or Cap, if you prefer; that's what the boys call me. Yes, we've had a meeting at the town-hall, and everybody has volunteered; and they selected me for captain, and I'm going to the war, the big war, the glorious war, the holy war ordained by the pocket Providence that blesses butchery. Come along; let's tell the whole family about it. Call them from their downy beds, father, mother, Aunt Hitty and all the folks!"

But when they mounted the veranda steps he did not wait for a larger audience; he poured the story out upon Editha alone.

"There was a lot of speaking, and then some of the fools set up a shout for me. It was all going one way, and I thought it would be a good joke to sprinkle a little cold water on them. But you can't do that with a crowd that adores you. The first thing I knew I was sprinkling hell-fire on them. 'Cry havoc, and let slip the dogs of war.' That was the style. Now that it had come to a fight, there were no two parties; there was one country, and the thing was to fight to a finish as quick as possible. I suggested volunteering then and there, and I wrote my name first of all on the roster. Then they elected me—that's all. I wish I had some ice-water."

She left him walking up and down the veranda, while she ran for the ice-pitcher and goblet, and when she came back he was still walking up and down shouting the story he had told her to her father and mother, who had come out more sketchily dressed than they commonly were by day. He drank goblet after goblet of the ice-water without noticing who was giving it, and kept on talking, and laughing through his talk wildly. "It's astonishing," he said, "how well the worse reason looks when you try to make it appear the better. Why, I believe I was the first convert to the war in that crowd to-night! I never thought I should like to kill a man; but now I shouldn't care; and the smokeless powder lets you see the man drop that you kill. It's all for the country! What a thing it is to have a country that *can't* be wrong, but if it is, is right, anyway!"

Editha had a great, vital thought, an inspiration. She set down the ice-pitcher on the veranda floor, and ran up-stairs and got the letter she had written him. When at last he noisily bade her father and mother, "Well, good-night. I forgot I woke you up; I sha'n't want any sleep myself," she followed him down the avenue to the gate. There, after the whirling words that seemed to fly away from her thoughts and refuse to serve them, she made a last effort to solemnize the moment that seemed so crazy, and pressed the letter she had written upon him.

"What's this?" he said. "Want me to mail it?"

"No, no. It's for you. I wrote it after you went this morning. Keep it—keep it—and read it sometime—" She thought, and then her inspiration came: "Read it if you ever doubt what you've done, or fear that I regret your having done it. Read it after you've started."

They strained each other in embraces that seemed as ineffective as their words, and he kissed her face with quick, hot breaths that were so unlike him, that made her feel as if she had lost her old lover and found a stranger in his place. The stranger said: "What a gorgeous flower you are, with your red hair, and your blue eyes that look black now, and your face with the color painted out by the white moonshine! Let me hold you under the chin, to see whether I love blood, you tiger-lily!" Then he laughed Gearson's laugh, and released her, scared and giddy. With her wilfulness she had been frightened by a sense of subtler force in him, and mystically mastered as she had never been before.

She ran all the way back to the house, and mounted the steps panting. Her mother and father were talking of the great affair. Her mother said: "Wa'n't Mr. Gearson in rather of an excited state of mind? Didn't you think he acted curious?"

"Well, not for a man who's just been elected captain and has set 'em up for the whole of Company A," her father chuckled back.

"What in the world do you mean, Mr. Balcom? Oh! There's Editha!" She offered to follow the girl indoors.

"Don't come, mother!" Editha called, vanishing.

Mrs. Balcom remained to reproach her husband. "I don't see much anything to laugh at."

"Well, it's catching. Caught it from Gearson. I guess it won't be much of a war, and I guess Gearson don't think so, either. The other fellows will back down as soon as they see we mean it. I wouldn't lose any sleep over it. I'm going back to bed, myself."

Gearson came back again next afternoon, looking pale and rather sick, but quite himself, even to his languid irony. "I guess I'd better tell you, Editha, that I consecrated myself to your god of battles last night by pouring too many libations to him down my throat. But I'm all right now. One has to carry off the excitement, somehow."

"Promise me," she commanded, "that you'll never touch it again!"

"What! Not let the cannikin clink? Not let the soldier drink? Well, I promise."

"You don't belong to yourself now; you don't even belong to *me*. You belong to your country, and you have a sacred charge to keep yourself strong and well for your country's sake. I have been thinking, thinking all night and all day long."

"You look as if you've been crying a little, too," he said, with his queer smile.

"That's all past. I've been thinking, and worshiping *you*. Don't you suppose I know all that you've been through, to come to this? I've followed you every step from your old theories and opinions."

"Well, you've had a long road to hoe."

"And I know you've done this from the highest motives—"

"Oh, there won't be much pettifogging to do till this cruel war is—"

"And you haven't simply done it for my sake. I couldn't respect you if you had."

"Well, then let's say I haven't. A man that hasn't got his own respect wants the respect of all the other people he can corner. But we won't go into that. I'm in for the thing now, and we've got to face our future. My idea is that this isn't going to be a very protracted struggle; we shall just scare the enemy to death before we fight at all. But we must provide for contingencies, Editha. If anything happens to me—"

"Oh, George!" She clung to him, sobbing.

"I don't want you to be foolishly bound to my memory. I should hate that, wherever I happened to be."

"I am yours, for time and eternity—time and eternity." She liked the words; they satisfied her famine for phrases.

"Well, say eternity; that's all right; but time's another thing; and I'm talking about time. But there is something! My mother! If anything happens—"

She winced, and he laughed. "You're not the bold soldier-girl of yesterday!" Then he sobered. "If anything happens, I want you to help my mother out. She won't like my doing this thing. She brought me up to think war is a fool thing as well as a bad thing. My father was in the Civil War; all through it; lost his arm in it." She thrilled with the sense of the arm around her; what if that should be lost? He laughed as if divining her: "Oh, it doesn't run in the family, as far as I know!" Then he added, gravely : "He came home with misgivings about war, and they grew on him. I guess he and mother agreed between them that I was to be brought up in his final mind about it; but that was before my time. I only knew him from my mother's report of him and his opinions; I don't know whether they were hers first; but they were hers last. This will be a blow to her. I shall have to write and tell her—"

He stopped and she asked: "Would you like me to write, too, George?"

"I don't believe that would do. No, I'll do the writing. She'll understand a little if I say that the way to minimize it was to make the war on the largest possible scale at once—that I felt I must have been helping on the war somehow if I hadn't helped keep it from coming, and I knew I hadn't; when it came, I had no right to stay out of it."

Whether his sophistries satisfied him or not, they satisfied her. She clung to his breast, and whispered, with closed eyes and quivering lips: "Yes, yes, yes!"

"But if anything should happen, you might go to her and see what you could do for her. You know? It's rather far off; she can't leave her chair—"

"Oh, I'll go, if it's the ends of the earth! But nothing will happen! Nothing *can*! I—"

She felt herself lifted with his rising, and Gearson was saying, with his arm still round her, to her father: "Well, we're off at once, Mr. Balcom. We're to be formally accepted at the capital, and then bunched up with the rest somehow, and sent into camp somewhere, and got to the front as soon as possible. We all want to be in the van, of course; we're the first company to report to the Governor. I came to tell Editha, but I hadn't got around to it."

She saw him again for a moment at the capital, in the station, just before the train started southward with his regiment. He looked well, in his uniform, and very soldierly, but somehow girlish, too, with his clean-shaven face and slim figure. The manly eyes and the strong voice satisfied her, and his preoccupation with some unexpected details of duty flattered her. Other girls were weeping and bemoaning themselves, but she felt a sort of noble distinction in the abstraction, the almost unconsciousness, with which they parted. Only at the last moment he said: "Don't forget my mother. It mayn't be such a walkover as I supposed," and he laughed at the notion.

He waved his hand to her, as the train moved off—she knew it among a score of hands that were waved to other girls from the platform of the car, for it held a letter which she knew was hers. Then he went inside the car to read it, doubtless, and she did not see him again. But she felt safe for him through the strength of what she called her love. What she called her God, always speaking the name in a deep voice and with the implication of a mutual understanding, would watch over him and keep him and bring him back to her. If with an empty sleeve, then he should have three arms instead of two, for both of hers should be his for life. She did not see, though, why she should always be thinking of the arm his father had lost.

There were not many letters from him, but they were such as she could have wished, and she put her whole strength into making hers such as she imagined he could have wished, glorifying and supporting him. She wrote to his mother glorifying him as their hero, but the brief answer she got was merely to the effect that Mrs. Gearson was not well enough to write herself, and thanking her for her letter by the hand of someone who called herself "Yrs truly, Mrs. W. J. Andrews."

Editha determined not to be hurt, but to write again quite as if the answer had been all she expected. Before it seemed as if she could have written, there came news of the first skirmish, and in the list of the killed, which was telegraphed as a trifling loss on our side, was Gearson's name. There was a frantic time of trying to make out that it might be, must be, some other Gearson; but the name and company and the regiment and the State were too definitely given.

Then there was a lapse into the depths out of which it seemed as if she could never rise again; then a lift into clouds far above all grief, black clouds, that blotted out the sun, but where she soared with him, with George— George! She had the fever that she expected of herself, but she did not die in it; she was not even delirious, and it did not last long. When she was well enough to leave her bed, her one thought was of George's mother, of his strangely worded wish that she should go to her and see what she could do for her. In the exaltation of the duty laid upon her—it buoyed her up instead of burdening her—she rapidly recovered.

Her father went with her on the long railroad journey from northern New York to western Iowa; he had business out in Davenport, and he said he could just as well go then as anytime; and he went with her to the little country town where George's mother lived in a little house on the edge of the illimitable cornfields, under trees pushed to a top of the rolling prairie. George's father had settled there after the Civil War, as so many other old soldiers had done; but they were Eastern people, and Editha fancied touches of the East in the June rose overhanging the front door, and the garden with early summer flowers stretching from the gate of the paling fence.

It was very low inside the house, and so dim, with the closed blinds, that they could scarcely see one another: Editha tall and black in her crapes which filled the air with the smell of their dyes; her father standing decorously apart with his hat on his forearm, as at funerals; a woman rested in a deep arm-chair, and the woman who had let the strangers in stood behind the chair.

The seated woman turned her head round and up, and asked the woman behind her chair: "*Who* did you say?"

Editha, if she had done what she had expected of herself, would have gone down on her knees at the feet of the seated figure and said, "I am George's Editha," for answer.

But instead of her own voice she heard that other woman's voice saying "Well, I don't know as I *did* get the name just right. I guess I'll have to make a little more light in here," and she went and pushed two of the shutters ajar.

Then Editha's father said, in his public will-now-address-a-few-remarks tone: "My name is Balcom, ma'am—Junius H. Balcom, of Balcom's Works, New York; my daughter—"

"Oh!" the seated woman broke in, with a powerful voice, the voice that always surprised Editha from Gearson's slender frame. "Let me see you. Stand round where the light can strike on your face," and Editha dumbly obeyed. "So, you're Editha Balcom," she sighed.

"Yes," Editha said, sounding more like a culprit than a comforter.

"What did you come for?" Mrs. Gearson asked.

Editha's face quivered and her knees shook. "I came—because—because George—" She could go no further.

"Yes," the mother said, "he told me that he had asked you to come if he got killed. You didn't expect that, I suppose, when you sent him."

"I would rather have died myself than done it!" Editha said, with more truth in her deep voice than she ordinarily found in it. "I tried to leave him free"—

"Yes, that letter of yours, that came back with his other things, that left him free."

Editha saw now where George's irony came from.

"It was not to be read before—unless—until—I told him so," she faltered.

"Of course, he wouldn't read a letter of yours, under the circumstances, till he thought you wanted him to. Been sick?" the woman abruptly demanded.

"Very sick," Editha said, with self-pity.

"Daughter's life," her father interposed, "was almost despaired of, at one time."

Mrs. Gearson gave him no heed. "I suppose you would have been glad to die, such a brave person as you! I don't believe *he* was glad to die. He was always a timid boy, that way; he was afraid of a good many things; but if he was afraid he did what he made up his mind to. I suppose he made up his mind to go, but I knew what it cost him by what it cost me when I heard of it. I had been through *one* war before. When you sent him you didn't expect he would get killed."

The voice seemed to compassionate Editha, and it was time. "No," she huskily murmured.

"No, girls don't; women don't, when they give their men up to their country. They think they'll come marching back, somehow, just as gay as they went, or if it's an empty sleeve, or even an empty pantaloon, it's all the more glory, and they're so much the prouder of them, poor things!"

The tears began to run down Editha's face; she had not wept till then; but it was now such a relief to be understood that the tears came.

"No, you didn't expect him to get killed," Mrs. Gearson repeated, in a voice which was startlingly like George's again. "You just expected him to kill some one else, some of those foreigners, that weren't there because they had any say about it, but because they had to be there, poor wretches—conscripts, or whatever you call 'em. You thought it would be all right for my George, *your* George, to kill the sons of those miserable mothers and the husbands of those girls that you would never see the faces of." The woman lifted her powerful voice in a psalmlike note. "I thank my God he didn't live to do it! I thank my God they killed him first, and that he ain't livin' with their blood on his hands!" She dropped her eyes, which she had raised with her voice, and glared at Editha. "What you got that black on for?" She lifted herself by her powerful arms so high that her helpless body seemed to hang limp its full length. "Take it off, take it off, before I tear it from your back!"

The lady who was passing the summer near Balcom's Works was sketching Editha's beauty, which lent itself wonderfully to the effects of a colorist. It had come to that confidence which is rather apt to grow between artist and sitter, and Editha had told her everything.

"To think of your having such a tragedy in your life!" the lady said. She added: "I suppose there are people who feel that way about war. But when you consider the good this war has done—how much it has done for the country! I can't understand such people, for my part. And when you had come all the way out there to console her—got up out of a sick-bed! Well!"

"I think," Editha said, magnanimously, "she wasn't quite in her right mind; and so did papa."

"Yes," the lady said, looking at Editha's lips in nature and then at her lips in art, and giving an empirical touch to them in the picture. "But how dreadful of her! How perfectly—excuse me—how *vulgar!*"

A light broke upon Editha in the darkness which she felt had been without a gleam of brightness for weeks and months. The mystery that had bewildered her was solved by the word; and from that moment she rose from groveling in shame and self-pity, and began to live again in the ideal.

The Eidolons of Brooks Alford

1906

"THE EIDOLONS OF BROOKS ALFORD" was first published in the August 1906 issue of *Harper's Monthly* and was reprinted the following year in *Between the Dark and the Daylight*. It was the sixth of Howells's nine Turkish Room stories. (See above pp. 122–24 for a fuller discussion of the Turkish Room stories.) "Eidolons" displays two primary characteristics of these stories: the treatment of abnormal psychic phenomena, and the focus on the interpretation of events rather than on the events themselves. And, like most of the other stories, it is framed, told at secondhand by Acton, the writer, who is recollecting an earlier narration by Wanhope, the psychologist.

The psychic phenomena in this story, as in "The Angel of the Lord," are eidolons or visions—but here they are seen as purely "the effects of a mental process" and not as messages from the spirit world. In this way, "Eidolons" differs from the two stories with which it will most likely be compared, Howells's "His Apparition" and Henry James's "The Beast in the Jungle."[1] In both of these, there is at least a suggestion that the vision seen is of spiritual importance and has its origin outside the mind of the observer. In "His

Apparition," Hewson is convinced that his apparition was "a supernatural incident" (13); "that it was a veridical phantom which had appeared to him he did not in his inmost at all doubt" (27). Furthermore, he believes that "an occurrence so out of the course of events must have had some message for him, and it must have been his fault that he could not divine it" (30). Similarly, John Marcher, in "The Beast in the Jungle," feels "the sense of being kept for something rare and strange, possibly prodigious and terrible, that was sooner or later to happen" (282). But Brooks Alford, although he feels "a sense of approaching creepiness in his experience," sees it as a purely psychological experience. His reaction is to see his doctor, to "mention his eidolons, and ask if they were at all related to the condition of his nerves." When the eidolons recur, he "said to himself that he was making the whole thing, but the very subjectivity was what filled him with a deep and hopeless dread." And when he has to put his experience in words, his description is "I'm afraid I'm losing my mind."

Like Hewson and Marcher, however, Alford is at first "proud of what had happened to him as out of the ordinary." And, like these fictional counterparts, he relies on the help of a woman to interpret or to cure his condition. In all three stories, the woman is closely linked to the abnormal vision—and the hero's ability to understand this link determines his fate. But in "Eidolons," again, the link is earthly and pragmatic, rather than mystical. Mrs. Yarrow is, in her own blunt words, "a prescription," in contrast to Hewson's Rosalie and Marcher's May, who, it is suggested, are linked by the psychic phenomena to the supernatural.

In "Eidolons," Howells clearly rejects psychic explanations. This story thus differs from stories in which psychic and psychological explanations are given equal weight, such as the earlier "His Apparition" and "Though One Rose from the Dead," and from those which lean toward psychic explanations, such as the later "Talking of Presentiments," "Fulfillment of the Pact" and, to a lesser extent, "An Experience." Any discussion of Howells's psychic romances must take into account his oscillation between the psychic and the psychological approaches, and his tendency to favor the latter. Although Howells's interest in the psychic is well established and is evidenced by many of the stories, he rarely abandoned his role as a psychological writer.

"Eidolons," like the other Turkish Room stories, draws attention away from narrated events and toward the interpretation of these events by using the varied comments of the Turkish Room habitués as a chorus and by the striking lack of a dramatic conclusion. The ending of "Eidolons" is a good example of both techniques. The reader's attention has been diverted from the expected conclusion—revelation of the success or failure of Dr. Enderby's "prescription" for the eidolons—to a consideration of the psychological requirements of love and marriage. It is only with Rulledge's final exclamation that we are reminded of how this story, were it conventionally dramatic, would end.

"Eidolons," like most or all of the *Between the Dark and the Daylight* and *Questionable Shapes* stories, was apparently based on Howells's own experiences (Cady, *Road* 243; Brooks 223). The narrator's opening comment that "It was undoubtedly overwork which preceded Alford's experiences if it did not cause them" recalls Howells's own mental breakdowns, many of which he attributed to overwork (Cady, *Road* 59 and passim). And the form that Alford's "breakdown" takes is reminiscent of the "almost palpably vivid dream-experiences" that Howells "recurrently suffered" throughout his life (Cady, *Road* 243). Althought "Eidolons" is light and amusing, a "romance," according to the full title of the volume in which it was included, it is composed of some of the more disturbing elements of Howells's own life; and Alford's apparent discovery that love and marriage can help to suppress the "demons" of mental instability surely reflects the haven from psychological terrors that Howells found in his own marriage (Cady, *Road* 99).

Notes

1. It may also be compared to some extent with *The Shadow of a Dream*; in both, the plot is advanced by the actions or advice of a Boston doctor who has been consulted about psychological problems.

The Eidolons of Brooks Alford

I should like to give the story of Alford's experiences just as Wanhope told it, sitting with us before the glowing hearth in the Turkish room, one night after the other diners at our club had gone away to digest their dinners at the theatre, or in their bachelor apartments up-town, or on the late trains which they were taking north, south, and west; or had hurried back to their offices to spend the time stolen from rest in overwork for which their famished nerves would duly revenge themselves. It was undoubtedly overwork which preceded Alford's experiences if it did not cause them, for he was pretty well broken from it when he took himself off in the early summer, to put the pieces together as best he could by the seaside. But this was a fact which Wanhope was not obliged to note to us, and there were certain other commonplaces of our knowledge of Alford which he could omit without omitting anything essential to our understanding of the facts which he dealt with so delicately, so electly, almost affectionately, coaxing each point into the fittest light, and then lifting his phrase from it, and letting it stand alone in our consciousness. I remember particularly how he touched upon the love-affair which was supposed to have so much to do with Alford's break-up, and how he dismissed it to its proper place in the story. As he talked on, with scarcely an interruption either from the eager credulity of Rulledge or the doubt of Minver, I heard with a sensuous comfort—I can use no other word —the far-off click of the dishes in the club kitchen, putting away till next day, with the musical murmur of a smitten glass or the jingle of a dropped spoon. But if I should try to render his words, I should spoil their impression in the vain attempt, and I feel that it is best to give the story as best I can in words of my own, so far from responsive to the requisitions of the occult incident.

The first intimation Alford had of the strange effect, which from first to last was rather an obsession than a possession of his, was after a morning of idle satisfaction spent in watching the target practice from the fort in the neighborhood of the little fishing-village where he was spending the summer. The target was two or three miles out in the open water beyond the harbor, and he found his pleasure in watching the smoke of the gun for that discrete interval before the report reached him, and then for that somewhat longer interval before he saw the magnificent splash of the shot which, as it plunged into the sea, sent a fan-shaped fountain thirty or forty feet into the air. He did not know and he did not care whether the target was ever hit or not. That fact was no part of his concern. His affair was to watch the burst of smoke from the fort and then to watch the upward gush of water, almost as light and vaporous to the eye, where the ball struck. He did not miss one of the shots fired during the forenoon, and when he met the other people who sat down with him at the midday dinner in the hotel, his talk with them was naturally of the morning's practice. They one and all declared it a great nuisance, and said that it had shattered their nerves terribly, which was not perhaps so strange, since they were all women. But when they asked him in his quality of nervous wreck whether he had not suffered from the prolonged and repeated explosions, too, he found himself able to say no, that he had enjoyed every moment of the firing. He added that he did not believe he had even noticed the noise after the first shot, he was so wholly taken by the beauty of the fountain-burst from the sea which followed; and as he spoke the fan-like spray rose and expanded itself before his eyes, quite blotting out the visage of a young widow across the table. In his swift recognition of the fact and his reflection on it, he realized that the effect was quite as if he had been looking at some intense light, almost as if he had been looking at the sun, and that the illusion which had blotted out the agreeable reality opposite was of the quality of those flying shapes which repeat themselves here, there, and everywhere that one looks, after lifting the gaze from a dazzling object. When his consciousness had duly registered this perception, there instantly followed a recognition of the fact that the eidolon now filling his vision was not the effect of the dazzled eyes, but of a mental process, of thinking how the thing which it reported had looked.

By the time Alford had co-ordinated this reflection with the other, the eidolon had faded from the lady's face, which again presented itself in uninterrupted loveliness with the added attraction of a distinct pout.

"Well, Mr. Alford!" she bantered him.

"Oh, I beg your pardon! I was thinking—"

"Not of what I was saying," she broke in, laughingly, forgivingly.

"No, I certainly wasn't," he assented, with such a sense of approaching creepiness in his experience that when she challenged him to say what he *was* thinking of, he could not, or would not; she professed to believe that he would not.

In the joking that followed he soon lost the sense of approaching creepiness, and began to be proud of what had happened to him as out of the ordinary, as a species of psychological ecstasy almost of spiritual value. From time to time he tried, by thinking of the splash and upward gush from the cannon-shot's plunge in the sea, to recall the vision, but it would not come again, and at the end of an afternoon somewhat distraughtly spent he decided to put the matter away, as one of the odd things of no significance which happen in life and must be dealt with as mysteries none the less trifling because they are inexplicable.

"Well, you've got over it?" the widow joked him as he drew up towards her, smiling from her rocker on the veranda after supper. At first, all the women in the hotel had petted him; but with their own cares and ailments to reclaim them they had let the invalid fall to the peculiar charge of the childless widow who had nothing else to do, and was so well and strong that she could look after the invalid Professor of Archæology (at the Champlain University) without the fatigues they must feel.

"Yes, I've got over it," he said.

"And what was it?" she boldly pursued.

He was about to say, and then he could not.

"You won't tell?"

"Not yet," he answered. He added, after a moment, "I don't believe I can."

"Because it's confidential?"

"No; not exactly that. Because it's impossible."

"Oh, that's simple enough. I understand exactly what you mean. Well, if ever it becomes less difficult, remember that I should always like to know. It seemed a little—personal."

"How in the world?"

"Well, when one is stared at in that way—"

"Did I stare?"

"Don't you *always* stare? But in this case you stared as if there was something wrong with my hair."

"There wasn't," Alford protested, simple-heartedly. Then he recollected his sophistication to say: "Unless its being of that particular shade between brown and red was wrong."

"Oh, thank you, Mr. Alford! After that I *must* believe you."

They talked on the veranda till the night fell, and then they came in among the lamps, in the parlor, and she sat down with a certain provisionality, putting herself sideways on a light chair by a window, and as she chatted and laughed with one cheek towards him she now and then beat the back of her chair with her open hand. The other people were reading or severely playing cards, and they, too, kept their tones down to a respectful level, while she lingered, and when she rose and said good-night he went out and took some turns on the veranda before going up to bed. She was certainly, he realized, a very pretty woman, and very graceful and very amusing, and though she probably knew all about it, she was the franker and honester for her knowledge.

He had arrived at this conclusion just as he turned the switch of the electric light inside his door, and in the first flash of the carbon film he saw her sitting beside the window in such a chair as she had taken and in the very pose which she had kept in the parlor. Her half-averted face was lit as from laughing, and she had her hand lifted as if to beat the back of her chair.

"Good Heavens, Mrs. Yarrow!" he said, in a sort of whispered shout, while he mechanically closed the door behind him as if to keep the fact to himself. "What in the world are you doing here?"

Then she was not there. Nothing was there; not even a chair beside the window.

Alford dropped weakly into the only chair in the room, which stood next the door by the head of his bed, and abandoned himself a helpless prey to the logic of the events.

It was at this point, which I have been able to give in Wanhope's exact words, that, in the ensuing pause, Rulledge asked, as if he thought some detail might be denied him: "And what was the logic of these events?"

Minver gave a fleering laugh. "Don't be premature, Rulledge. If you have the logic now, you will spoil everything. You can't have the moral until you've had the whole story. Go on, Wanhope. You're so much more interesting than usual that I won't ask how you got hold of all these compromising minutiæ."

"Of course," Wanhope returned, "they're not for the general ear. I go rather further, for the sake of the curious fact, than I should be warranted in doing if I did not know my audience so well."

We joined in a murmur of gratification, and he went on to say that Alford's first coherent thought was that he was dreaming one of those unwarranted dreams in which we make our acquaintance privy to all sorts of strange incidents. Then he knew that he was not dreaming, and that his eye had merely externated a mental vision, as in the case of the cannon-shot splash of which he had seen the phantom as soon as it was mentioned. He remembered afterwards asking himself in a sort of terror how far it was going to go with him; how far his thought was going to report itself objectively hereafter, and what were the reasonable implications of his abnormal experiences. He did not know just how long he sat by his bedside trying to think, only to have his conclusions whir away like a flock of startled birds when he approached them. He went to bed because he was exhausted rather than because he was sleepy, but he could not recall a moment of wakefulness after his head touched the pillow.

He woke surprisingly refreshed, but at the belated breakfast where he found Mrs. Yarrow still lingering he thought her not looking well. She confessed, listlessly, that she had not rested well. She was not sure, she said, whether the sea agreed with her; she might try the mountains a little later. She was not inclined to talk, and that day he scarcely spoke with her except in commonplaces at the table. They had no return to the little mystery they had mocked together the day before.

More days passed, and Alford had no recurrence of his visions. His acquaintance with Mrs. Yarrow made no further advance; there was no one else in the hotel who interested him; and he bored himself. At the same time his recovery seemed retarded; he lost tone, and after a fortnight he ran up to talk himself over with his doctor in Boston. He rather thought he would mention his eidolons, and ask if they were at all related to the condition of his nerves. It was a keen disappointment, but it ought not to have been a surprise, for him to find that his doctor was off on his summer vacation. The caretaker who opened the door to Alford named a young physician in the same block of Marlborough Street who had his doctor's practice for the summer, but Alford had not the heart to go to this alternate.

He started down to his hotel on a late afternoon train that would bring him to the station after dusk, and before he reached it the lamps had been lighted in his car. Alford sat in a sparsely peopled smoker, where he found a place away from the crowd in the other coaches, and looked out the window into the reflected interior of his car, which now and then thinned away and let him see the weeds and gravel of the railroad banks, with the bushes that topped them and the woods that backed them. The train at one point stopped rather suddenly and then went on, for no reason that he ever cared to inquire; but as it slowly moved forward again he was reminded of something he had seen one night in going to New York just before the train drew into Springfield. It had then made such another apparently reasonless stop; but before it resumed its course Alford saw from his window a group of trainmen, and his own Pullman conductor with his lantern on his arm, bending over the figure of a man defined in his dark clothing against the snow of the bank where he lay propped. His face was waxen white, and Alford noted how particularly black the mustache looked traversing the pallid visage. He never knew whether the man was killed or merely stunned; you learn nothing with certainty of such things on trains; but now, as he thought of the incident, its eidolon showed itself outside of his mind, and followed in every detail, even to a snowy stretch of the embankment, until the increasing speed of the train seemed to sweep it back out of sight.

Alford turned his eyes to the interior of the smoker, which, except for two or three dozing commuters and a noisy euchre-party, had been empty of everything but the fumes and stale odors of tobacco, and found it swarming with visions, the eidolons of everything he remembered from his past life. Whatever had once strongly impressed itself upon his nerves was reported there again as instantly as he thought of it. It was largely a whirling chaos, a kaleidoscopic jumble of facts; but from time to time some more memorable and important experience visualized itself alone. Such was the death-bed of the little sister whom he had been wakened, a child, to see going to heaven, as they told him. Such was the pathetic, foolish face of the girl whom long ago he had made believe he cared for, and then had abruptly broken with: he saw again, with heartache, her silly, tender amaze when he said he was going away. Such was the look of mute astonishment, of gentle reproach, in the eyes of a friend, now long dead, whom in a moment of insensate fury he had struck on the mouth, and who put his hand to his bleeding lips as he bent that gaze of wonder and bewilderment upon him. But it was not alone the dreadful impressions that reported themselves. There were others, as vivid, which came back in the original joyousness: the face of his mother looking up at him from the crowd on a day of college triumph when he was delivering the valedictory of his class; the collective gayety of the whole table on a particularly delightful evening at his dining-club; his own image in the glass as he caught sight of it on coming home accepted by the woman who afterwards jilted him; the transport which lighted up his father's visage when he stepped ashore from the vessel which had been rumored lost, and he could be verified by the senses as still alive; the comical, bashful ecstasy of the good fellow, his ancient chum, in telling him he had had a son the night before, and the mother was doing well, and how he laughed and danced, and skipped into the air.

The smoker was full of these eidolons and of others which came and went with constant vicissitude. But what was of a greater weirdness than seeing them within it was seeing them without in that reflection of the interior which traveled with it through the summer night, and repeated it, now dimly, now brilliantly, in every detail. Alford sat in a daze, with a smile which he was aware of, fixed and stiff as if in plaster, on his face, and with his gaze bent on this or that eidolon, and then on all of them together. He was not so much afraid of them as of being noticed by the other passengers in the smoker, to whom he knew he might look very queer. He said to himself that he was making the whole thing, but the very subjectivity was what filled him with a deep and hopeless dread. At last the train ceased its long leaping through the dark, and with its coming to a stand the whole illusion vanished. He heard a gay voice which he knew bidding some one good-bye who was getting into the car just back of the smoker, and as he descended to the platform he almost walked into the arms of Mrs. Yarrow.

"Why, Mr. Alford! We had given you up. We thought you wouldn't come back till to-morrow—or perhaps ever. What in the world will you do for supper? The kitchen fires were out ages ago!"

In the light of the station electrics she beamed upon him, and he felt glad at heart, as if he had been saved from something, a mortal danger or a threatened shame. But he could not speak at once; his teeth closed with tetanic force upon each other. Later, as they walked to the hotel, through the warm, soft night in which the south wind was roaming the starless heavens for rain, he found his voice, and although he felt that he was speaking unnaturally, he made out to answer the lively questions with which she pelted him too thickly to be answered severally. She told him all the news of the day, and when she began on yesterday's news she checked herself with a laugh and said she had forgotten that he had only been gone since morning. "But now," she said, "you see how you've been missed—how *any* man must be missed in a hotel full of women."

She took charge of him when they got to the house, and said if he would go boldly into the dining-room, where they detected, as they approached, one lamp scantly shining from the else darkened windows, she would beard the lioness in her den, by which she meant the cook in the kitchen, and see what she could get him for supper. Apparently she could get nothing warm, for when a reluctant waitress appeared it was with such a chilly refection on her tray that Alford, though he was not very hungry, returned from interrogating the obscurity for eidolons, and shivered at it. At the same time the swing-door of the long, dim room opened to admit a gush of the outer radiance on which Mrs. Yarrow drifted in with a chafing-dish in one hand and a tea-basket in the other. She floated towards him like, he thought, a pretty little ship, and sent a cheery hail before.

"I've been trying to get somebody to join you at a premature Welsh-rarebit and a belated cup of tea, but I can't tear one of the tabbies from their cards or the kittens from their gambols in the amusement-hall in the basement. Do you mind so very much having it alone? Because you'll have to, whether you do or not. Unless you call me company, when I'm merely cook."

She put her utensils on the table beside the forbidding tray the waitress had left, and helped lift herself by pressing one hand on the top of a chair towards the electric, which she flashed up to keep the dismal lamp in countenance. Alford let her do it. He durst not, he felt, stir from his place, lest any movement should summon back the eidolons; and now, in the sudden glare of light he shyly, slyly searched the room for them. Not one, fair or foul, showed itself, and slowly he felt a great weight lifting from his heart. In its place there sprang up a joyous gratitude towards Mrs. Yarrow, who had saved him from them, from himself. An inexpressible tenderness filled his breast; the tears rose to his eyes; a soft glow enveloped his whole being, a warmth of hope, a freshness of life renewed, encompassed him. He wished to take her in his arms, to tell her how he loved her; and as she bustled about, lighting the lamp of her chafing-dish, and kindling the little spirit-stove she had brought with her to make tea, he let his gaze dwell upon every pose, every motion of her with a glad hunger in which no smallest detail was lost. He now believed that without her he must die, without her he could not wish to live.

"Jove," Rulledge broke in at this point of Wanhope's story, which I am telling again so badly, "I think Alford was in luck."

Minver gave a harsh cackle. "The only thing Rulledge finds fault with in this club is 'the lack of woman's nursing and the lack of woman's tears.' Nothing is wanting to his enjoyment of his victuals but the fact that they are not served by a neat-handed Phyllis, like Alford's."

Rulledge glanced towards Wanhope, and innocently inquired, "Was that her first name?"

Minver burst into a scream, and Rulledge looked red and silly for having given himself away; but he made an excursion to the buffet outside, and returned with a sandwich with which he supported himself stolidly under Minver's derision, until Wanhope came to his relief by resuming his story, or rather his study, of Alford's strange experience.

Mrs. Yarrow first gave Alford his tea, as being of a prompter brew than the rarebit, but she was very quick and apt with that, too; and pretty soon she leaned forward, and in the glow from the lamp under the chafing-dish, which spiritualized her charming face with its thin radiance, puffed the flame out with her pouted lips, and drew back with a long-sighed "There! That will make you see your grandmother, if anything will."

"My grandmother?" Alford repeated.

"Yes. Wouldn't you like to?" Mrs. Yarrow asked, pouring the thick composition over the toast (rescued stone-cold from the frigid tray) on Alford's plate. "I'm sure I should like to see mine—dear old gran! Not that I ever saw her—either of her—or should know how she looked. Did you ever see yours—either of her?" she pursued, impulsively.

"Oh, yes," Alford answered, looking intently at her, but with so little speculation in the eyes he glared so with that he knew her to be uneasy under them.

She laughed a little, and stayed her hand on the bail of the teapot. "Which of her?"

"Oh, both!"

"And—and—did she look so much like *me*?" she asked, with an added laugh, that he perceived had an hysterical note in it. "You're letting your rarebit get cold!"

He laughed himself, now, a great laugh of relaxation, of relief. "Not the least in the world! She was not exactly a phantom of delight."

"Oh, thank you, Mr. Alford. Now, it's your tea's getting cold."

They laughed together, and he gave himself to his victual with a relish that she visibly enjoyed. When that question of his grandmother had been pushed he thought of an awful experience of his childhood, which left on his infant mind an indelible impression, a scar, to remain from the original wound forever. He had been caught in a lie, the first he could remember, but by no means the last, by many immemorable thousands. His poor little wickedness had impugned the veracity of both these terrible old ladies, who, habitually at odds with each other, now united, for once, against him. He could always see himself, a mean little blubbering-faced rascal, stealing guilty looks of imploring at their faces, set unmercifully against him, one in sorrow and one in anger, requiring his mother to whip him, and insisting till he was led, loudly roaring, into the parlor, and there made a liar of for all time, so far as fear could do it.

When Mrs. Yarrow asked if had ever seen his grandmother he expected instantly to see her, in duplicate, and as a sole refuge, but with little hope that it would save him, he kept his eyes fast on hers, and to his unspeakable joy it did avail. No other face, of sorrow or of anger, rose between them. For the time his thought was quit of its consequence; no eidolon outwardly repeated his inner vision. A warm gush of gratitude seemed to burst from his heart, and to bathe his whole being, and then to flow in a tide of ineffable tenderness toward Mrs. Yarrow, and involve her and bear them together heavenward. It was not passion, it was not love, he perceived well enough; it was the utterance of a vital conviction that she had saved him from an overwhelming subjective horror, and that in her sweet objectivity there was a security and peace to be found nowhere else.

He greedily ate every atom of his rarebit, he absorbed every drop of the moisture in the teapot, so that when she shook it, and shook it, and then tried to pour something from it, there was no slightest dribble at the spout. But they lingered, talking and laughing, and perhaps they might never have left the place if the hard handmaiden who had brought the tea-tray had not first tried putting her head in at the swing-door from the kitchen, and then, later, come boldly in and taken the tray away.

Mrs. Yarrow waited self-respectfully for her disappearance, and then she said, "I'm afraid that was a hint, Mr. Alford."

"It seemed like one," he owned.

They went out together, gayly chatting, but she would not encourage the movement he made towards the veranda. She remained firmly attached to the newel-post of the stairs, and at the first chance he gave her she said good-night and bounded lightly upward. At the turn of the stairs she stopped and looked laughing down at him over the rail. "I hope you won't see your grand-mother."

"Oh, not a bit of it," he called back. He felt that he failed to give his reply the quality of epigram, but he was not unhappy in his failure.

Many light-hearted days followed this joyous evening. No eidolons haunted Alford's horizon, perhaps because Mrs. Yarrow filled his whole heaven. She was very constantly with him, guiding his wavering steps up the hill of re-covery, which he climbed with more and more activity, and keeping him com-pany in those valleys of relapse into which he now and then fell back from the difficult steeps. It came to be tacitly, or at least passively, conceded by the other ladies that she had somehow earned the exclusive right to what had once been the common charge; or that if one of their number had a claim to keep Mr. Alford from killing himself by all sorts of imprudences, which in his case amounted to impieties, it was certainly Mrs. Yarrow. They did not put this in terms, but they felt it and acted it.

She was all the safer guardian for a delicate invalid because she loathed manly sports so entirely that she did not even pretend to like them, as most women, poor things, think themselves obliged to do. In her hands there was no danger that he would be tempted to excesses in golf. She was really afraid of all boats, but she was willing to go out with him in the sail-boat of a su-perannuated skipper, because to sit talking in the stern and swoop for the va-garies of the boom in tacking was such good exercise. She would join him in fishing from the rotting pier, but with no certainty which was a cunner and which was a sculpin, when she caught it, and with an equal horror of both the nasty, wriggling things. When they went for a walk together, her notion of a healthful tramp was to find a nice place among the sweet-fern or the pine-needles, and sit down in it and talk, or make a lap, to which he could bring the berries he gathered for her to arrange in the shallow leaf-trays she pinned to-gether with twigs. She really preferred a rocking chair on the veranda to any-thing else; but if he wished to go to those other excesses, she would go with him, to keep him out of mischief.

There could be only one credible reading of the situation, but Alford let the summer pass in this pleasant dreaming without waking up till too late to the pleasanter reality. It will seem strange enough, but it is true, that it was no part of his dream to fancy that Mrs. Yarrow was in love with him. He knew very well, long before the end, that he was in love with her; but, remaining in the dark otherwise, he considered only himself in forebearing verbally to make love to her.

"Well!" Rulledge snarled at this point, "he *was* a chump."

Wanhope at the moment opposed nothing directly to the censure, but said that something pathetically reproachful in Mrs. Yarrow's smiling looks penetrated to Alford as she nodded gayly from the car window to him in the little group which had assembled to see her off at the station when she left, by no means the first of their happy hotel circle to go.

"Somebody," Rulledge burst out again, "ought to have kicked him."

"What's become," Minver asked, "of all the dear maids and widows that you've failed to marry at the end of each summer, Rulledge?"

The satire involved flattery so sweet that Rulledge could not perhaps wish to make any retort. He frowned sternly, and said, with a face averted from Minver: "Go on, Wanhope!"

Wanhope here permitted himself a philosophical excursion in which I will not accompany him. It was apparently to prepare us for the dramatic fact which followed, and which I suppose he was trying rather to work away from than work up to. It included some facts which he had failed to touch on before, and which led to a discussion very interesting in itself, but of a range too great for the limits I am trying to keep here. It seems Alford had been stayed from declaring his love not only because he doubted of its nature, but also because he questioned whether a man in his broken health had any right to offer himself to a woman, and because from a yet finer scruple he hesitated in his poverty to ask the hand of a rich woman. On the first point, we were pretty well agreed, but on the second we divided again, especially Rulledge and Minver, who held, the one, that his hesitation did Alford honor, and quite relieved him from the imputation of being a chump; and the other that he was an ass to keep quiet for any such silly reason. Minver contended that every woman had a right, whether rich or poor, to the man who loved her; and moreover, there were now so many rich women that, if they were not allowed to marry poor men, their chances of marriage were indefinitely reduced. What better could a widow do with the money she had inherited from a husband she probably did not love than give it to a man like Alford—or to an ass like Alford, Minver corrected himself.

His *reductio ad absurdum* allowed Wanhope to resume with a laugh, and say that Alford waited at the station in the singleness to which the tactful dispersion of the others had left him, and watched the train rapidly dwindle in the perspective, till an abrupt turn of the road carried it out of sight. Then he lifted his eyes with a long sigh, and looked around. Everywhere he saw Mrs.

Yarrow's smiling face with that inner pathos. It swarmed upon him from all points; and wherever he turned it repeated itself in the distances like that succession of faces you see when you stand between two mirrors.

It was not merely a lapse from his lately hopeful state with Alford, it was a collapse. The man withered and dwindled away, till he felt that he must audibly rattle in his clothes as he walked by people. He did not walk much. Mostly he remained shrunken in the arm-chair where he used to sit beside Mrs. Yarrow's rocker, and the ladies, the older and the older-fashioned, who were "sticking it out" at the hotel till it should close on the 15th of September, observed him, some compassionately, some censoriously, but all in the same conviction.

"It's plain to see what ails Mr. Alford, *now*."

"Well, I guess it *is*."

"*I* guess so."

"I *guess* it is."

"Seems kind of heartless, her going and leaving him so."

"Like a sick kitten!"

"Well, I should say as *much*."

"Your eyes bother you, Mr. Alford?" one of them chanted, breaking from their discussion of him to appeal directly to him. He was rubbing his eyes, to relieve himself for the moment from the intolerable affliction of those swarming eidolons, which, whenever he thought of this thing or that, thickened about him. They now no longer displaced one another, but those which came first remained fadedly beside or behind the fresher appearances, like the earlier rainbow which loses depth and color when a later arch defines itself.

"Yes," he said, glad of the subterfuge. "They annoy me a great deal of late."

"You want to get fitted for a good pair of glasses. I kept letting it go, when I first began to get old-sighted."

Another lady came to Alford's rescue. "I guess Mr. Alford has no need to get fitted for old sight yet for a while. You got little spidery things—specks and dots—in your eyes?"

"Yes—multitudes," he said, hopelessly.

"Well, I'll tell you what: you want to build up. That was the way with me, and the oculist said it was from getting all run down. I built up, and the first thing I knew my sight was as clear as a bell. You want to build up."

"You want to go to the mountains," a third interposed. "That's where Mrs. Yarrow's gone, and I guess it'll do her more good than sticking it out here would ever have done."

Alford would have been glad enough to go to the mountains, but with those illusions hovering closer and closer about him, he no longer had the courage, the strength. He had barely enough of either to get away to Boston. He found his doctor this time, after winning and losing the wager he made himself that he would not have returned to town yet, and the good-fortune was almost too much for his shaken nerves. The cordial of his friend's greeting—they had been chums at Harvard—completed his overthrow. As he sank upon the professional sofa, where so many other cases had been diagnosticated, he broke into tears. "Hello, old fellow!" the doctor said, encouragingly, and more tenderly than he would have dealt with some women. "What's up?"

"Jim," Alford found voice to say, "I'm afraid I'm losing my mind."

The doctor smiled provisionally. "Well, that's *one* of the signs you're not. Can you say how?"

"Oh yes. In a minute," Alford sobbed, and when he had got the better of himself he told his friend the whole story. In the direct examination he suppressed Mrs. Yarrow's part, but when the doctor, who had listened with smiling seriousness, began to cross-examine him with the question, "And you don't remember that any outside influence affected the recurrence of the illusions, or did anything to prevent it?" Alford answered promptly: "Oh yes. There was a woman who did."

"A woman? What sort of woman?"

Alford told.

"That is very curious," the doctor said. "I know a man who used to have a distressing dream. He broke it up by telling his wife about it every morning after he had dreamt it."

"Unluckily, she isn't my wife," Alford said, gloomily.

"But when she was with you, you got rid of the illusions?"

"At first, I used to see hers; then I stopped seeing any."

"Did you ever tell her of them?"

"No; I didn't."

"Never tell anybody?"

"No one but you."

"And do you see them now?"

"No."

"Do you think, because you've told me of them?"

"It seems so."

The doctor was silent for a marked space. Then he asked, smiling: "Well, why not?"

"Why not what?"

"Tell your wife."

"How, my wife?"

"By marriage."

Alford looked dazed. "Do you mean Mrs. Yarrow?"

"If that's her name, and she's a widow."

"And do you think it would be the fair thing for a man on the verge of insanity—a physical and mental wreck—to ask a woman to marry him?"

"In your case, yes. In the first place, you're not so bad as all that. You need nothing but rest for your body and change for your mind. I believe you'll get rid of your illusions as soon as you form the habit of speaking of them promptly when they begin to trouble you. You ought to speak of them to some one. You can't always have me around, and Mrs. Yarrow would be the next best thing."

"She's rich, and you know what I am. I'll have to borrow the money to rest on, I'm so poor."

"Not if you marry it."

Alford rose, somewhat more vigorously than he had sat down. But that day he did not go beyond ascertaining that Mrs. Yarrow was in town. He found out the fact from the maid at her door, who said that she was nearly always at home after dinner, and, without waiting for the evening of another day, Alford went to call upon her.

She said, coming down to him in a rather old-fashioned, impersonal drawing-room which looked distinctly as if it had been left to her: "I was so glad to get your card. When did you leave Woodbeach?"

"Mrs. Yarrow," he returned, as if that were the answer, "I think I owe you an explanation."

"Pay it!" she bantered, putting out her hand.

"I'm so poverty-stricken that I don't know whether I can. Did you ever notice anything odd about me?"

His directness seemed to have a right to directness from her. "I noticed that you stared a good deal—or used to. But people *do* stare."

"I stared because I saw things."

"Saw things?"

"I saw whatever I thought of. Whatever came into my mind was externated in a vision."

She smiled, he could not make out whether uneasily or not. "It sounds rather creepy, doesn't it? But it's very interesting."

"That's what the doctor said; I've been to see him this morning. May I tell you about my visions? They're not so creepy as they sound, I believe, and I don't think they'll keep you awake."

"Yes, do," she said. "I should like of all things to hear about them. Perhaps I've been one of them."

"You have."

"Oh! Isn't that rather personal?"

"I hope not offensively."

He went on to tell her, with even greater fulness than he had told the doctor. She listened with the interest women take in anything weird, and with a compassion for him which she did not conceal so perfectly but that he saw it. At the end he said: "You may wonder that I come to you with all this, which must sound like the ravings of a madman."

"No—no," she hesitated.

"I came because I wished you to know everything about me before—before—I wouldn't have come, you'll believe me, if I hadn't had the doctor's assurance that my trouble was merely a part of my being physically out of kilter, and had nothing to do with my sanity—Good Heavens! What am I saying? But the thought has tormented me so! And in the midst of it I've allowed myself to—Mrs. Yarrow, I love you. Don't you know that?"

Alford may have had a divided mind in this declaration, but after that one word Mrs. Yarrow had no mind for anything else. He went on.

"I'm not only sick—so sick that I sha'n't be able to do any work for a year at least—but I'm poor, so poor that I can't afford to be sick."

She lifted her eyes and looked at him, where he sat oddly aloof from those possessions of hers, to which she seemed so little related, and said, with a smile quivering at the corners of her pretty mouth, "I don't see what that has to do with it."

"What do you mean?" He stared at her hard.

"Am I in duplicate or triplicate, this time?"

"No, you're only one, and there's none like you! I could never see any one else when I looked at you!" he cried, only half aware of his poetry, and meaning what he said very literally.

But she only took the poetry. "I shouldn't wish you to," she said, and she laughed.

He could not believe yet in his good-fortune. His countenance fell. "I'm afraid I don't understand, or that you don't. It doesn't seem as if I could get to the end of my unworthiness, which isn't voluntary. It seems altogether too base. I can't let you say what you do, if you mean it, till you know that I come to you in despair as well as in love. You saved me from the fear I was in, again and again, and I believe that without you I shall—Ah, it seems very base! But the doctor—If I could always tell some one—if I could tell *you* when these things were obsessing me—haunting me—they would cease—"

Mrs. Yarrow rose, with rather a piteous smile. "Then, I am a prescription!" She hoped, woman-like, that she was solely a passion: but is any woman worth having, ever solely a passion?

"Don't!" Alford implored, rising too. "Don't, in mercy, take it that way! It's only that I wish you to know everything that's in me; to know how utterly helpless and worthless I am. You needn't have a pang in throwing such a thing away."

She put out her hand to him, but at arm's-length. "I sha'n't throw you away—at least, not to-night. I want to think." It was a way of saying she wished him to go, and he had no desire to stay. He asked if he might come again, and she said, "Oh yes."

"To-morrow?"

"Not to-morrow, perhaps. When I send. Was it *young* Dr. Enderby?"

They had rather a sad, dry parting; and when her door closed upon him he felt that it had shut him out forever. His shame and his defeat were so great that he did not think of his eidolons, and they did not come to trouble him. He woke in the morning, asking himself, bitterly, if he were cured already. His humiliation was such that he closed his eyes to the light, and wished he might never again open them to it.

The question that Mrs. Yarrow had to ask Dr. Enderby was not the question he had instantly forecast for her when she put aside her veil in his office and told him who she was. She did not seem anxious to be assured about Alford's mental condition, or as to any risks in marrying him. Her inquiry was much more psychological; it was almost impersonal, and yet Dr. Enderby thought she looked as if she had been crying.

She had a difficulty in formulating her question, and when it came it was almost a speculation.

"Women," she said, a little hoarsely, "have no right, I suppose, to expect the ideal in life. The best they can do seems to be to make the real look like it."

Dr. Enderby reflected. "Well, yes. But I don't know that I ever put it to myself in just those terms."

Then she remarked, as if that were the next thing: "You've known Mr. Alford a long time."

"We were at school together, and we shared the same rooms at Harvard."

"He is very sincere," she added, as if this were relevant.

"He's a man who likes to have a little worse than the worst known about him. One might say he was excessively sincere." Enderby divined that Alford had been bungling the matter, and he was willing to help him out, if he could.

Mrs. Yarrow fixed dimly beautiful eyes upon him. "I don't know," she said, "why it wouldn't be ideal—as much ideal as anything—to give one's self absolutely to—to—a duty—or not duty, exactly; I don't mean that. Especially," she added, showing a light through the mist, "if one wanted to do it."

Then he knew she had made up her mind, and though on some accounts he would have liked to laugh with her, on other accounts he felt that he owed it to her to be serious.

"If women could not fulfil the ideal in that way—if they did not constantly do it—there would be no marriages for love."

"Do you think so?" she asked, with a shaking voice. "But men—men are ideal, too."

"Not as women are—except now and then some fool like Alford." Now, indeed, he laughed, and he began to praise Alford from his heart, so delicately, so tenderly, so reverently, that Mrs. Yarrow laughed too before he was done, and cried a little, and when she rose to leave she could not speak; but clung to his hand, on turning away, and so flung it from behind her with a gesture that Enderby thought pretty.

At this point, Wanhope stopped as if that were the end.

"And did she let Alford come to see her again?" Rulledge, at once romantic and literal, demanded.

"Oh yes. At any rate, they were married that fall. They are—I believe he's pursuing his archaeological studies there—living in Athens."

"Together?" Minver smoothly inquired.

At this expression of cynicism Rulledge gave him a look that would have incinerated another. Wanhope went out with Minver, and then, after a moment's daze, Rulledge exclaimed: "Jove! I forgot to ask him whether it's stopped Alford's illusions!"

A Memory That
Worked Overtime

1907

A MEMORY THAT WORKED OVERTIME" was the seventh of Howells's
nine Turkish Room stories (see above pp. 122–24 for a fuller discussion of these stories). It first appeared in *Harper's Monthly* in
August 1907, and was reprinted later that year in *Between the Dark and the
Daylight*. While it is not actually set in the Turkish Room, it resembles the
other stories in that it is told at secondhand by Acton and is based on an incident of psychological interest. If "A Memory" is a slight piece, it is nonethe-
less significant in that it demonstrates Howells's interest in the mechanics of
thought and memory; and it may reveal his awareness of the subtle and mysterious link between the creative imagination and the unconscious.

Much has been made of Howells's claim, in *Years of My Youth* (1916), that
"No man, unless he puts on the mask of fiction, can show his real face or the
will behind it. For this reason the only real biographies are the novels, and
every novel if it is honest will be the autobiography of the author" (110). John
Crowley, who uses Howells's statement as the starting point for many of his
critical inquiries, explicates these words by recalling Howells's statement
that in his youth he "learnt to practise a psychological juggle; I came to deal

with my own state of mind as another would deal with it, and to combat my fears as if they were alien" (*YY* 81). Howells practised his "juggle," Crowley points out, by writing; fictional creation—the act of telling a story—could be for Howells an act of coming to terms with his past and of understanding the present. Crowley further notes that Howells, "unlike his circus counterpart, did not permit the right hand to know what the left hand was doing." Instead, he "was given to splitting off conscious control from unconscious inspiration," which led to "unwonted eruptions of unconscious material . . . not assimilated into the conscious design of the fiction" (*Mask* 9). This phenomenon —the "eruption" of unintended material into fiction—is akin to what happens in "A Memory." The process of telling a story is distorted by "unconscious inspiration," and the more that the story is viewed by the teller *as* a story, the stronger the distortion becomes. Minver's brother testifies to this phenomenon, noting that after four tellings (to the stationmaster, General Filbert, the man at the stables, and his fiancée), "I had got my story pretty glib. . . . I was so letter-perfect that I had a vision of the whole thing, especially of my talking with the general while I kept my hand on the picture." (Crowley is quick to note that his theories represent one end of a spectrum of opinion about Howells's degree of control over his material—*Mask* 10–11. Crowley's "revisionist" views, like those of George Carrington, Kermit Vanderbilt, and Kenneth Lynn, stress Howells's neuroticism and the intensity of his inner conflicts; while the "revivalist" position, represented by Everett Carter, George Bennett, and Don L. Cook, among others, focuses on Howells's imaginative control and his solid realism.)

Crowley argues that Howells eventually became aware of the peculiar mechanics of his muse, and if this is true, then "A Memory" may testify to his understanding of the ways in which the unconscious may usurp fictional creations and recast memories. At the same time, the story may involve a gentle self-satire. Both the story's title and its concluding line deflate the philosophical speculations of Acton and Mrs. Minver, and also of the overly zealous reader who may exaggerate the seriousness of Howells's intention.

"A Memory" is clearly an examination of the psychological, rather than the psychic,[1] and as such it can be contrasted with "A Presentiment" (see p. 257), which followed it by only four months. Acton's coining of the phrase "inverted presentiment" to describe Minver's brother's experience not only looks forward to this story, but in a way recalls "The Eidolons of Brooks Alford," the account of a man haunted by "presentiments" of the past.

Notes

1. Cady overgeneralizes when he uses both "The Eidolons of Brooks Alford" and "The Memory that Worked Overtime" [*sic*] as examples of psychic, rather than psychological, stories (*Road* 243).

₡

A Memory That Worked Overtime

Minver's brother took down from the top of the low bookshelf a small painting on panel, which he first studied in the obverse, and then turned and contemplated on the back with the same dreamy smile. "I don't see how that got *here*," he said, absently.

"Well," Minver returned, "you don't expect *me* to tell you, except on the principle that any one would naturally know more about anything of yours than you would." He took it from his brother and looked at the front of it. "It isn't bad. It's pretty good!" He turned it round. "Why, it's one of old Blakey's! How did *you* come by it?"

"Stole it, probably," Minver's brother said, still thoughtfully. Then with an effect of recollecting: "No, come to think of it," he added, "Blakey gave it to me." The Minvers played these little comedies together, quite as much to satisfy their tenderness for each other as to give their friends pleasure. "Think you're the only painter that gets me to take his truck as a gift? He gave it to me, let's see, about ten years ago, when he was trying to make a die of it, and failed; I thought he would succeed. But it's been in my wife's room nearly ever since, and what I can't understand is what she's doing with it down here."

"Probably to make trouble for you, somehow," Minver suggested.

"No, I don't think it's *that*, quite," his brother returned, with a false air of scrupulosity, which was part of their game with each other. He looked some more at the picture, and then he glanced from it at me. "There's a very curious story connected with that sketch."

"Oh, well, tell it," Minver said. "Tell it! I suppose I can stand it again. Acton's never heard it, I believe. But you needn't make a show of sparing him. I *couldn't* stand that."

"I certainly haven't heard the story," I said, "and if I had I would be too polite to own it."

Minver's brother looked towards the open door over his shoulder, and Minver interpreted for him: "She's not coming. I'll give you due warning."

"It was before we were married, but not much before, and the picture was a sort of wedding present for my wife, though Blakey made a show of giving it to me. Said he had painted it for me, because he had a prophetic soul, and felt in his bones that I was going to want a picture of the place where I first met her. You see, it's the little villa her mother had taken that winter on the Viale Petrarca, just outside of Florence. It *was* the first place I met her, but not the last."

"Don't be obvious," Minver ordered.

His brother did not mind him. "I thought it was mighty nice of Blakey. He was barking away, all the time he was talking, and when he wasn't coughing he was so hoarse he could hardly speak above a whisper; but he kept talking on, and wishing me happy, and fending off my gratitude, while he was finding a piece of manila paper to wrap the sketch in, and then hunting for a piece of string to tie it. When he handed it to me at last, he gasped out: 'I don't mind her knowing that I partly meant it as the place where *she* first met *you*, too. I'm not ashamed of it as a bit of color. Anyway, I sha'n't live to do anything better.'

"'Oh, yes, you will,' I came back in that lying way we think is kind with dying people. I suppose it is; anyway, it turned out all right with Blakey, as he'll testify if you look him up when you go to Florence. By the way, he lives in that villa *now*."

"No?" I said. "How charming!"

Minver's brother went on: "I made up my mind to be awfully careful of that picture, and not let it out of my hand till I left it with 'her' mother, to be put among the other wedding presents that were accumulating at their house in Exeter Street. So I held it on my lap going in by train from Lexington, where Blakey lived, and when I got out at the old Lowell depot—North Station, now—and got into the little tinkle-tankle horse-car that took me up to where I was to get the Back Bay car—Those were the prehistoric times before trolleys, and there were odds in horse-cars.* We considered the blue-painted Back Bay cars very swell. *You* remember them?" he asked Minver.

---

* Horse-cars were railroad cars or streetcars drawn by horses, while trolleys were electric cars attached to an overhead wire.

"Not when I can help it," Minver answered. "When I broke with Boston, and went to New York, I burnt my horse-cars behind me, and never wanted to know what they looked like, one from another."

"Well, as I was saying," Minver's brother went on, without regarding his impatriotism, "when I got into the horse-car at the depot, I rushed for a corner seat, and I put the picture, with its face next the car-end, between me and the wall, and kept my hand on it; and when I changed to the Back Bay car, I did the same thing. There was a florist's just there, and I couldn't resist some Mayflowers in the window; I was in that condition, you know, when flowers seemed to be made for her, and I had to take her own to her wherever I found them. I put the bunch between my knees, and kept one hand on it, while I kept my other hand on the picture at my side. I was feeling first-rate, and when General Filbert got in after we started, and stood before me hanging by a strap and talking down to me, I had the decency to propose giving him my seat, as he was about ten years older."

"Sure?" Minver asked.

"Well, say fifteen. I don't pretend to be a chicken, and never did. But he wouldn't hear of it. Said I had a bundle, and winked at the bunch of Mayflowers. We had such a jolly talk that I let the car carry me a block by and had to get out at Gloucester and run back to Exeter. I rang, and, when the maid came to the door, there I stood with nothing but the Mayflowers in my hand."

"Good *coup de théâtre*," Minver jeered. "Curtain?"

His brother disdained reply, or was too much absorbed in his tale to think of any. "When the girl opened the door and I discovered my fix I burst out, 'Good Lord!' and I stuck the bunch of flowers at her, and turned and ran. I suppose I must have had some notion of overtaking the car with my picture in it. But the best I could do was to let the next one overtake me several blocks down Marlborough Street, and carry me to the little jumping-off station on Westchester Park, as we used to call it in those days, at the end of the Back Bay line.

"As I pushed into the railroad office, I bet myself that the picture would not be there, and, sure enough, I won."

"You were always a lucky dog," Minver said.

"But the man in charge was very encouraging, and said it was sure to be turned in; and he asked me what time the car had passed the corner of Gloucester Street. I happened to know, and then he said, Oh yes, that conductor was a substitute, and he wouldn't be on again till morning; then he would be certain to bring the picture with him. I was not to worry, for it would be all right. Nothing left in the Back Bay cars was ever lost; the character of the abutters* was guarantee for that, and they were practically the only passengers. The conductors and the drivers were as honest as the passengers, and I could consider myself in the hands of friends.

"He was so reassuring that I went away smiling at my fears, and promising to be round bright and early, as soon, the official suggested—the morrow being Sunday—as soon as the men and horses had had their baked beans.

"Still, after dinner, I had a lurking anxiety, which I turned into a friendly impulse to go and call on Mrs. Filbert, whom I really owed a bread-and-butter visit, and who, I knew, would not mind my coming in the evening. The general, she said, had been telling her about our pleasant chat in the car, and would be glad to smoke his after-dinner cigar with me, and why wouldn't I come into the library?

"We were so very jolly together, all three, that I made light of my misadventure about the picture. The general inquired about the flowers first. He remembered the flowers perfectly, and hoped they were acceptable; he thought he remembered the picture, too, now I mentioned it; but he would not have noticed it so much, there by my side, with my hand on it. I would be sure to get it. He gave several instances, personal to him and his friends, of recoveries of lost articles; it was really astonishing how careful the horse-car people were, especially on the Back Bay line. I would find my picture all right at the Westchester Park station in the morning; never fear.

"I feared so little that I slept well, and even overslept; and I went to get my picture quite confidently, and I could hardly believe it had not been turned in yet, though the station-master told me so. The substitute conductor had not seen it, but more than likely it was at the stables, where the cleaners would have found it in the car and turned it in. He was as robustly cheerful about it as ever, and offered to send an inquiry by the next car; but I said, Why shouldn't I go myself; and he said that was a good idea. So I went, and it was well I did, for my picture was not there, and I had saved time by going. It was not there, but the head man said I need not worry a mite about it; I was certain to get it sooner or later; it would be turned in, to a dead certainty. We became rather confidential, and I went so far as to explain about wanting to make my inquiries very quietly on Blakey's account: he would be annoyed if he heard of its loss, and it might react unfavorably on his health.

"The head man said that was so; and he would tell me what I wanted to do:

---

* According to *Webster's*, "the owners of a contiguous property (the abutters on a street)," i.e., the neighborhood shopowners.

I wanted to go to the Company's General Offices in Milk Street, and tell them about it. That was where everything went as a last resort, and he would bet any money that I would see my picture there the first thing I got inside the door. I thanked him with the fervor I thought he merited, and said I would go at once.

"'Well,' he said, 'you don't want to go to-day, you know. The offices are not open Sunday. And tomorrow's a holiday. But you're all right. You'll find your picture there, don't you have any doubts about it.'

"That was my next to last Sunday supper with my wife, before she became my wife, at her mother's house, and I went to the feast with as little gayety as I suppose any young man ever carried to a supper of the kind. I was told, afterwards, that my behavior up to a certain point was so suggestive either of secret crime or of secret regret, that the only question was whether they should have in the police or I should be given back my engagement ring and advised to go. Luckily I ceased to bear my anguish just in time.

"The fact is, I could not stand it any longer, and as soon as I was alone with her I made a clean breast of it; partially clean, that is: I suppose a fellow never tells *all* to a girl, if he truly loves her." Minver's brother glanced round at us and gathered the harvest of our approving smiles. "I said to her, 'I've been having a wedding present.' 'Well,' she said, 'you've come as near having no use for a wedding present as anybody *I* know. Was having a wedding present what made you so gloomy at supper? Who gave it to you, anyway?' 'Old Blakey.' 'A painting?' 'Yes—a sketch.' 'What of?' This was where I qualified. I said: 'Oh, just one of those Sorrento things of his.' You see, if I told her that it was the villa where we first met, and then said I had left it in the horse-car, she would take it as proof positive that I did not really care anything about her or I never could have forgotten it."

"You were wise as far as you went," Minver said. "Go on."

"Well, I told her the whole story circumstantially: how I had kept the sketch religiously in my lap in the train, and then held it down with my hand all the while beside me in the first horse-car, and did the same thing in the Back Bay car I changed to; and felt of it the whole time I was talking with General Filbert, and then left it there when I got out to leave the flowers at her door, when the awful fact came over me like a flash. 'Yes,' she said, 'Norah said you poked the flowers at her without a word, and she had to guess they were for me.'

"I had got my story pretty glib by this time; I had reeled it off with increasing particulars to the Westchester Park station-master, and the head man at the stables, and General Filbert, and I was so letter-perfect that I had a vision of the whole thing, especially of my talking with the general while I kept my hand on the picture—and then all was dark.

"At the end she said we must advertise for the picture. I said it would kill Blakey if he saw it; and she said: No matter, *let* it kill him; it would show him that we valued his gift, and were moving heaven and earth to find it; and, at any rate, it would kill *me* if I kept myself in suspense. I said I should not care for that; but with her sympathy I guessed I could live through the night, and I was sure I should find the thing at the Milk Street office in the morning.

"'Why,' said she, 'to-morrow it'll be shut!' and then I really didn't know what to say, and I agreed to drawing up an advertisement then and there, so as not to lose an instant's time after I had been at the Milk Street office on Tuesday and found the picture had not been turned in. She said I could dictate the advertisement and she would write it down, and she asked: 'Which one of his Sorrento things was it? You must describe it exactly, you know.' That made me feel awfully, and I said I was not going to have my next-to-last Sunday evening with her spoiled by writing advertisements; and I got away, somehow, with all sorts of comforting reassurances from her. I could see that she was feigning them to encourage me.

"The next morning, I simply could not keep away from the Milk Street office, and my unreasonable impatience was rewarded by finding it at least ajar, if not open. There was the nicest kind of a young fellow there, and he said he was not officially present; but what could he do for me? Then I told him the whole story, with details I had not thought of before; and he was just as enthusiastic about my getting my picture as the Westchester Park station-master or the head man of the stables. It was morally certain to be turned in, the first thing in the morning; but he would take a description of it, and send out inquiries to all the conductors and drivers and car-cleaners, and make a special thing of it. He entered into the spirit of the affair, and I felt that I had such a friend in him that I confided a little more and hinted at the double interest I had in the picture. I didn't pretend that it was one of Blakey's Sorrento things, but I gave him a full and true description of it, with its length, breadth, and thickness, in exact measure."

Here Minver's brother stopped and lost himself in contemplation of the sketch, as he held it at arm's-length.

"Well, did you get your picture?" I prompted, after a moment.

"Oh, yes," he said, with a quick turn towards me. "This is it. A District Messenger brought it round the first thing Tuesday morning. He brought it," Minver's brother added, with a certain effectiveness, "from the florist's, where I had stopped to get those Mayflowers. I had left it there."

"You've told it very well, this time, Joe," Minver said. "But Acton here is waiting for the psychology. Poor old Wanhope ought to be here," he added to me. He looked about for a match to light his pipe, and his brother jerked his head in the direction of the chimney.

"Box on the mantel. Yes," he sighed, "that was really something very curious. You see, I had invented the whole history of the case from the time I got into the Back Bay car with my flowers. Absolutely nothing happened of all I had remembered till I got out of the car. I did not put the picture beside me at the end of the car; I did not keep my hand on it while I talked with General Filbert; I did not leave it behind me when I left the car. Nothing of the kind happened. I had already left it at the florist's, and the whole passage of experience which was so vividly and circumstantially stamped in my memory that I related it four or five times over, and would have made oath to every detail of it, was pure invention, or, rather, it was something less positive: the reflex of the first half of my horse-car experience, when I really did put the picture in the corner next me, and did keep my hand on it."

"Very strange," I was beginning, but just then the door opened and Mrs. Minver came in, and I was presented.

She gave me a distracted hand, as she said to her husband: "Have you been telling the story about that picture again?" He was still holding it. "Silly!"

She was a mighty pretty woman, but full of vim and fun and sense.

"It's one of the most curious freaks of memory I ever heard of, Mrs. Minver," I said.

Then she showed that she was proud of it, though she had called him silly. "Have you told," she demanded of her husband, "how oddly your memory behaved about the subject of the picture, too?"

"I have again eaten that particular piece of humble-pie," Minver's brother replied.

"Well," she said to me, "*I* think he was simply so possessed with the awfulness of having lost the picture that all the rest took place prophetically, but unconsciously."

"By a species of inverted presentiment?" I suggested.

"Yes," she assented, slowly, as if the formulation were new to her, but not unacceptable. "Something of the kind. I never heard of anyone else having it."

Minver had got his pipe alight, and was enjoying it. "*I* think Joe was simply off his nut, for the time being."

The Critical Bookstore

1913

"HE CRITICAL BOOKSTORE" first appeared in *Harper's Monthly* in August, 1913, and was reprinted three years later in *The Daughter of the Storage*, Howells's last collection of "Things in Prose and Verse." Except for brief contemporary notices (Eichelberger 292–94) and two quick comments by Edward Wagenknecht, one on Margaret Green's habitually open mouth (74, 79), the story has been largely ignored since its publication. The exception is an analysis by Lewis P. Simpson, who, in "The Treason of William Dean Howells," uses "The Critical Bookstore" to help bolster his contention that Howells's literary emancipation from New England came at the expense of admired Bostonian ideals; that Howells, in fact, consciously betrayed the ideal of the literary life for the realities of commercial America. The lack of greater attention to the story is regrettable, as it reflects, more than any other fictional work by Howells, his career as an editor and a literary businessman; and the issues that it raises and treats lightly and comically are still relevant today.

"The Critical Bookstore," as Simpson points out, is a fictional treatment of issues that Howells addressed at length in his nonfiction. For example, in "The Man of Letters as a Man of Business" (1893) and, to a lesser extent, in "The Art of the Adsmith" (1896), both republished in *Literature and Life* (1902), Howells examined the regrettable connection between art and moneymaking—in his words, "the dishonor which money-purchase does to art" ("Man of Letters" 3). His countless book reviews and his essays on the possibilities and responsibilities of literature are further testimony to his concern with the frequent rift between the ideals of literary art and the weaknesses of popular taste. These issues, of course, were not merely theoretical for Howells. As editor-in-chief of the *Atlantic Monthly* from 1871 to 1881, as contributor, advisor, and editor for the House of Harper from 1886 onwards, and as co-editor, briefly, of *Cosmopolitan* in 1892, Howells was called upon to balance his sense of the worthy with his instinct for the marketable. "The Critical Bookstore"'s Frederick Erlcort is of course a bookseller, rather than an editor, but in his efforts to direct and educate the tastes of the reading public, he stands in for Howells, or for any literary journalist. The problems he faces —the unpleasantness of rejecting authors and of disagreeing with critics, the public's appetite for the new and disdain for the old, its prudishness and conformity, and the not infrequent contradiction between commercial and artistic success—mirror those of Howells's own career. Erlcort's eventual decision that "literature is the whole world" is admirable, but in making it, he abandons altogether the role of editor and suggests that judgments about literature are, if not impossible, undesirable. In this way Erlcort anticipates some of the tenets of current literary theory.

"The Critical Bookstore" reveals Howells's understanding of the business of literature in other ways as well. Erlcort's regard for women readers, his respect for literary reviews, and his defense of the "frightful episode" all reflect positions held by Howells. Erlcort's awareness of the manipulations of advertising and of merchandising (Margaret Green's "immoral" mirrors, for example) reveal Howells's shrewdness. Howells's parodic presentation of the mentality of the best-selling novelist—the episode of the eggbeater—seems especially accurate. But the story is a romance as well as a business story, and as such it enters some new territory as well. While Margaret Green, the plain and intense "elderly girl," is reminiscent of Penelope Lapham in being smart rather than pretty, she stands out as one of the most independent and mature of Howells's heroines. (Frederick Erlcort and Margaret Green reappeared in 1916 in "The Rotational Tenants.")

"The Critical Bookstore," like *A Hazard of New Fortunes*, is a story of New York; it is as specific about its New York locations as "The Memory That Worked Overtime" or *The Rise of Silas Lapham*, for example, are about those of Boston. Finally, the story, like so much of Howells's work, reflects contemporary details—but in the case of "The Critical Bookstore," the details are surprisingly familiar. The story abounds with references to the conveniences and paraphernalia of the "modern" city—from the department store to the "electric runabout." The reader who associates Howells primarily with the 1880s will be pleased to find in "The Critical Bookstore" a writer fully at home in the twentieth century.

ℰ

The Critical Bookstore

It had long been the notion of Frederick Erlcort, who held it playfully, held it seriously, according to the company he was in, that there might be a censorship of taste and conscience in literary matters strictly affiliated with the retail commerce in books. When he first began to propose it, playfully, seriously, as his listener chose, he said that he had noticed how in the great department stores where nearly everything to supply human need was sold, the shopmen and shopwomen seemed instructed by the ownership or the management to deal in absolute good faith with the customers, and not to misrepresent the quality, the make, or the material of any article in the slightest degree. A thing was not to be called silk or wool when it was partly cotton; it was not to be said that it would wash when it would not wash, or that the color would not come off when it would come off, or that the stuff was English or French when it was American.

When Erlcort once noted his interest in the fact to a floor-walker whom he happened to find at leisure, the floor-walker said, Yes, that was so; and the house did it because it was business, good business, the only good business. He was instantly enthusiastic, and he said that just in the same way, as an extension of its good faith with the public, the house had established the rule of taking back any article which a customer did not like, or did not find what she had supposed when she got it home, and refunding the money. This was the best sort of business; it held custom; the woman became a customer for life. The floor-walker laughed, and after he had told an anxious applicant, "Second aisle to the left, lady; three counters back," he concluded to Elcort, "I say *she* because a man never brings a thing back when he's made a mistake; but a woman can always blame it on the house. That so?"

Erlcort laughed with him, and in going out he stopped at the book-counter. Rather it was a bookstore, and no small one, with ranks of new books covering the large tables and mounting to their level from the floor, neatly piled, and with shelves of complete editions and soberer-looking volumes stretching along the wall as high as the ceiling. "Do you happen to have a good book—a book that would read good, I mean—in your stock here?" he asked the neat blonde behind the literary barricade.

"Well, here's a book that a good many are reading," she answered, with prompt interest and a smile that told in the book's favor; it was a protectingly filial and guardedly ladylike smile.

"Yes, but is it a book worth reading—worth the money?"

"Well, I don't know as I'm a judge," the kind little blonde replied. She added, daringly, "All I can say is, I set up till two last night to finish it."

"And you advise me to buy it?"

"Well, we're not allowed to do that, exactly. I can only tell you what I know."

"But if I take it, and it isn't what I expected, I can return it and get my money back?"

"That's something I never was asked before. Mr. Jeffers! Mr. Jeffers!" she called to a floor-walker passing near; and when he stopped and came up to the counter, she put the case to him.

He took the book from Elcort's hand and examined the outside of it curiously if not critically. Then he looked from it to Elcort and said, "Oh, how do you do again! Well, no, sir; I don't know as we could do that. You see, you would have to read it to find out that you didn't want it, and that would be like using or wearing an article, wouldn't it? We couldn't take back a thing that had been used or worn—heigh?"

"But you might have some means of knowing whether a book is good or not?"

"Well, yes, we might. That's a point we have never had raised before. Miss Prittiman, haven't we any means of knowing whether a book's something we can guarantee or not?"

"Well, Mr. Jeffers, there's the publisher's advertisement."

"Why, yes, so there is! And a respectable publisher wouldn't indorse a book that wasn't the genuine article, would he now, sir?"

"He mightn't," Erlcort said, as if he felt the force of the argument.

"And there are the notices in the newspapers. They ought to tell," Miss Prittiman added, more convincingly. "I don't know," she said, as from a sensitive conscience, "whether there have been any about this book yet, but I should think there would be."

"And in the mean time, as you wouldn't guarantee the book so that I can bring it back and get my money if I find it worthless, I must accept the publisher's word?" Erlcort pressed further.

"I should think you could do that," the floor-walker suggested, with the appearance of being tired.

"Well, I think I will, for once," Erlcort relented. "But wait! What does the publisher say?"

"It's all printed on this slip inside," the blonde said, and she showed it as she took the book from him. "Shall I send it? Or will you—"

"No, no, thank you, I'll take it with me. Let me—"

He kept the printed slip and began to read it. The blonde wrapped the book up and laid it with a half-dollar in change on the counter before Erlcort. The floor-walker went away; Erlcort heard him saying, "No, madam; toys on the fifth floor, at the extreme rear, left," while he lost himself in the glowing promises of the publisher. It appeared that the book he had just bought was by a perfectly new author, an old lady of seventy who had never written a novel before, and might therefore be trusted for an entire freshness of thought and feeling. The plot was of a gripping intensity; the characters were painted with large, bold strokes, and were of an unexampled virility; the story was packed with passion from cover to cover; and the reader would be held breathless by the author's skill in working from the tragic conditions to an all-round happy conclusion.

From time to time Erlcort heard the gentle blonde saying such things as, "Oh yes; it's the best-seller, all right," and, "All I can say is I set up till two o'clock in the morning to finish it," and, "Yes ma'am; it's by a new writer; a very old lady of seventy who is just beginning to write; well, that's what I *heard*."

On his way up-town in the Subway he clung to the wonted strap, unsupported by anything in the romance which he had bought; and yet he could not take the book back and get his money, or even exchange it for some article of neckwear or footwear. In his extremity he thought he would try giving it to the trainman just before he reached his stop.

"You want to *give* it to me? Well, that's something that never happened to me on *this* line before. I guess my wife will like it. I—*1009th Street! [sic] Change for East Brooklyn and the Bronx!*" the guard shouted, and he let Erlcort out of the car, the very first of the tide that spilled itself forth at the station. He called after him, "Do as much for you sometime."

The incident first amused Erlcort, and then it began to trouble him; but he appeased his remorse by toying with his old notion of a critical bookstore. His mind was still at play with it when he stopped at the bell-pull of an elderly girl of his acquaintance who had a studio ten stories above, and the habit of giving him afternoon tea in it if he called there about five o'clock. She had her ugly painting-apron still on, and her thumb through the hole in her palette, when she opened her door to him.

"Too soon?" he asked.

She answered as well as she could with the brush held horizontally in her mouth while she glared inhospitably at him. "Well, not much," and then she let him in, and went and lighted her spirit-lamp.

He began at once to tell her of his strange experience, and went on till she said: "Well, there's your tea. *I* don't know what you've been driving at, but I suppose you do. Is it the old thing?"

"It's my critical bookstore, if that's what you call the old thing."

"Oh! *That!* I thought it had failed 'way back in the dark ages."

"The dark ages are not *back*, please; they're all 'round, and you know very well that my critical bookstore has never been tried yet. But tell me one thing: should you wish to live with a picture, even for a few hours, which had been painted by an old lady of seventy who had never tried to paint before?"

"If I intended to go crazy, yes. What has all that got to do with it?"

"That's the joint commendation of the publisher and the kind little blonde who united to sell me the book I just gave to that poor Subway trainman. Do you ever buy a new book?"

"No; I always borrow an old one."

"But if you *had* to buy a new one, wouldn't you like to know of a place where you could be sure of getting a good one?"

"I shouldn't mind. Or, yes, I should, rather. Where's it to be?"

"Oh, I know. I've had my eye on the place for a good while. It's a funny old place in Sixth Avenue—"

"Sixth *Avenue!*"

"Don't interrupt—where the dearest old codger in the world is just going out of the house furnishing business in a small way. It's kept getting smaller and smaller—I've watched it shrink—till now it can't stand up against the big shops, and the old codger told me the other day that it was no use."

"Poor fellow!"

"No. He's not badly off, and he's going back up-state where he came from about forty years ago, and he can live—or die—very well on what he's put by. I've known him rather a good while, and we've been friends ever since we've been acquainted."

"Go on," the elderly girl said.

Erlcort was not stopping, but she spoke so as to close her mouth, which she was apt to let hang open in a way that she did not like; she had her intimates pledged to tell her when she was doing it, but she could not make a man promise, and she had to look after her mouth herself with Erlcort. It was not a bad mouth; her eyes were large, and it was merely large to match them.

"When shall you begin—open shop?" she asked.

"My old codger's lease expires in the fall," he answered, "but he would be glad to have me take it off his hands this spring. I could give the summer to changing and decorating, and begin my campaign in the fall—the first of October, say. Wouldn't you like to come some day and see the old place?"

"I should love it. But you're not supposing that I shall be of the least use, I hope? I'm not decorational, you know. Easel pictures, and small ones at that."

"Of course. But you are a woman, and have ideas of the cozy. I mean that the place shall be made attractive."

"Do you think the situation will be—on Sixth Avenue?"

"It will be quaint. It's in a retarded region of low buildings, with a carpenter's shop two doors off. The L roars overhead and the surface cars squeal before, but that is New York, you know, and it's very central. Besides, at the back of the shop, with the front door shut, it is very quiet."

The next day the friends lunched together at an Italian restaurant very near the place, and rather hurried themselves away to the old codger's store.

"He *is* a dear," Margaret whispered to Erlcort in following him about to see the advantages of the place.

"Oh, mine's setting-hen's time," he justified his hospitality in finally asking them to take seats on a nail-keg apiece. "You mustn't think you're interruptin'. Look 'round all ye want to, or set down and rest ye."

"That would be a good motto for your book-store," she screamed to Erlcort, when they got out into the roar of the avenue. "'Look 'round all ye want to, or set down and rest ye.' Wasn't he sweet? And I don't wonder you're taken with the place: it *has* such capabilities. You might as well begin imagining how you will arrange it."

They were walking involuntarily up the avenue, and when they came to the Park they went into it, and in the excitement of their planning they went as far as the Ramble, where they sat down on a bench and disappointed some squirrels who supposed they had brought peanuts with them.

They decided that the front of the shop should be elaborately simple; perhaps the door should be painted black, with a small-paned sash and a heavy brass latch. On each side should be a small-paned show-window, with books laid inside on an inclined shelving; on the door should be a modest bronze plate, reading, "The Critical Bookstore." They rejected *shop* as an affectation, and they hooted the notion of "Ye Critical Bookstore" as altogether loathsome. The door and window would be in a rather belated taste, but the beautiful is never out of date, and black paint and small panes might be found rococo in their old-fashionedness now. There should be a fireplace, or perhaps a Franklin stove, at the rear of the room, with a high-shouldered, small-paned sash on each side letting in the light from the yard of the carpenter-shop. On the chimneypiece should be lettered, "Look 'round all ye want to, or set down and rest ye."

The genius of the place should be a refined hospitality, such as the gentle old codger had practised with them, and to facilitate this there should be a pair of high-backed settles, one under each window. The book-counter should stretch the whole length of the store, and at intervals beside it, against the book-shelving, should be set old-fashioned chairs, but not too old-fashioned. Against the lower book-shelves on a deeper shelf might be stood against the books a few sketches in water-color, or even oil.

This was Margaret Green's idea.

"And would you guarantee the quality?" Erlcort asked.

"Perhaps they wouldn't be for sale; though if any one insisted—"

"I see. Well, pass the sketches. What else?"

"Well, a few little figures in plaster, or even marble or bronze, very Greek, or very American; things in low relief."

"Pass the little figures and low reliefs. But don't forget it's a *bookstore*."

"Oh, I won't. The sketches of all kinds would be strictly subordinated to the books. If I had a tea-room handy here, with a table and the backs of some menus to draw on, I could show you just how it would look."

"What's the matter with the Casino?"

"Nothing; only it's rather early for tea yet."

"It isn't for soda-lemonade."

She set him the example of instantly rising, and led the way back along the lake to the Casino, resting at that afternoon hour among its spring flowers and blossoms innocent of its lurid afterdark frequentation. He got some paper from the waiter who came to take their order. She began to draw rapidly, and by the time the waiter came again she was giving Erlcort the last scrap of paper.

"Well," he said, "I had no idea that I had imagined anything so charming!

If this critical bookstore doesn't succeed, it'll be because there are no critics. But what—what are these little things hung against the partitions of the shelves?"

"Oh—mirrors. Little round ones."

"But why mirrors of any shape?"

"Nothing; only people like to see themselves in a glass of any shape. And when," Margaret added, in a burst of candor, "a woman looks up and sees herself with a book in her hand, she will feel so intellectual she will never put it down. She will buy it."

"Margaret Green, this is immoral. Strike out those mirrors, or I will smash them every one!"

"Oh, very well!" she said, and she rubbed them out with the top of her pencil. "If you want your place a howling wilderness."

He looked at the ruin her rubber had wrought. "They *were* rather nice. Could—could you rub them in again?"

"Not if I tried a hundred years. Besides, they *were* rather impudent. What time is it?"

"No time at all. It's half-past three."

"Dear me! I must be going. And if you're really going to start that precious critical bookstore in the fall, you must begin work on it right away."

"Work?"

"Reading up for it. If you're going to guarantee the books, you must know what's in them, mustn't you?"

He realized that he must do what she said; he must know from his own knowledge what was in the books he offered for sale, and he began reading, or reading *at*, the new books immediately. He was a good deal occupied by day with the arrangement of his store, though he left it mainly with the lively young decorator who undertook for a lump sum to realize Margaret Green's ideas. It was at night that he did most of his reading in the spring books which the publishers were willing to send him gratis, when they understood he was going to open a bookstore, and only wanted sample copies. As long as she remained in town Margaret Green helped him read, and they talked the books over, and mostly rejected them. By the time she went to Europe in August with another elderly girl they had not chosen more than eight to ten books; but they hoped for better things in the fall.

Word of what he was doing had gone out from Margaret, and a great many women of their rather esthetic circle began writing to him about the books they were reading, and commending them to him or warning him against them. The circle of his volunteer associates enlarged itself in the nature of an endless chain, and before society quite broke up for the summer a Sympathetic Tea was offered to Erlcort by a Leading Society Woman at the Intellectual Club, where he was invited to address the Intellectuals in explanation of his project. This was before Margaret sailed, and he hurried to her in horror.

"Why, of course you must accept. You're not going to hide your Critical Bookstore under a bushel; you can't have too much publicity."

The Leading Society Woman flowed in fulsome gratitude at his acceptance, and promised no one but the club should be there; he had hinted his reluctance. She kept her promise, but among the Intellectuals there was a girl who was a just beginning journalist, and who pumped Erlcort's whole scheme out of him, unsuspicious of what she was doing, till he saw it all, with his picture, in the Sunday Supplement. She rightly judged that the intimacy of an interview would be more popular with her readers than the cold and distant report of his formal address, which she must give, though she received it so ardently with all the other Intellectuals. They flocked flatteringly, almost suffocatingly, around him at the end. His scheme was just what every one had vaguely thought of: something must be done to stem the tide of worthless fiction, which was so often shocking as well as silly, and they would only be too glad to help read for him. They were nearly all just going to sail, but they would each take a spring book on the ship, and write him about it from the other side; they would each get a fall book coming home, and report as soon as they got back.

His scheme was discussed seriously and satirically by the press; it became a joke with many papers, and a byword quickly worn out, so that people thought that it had been dropped. But Erlcort gave his days and nights to preparation for his autumnal campaign. He studied in careful comparison the reviews of the different literary authorities, and was a little surprised to find, when he came to read the books they reviewed, how honest and adequate they often were. He was obliged to own to himself that if people were guided by them, few worthless books would be sold, and he decided that the immense majority of the book-buyers were not guided by the critics. The publishers themselves seemed not so much to blame when he went to see them and explained his wish to deal with them on the basis of a critical bookseller. They said they wished all the booksellers were like him, for they would ask nothing better than to publish only good books. The trouble, they said, lay with the authors; they wrote such worthless books. Or if now and then one of them did write a good book and they were over-tempted to publish it, the public united in refusing to buy it. So he saw? But if the booksellers persisted in selling none but good books, perhaps something might be done. At any rate they would like to see the experiment tried.

Erlcort felt obliged to read the books suggested to him by the endless chain of readers who volunteered to read for him, on both sides of the ocean, or going and coming on the ocean. Mostly the books they praised were abject rubbish, but it took time to find this out, and he formed the habit of reading far into the night, and if he was very much vexed at discovering that the book recommended to him was trash, he could not sleep unless he took veronal, and then he had a ghastly next day.

He did not go out of town except for a few brief sojourns at places where he knew cultivated people were staying, and could give him their opinions of the books they were reading. When the publishers began, as they had agreed, to send him their advance sheets, the stitched but unbound volumes roused so much interest by the novelty of their form that his readers could not give an undivided attention to their contents. He foresaw that in the end he should have to rely upon the taste of mercenaries in his warfare against rubbish, and more and more he found it necessary to expend himself in it, to read at second hand as well as at first. His greatest relief was in returning to town and watching the magical changes which the decorator was working in his store. This was consolation, this was inspiration, but he longed for the return of Margaret Green, that she might help him enjoy the realization of her ideas in the equipment of the place; and he held the decorator to the most slavish obedience through the carpenters and painters who created at his bidding a miraculous interior, all white, or just off-white, such as had never been imagined of a bookstore in New York before. It was actually ready by the end of August, though smelling a little of turpentine still, and Erlcort, letting himself in at the small-paned black door, and ranging up and down the long, beautiful room, and round and round the central book-table, and in and out between the side tables, under the soft, bright shelving of the walls, could hardly wait the arrival of the *Minnedingdong* in which the elderly girl had taken her passage back. One day, ten days ahead of time, she blew in at the front door in a paroxysm of explanation; she had swapped passages home with another girl who wanted to come back later, while she herself wanted to come back earlier. She had no very convincing reason for this as she gave it, but Erlcort did not listen to her reason, whatever it was. He said, between the raptures with the place that she fell in and out of, that now she was just in time for the furnishing, which he never could have dared to undertake alone.

In the gay September weather they visited all the antiquity shops in Fourth

Avenue, and then threw themselves frankly upon reproductions, which they bought in the native wood and ordered painted, the settles and the spindle-backed chairs in the cool gray which she decided was the thing. In the same spirit they bought new brass fire-irons and new shovel and tongs, but all very tall and antique-looking, and then they got those little immoral mirrors, which Margaret Green attached with her own hands to the partitions of the shelving. She also got soft green silk curtains for the chimney windows and for the sash of the front door; even the front windows she curtained, but very low, so that a salesman or saleswoman could easily reach over from the interior and get a book that any customer had seen from the outside.

One day when all this was done, and Erlcort had begun ordering in a stock of such books as he had selected to start with, she said: "You're looking rather peakéd, aren't you?"

"Well, I've been *feeling* rather peakéd, until lately, keeping awake to read and read *after* the volunteer readers."

"You mean you've lost sleep?"

"Something like that."

"Well, you mustn't. How many books do you start with?"

"About twenty-five."

"Good ones? It's a lot, isn't it? I didn't suppose there were so many."

"Well, to fill our shelves I shall have to order about a thousand of each."

"You'll never sell them in the world! You'll be ruined."

"Oh no; the publishers will take them back."

"How nice of them! But that's only what painters have to do when the dealers can't sell their pictures."

A month off, the prospect was brilliant, and when the shelves and tables were filled and the sketches and bas-reliefs were stuck about and the little immoral mirrors were hung, the place was charming. The chairs and settles were all that could be asked; Margaret Green helped put them about; and he let her light the low fire on the hearth of the Franklin stove; he said he should not always burn hickory, but he had got twenty-four sticks for two dollars from an Italian in a cellar near by, and he meant to burn that much. She upbraided him for his extravagance while touching the match to the paper underneath the kindling; but October opened cold, and he needed the fire.

The enterprise seemed rather to mystify the neighborhood, and some old customers of the old codger's came in upon one fictitious errand and another to see about it, and went away without quite making it out. It was a bookstore, all right, they owned in conference, but what did he mean by "critical"?

The first *bona fide* buyer appeared in a girl who could just get her chin on the counter, and who asked for an egg-beater. Erlcort had begun with only one assistant, the young lady who typed his letters and who said she guessed she could help him when she was not working. She leaned over and tried to understand the little girl, and then she called to Erlcort where he stood with his back to the fire and the morning paper open before his face.

"Mr Erlcort, have we got a book called *The Egg-beater?*"

"*The Egg-beater?*" he echoed, letting his paper drop below his face.

"No, no!" the little girl shouted, angrily. "It *ain't* a book. It's a thing to beat eggs with. Mother said to come here and get it."

"Well, she's sent you to the wrong place, little girl. You want to go to a hardware-store," the young lady argued.

"Ain't this No. 1232?"

"Yes."

"Well, this is the *right* place. Mother said to go to 1232. I guess she knows. She's an old customer."

"*The Egg-beater! The Egg-beater!*" the blithe young novelist to whom Erlcort told the story repeated. He was still happy in his original success as a best-seller, and he had come to the Critical Bookstore to spy out the stock and see whether his last novel was in it; but though it was not, he joyously extended an acquaintance with Erlcort which had begun elsewhere. "*The Egg-beater?* What a splendid title for a story of adventure! Keep the secret of its applicability to the last word, or perhaps never reveal it at all, and leave the reader worrying. That's one way; makes him go and talk about the book to all the girls he knows and gets them guessing. Best ad. in the world. *The Egg-beater!* Doesn't it suggest desert islands and penguins' nests in the rocks? Fellow and girl shipwrecked, and girl wants to make an omelette after they've got sick of plain eggs, and can't for want of an egg-beater. Heigh? He invents one—makes it out of some wire that floats off from the wreck. See? When they are rescued, she brings it away, and doesn't let him know it till their Iron Wedding Day. They keep it over his study fireplace always."

This author was the first to stretch his legs before Erlcort's fire from his seat on one of the reproductions. He could not say enough of the beauty of the place, and he asked if he might sit there and watch for the old codger's old customers coming to buy hardware. There might be copy in it.

But the old customers did not come so often as he hoped and Erlcort feared. Instead there came *bona fide* book-buyers, who asked some for a book and some for a particular book. The first were not satisfied with the books that Erlcort or his acting saleslady recommended, and went away without buying. The last were indignant at not finding what they wanted in Erlcort's selection.

"Why don't you stock it?" they demanded.

"Because I don't think it's worth reading."

"Oh, indeed!" The sarcastic customers were commonly ladies. "I thought you let the public judge of that!"

"There are bookstores where they do. This is a critical bookstore. I sell only the books that *I* think worth reading. If you had noticed my sign—"

"Oh!" the customer would say, and she, too, would go away without buying.

There were other ladies who came, links of the endless chain of volunteer readers who had tried to help Erlcort in making his selection, and he could see them slyly looking his stock over for the books they had praised to him. Mostly they went away without comment, but with heads held high in the offense which he felt even more than saw. One, indeed, did ask him why he had not stocked her chosen book, and he had to say, "Well, when I came to go through it carefully, I didn't think it quite—"

"But here is *The Green Bay Tree*, and *The Biggest Toad in the Puddle*, and—"*

"I know. For one reason and another I thought them worth stocking."

Then another head went away high in the air, with its plumes quivering. One afternoon late a lady came flying in with all the marks, whatever they are, of transatlantic travel upon her.

"I'm just through the customs, and I've motored up here the first thing, even before I went home, to stop you from selling that book I recommended. It's dreadful; and, horrors! horrors! here it is by the hundreds! Oh, Mr. Erlcort! You mustn't sell that dreadful book! You see, I had skipped through it in my berth going out, and posted my letter the first thing; and just now, coming home, I found it in the ship's library and came on that frightful episode. You know! Where—How *could* you order it without reading it, on a mere say-so? It's utterly immoral!"

"I don't agree with you," Erlcort answered, dryly. "I consider that passage one of the finest in modern fiction—one of the most ennobling and illumin-ing—"

"Ennobling!" The lady made a gesture of horror. "Very well! If *that* is your idea of a critical bookstore, all I've got to say is—"

But she had apparently no words to say it in, and she went out banging but failing to latch the door which let through the indignant snort of her car as it whirled her away. She left Erlcort and his assistant to a common silence, but he imagined somehow a resolution in the stenographer not to let the book go unsearched till she had grasped the full iniquity of that episode and felt all its ennobling force. He was not consoled when another lady came in and, after drifting unmolestedly about (it was the primary rule of the place not to fol-

---

* Howells apparently invented these titles.

low people up), stopped before the side shelf where the book was ranged in dozens and scores. She took a copy from the neat ranks, and opened it; then she lifted her head by chance and caught sight of her plume in one of the little mirrors. She stealthily lifted herself on tiptoe till she could see her face, and then she turned to the assistant and said, gently, "I believe I should like *this* book, please," and paid for it and went out.

It was now almost on the stroke of six, and Erlcort said to his assistant: "I'll close the store, Miss Pearsall. You needn't stay any longer."

"All right, sir," the girl said, and went into the little closet at the rear for her hat and coat. Did she contrive to get a copy of that book under her coat as she passed the shelf where it lay?

When she was gone, he turned the key in the door and went back and sat down before the fire dying down on the hearth of the Franklin stove. It was not a very cheerful moment with him, but he could not have said that the day had been unprofitable, either spiritually or pecuniarily. In its experiences it had been a varied day, and he had really sold a good many books. More people than he could have expected had taken him seriously and even intelligently. It is true that he had been somewhat vexed by the sort of authority the president of the Intellectual Club had shown in the way she swelled into the store and patronized him and it, as if she had invented them both, and blamed him in a high, sweet voice for having so many *old* books. "My idea was that it would be a place where one could come for the best of the *new* books. But here! Why, half of them I saw in June before I sailed!" She chided him merrily, and she acted as if it were quite part of the joke when he said that he did not think a good book could age much in four months. She laughed patronizingly at his conceit of getting in the fall books by Thanksgiving; but even for the humor of it she could not let him say he should not do anything in holiday books. "I had expected to get *all* my Christmas books of you, Mr. Erlcort," she crowed, but for the present she bought nothing. In compensation he recalled the gratitude, almost humble gratitude, of a lady (she *was* a lady!) who had come that day, bringing her daughter to get a book, any book in his stock, and to thank him for his enterprise, which she had found worked perfectly in the case of the book she had got the week before; the book had been an unalloyed delight, and had left a sense of heightened self-respect with her: that book of the dreadful episode.

He wished Margaret Green had been there; but she had been there only once since his opening; he could not think why. He heard a rattling at the door-latch, and he said before he turned to look, "What if it should be she *now*?" But when he went to peer through the door-curtain it was only an old fellow who had spent the better part of the afternoon in the best chair, reading a book. Erlcort went back to the fire and let him rattle, which he did rather a long time, and then went away, Erlcort hoped, in dudgeon. He was one of a number of customers who had acted on the half of his motto asking them to sit down and rest them, after acting on the other half to look round all they wanted. Most of them did not read, even; they seemed to know one another, and they talked comfortably together. Erlcort recognized a companionship of four whom he had noticed in the Park formerly; they were clean-enough-looking elderly men, but occupied nearly all the chairs and settles, so that lady customers did not like to bring books and look over them in the few places left, and Erlcort foresaw the time when he should have to ask the old fellows to look around more and rest them less. In resuming his own place before the fire he felt the fleeting ache of a desire to ask Margaret Green whether it would not be a good plan to remove the motto from the chimneypiece. He would not have liked to do it without asking her; it had been her notion to put it there, and her other notion of the immoral mirrors had certainly worked well. The thoughtful expression they had reflected on the faces of lady customers had sold a good many books; not that Erlcort wished to sell books that way, though he argued with himself that his responsibility ought strictly to end with the provision of books which he had critically approved before offering them for sale.

His conscience was not wholly at peace as to his stock, not only the books which he had included, but also those he had excluded. Some of these tacitly pleaded against his severity; in one case an author came and personally protested. This was the case of a book by the ex-best-seller, who held that his last book was so much better than his first that it ought certainly to be found in any critical bookstore. The proceeds of his best-seller had enabled him to buy an electric runabout, and he purred up to Erlcort's door in it to argue the matter with him. He sat down in a reproduction and proved, gaily, that Erlcort was quite wrong about it. He had the book with him, and read passages from it; then he read passages from some of the books on sale and defied Erlcort to say that his passages were not just as good, or, as he put it merrily, the same as. He held that his marked improvement entitled him to the favor of a critical bookstore; without this, what motive had he in keeping from a reversion to the errors which had won him the vicious prosperity of his first venture? Hadn't Erlcort a duty to perform in preventing his going back to the bad? Refuse this markedly improved fiction, and you drove him to writing nothing but best-sellers from now on. He urged Erlcort to reflect.

They had a jolly time, and the ex-best-seller went away in high spirits, prophesying that Erlcort would come to his fiction yet.

There were authors who did not leave Erlcort so cheerful when they failed to see their books on his shelves or tables. Some of them were young authors who had written their worthless books with a devout faith in their worth, and they went away more in sorrow than in anger, and yet more in bewilderment. Some were old authors who had been all their lives acceptably writing second-rate books and trying to make them unacceptably first-rate. If he knew them he kept out of their way, but the dejection of their looks was not less a pang to him if he saw them searching his stock for their books in vain.

He had his own moments of dejection. The interest of the press in his enterprise had flashed through the Sunday issues of a single week, and then flashed out in lasting darkness. He wondered vaguely if he had counted without the counting-house in hoping for their continued favor; he could not realize that nothing is so stale as old news, and that no excess of advertising would have relumed those fitful fires.

He would have liked to talk the case over with Margaret Green. After his first revolt from the easy publicity the reporters had first given him, he was aware of having enjoyed it—perhaps vulgarly enjoyed it. But he hoped not quite that; he hoped that in his fleeting celebrity he had cared for his scheme rather than himself. He had really believed in it, and he liked having it recognized as a feature of modern civilization, an innovation which did his city and his country credit. Now and then an essayist of those who wrote thoughtful articles in the Sunday or Saturday-evening editions had dropped in, and he had opened his heart to them in a way he would not have minded their taking advantage of. Secretly he hoped they would see a topic in his enterprise and his philosophy of it. But they never did, and he was left to the shame of hopes which had held nothing to support defeat. He would have liked to confess his shame and own the justice of his punishment to Margaret Green, but she seemed the only friend who never came near. Other friends came, and many strangers, the friends to look and the strangers to buy. He had no reason to complain of his sales; the fame of his critical bookstore might have ceased in New York, because it had gone abroad to Chicago and St. Louis and Pittsburg [*sic*]; people who were clearly from these commercial capitals and others came and bought copiously of his criticized stock, and they praised the notion of it in telling him that he ought to open branches in their several cities.

They were all women, and it was nearly all women who frequented the Critical Bookstore, but in their multitude Margaret Green was not. He thought it the greater pity because she would have enjoyed many of them with him, and would have divined such as hoped the culture implicated by a critical bookstore would come off on them without great effort of their own; she would have known the sincere spirits, too, and could have helped direct their choice of the best where all was so good. He smiled to find that he was invoking her help, which he had no right to.

His longing had no effect upon her till deep in January, when the weather was engaged late one afternoon in keeping the promise of a January thaw in the form of the worst snow-storm of the winter. Then she came thumping with her umbrella-handle at his door as if, he divined, she were too stiff-handed or too package-laden to press the latch and let herself in, and she almost fell in, but saved herself by spilling on the floor some canvases and other things which she had been getting at the artist's-materials store near by. "Don't bother about them," she said, "but take me to the fire as fast as you can," and when she had turned from snow to rain and had dripped partially dry before the Franklin stove, she asked, "Where have you been all the time?"

"Waiting here for you," he answered.

"Well, you needn't. I wasn't going to come—or at least not till you sent for me, or said you wanted my advice."

"I don't want your advice now."

"I didn't come to give it. I just dropped in because if I hadn't I should have just dropped outside. How have you been getting along with your ridiculous critical bookstore?"

"Well, things are rather quiet with us just now, as the publishers say to the authors when they don't want to publish their books."

"Yes, I know that saying. Why didn't you go in for the holiday books?"

"How did you know I didn't?"

"Lots of people told me."

"Well, then, I'll tell you why. I would have had to read them first, and no human being could do that—not even a volunteer link in an endless chain."

"I see. But since Christmas?"

"You know very well that after Christmas the book market drops dead."

"Yes, so I've been told." She had flung her wet veil back over her shoulders, and he thought she had never looked so adorably plain before; if she could have seen herself in a glass she would have found her whole face out of drawing. It seemed as if his thinking had put her in mind of them, and she said, "Those immoral mirrors are shameful."

"They've sold more of the best books than anything else."

"Very well. *I* didn't put them up." He laid a log of hickory on the fire. "I'm not doing it to dry you quicker."

"Oh, I know. I'll tell you one thing. You ought to keep the magazines, or at least the Big Four. You could keep them with a good conscience, and you could sell them without reading; they're always good."

"There's an idea in that. I believe I'll try it."

Margaret Green was now dry enough, and she rose and removed the mirrors. In doing this she noticed that Erlcort had apparently sold a good many of his best books, and she said: "Well, I don't see why *you* should be discouraged."

"Who said I was? I'm exultant." ·

"Then you were exulting with the corners of your mouth down just now. Well, I must be going. Will you get a taxi to flounder over to the Subway with me?" While Erlcort was telephoning she was talking to him. "I believe the magazines will revive public interest in your scheme. Put them in your window. Try to get advance copies for it."

"You have a commercial genius, Margaret Green."

"When it comes to selling literature, I have. Selling art is where I fall down."

"That's because you always try to sell your own art. I should fall down, too, if I tried to sell my own literature."

They got quite back to their old friendliness; the coming of the taxi gave them plenty of time. The electric lights were turned brilliantly on, but there, at the far end of the store, before the Franklin stove, they had a cozy privacy. At the moment of parting she said:

"If I were you I should take out these settles. They simply invite loafing."

"I've noticed that they seem to do that."

"And better paint out that motto."

"I've sometimes fancied I'd better. *That* invites loafing, too; though some nice people like it."

"Nice people? Why haven't some of them bought a picture?" He perceived that she had taken in the persistent presence of the sketches when removing the mirrors, and he shared the indignation she expressed: "Shabby things!"

She stood with the mirrors under her arm, and he asked what she was going to do with them, as he followed her to the door with her other things.

"Put them around the studio. But you needn't come to see the effect."

"No. I shall come to see you."

But when he came in a lull of February, and he could walk part of the way up through the Park on the sunny Saturday afternoon, she said:

"I suppose you've come to pour out some more of your griefs. Well, pour away! Has the magazine project failed?"

"On the contrary, it has been a *succès fou*. But I don't feel altogether easy in my mind about it. The fact is, they seem to print much more rubbish than I supposed."

"Of course they do; they must; rubbish is the breath in their nostrils."

She painted away, screwing her eyes almost shut and getting very close to her picture. He had never thought her so plain; she was letting her mouth hang open. He wondered why she was so charming; but when she stepped back rhythmically, tilting her pretty head this way and that, he saw why: it was her unfailing grace. She suddenly remembered her mouth and shut it to say, "Well?"

"Well, some people have come back to me. They've said, What a rotten number this or that was! They were right; and yet there were things in all those magazines better than anything they had ever printed. What's to be done about it? I can't ask people to buy truck or read truck because it comes bound up with essays and stories and poems of the first quality."

"No. You can't. Why," she asked, drifting up to her picture again, "don't you tear the bad out, and sell the good?"

Erlcort gave a disdainful sound, such as cannot be spelled in English. "Do you know how defiantly the bad is bound up with the good in the magazines? They're wired together, and you could no more tear out the bad and leave the good than you could part vice from virtue in human nature."

"I see," Margaret Green said, but she saw no further, and she had to let him go disconsolate. After waiting a decent time she went to find him in his critical bookstore. It was late in an afternoon of the days that were getting longer, and only one electric was lighted in the rear of the room, where Erlcort sat before the fireless Franklin stove, so busy at something that he scarcely seemed aware of her.

"What in the world are you doing?" she demanded.

He looked up. "Who? I? Oh, it's you! Why, I'm merely censoring the truck in the May number of this magazine." He held up a little roller, as long as the magazine was wide, blacked with printer's ink, which he had been applying to the open periodical. "I've taken a hint from the way the Russian censorship blots out seditious literature before it lets it go to the public."

"And *what* a mess you're making!"

"Of course it will have to dry before it's put on sale."

"I should think so. Listen to me, Frederick Erlcort: you're going crazy."

"I've sometimes thought so: crazy with conceit and vanity and arrogance. Who am I that I should set up for a critical bookstore-keeper? What is the Republic of Letters, anyway? A vast, benevolent, generous democracy, where one may have what one likes, or a cold oligarchy where he is compelled to take what is good for him? Is it a restricted citizenship, with a minority representation, or is it universal suffrage?"

"Now," Margaret Green said, "you are talking sense. Why didn't you think of this in the beginning?"

"Is it a world, a whole earth," he went on, "where the weeds mostly out-flourish the flowers, or is it a wretched little florist's conservatory where the watering-pot assumes to better the instruction of the rain which falls upon the just and the unjust? What is all the worthy family of asses to do if there are no thistles to feed them? Because the succulent fruits and nourishing cereals are better for the finer organisms, are the coarser not to have fodder? No; I have made a mistake. Literature is the whole world; it is the expression of the gross, the fatuous, and the foolish, and it is the pleasure of the gross, the fatuous, and the foolish, as well as the expression and the pleasure of the wise, the fine, the elect. Let the multitude have their truck, their rubbish, their rot; it may not be the truck, the rubbish, the rot that it would be to us, or may slowly and by natural selection become to certain of them. But let there be no artificial selection, no survival of the fittest by main force—the force of the spectator, who thinks he knows better than the creator of the ugly and the beautiful, the fair and foul, the evil and good."

"Oh, *now* if the Intellectual Club could hear you!" Margaret Green said, with a long, deep, admiring suspiration. "And what are you going to do with your critical bookstore?"

"I'm going to sell it. I've had an offer from the author of that best-seller— I've told you about him. I was just trying to censor that magazine while I was thinking it over. He's got an idea. He's going to keep it a critical bookstore, but the criticism is to be made by universal suffrage and the will of the majority. The latest books will be put to a vote; and the one getting the greatest number of votes will be the first offered for sale, and the author will receive a free passage to Europe by the southern route."

"The southern route!" Margaret mused. "I've never been that way. It must be delightful."

"Then come with *me! I'm* going."

"But how can I?"

"By marrying me!"

"I never thought of that," she said. Then, with the conscientious resolution of an elderly girl who puts her fate to the touch of any risk the truth compels, she added: "Or, yes! I *have*. But I never supposed you would ask me." She stared at him, and she was aware she was letting her mouth hang open. While she was trying for some word to close it with he closed it for her.

The Pearl
A Tale Untold

1916 & 1917

"THE PEARL" AND "A TALE UNTOLD" are two of Howells's latest stories, although he continued to write "Easy Chair" columns, reviews,
essays, and poetry until his death in 1920 at the age of eighty-three.
(Howells also completed one novel, *The Leatherwood God*, and one volume of
autobiography, *Years of My Youth*, in 1916.) "The Pearl" appeared in *Harper's
Monthly* in August of 1916, and "A Tale Untold" in the *Atlantic Monthly* one
year later. To my knowledge, neither has been reprinted since. Both stories
focus on the coming of age of a young Midwesterner, Stephen West, and both
are set on steamboats travelling west from Pittsburgh (which Howells habitually spells as "Pittsburg") to St. Louis on the Ohio and then the Mississippi
Rivers. Both, too, are more or less autobiographical, but "A Tale Untold" is
less of an autobiographical sketch than a reworking of old themes along new
lines.

In both "The Pearl" and "A Tale Untold," the setting plays an important
role. Edwin Cady, in his biography of Howells and in his more recent
"Howells on the River," draws attention to the significance of the Ohio River
and its steamboats in Howells's life, noting his affection for his two steamboat-

captain uncles, his early memory of seeing a man drown as he tried to board an Ohio River steamboat, his brother Joe's brief career as a river pilot, and the wide variety of his writing about river life, including "The Pilot's Story" in 1860, *A Boy's Town* in 1890, "Floating Down the River on the O-hi-o" in 1902, and concluding with "The Pearl" and "A Tale Untold" (*Road* 8, 13, 38).

All of these except "The Pilot's Story"—a melodramatic antislavery poem —treat the river nostalgically, and many combine descriptions of contemporary river life with memories of its past. "Floating Down the River on the O-hi-o," for example, describes the experience of some "light-hearted youngsters of sixty-five and seventy" ("Floating" 309) whose journey on a stern-wheel steamboat enables them to recall similar journeys in the 1850s. Their reflections are all on the differences between those past journeys and the present, and their pleasure increases as they note the insignificance of the changes. The main incidents of both "The Pearl" and "A Tale Untold," on the other hand, are explicitly set "sixty years ago"—that is, in the 1850s—but both stories end years later, when the earlier events are being recalled by the now mature protagonist. Cady sensibly notes that Howells's ingrained knowledge of river life "made his later intimacy with Mark Twain, and his ability to support Twain's work, possible" (*Road* 13).

"The Pearl" and "A Tale Untold" are linked not only by their setting but by a common protagonist, Stephen West, who is depicted in each at a moment of humiliation that painfully leads to illumination and growth. Stephen bears a strong resemblance to Sherwood Anderson's George Willard of *Winesburg, Ohio;* indeed the two Stephen West stories are Andersonesque not only in their content but in their tone and, to a degree, in their style.[1] Just as George and Winesburg stand in fictionally for Anderson and Clyde, Ohio, Stephen, more than most Howellsian heroes (after "A Dream" and other very early works) stands in for the young Howells.

"The Pearl," according to Cady (*Road* 13), Lynn (49), Wagenknecht (145), and Gibson and Arms (155) is directly autobiographical. Lynn further connects the story to an episode of Howells's youth described in *A Boy's Town.* Referring to himself in the third person, as "my boy," Howells writes:

> A girl at school mislaid a pencil which she thought she had lent him, and he began to have a morbid belief that he must have stolen it; he became frantic with the mere dread of guilt; he could not eat or sleep, and it was not till he went to make good the loss with a pencil which his grandfather gave him that the girl said she had found her pencil in her desk, and saved him from the despair of a self-convicted criminal. (198)

Howells uses this incident as an example of his extreme "desire to lead an up-right life" and his consequent "anguish" over the slightest connection with any wrongdoing (198). Although he does not explicitly point out the moral that such self-induced guilt is one path to compassion in later life, there is a clear connection between Howells's youthful neurotic guilt and his later rep-utation for kindness and understanding—in the terms of the story, between the grain of sand that makes "a kind of a sick oyster" and the "pearl of great price" that "costs a man his peace, but . . . keeps him merciful to others."

"A Tale Untold" has not been linked directly to Howells's autobiography (indeed, it has hardly been treated at all) but it is clearly a miniature *Künstler-roman*, and a reflection of Howells's youthful naïveté. Indeed, the story it most resembles is "A Romance of Real Life." Stephen's considerations of the fictional uses of his experiences mirror the contributor's attempts to turn "real life" into a "romance," as does his adoption and rejection of various lit-erary treatments. And, like "A Romance of Real Life," the story concludes by moving outside of its initial fictional situation into the realm of metafiction—it becomes the story *of* a story, in this case, a story "untold." (It's interesting that Stephen's immediate reaction to the confirmation of his fears about the actual value of his watch guard is not embarrassment but "pleasure": he im-mediately turns away from his actual experience and exults in its fictional possibilities: "What had happened was nothing to what could happen.")

"A Tale Untold" resembles "A Romance of Real Life" as well in that each concerns a writer duped by a con man.[2] The contributor's gullibility is treated comically, as the contributor is not essentially hurt by his foolishness and instead recalls his experience as having a "most agreeable charm." Stephen West, on the other hand, is humiliated and financially victimized, and his final reaction to the events of the story is a helpless silence; his in-ability to gain "mastery" as a writer over the materials of his life is the mirror image of his earlier inability to master the men who set out to swindle him.

"The Pearl" and "A Tale Untold" are further linked by an emphasis on the inequities of race and class. The three cousins in "The Pearl" are keenly aware of their own social standing and of the black cabin boy's lack of any standing at all. And in "A Tale Untold," Stephen carefully observes the social strata represented by the steamboat's passengers, and his falling out with the river pilot occurs over the question of slavery. (Similarly, "Floating Down the River on the O-hi-o" ends with an abrupt and unexpected lament on the hopeless lives of black laborers specifically and on "the struggle of toiling men" in general—323.) The stories, taken together, form an appropriate coda to Howells's career as a short story writer as they treat, if only lightly, recurrent themes of his work: moral growth, social awareness, and the tenuous connections between literature and life.

Notes

1. Kenneth Lynn finds interesting parallels between the mothers of Howells and Anderson (31).
2. Cady links the con man of "A Tale Untold" to the riverboat gamblers that appear both in Howells's "The Pilot's Story" and in the early series of epistolary essays that Wortham has published in his *Early Prose Writings of William Dean Howells* under the title "Pictures of River Travel" ("Howells on the River" 39).

ℰ̃

The Pearl

The cousins were going round from Pittsburg [*sic*] to St. Louis on their uncle's boat in the spring of the year sixty years ago, and the boat was expected to get in early in the afternoon. The weather was already warm, and the scent of the young willows in blossom along the shores blew at the open doors and lattices of the texas,* where the cousins were putting on their summer clothes. Their youth, and their community of hope, and their uncertainty of the future made them friends; otherwise, except that they had nothing against each other, there was nothing but their cousinship to unite them. One had thought he was going to be a painter, but under correction of a business father he now thought not. From time to time he made some sketches which surprised one of the others, but which he did not much care for himself. This other, who was not akin to him, but only to his cousin, had never seen anybody sketching before; he was intensely, almost bitterly literary; he was going to be an author, and above all he was going to be a poet. His cousin did not know quite what he was going to be, but he was going to be rich, though cer-

---

* According to *Webster's*, "a structure on the awning deck of a steamer containing the officers' cabins and having the pilot house in front or on top (fr. the practice on Mississippi steamboats of naming the cabins after the states, the officers' cabin being the largest)".

tainly not by favor of the river life, for the good reason that his father and his father's three brothers and brothers-in-law had all prospered in that life.

What united the cousins at the beginning was their common doubt whether putting them up in the texas was not a flaw in the hospitality of the uncle who had asked them to be his guests for the trip to St. Louis and back. His hospitality would have been perfecter if he had welcomed them, like paying passengers, to staterooms in the long, shining sweep of the grand saloon below. It was all right to be quartered with the upper officers; they could well be proud to be of the company of the captain and the two pilots and the two boat's clerks in the texas; but the mates, the watchmen? Before they could put their misgiving into words, or make any overt sign of it to one another, they suddenly found themselves more than satisifed to be in the texas, which rose from the hurricane-deck above the long saloon just aft of the pilot-house. They now realized that it was a distinction to be in the texas, white, clean, and cool, an obvious mystery to the young lady passengers, drifting by in their promenade of the hurricane deck and throwing respectful glances in at the lattice doors.

The cousins ate at the great table in the saloon not far from the captain and whichever pilot was off watch; and in their quarters they had almost the sole use of a cabin-boy. He was the captain's special boy, and was supposed to be the best cabin-boy on the boat. In the nature of his calling he would have been black, and he might really have been black in everything but his complexion, which was white. He served the cousins, and whether he was black or not, they liked him without much thought, if any, of his personal or social quality. He was Jim, and when they wanted him they called for him by that name, but mostly they preferred to do without his help.

They had now got their summer clothes out of the valises which held these as their sole change, and laid them on the backs of chairs in the little cabin room which they used as a common dressing-room. Their clothes were all of the white linen which men wore in those days, but the cousin who was going to be a poet was from a country town, and he felt a difference in the make of his coat and trousers from that of the other cousins' clothes when he saw them together; he had said he would change in his state-room, and he took his things back there. The cousin who was not now going to be a painter did not mind the comparison challenged by the clothes of the cousin who was going to be rich. He sat, delaying his change and making idle studies of this cousin, who had begun by clothing himself like one who was rich already. He was going to put on shoes of patent leather, and a pleated shirt, and trousers of snowy drilling, and a coat of snowy duck, and above all he was going to wear a blue-silk neckerchief, with a violin-shaped scarf-pin of fine gold set with a precious stone, which he said had cost fifteen dollars.

While he dressed he buzzed softly through his teeth as well as his talking would allow, and the intending poet, where he sat with a book in his state-room, involuntarily followed the different events as his cousin advanced from one garment to another. He knew when his cousin was pulling up and buttoning his trousers, and when he was buttoning his collar before the glass. He had a mounting interest in the events, from the gaiety of the buzzing and the blitheness of the talk; till all at once both stopped, and he heard his cousin call out in a note of conditional grief:

"Why, look here, Lorry; where's my scarf?"

"You had it last, Dan, didn't you?" the cousin who was with him asked, placidly.

"Yes, I did; and I hung it here with my other things on the back of this chair."

"It must be there yet, then," Lorry suggested.

"No; it isn't," Dan returned.

"Then you didn't put it there."

"I believe in my heart I didn't." The intending poet followed from his place his cousin's rush to his state-room; his quick, noisy search, and his swift return. "Well, I *did*. What do you suppose has become of it?"

"I should say I stole it," Lorry answered, with the effect of wishing to help in any way he could.

Dan ignored him. "Look here, Stephen!" he called to the intending poet. "I wish you'd come out here." Stephen West appeared, dreamy-eyed, with his finger between the pages of his book, and Dan hurried on. "I've lost my necktie with that fifteen-dollar pin of mine in it. I brought it out with my other things, before I began to dress here, and put it on the back of this chair here, and now—it's gone. Where did you put your things when you brought them out here first?"

Stephen pulled himself up out of the poem he had been reading. "I don't know," he began, hazily.

"Well, now look here," Dan cheered himself on. "We've all had our things out here, and got them mixed up more than once. Suppose we all go into our rooms and give a good look, and see if we can find it anywhere. Very likely I didn't bring it out, as you say, Lorry." He turned from Stephen with his appeal. He was serious, almost tragical, and the others said, each in his way:

"Why, of course, Dan," and went to make the search.

They came back from different quarters when they came back, and their looks confirmed their failure. "Well, what ought I to do, boys?" the owner of the pin lamented.

"You might search us," Lorry proposed.

"I'll tell you what," Dan plaintively ignored him. "I don't like to suggest it, but I don't see what we can do now except to get Jim in here and ask him."

"Accuse him?" Stephen said.

"No; just ask him if he's seen it."

"That will be the same as telling him he's taken it," Lorry said.

"I don't think so," Dan argued. "Did I tell you fellows you'd taken it when I asked if you'd seen it?"

"Well," Lorry teased, "you hinted as much."

"Did I, Stephen?"

"I don't think I noticed. I shouldn't have dreamed of your suspecting me."

"Oh, have Jim in! I don't suppose even such a pale black has got any feelings that a white man is bound to respect." Lorry parodied a phrase that had lately come in from a decision of the Supreme Court.

Dan went to the inner door, and called into the corridor. "Jim, I wish you'd come here a minute."

Jim came smiling, but anxiously smiling.

"Oh!" Dan began. "I was just wondering if you'd happened to see anything of my blue tie—with my pin in it. I thought I brought it and put it on the chair here with my other things."

The smile faded out of Jim's anxiety. "No, Mister Dan. I ha'n't seen it at all."

"You know the pin I mean?"

"Oh yes, I know that pin."

"And you haven't seen it this morning, anywhere?"

"No, Mr. Dan. Why—why—my Lord! You don't think I *took* it, do you, Mr. Dan?"

"Did I say you did?" Dan's anger flamed up. "Well, that's all. Go along." The cabin-boy shrank out; Lorry snickered, and Dan turned upon him. "Well, I hope you're satisfied, now. He took that pin as plain as day, and if it hadn't been for you, there, with your dog-gone doubts, I'd have had it out of him. Oh, well, let it go!"

They started upon an argument of the case, which lasted a long time. At the end Dan borrowed a tie from Lorry, and finished dressing. Stephen tried at first to read where they were arguing, and then he recollected himself sufficiently to go back into his state-room and read there. Through the Tennysonian cadences of his book he was aware of their disputing voices; once he saw the cabin-boy pass his inner door; he seemed to have been crying; the watchman went by his outer door, and looked hesitatingly in at Stephen where he sat hunched over on a camp-stool, with his valise between his feet; he had pulled it up from under his berth when he opened it to look if he might have happened to put Dan's tie into it.

He had got to the end of "Morte d'Arthur," and had sweet in his sense the music of the line,

And on the ear their wailing died away,

when he heard his cousin calling him.

"Stephen! Oh, Stephen! Come in here a minute, will you?"

Stephen went, purblindly stumbling in where Dan and Lorry seemed at the close of a useless debate.

"Look here," his cousin said. "I don't want to leave Jim under suspicion. I know he took my pin, but I want to give him the benefit of the doubt, and what I say now is, let's all go and give another *good* look among our things. It's so easy getting the tie mixed up with them. You go into your room and I'll go into mine, and we'll try to see if we can't find it. If we can't, all right; only I think we ought to tell uncle about Jim."

"I don't believe he's got your pin," Stephen said, "and I'm certainly willing to look again. Suppose you both come and help me look, and make perfectly sure."

"That's a good idea! We'll all help one another," Dan said.

Stephen went first, and the other cousins followed him. "All my things except what I have on are in this bag," he said, as he lifted the old-fashioned oil-cloth sack, lank still, with his whole wardrobe in it, and set it on his berth.

He somewhat fiercely pulled its frogmouth open, and showed the tie with the pin in it lying on the top of his few clothes. All life seemed to stop with a jolt.

None of them said anything for a moment. Then Dan leaned over and took up his tie. "Well, I'm glad we found it at last," he said, but they did not look at one another. Dan went out with Lorry, and put on his own tie. Stephen remained, where he had sunk on his camp-stool, till Dan came back fully clothed, and said, "Of course Jim slipped in here, while we were talking, and put it into your bag."

"He must have," Stephen said.

"That's what I think, and that's what Lorry thinks. What's the matter with you?"

"Nothing. Only—"

"Why, look here, Stephen! You don't suppose I think or Lorry thinks—"

"Oh, no! But if I were among strangers and had been found with stolen property—"

"Well, you're *not* among strangers. Lorry's my cousin if he isn't yours, and we're all the same as one family. Get on your things quick, now, and let's go and see them bring her in. But look out you don't speak to the captain while he's forward making motions to the pilot!" Dan laughed for pleasure in the impossible notion. He glanced into the little mirror over Stephen's dejected head, and pressed the tie further into the pleated bosom of his shirt with joy in the touch of it. "Hurry up, now!"

In the gaiety of the bright air outside, Stephen did not feel so sick, physically and spiritually, but the nightmare thing that had happened lurked in his consciousness and haunted him through all that was passing. His uncle's fierce intensity in making a safe landing, and his way of turning upon an ill-advised passenger who offered him an untimely pleasantry, sickened him again. A girl in a green-silk dress and a tilting hoop-skirt, who stood about twisting her parasol on her shoulder, did not distract him, though he was nineteen and instantly in love with such looks as hers whenever he saw them.

The boat lay a week at St. Louis before she got a return freight for Pittsburg, and the cousins gave themselves to a tireless exploration of the city, from the thronged and burdened levee, with its row of old stone houses of the French time at top, to every farthest limit of the actual American prosperity beyond. They drank as much soda-water and ate as many ice-creams as they had money for; and under their favoring influences Stephen's nightmare lifted. But one night after they saw an actor, then almost as young as themselves, in "Richard III," the pangs of that guilty wretch's conscience as Edwin Booth proclaimed them in waking from his midnight dream, brought Stephen's trouble back again, and he stumbled heavily under it through the soft darkness to the boat with the other cousins.

The other cousins seemed to have quite forgotten. Dan wore his blue tie and pin every day, and Lorry made some studies of the old French houses which Stephen easily identified with the originals. It would have been a time of perfect happiness if it had not been for that strange thing, which still did not constantly obsess the boy with its dreadfulness. From time to time he figured its having chanced among people who did not know him, and then his fancy painted the circumstances of shame and horror, the court and the prison, with sickening vividness. In these moments he was humbly grateful to his comrades, though he kept his gratitude and his humility silent with his misery. He had other moments, of defiant innocence, when the sense of what he was and had always been emboldened him to defy all doubt, and to reject all acquittal which did not reject the thing as if it had not been, which did not go behind it and forbid it. It was not till looking back at it after years that he realized how beautiful and delicate the behavior of the others was. They were boys like himself, ignorant and inexperienced, without chivalrous ideas; but nothing in those "Idylls of the King," which he was reading, could surpass the gentle chivalry of their tacit faith in him.

He believed, as they did, that the cabin-boy had stolen the scarf with the pin, and while they were talking together had slipped into his room and put them into his bag. They had not been there when he first looked, and when he looked the second time they were there; he could not tell how unless it was by the boy's act. He thought that Jim would leave the boat at St. Louis, and he hoped that his doubt of him would have this confirmation; but Jim did not leave, and when the boat started on her return trip he was there on duty in the texas, as before.

The sore place in Stephen's soul, which was not always sore, which was perhaps not even often sore, began to cicatrize, to callous, even in the fort-night that followed. If he laid his touch on the place, the sore would burn and beat, but he could keep himself from touching it.

The night before the boat got into Pittsburg Stephen suddenly could not bear it. He heard Jim stealthily passing his inner door, and he called to him.

"Jim, come in here a moment, won't you?"

The boy stopped, and after a pause put his head in at the open door. "Yes, Mr. Stephen."

"Jim," Stephen began again, "I want you to tell me the truth; I won't do anything to you. Did you put Dan's scarf and pin in my bag?"

"No, Mr. Stephen. As sure as there's a living God, I didn't; I hope I may die; I hope He may strike me dead this minute, if I done it."

After a moment, Stephen said: "That's all. I believe you, Jim. Good night."

"Oh, thank you, Mr. Stephen! Thank you, thank you, thank you!"

"Oh, all right, Jim. I knew you didn't do it."

The boy went out, and Stephen drew the sheet up over his head.

In the morning everything was different. He went home with his cousin, and had a glad visit there, in the glory of their travels; and after a week he went on to the little town where he lived.

He lived afterward in larger towns and famous cities, and, as the years passed, by operation of that law which enables us to endure the remembrance of what we have done and suffered, and which will doubtless strengthen us to support it through eternity, he grew indifferent to his experience. He even became rather proud of it as something unique; he liked telling it, though he saw that it did not greatly interest people; that they did not even get his point of view; that they hastened to try matching it from their own experience with something not at all equivalent.

"But I have always thought," he would say, "how, if it had happened to me among strangers—"

"Oh, yes—yes," they would consent. "*That*, of course."

It seemed to him at last that once a listener passed from indifference, and, however delicately, evinced a certain compassion for him as the prey of a guilty conscience, as a sinner who was trying for the help of others in disowning his sin.

He recoiled in horror, and quite ceased to speak of the incident which still, from time to time, recurred to him in lasting baffle. Many years afterward he met his cousin; the kind, gay Lorry had died, and from speaking of him they recurred to their trip on the river, and Stephen could not help touching upon that place in his memory where this fact of the theft always lurked.

"You never found out anything about that pin of yours which I stole?" he asked with forced irony.

Dan at first humored his joke; then he said, gravely, "I always believed Jim took it and slipped it into your bag while we were talking."

"I never did," Stephen maintained stiffly.

"Well, then, who do you think did do it?"

"The evidence was all against *me*."

"Oh, pshaw, now, Steve! You're morbid. Have you been letting that thing bedevil you all these years? Forget it!"

"I can't. I don't mind it, except when I think of it; that is, I'm not always conscious of it."

"Why, but look here, Steve! If you'd taken it, would you have put it into the mouth of your bag, like Benjamin's cup, and then have opened the bag before us to show us it wasn't there?"

"That's the one point in my favor. But you might say that was a bluff."

Stephen spoke without feeling, and he listened with apathy while his cousin argued the question academically with him. "I can understand how it is with you," Dan ended, with a psychological reach impredicable of him. "Every one of us has a grain of sand in him that keeps him a kind of a sick oyster. He coats it over with his juice and hides it away in his shell somewhere; and that's what turns into a pearl, they say; I mean in a real oyster."

"The pearl of great price," West commented, bitterly.

"Why, yes, you may call it that. It costs a man his peace, but it keeps him merciful to others. Why, if a man had nothing on his conscience, he'd be a perfect devil."

"And you mean that I've got stealing your pin on my conscience?"

"Ah, there you go again! As sure as there's a God in heaven I never doubted you a second, because you were *you*. You just *couldn't* have. Will that do you?"

"It must. I don't feel my pearl all the time; I only know it's there when I feel round for it. Thank you, Dan."

They were parting, and they took each other's hands. Dan put his left arm on his cousin's shoulder, and pulled him affectionately toward him. "Goodby, you old sick oyster! Don't feel round for your pearl, and then it won't be there."

$\widetilde{\mathbf{c}}$

A Tale Untold

The stranger was not of the age to be called venerable, but his silvered hair and the bloom of his elderly good looks had won upon the serious favor of the ladies, and they made him welcome in their cabin at the stern of the boat. In the fashion of Western river-travel sixty years ago, they sat there with their sewing and knitting in the morning, and played and sang at the melodeon* in the afternoon. Usually they played and sang hymns, and then the stranger led what might be called their devotions, from a better acquaintance with the hymns.

When he left them, with polite excuses, for a walk on the hurricane-deck, he had to pass the men who sat at euchre around a table in the forward cabin. He always faltered for a glance at the cards they held and for a glance from the cards to their faces, while he kept humming the psalm-tune he had been singing. At last one of the men asked him with humorous deference if he would not sit down.

"But you don't like the sight of this, deacon," the gambler suggested.

"Then I wish he would lump it, damn him!" another gambler broke out. He

---

* organ

had been losing heavily. "Move on, now," he called savagely up at the stranger, who hurried away.

"Well, I don't know," the other gambler objected, "as I would want to damn him away, exactly."

"You take this hand," the loser blazed back, "and you may do the damnin' yourself."

The stranger put himself beyond hearing, and after that he seemed anxious not to glance at the gamblers as he passed, though other people stopped and followed the game to the end from the hands of the players.

A day or two later, as he stole by with his face carefully turned from the players, the losing gambler jumped to his feet and shouted, "Now you see here, will you! I ain't goin' to have you overlookin' my hand and settin' the cards ag'inst me. If I didn't know we was all gentlemen at this game, I would say you was in cahoots with somebody; but I ain't a goin' to have it, anyway. Now you just leave! You go back to your psalm-singin'."

He shook his cards in the stranger's face and roared away his protest that he had not meant to look at them, much less tried to overlook them; that he did not believe in the power of overlooking a hand, and should consider it wrong to use the power if he had it. The other players sided with the stranger and clamored at the man to sit down, to go on with the game, and not be a fool. The gambler said he wanted the stranger to keep away, that was all, and he violently shrugged off the touch which the stranger laid on his shoulder in mild entreaty, and slumped back into his chair. He studied the cards he held, and "Can't tell," he growled, "what the hell I *have* got, any more."

The sight and sound of the affair sickened Stephen West, who had stopped on his way to the hurricane-deck. The voyage was his farthest travel from the village where he had lived in a vision of the world, and he knew it equally from Tennyson and Longfellow and from Thackeray and Cervantes. In this vision the good and the evil of the world had the same charm for him, but he liked to verify it from the experience of a practical man like the pilot, and he had the habit of talking with him about life. Stephen's reading and thinking had aged him beyond his years, but the pilot was of a worldly wisdom which he could not hope to gain when the years had made them contemporaries.

The pilot's worldly wisdom, though it was so wide and varied, was of a decency which the boy could share without fear or shame. Stephen came away refreshed and strengthened in his ideals, with increasing respect for a person who seemed to be as fearless with men as he was blameless with women, and able to meet danger from either with steady courage. There seemed few incidents which the pilot's experience had not included. In Stephen's unenvious eyes he bore himself becomingly in a tall silk hat, a broadcloth coat, and a velvet waistcoat. He wore very thin-soled, high-heeled boots, such as Stephen never found for sale in his village.

Stephen was not going to talk with him now, or even willingly look at him. A few days before, in the wide range which their conversation often took, the pilot had come out with the abominable doctrine that the Declaration of Independence could not apply to negroes in its axiom that all men were created equal, because negroes had no souls and might be fitly enslaved for their defect. Stephen had heard this doctrine before, but in his amazement at hearing it from the pilot, he lost hold of the counter-arguments commonly used in that day against it. He could only allege the example of the fathers of the country in their abhorrence of slavery, and he recalled the saying of Jefferson that he trembled for his country when he remembered that God was just. He thrilled with the poetic solemnity of the words as he pronounced them; but the pilot flew into a sudden Celtic fury and cursed himself, and swore that he did not care for what Jefferson said, or for any fool who did care.

Stephen could scarcely believe that the thing had happened. He got himself somehow out of the place and went about trying to think how he could best resent the outrage put upon him. He was still boy enough to feel that a blow could be the only fit retort to such an insult, but he had not sufficiently dramatized the action when he saw the stranger, who had followed him up to the hurricane-deck and was now making towards the pilot-house. He felt that the right moment had come and that he could not do better than follow him and deal with the pilot in his presence; he had not contrived just how he should knock the pilot over his wheel and then have the stranger interpose and quiet the passions of both, but the scene enacted itself in his seething fancy without specific details, while he walked back and forth across the deck. Through the vindictive tumult of his revery he kept fitting certain aspects of the river with apt phrases, and it embittered his resentment the more to realize that a person who could do this should have been so vulgarly insulted. He controlled his impulse to burst into the pilot-house and fling himself on the pilot, no matter how the boat ran wild among the snags and sandbars; and he set his teeth hard and clenched his fists so tight that the nails cut into the palms of his hands. But the pilot stretched forward on tip-toe and called through his open window, "Come in here a minute, Mr. West, won't you?" Stephen eagerly construed his appeal as an overture to apology, and obeyed.

The stranger was sitting on the benching behind the pilot and humming one of his psalm tunes, with an air of courteous abstraction. He saluted Stephen blandly, but offered no reason for the pilot's invitation, and the pilot gave none. He said to the stranger, over his shoulder, "Just show them to him, will you?"

The stranger returned from his absence. "Oh! I was merely letting our friend here see some pieces of jewelry which I secured at a low rate from a bankrupt stock a few days before we left Cincinnati."

He had a tone of excuse, as if the fact was something too trivial to be more than passingly noted to a person of Stephen's quality; but the glitter of the things dazzled the boy in their variety of brooches, bracelets, rings, neck-chains, and watch-charms.

Stephen had a silver watch, with no present hope of a gold one; he had meant some time to have his watch plated, but he did not like the notion, and he had thought he would wait; but now the sight of a guard very rich and massive tempted him. Until he could buy a gold watch he might wear such a chain, and leave the spectators to imagine a gold watch at the end of it in his pocket. He did not like the notion of that, either, and he stood looking at the jewelry and then at the stranger who had not offered it for sale to him.

"I was just saying to our friend the captain," the stranger remarked, giving the pilot his courtesy-title, "that these guards were such a bargain, that I doubted whether the auctioneer knew their value; but I did not feel bound to inform him that they were 18-karats fine."

"Tell him," the pilot commanded, "what you offered one to me for."

"Oh, well, captain," the stranger deprecated, "that was to *you*." But he lifted the chain which he seemed to have seen Stephen admire, and viewed it with something like surprise, as he spread it with his thumb and finger. "I am not sure that I could let another go for that." He dropped the chain back into the shining heap in the handkerchief opened on his knees, and began to muse his hymn tune again.

"Would you say, Mr. West," the pilot asked, more to give dignity to the transaction than to Stephen, as the boy felt, by the ceremonious use of his surname, "that a watch-guard like that was worth three dollars?"

"Oh, no, captain!" the stranger interposed, "three-fifty, three-fifty!"

"Three," the pilot insisted.

The stranger was sure of three-fifty, the pilot of three, and the pilot was reddening under the contradiction. The stranger made a courteous inclination toward him, and waved his hand in concession. "Very well, three, if that is your recollection, captain."

"What do you say, Stephen?" the pilot repeated toward West.

"I don't know, Captain Ryan," Stephen answered stiffly. "I never bought anything like it."

"I would put one to you, as a friend of the captain here, on the same terms," the stranger suggested. "There are two, I see, exactly alike." He examined the jewelry as if he had not observed the fact before."I bid off the lot together, and I can't tell whether I am losing money or not, but I should like to get back a little cash. I will let the two go at the same figure. The figure Captain Ryan says."

He held up a guard in each hand.

It was very convincing. If Stephen should yet decide to have his watch gold-plated, a gold watch-guard was the irresistible logic of the event. He drew a deep sigh, but he shook his head. "I couldn't afford it," he said finally.

The stranger smiled benignly. "I know just how you feel, and I can't help approving of your caution in a young man; but there is this to be said on the other hand. If this guard here is the same as cash and more than the same, why it isn't parting with your money at all. It's like putting it in the bank where you can draw against it whenever you want it."

In treating the case as a hypothetical abstraction the stranger appealed to the caution which was a strong principle in Stephen's nature.

The boy heaved another sigh. "I couldn't, I couldn't."

"The boy is right," the pilot violently interposed. "I didn't ask him to buy one of them guards. I asked his opinion, but I don't want him to take mine."

He was holding the wheel with one hand and with the other rummaging in his waistcoat pocket. He drew out some bank-notes and flung them toward the stranger. "How much is there there?"

The stranger caught them without dropping his jewelry and counted the bank-notes. "Just three. I thought there were four. All right, captain."

He held the notes in one hand while he reached the watch-guard to the pilot with the other. The pilot pushed it into his pocket without looking round. The stranger remained seated and began absent-mindedly humming again. Then he began to speak to Stephen of the scenery and of the high water. By a natural transition he spoke of the life on the steamboats of our Western rivers and its differing character from north to south. He touched upon its darker aspects, and he said he would take the privilege of an elder man in warning Stephen against the games of chance which might tempt him by the sight of the easy winnings. Then, as if unwilling to remind him of the treatment Stephen had seen him suffer from that blackleg, he turned from the point and remarked that he had not met Stephen at the evening singing in the ladies' cabin. Every one was welcome; he asked Stephen if he sang.

He let himself, blandly smiling, out of the pilot-house; but when he had pulled the door shut, Stephen suddenly pulled it open and bounded after him. "Have you,—have you," he panted, "another one of those watchguards? But, of course—I mean I want one, if it's three dollars."

All the time that the pilot had been buying the chain his example had wrought with the boy as one that might be followed with honor and profit. He had not in the least forgiven him for his brutality, but he fancied that his apology had been delayed by the presence of the stranger. From the first sight of the jewelry he had been tempted by the fitness of acquiring a watch-guard, and his contempt for the pilot as an unreasonable ruffian rested on unbroken faith in him as a man of worldly knowledge who might be safely trusted in such a matter. He had been struck by his ease in meeting the stranger's recollection of the price and his own figure of three dollars. A person less versed in business matters might have yielded the point of half a dollar in the purchase of a thing clearly worth three or four times the stranger's demand.

"But I couldn't—I couldn't give more than three dollars," he cautioned the stranger, who had drawn the chain promptly from his pocket again.

The stranger hesitated almost imperceptibly. Then he said, "I really ought to have more for the value, but as a friend of the captain, well, we will say three dollars. And let me caution you, my young friend," he added, while taking Stephen's money and giving him the watch-guard wrapped in tissue paper, "to beware of your dealings with strangers in the course of your travels, and try to have witnesses to every transaction. Is this the guard you wanted? Look at it, please. Though I don't know that there is any difference in the chains. Is it all right? If you find it different I may be able to exchange it for you during the day. I couldn't say later; I shall be showing them—"

"Yes, yes; it is all right." Stephen stopped him, and put the chain into his pocket with a feeling of shame, and walked rather giddily away to his stateroom. He felt that he was taking an advantage of the stranger in letting him suppose he was a friend of the pilot. But it was some comfort to take the watch-guard out and look at it, alone there in his stateroom—to try it across from his waistcoat pocket to the buttonhole where he meant to hook it, and to hold it up in different lights. He attached it to his watch for the effect; but because the watch was still silver and the guard was gold, the effect was not good. If he pulled it out suddenly the effect would be ridiculous; he must wait to get his watch gold-plated.

When he went to dinner he glanced at the pilot, who was already there, and he did not know whether it was a relief or not to find that he was not wearing his watch-guard. If the stranger had sold other guards, they were not to be seen. Toward evening Stephen noticed some of the ladies with neck-chains; one wore a bracelet, and the things all looked as if they were out of the stranger's lot of jewelry.

The gamblers went back to their cards after dinner and played until supper. Sometimes the stranger's enemy seemed to be winning, but mostly he was losing. Stephen noticed that the stranger avoided looking at the player's hand as he passed the card-table, and otherwise kept quite away from him. There was a good deal of loud talking and quarreling among the gamblers. Now and then one of them left his place and went to the bar, and came back with his face redder than before. All their faces were red.

The enchantment of the river, with its life afloat and ashore, continued for Stephen. They met some of the large New Orleans side-wheel packets whose swelling vastness dwarfed the stern-wheeler from the Ohio; but when this had the river to itself, it seemed of no mean size, as it pushed among the flat boats and traders. When it stopped beside a wharf-boat in landing or loading freight it was of even towering grandeur.

Sometimes it stopped at little towns where there was no wharf-boat; but at night there were beacons of blazing fat-pine, swinging from iron-shod poles driven into the bank to light the embarking or disembarking passengers. At such point a planter, dazzling in white linen from head to foot, came aboard through the glare of the beacons, with his wife and daughters, and slave-women bringing their handbags after them.

Stephen instantly contrived how, by a happy chance, he should get to speak with one of the girls whom he had fallen in love with more than the others and who loved him again. He overcame her father's ill-will and married her, and she freed her portion of the slaves. In a swift process of time the planter freed all the other slaves, and came to live with Stephen in the North, or perhaps, England. "Slaves cannot breathe in England," he remembered. At the same time, before the gangplank could be pulled in after the embarkation of the planter's family, he was aware of the second mate pushing one of those drunken gamblers down to the shore on it. It was the one who had been so brutal to the stranger; he was swearing at the mate over his shoulder; their faces almost touched, and it was as if their curses clashed together.

The deck-hands began to lift the gang-plank, when a passenger carrying a carpet-bag in one hand and holding his hat on with the other ran tottering over it to the land. He stumbled up the bank on the heels of the gambler, and kept himself from falling by catching his hand through the gambler's arm and pulling himself up close to him. He lifted his face and Stephen saw in the light of the beacon at their shoulders that it was the face of the stranger. He was smiling on his enemy as if he might have chosen to follow him and share his banishment and disgrace. Then the two burst into a jeering laugh together and wagged their hands in mockery at the boat.

Stephen kept his watch-guard in his pocket till the boat got back to Pittsburg, and the pilot never wore his chain so far as Stephen saw. They did not speak of the man who had sold it to them; Stephen in fact did not make friends with the pilot again. Certain of the ladies wore their neck-chains for a day or two; but as if some rumor went about that made then ashamed, they ceased to wear them.

At Pittsburg Stephen carried his watch-guard to have it tested by a jeweler. The jeweler took a little bottle and touched the chain with the acid from it. Then he pushed it across the showcase.

"Is it good?" Stephen faltered.

"Good to throw at a dog," the jeweler said.

Stephen knew this or the like of it already, but now he had the final authority to drop the thing into the street when he went out. A skulking loafer slipped from a doorway and picked it up, in the delusion that he was stealing value.

This was the beginning of Stephen's pleasure in the ironical color of his experience and the ending of his wrath for being the easy prey of a plausible scoundrel. What had happened was nothing to what could happen. He thought how he might turn the adventure to account in the sort of literature which he loved almost as much as he loved the highest poetry. He wondered whether he should treat it like certain of the episodes in *Don Quixote*, or like Thackeray in some of those picaresque sketches of his. But he was aware of a certain crudeness in the setting. Could polite lovers of such fiction be made to care for something that happened on a stern-wheel steamboat between Pittsburg and St. Louis? At the same time, did not that very crudeness of the setting give a novel value to the facts? He played with the amusing risks and chances of his rascals, their scrapes and escapes; their cunning flourished under the magic of his fancy; he became fond of them in the growth of their qualities which were the defects of other men's virtues. He exulted in their iniquitous courage, their wicked self-devotion. He tasted a deleterious delight in working out their devices of cheating and swindling. Without really beginning their story, by a quite original stroke of invention he had them end in a prosperity defiant of both literary and moral convention. He admired the boldness and novelty of the thing; he imagined its flattering recognition by criticism.

But when he looked again at the material which fortune had thrown into his hands, he saw its chances of tragedy increasing with the passage of time. The field of his rascal's adventures narrowed each year; always haunting the rivers, they must often take the same boat at such short intervals that the officers would come to know them; they must often escape at the same landing, where they would be recognized with welcome more and more ironical; their game would often be spoiled from the start; their dupes would know them and their lives would never be safe; they would be in constant danger of violence. He followed them from one squalid event to another, through the mud or the dust of the brutal little riverside towns, where they were tarred and feathered and ridden on rails by the hooting mob, or stabbed or shot.

When the law sometimes saved them from the mob and sent them to prison, he saw them come out white and weak and bewildered, in a world where they could find nothing but harm to do. They grew old on his hands and became each other's foes in the lapse of the black arts which had kept them friends. At last, one of them would sicken and die, after weeks, or months, or years; Stephen rejected a melodramatic chance that should take them off together. The one who was left would wander back to the village where he had been a worthless boy and end there a friendless pauper.

If the right moral could be read from it, Stephen felt that their tale would be one of the saddest of the human stories. In the hands of a master it would be one of the most powerful, because the elements were the dust of the earth which all men were made from; but Stephen knew himself wanting in the mastery needed. Perhaps some day he would win that mastery, but now he could only wait; and as he did not write the comedy of those evil lives, because he rejected it, so he did not write the tragedy of them, because it rejected him. Their story remained with him a tale untold.

Annotated Story List

THIS ANNOTATED BIBLIOGRAPHY was compiled using William Gibson and George Arms's *Bibliography of William Dean Howells*, George Carrington and Ildikó de Papp Carrington's *Plots and Characters in the Fiction of William Dean Howells*, and Thomas Wortham's *The Early Prose Writings of William Dean Howells 1853–1861*. Unless otherwise indicated, all items on this list were signed by Howells. Each entry includes basic bibliographical information: the story's title and the location and date of its first publication. I have noted items that were unsigned or signed with a pseudonym. I have also used the following parenthetical abbreviations: (C&C) to indicate that the story is listed in Carrington and Carrington's volume; (VB) to indicate that the story is listed in Vito Brenni's generally unreliable list of Howells's short stories; (W) to show that the story is reprinted in full in Thomas Wortham's book; and (TR) to show that the story is one of Howells's nine Turkish Room stories.

Most of Howells's stories were published first in periodicals and reprinted later in collections. The name of the collection in which a story was reprinted is, in most cases, the last item of information included in each entry. If the story has an unusual publishing history or was reprinted independently, I note that as well, but I do not pretend to provide a complete record of the publishing history of all the stories. ("Editha," for example, was republished quite a number of times, but I list only its first publication, in *Harper's Monthly,* and its subsequent publication in *Between the Dark and Daylight.*)

The bibliographical listings for the stories that are included in this selected edition are followed by the instruction to "see" the page number on which they appear. Listings for stories which I do not include in this edition are followed by brief annotations. I have tried, in my annotations, to avoid duplicating the work that was done by Carrington and Carrington, and so I keep my plot summaries to a minimum. Instead, my purpose is to comment on the stories critically, to guide the reader through any criticism that has been published about the stories, to point out ways in which the stories connect to other stories and to other works by Howells, to discuss autobiographical implications, and, at times, to express my opinion of the quality of the story in question. I also briefly discuss questions of attribution.

All references are to the Works Cited list which appears at the end of this work.

1853   "A Tale of Love and Politics, Adventures of a Printer Boy." *Ashtabula Sentinel* 1 Sept. 1853: 1. (C&C) unsigned

Apparently Howells's first published fiction, "A Tale of Love and Politics" is the "obvious daydream" (Cady, *Road* 49) of a sixteen-year-old romantic. George Wentworth, the printer-boy, wins the hearts of the citizens of a town in upstate New York with his courage, strength, patriotism, honor, and finally, his tremendous writing ability. The "love" is that between George and Ida S——; the "politics" is the Congressional campaign of Judge S——, Ida's father and George's patron. The newspaper and printshop setting is called "fresh . . ." by Cady (49), but "not uncommon" by Thomas Wortham (personal letter). Rodney Olsen, noting Howells's anxiety about leaving home, calls "A Tale of Love and Politics" a "success tale that countered family stories of desperation and failure" (99). He also comments on the importance of "chance or luck" in both Howells's story and in other success tales of the period (99, 302).

The attribution to Howells, made "through background and narrator of story and its publication in the Howells newspaper" (Gibson and Arms 74) is generally accepted, although not proven.

"The Journeyman's Secret, Stray Leaves from the Diary of a Journeyman Printer." *Ashtabula Sentinel* 3 Nov. 1853: 1. (C&C) (VB) unsigned

Howells's second story, unlike his first, has a unified plot and a first-
person narrator. Set in a print shop, it includes some realistic details
and believable dialogue. "The Journeyman's Secret" is the story of the
silent, hardworking "Quaker," whose unsociability and miserliness
are resented by his fellow printers. When their taunts finally goad
him into breaking his silence, he reveals that he is the sole support of
a large family and is saving for an operation for his blind sister. The
printers are tearfully repentant and raise enough money for the operation, which, we learn, is a success. The story is juvenile, but well
structured, and the emphasis on false perceptions is interesting in the
light of Howells's later work. As with "A Tale of Love and Politics,"
the attribution to Howells was made "through background and narrator of story and its publication in the Howells newspaper" (Gibson
and Arms 74).

1854   "Dropped Dead: A Ghost Story." *Ohio Farmer* 11 May 1854. signed
Will Narlie (W)

"Dropped Dead: A Ghost Story" is interesting primarily in the light
of Howells's later stories. As Thomas Wortham says, it is "hackneyed
and confused in its aim" (39), as it moves from the "local color" and
folk-dialogue of its opening to the inconclusive psychological portrai-
ture of Robert Glen, the mysterious and silent stranger who drops
dead, to the thoroughly Gothic climax, and finally to the Irvingesque
conclusion. "Dropped Dead" is the story of young Tom Smith, who
dares to visit a haunted tavern and is taken on a strange journey by
the ghost of Robert Glen—unless his whole experience was actually
a dream.

   The story has some noteworthy parallels in Howells's later fiction.
Glen, like Ransom Hilbrook of "A Difficult Case," hopes that there will
be no afterlife. The narrator's digression about his "old child-fears"
recalls Howells's childhood. And the ending, with its evasion of responsibility for the truth of the tale, sets the pattern to be found in all
of Howells's later psychic tales. The story has another parallel as well.
The characterization of Tom Smith ("He played truant, and passed
hours in the woods dreaming of Sinbad, when he should have been
cyphering, and in an old cabin near the village he dwelt—two or three
summer afternoons—as the wretched castaway, Crusoe, at times, and

again as the forty thieves"—42) anticipates the creation of Tom Sawyer more than twenty years later. [It should be noted that the pseudonym with which Howells signed this story—Will Narlie—had been used at least three times before (in "A New Year's Glimpse of Memory Land," "A Sunny Day in Winter," and "Letters from a Village," all published earlier in 1854); Gibson and Arms's conjecture that "Ye Childe and ye angell" may have been the first work to be signed with this name [75] was in error.]

"How I Lost a Wife, an Episode in the Life of a Bachelor." *Ashtabula Sentinel* 18 May 1854: 1. unsigned (C&C) (VB) (W)

"How I Lost a Wife" is certainly the best-known of Howells's early stories. Both Cady and Gibson and Arms link the story, in which the antics of a mischievous dog put the narrator in a humiliating position, with Howells's adolescent fear of dogs, specifically his hypochondriachal hydrophobia. Elizabeth Prioleau, although she does not specifically refer to "How I Lost a Wife," discusses Howells's use of dogs as personal and literary symbols of sexual evil (10) and notes that dogs are "also, significantly, symbols of lust in Emmanual Swedenborg, his family prophet" (189). (Prioleau's theories may be profitably applied to "How I Lost a Wife.") The most extensive treatment of the story is the Freudian analysis provided by John W. Crowley (*Truth* 24–25). Focusing on the narrator's irrationality, Crowley argues that the story implies a link between Howells's fear of dogs and the nervous breakdown he suffered soon after the story's publication. (Crowley also draws an interesting parallel between the narrator of "How I Lost a Wife" and some of Poe's mad narrators—165.) Autobiographical considerations aside, the story is lively and amusing, "a clever blend of Ik Marvel and Western humor" (Cady, *Road* 55). The attribution to Howells is "solely circumstantial" (Wortham 45), and is based on Howells's fear of dogs, the character of the story's narrator, and its prose style.

1859   "Not a Love Story." *Odd-Fellows Casket and Review* (Feb. 1859): 222–24. assigned in volume index (C&C) (VB) (W)

"Not a Love Story" is Howell's first published work to be explicitly set in "Dulldale." It presents the courtship of Arthur and Fanny, which, as we learn in an envoy to the story, leads to nothing, as Fanny marries Arthur's rival and Arthur remains a bachelor. "Not a Love Story" is interesting primarily because of the contrast between its self-conscious and romantic prose style and its realistic dialogue and conclusion. The story includes, for example, an interlude in which flowers, growing in the garden where Fanny and Arthur walk and flirt, whisper about "the rose's flirtation with the peony," and which concludes when the narrator wonders whether the subject of the flowers' gossip was "really the rose and the peony." This sort of precious digression is in sharp contrast to Fanny's mother's dialect, and to the envoy, which states that Fanny "is grown fat, and slaps her children when they are bad." Rodney Olsen points out that each of the story's three scenes ends with "a deflationary point" and that this amounts to a "devious undermining of sentimental expectation" (158). In this way, the story anticipates "A Dream." "Not a Love Story" is, for Howells, relatively lascivious, including kisses and embraces, and a surprising passage about the vicarious pleasure that novelists enjoy in describing "the caresses enjoyed by their heroes."

"The Valentine." *Ohio State Journal* 16 February 1859. unsigned (W)

"The Valentine" is a very slight piece, recounting the anxiety of Arabella as she waits to receive a valentine from Charles, her beau. The influence of Thackeray is readily apparent, as the story is marked by authorial intrusion and comment. "The Valentine" is thus noteworthy as an example of the narrative style that Howells later rejected. It is also an early indication of Howells's instinct for choosing the small unexceptional moment as the material of fiction. Perhaps the most interesting part of the story is the ending, in which the author abruptly grants privacy to his characters, declaring that "we do not believe in those novelists, poets and play-writers who impertinently follow their hero and heroine to the very threshold of wedded life, feasting an unnatural curiosity on . . . tender and enrapturing scenes." This forms a nice contrast to the apparent indulgence of "Not a Love Story," published in the same month. (The following April, Charles and Arabella reappeared in a sketch called "A Perfect Goose." It was published in the *Odd-Fellows Casket and Review* and signed by "Chispa.")

"Romance of the Crossing." *Odd-Fellows Casket and Review* (May 1859): 443–44. signed Chispa (C&C) (VB) (W)

"Romance of the Crossing" is a very slight, mannered piece about a lovers' quarrel between Edwin and Angelina. The quarrel is resolved when Edwin nobly steps with his freshly blackened boots into a muddy crossing, in order to let Angelina pass. Howells maintains a tone of mild satire and sarcasm throughout (e.g., "People in love are always the most reasonable creatures in the world"). The story demonstrates Howells's interest, from an early age, in the details of everyday life, and in the essential triviality of events that may rule our emotional lives. It is also noteworthy for the inconclusiveness of its ending, a hallmark of Howellsian fiction that continued throughout his career. For the most part, however, "Romance of the Crossing," along with the two other stories published in 1859, provides a standard by which to judge Howells's growth in the years ahead.

1861   "A Dream." *Knickerbocker* 58 (Aug. 1861): 146–50. (VB) (W)

See p. 1.

1868   "Tonelli's Marriage." *Atlantic Monthly* 22 (July 1868): 96–110. (C&C) (*A Fearful Responsibility*)

"Tonelli's Marriage," set in Venice, marks "Howell's first fictional use of his consular years" (Woodress 163). It also vividly demonstrates (as do the sketches that appear in *Venetian Life, Italian Journeys* and *Suburban Sketches*) the maturation of Howells's skill as a writer and as a prose stylist. Although Kenneth Eble is mistaken in calling this piece "Howells' first published short story" (49), his impression that this is the first story of the Howells we have come to know is not entirely wrong.

"Tonelli's Marriage" is a subtle and quietly humorous study of the relationship between a middle-aged bachelor and the family of his employer, which includes a strictly chaperoned young woman. Tomasso Tonelli's friendship with her family allows the girl a small measure of freedom, which she must lose when Tonelli finally marries. "Tonelli's Marriage" is briefly discussed by James Woodress, who notes that it "captures faithfully the atmosphere of the city, the economic conditions under the Austrian occupation, the social customs of the people, the gossiping in the cafes, and the suppressed patriotism of the *irredentisti*" (164). The situation and most of the characters of the story were drawn from Howells's own experience in Venice, and the biographical parallels are noted by Cady and Woodress.

The story is interesting not only biographically, but in its demonstration of Howells's interest in what Woodress calls "social protocol" (164). There is no doubt that Howells's observations of European customs drew his attention back to American customs—and of course the contrast between the two led to the development of the "international novel."

1870 "A Romance of Real Life." *Atlantic Monthly* 25 (March 1870): 305–12. (C&C) (VB) (*Suburban Sketches*)

See p. 11.

"A Day's Pleasure." *Atlantic Monthly* 26 (July–Sept. 1870): 107–14, 223–30, 341–46. (C&C) (VB) (*Suburban Sketches*) (Reprinted as *A Day's Pleasure*, Boston: J. R. Osgood, 1876, and in *A Day's Pleasure and Other Sketches*. Boston: Houghton, Mifflin, 1881.)

"A Day's Pleasure" is not very storylike, but it merits inclusion in this list because of the attention paid to it by George Carrington (*Drama*), who calls it, variously, "a slight but interesting tale" (8), an "easily moving sketch" (35), "an early attempt . . . at consecutive fictional narrative" (37), a "story," (62), and a "crucial link . . . between essay and anatomy-fiction" (153). "A Day's Pleasure" concerns a Boston family's attempt to spend a day at the beach and the many obstacles, imposed from both without and within, that they encounter instead. After a tiring day of disappointments, the family returns home to find a lost child in their home, who requires their attention and energy. Carrington notes that George Bennett, in *William Dean Howells: The Development of a Novelist*, explains that the episode of the lost child was added to the story so that it "could be 'stretched to three issues' [Bennett 13] of the *Atlantic*" (35). But, Carrington argues, this "filler" material is of considerable significance, as it may "uncover deeper areas of the psyche than materials chosen consciously to fit into some preexisting logical scheme" (35n). In a nutshell, Carrington equates the situation of the lost child, the "symbol of man lost in an alien world" (35), with that imposed upon the family by their day's misadventures. He draws attention to the resoundingly confident conclusion of the story (the child's reunion with his own family), comparing it to "the end of Howells' later, major novels" (63). (I would compare it also to the ambiguous endings of most of Howells's short stories.)

Aside from this atypical conclusion, "A Day's Pleasure" is typical of Howells. Like all of the *Suburban Sketches*, it applies the techniques of travel literature to the domestic American scene and in so doing subverts the stereotypes of the romantic and the real. The lost child episode has obvious parallels to "A Romance of Real Life," and the descriptions of travel by rail and water tie "A Day's Pleasure" to much of Howells's work.

1872   "Incident." *Pellet* 2 (17 April 1872): 4. (C&C) (VB)

     See p. 28.

1877   "At the Sign of the Savage." *Atlantic Monthly* 40 (July 1877): 36–48. (C&C) (VB) (*A Fearful Responsibility*)

"At the Sign of the Savage," an amusing story, is based on one of Howells's own experiences. The germ of the story is told again in "Overland to Venice," an autobiographical account of Howells's 1861 journey from northern Ohio to Venice, where he began his appointment as U.S. Consul. Upon arriving in Vienna, Howells (and his fictional counterpart, Colonel Ned Kenton) asked to be driven to the Kaiserin Elisabeth hotel, and it was only upon leaving the hotel the following morning for a day of sightseeing and then unsuccessfully trying to return that he learned that he had actually been brought to another hotel, its name and location unknown to him. Howells's, and then Kenton's, attempts to find out where he had in fact been staying (and in Kenton's case, to find the presumably distraught wife he had left there) provide the plot of the story.

In "At the Sign of the Savage," Howells's experience is used to explore his recurring theme of false perceptions. The story begins with an alternate, purely verbal, treatment of this theme, Kenton's extended joke about the "system of deception" practiced upon European travelers: "'Ah, they pretend this is Stuttgart, do they?' he said on arriving at the Suabian capital. 'A likely story! . . . It's outrageous, the way they let these swindling little towns palm themselves off upon the traveller for cities he's heard of'"(170). Kenton's satiric chorus on the slipperiness of perception and on the disparity between expectation, often fueled by literature, and reality is reflected in the action that follows. (Kenton's jokes, of course, bring to mind Twain's *The Innocents Abroad* [1869], which Howells had reviewed in the *Atlantic Monthly*.)

"At the Sign of the Savage" is of further interest because of its European setting and because of the relationship between Colonel and Mrs. Kenton, who are reminiscent of all of Howells's married couples. (Basil and Isabel March, of course, had made their first appearance just five years earlier, in *Their Wedding Journey*.)

1886   "Christmas Every Day." *Saint Nicholas* 13 (Jan. 1886): 163–67. (C&C) (VB) (*Christmas Every Day*)

     See p. 33.

1893 "Turkeys Turning the Tables." (C&C) (*Christmas Every Day*)

"Turkeys Turning the Tables," the second of Howells's stories for children, concerns a little girl who dreams that the Thanksgiving turkey she has just eaten comes back as a ghost to seek revenge. The story is linked to "Christmas Every Day" in a number of ways. Both are apparently set in the same year, "Christmas" shortly after Thanksgiving, and "Turkeys" on Christmas morning. Both deal with the consequences of self-indulgence and with the morally instructive role of storytelling. And both play with the contrast between fiction and truth, dream and reality (although "Turkeys" takes this dichotomy much further). But the most obvious link is the common fictional frame: both stories are told by a teasing, affectionate father to his daughter, who monitors the story's details and tries to direct its outcome. While the story within the story (the revenge of the Thanksgiving turkey) is not one of Howells's best, the depiction of family life in general and of the teasing ways of fathers in particular is delightful and authentic.

"The Pony Engine and the Pacific Express." (C&C) (*Christmas Every Day*)

"The Pony Engine and the Pacific Express" is the story of a little Pony Engine who longs to be a passenger locomotive and of its race across the country with the grand Pacific Express. The story is told by "the papa" to his son and daughter on Christmas Eve. Although this fictional frame links it to the other stories collected in *Christmas Every Day*, "The Pony Engine" is by far the darkest story in the volume; at its conclusion, the Pony Engine drowns in the Pacific Ocean and its grieving mother loses her mind. The father's clever personification of the trains in Fitchburg Depot and his detailed description of the cross-country race are the most amusing aspects of this rather odd tale. (When Edward Wagenknecht notes that this story "anticipates Carl Sandburg's Rootabaga Stories" [304], he is probably thinking of "How the Animals Lost Their Tails and Got Them Back Traveling from Philadelphia to Medicine Hat." In Sandburg's story, "[a] train jumped off the tracks down into the valley and cut across in a straight line on a cut-off, jumped on the tracks again and went on toward Ohio" [226], while in Howells's, "[the Pony Engine] couldn't wait, and so it slipped down from the track to the edge of the river and jumped across, and then scrambled up the embankment to the track again.")

"The Pumpkin-Glory." (C&C) (*Christmas Every Day*)

"The Pumpkin-Glory," like the other stories in *Christmas Every Day*, is told by a father to his children, but it differs from the rest in being a story that the children have heard many times before. It concerns two pumpkin seeds; while the good little seed dreams of becoming a pumpkin pie for a Thanksgiving dinner, the bad pumpkin seed wants to be a morning glory. It arduously climbs a fence and keeps its blossom open in the bright sun and so grows into an odd pear-shaped pumpkin—a pumpkin-glory. The pumpkin-glory is eventually made into a grand jack o' lantern but is finally, ignominiously, eaten by a pig. The personification of the pumpkin seeds and of the other garden vegetables is greatly helped by the illustrations, especially the wonderful picture of the "two little pumpkin seeds" (75).

"Butterflyflutterby and Flutterbybutterfly." (C&C) (*Christmas Every Day*)

"Butterflyflutterby and Flutterbybutterfly" is perhaps Howells's most delightfully unorganized story. Like the other *Christmas Every Day* stories, it is told by "the papa," but his audience this time is "the nephew and the niece," and the story is improvised nonsense, concerning the eponymous prince and princess, their friends the Khan and Khant of Tartary, and the royal prerogative of making a mess. The emphasis on the act of storytelling found throughout *Christmas Every Day* is here brought to the fore, as the father considers which story to tell, stalls in order to gain time for invention, threatens to stop telling the story and finally claims that "the rule of this story is that it has to go on as long as anyone listening remembers [which was Butterflyflutterby and which was Flutterbybutterfly]." Both the narrative itself and the dialogue between the father and the children are charming.

1894   "A Parting and a Meeting." *Cosmopolitan* 18 (Dec. 1894, Jan., Feb. 1895): 183–88, 307–16, 469–74. (Reprinted as *A Parting and a Meeting, Story.* New York: Harper & Brothers, 1896) (C&C)

"A Parting and a Meeting," one of Howells's longer stories, has been largely and undeservedly ignored. As the title suggests, it concerns the parting of a young engaged couple and their brief reunion years later. The couple, driving near their home, come upon a Shaker village and decide to visit it. The young man is immediately so struck by the apparent virtue and truth of the Shaker doctrine, which includes the rejection of marriage in an attempt to create "the angelic life" on earth (39), that he abruptly leaves his fiancée and joins the Shakers. The story resumes sixty years later as the couple, briefly reunited, compare their lives.

The interest of the tale lies in the inconclusive and moving ending, in which each character demonstrates that the angelic life, sought either through juvenile romance, through marriage and family, or through celibacy and devotion to religious doctrine, is unattainable, as human weaknesses and sorrows defeat any ideal. Howells approaches his usual romance/reality dichotomy from an unusual and penetrating angle, as all idealistic expectations of life, those founded in philosophy as well as in romantic dreams, are seen to be inadequate. (My reading of this story differs markedly from that of Carrington and Carrington, who state that at the end of the story, the old man "mixes regret for his loss of [his fiancée] with satisfaction in his Shaker years"—141. It is hard to reconcile this fairly rosy interpretation with the character's peevishness and irritability.)

"A Parting and a Meeting" may be profitably compared with *The Day of Their Wedding* (1896), which also depicts a couple trying to choose between marriage and the Shaker life.

1895 "A Circle in the Water." *Scribner's* 17 (March, April 1895): 293–303, 428–40. (C&C) (VB) (*A Pair of Patient Lovers*)

"A Circle in the Water" is one of Howells's more significant and masterful short stories. It deals with the large question of how and if evil deeds can be expiated and it does so, as was typical of Howells, within the small frame of family life and social manners. The central metaphor of a circle in the water that spreads and eventually ceases is used first to explore life's impermanence and the eventual obliteration of good deeds, and then as a symbol of sins and sorrows diminishing and ceasing in a sea of love.

"A Circle in the Water" is one of Howells's many Basil and Isabel March stories (see above pp. 14, 17n.4) and thus, as Jerome Klinkowitz points out, focuses on how the couple "face the responsibility of personal moral acts," especially acts motivated by aesthetic preferences rather than by ethical standards (304). The story concerns Tedham, a released convict in search of his estranged daughter. Tedham enlists the Marches' help in finding his daughter, and their ambivalent feel-

ings about the morality of uniting father and daughter pull them into
an ethical dilemma, so that the focus of the story changes from Tedham's expiation of sins to the "romantic" ("Circle" 349) and thus immoral acts of the Marches and their neighbors.

"A Circle in the Water" can be profitably compared to a number of
Howells's works, most notably *The Quality of Mercy* (1892) and the
much earlier "A Romance of Real Life," as it shares major plot elements with both (the criminal father, the long absence from an estranged daughter, the desire for forgiveness). It is also reminiscent, as
Kirk and Kirk point out (140), of "Materials of a Story," a poem from
Stops of Various Quills (1895). Elsa Nettels compares it to Fitzgerald's
"Babylon Revisited." And Cady notes that the story's title and central
metaphor may have come from a vision reported by George Fox, the
founder of the Society of Friends (*Realist* 202).

"A Circle in the Water" is also interesting in its exploration of the
bond between father and daughter (always worth examining in the
works that Howells wrote after the death of his daughter Winny in
1889) and in the contrast it draws between the instinctive morality of
"simple selfish" acts (349) and the frequently immoral requirements
of social duty and manners that ignore or discount the higher ethics
of love.

1897   "A Pair of Patient Lovers." *Harper's Monthly* 95 (Nov. 1897): 832–51.
(C&C) (VB) (*A Pair of Patient Lovers*)

"A Pair of Patient Lovers," a satisfying and memorable story, can serve
as an excellent introduction to Howells's work, as it includes many of
the characteristics and themes of his other stories and his novels. It
concerns the prolonged engagement of Arthur Glendenning and
Edith Bentley, who sacrifice their own happiness in order to please
Edith's imperious invalid mother. In its treatment of the moral dangers of self-sacrifice, this story strongly recalls the dangers that
Penelope Lapham faces in *The Rise of Silas Lapham*. Just as in that
novel the Reverend Mr. Sewell argues that prevailing romantic notions of self-sacrifice are "the figment of the shallowest sentimentality" (222) and contrary to the very essence of marriage, so in "A Pair
of Patient Lovers" Isabel March calls Miss Bentley's devotion to her
mother, rather than to her fiancé, "all wrong and—romantic. Her
mother has asked more than she had any right to ask, and Miss Bentley has tried to do more than she can perform" (37).

The emphasis on marriage and on the obligation of married (or in this case, engaged) couples to place their own needs ahead of the needs of outsiders ties "A Pair of Patient Lovers" to another work of Howells's, *The Shadow of a Dream*. It is also tied to this novella (and to other works as well) by being a Basil and Isabel March story, and as such, at least partly an examination of the habit of "fictionalizing" (see above pp. 45–46). Basil and Isabel's consideration of the plight of Glendenning and Miss Bentley as the material of fiction, in fact, forms the story as much as the actual engagement and its dramatic— almost melodramatic—denouement. As Jerome Klinkowitz points out in his excellent analysis of the Basil and Isabel March stories, "the Marches' sincere concern for their friends is [characteristically] mixed with a wish to fictionalize a more aesthetically pleasing ending to their experience" (316). Klinkowitz notes that in *The Shadow of a Dream*, Basil admits to having dealt with the main characters of that story, after their deaths, "as arbitrarily as with the personages in a fiction, and [having] placed and replaced them at our pleasure in the game, which they played so disastrously, so that we could bring it to a fortunate close for them" (Klinkowitz 316, *Shadow* 113), and that in "A Pair of Patient Lovers," Isabel feels "as if she had invented [Glendenning and Miss Bentley] and set them going in their advance toward each other, like two mechanical toys" (Klinkowitz 316, *Pair* 12).

"A Pair of Patient Lovers" is connected in a simpler way to the first Basil and Isabel March story, *Their Wedding Journey;* it begins as the Marches retrace the route of their wedding journey (as they do again in "Niagara Revisited"). But, as Carrington and Carrington point out, Howells commits an error of chronology in assigning the opening of this story to the year 1870, as Basil and Isabel marry in 1870, and in the beginning of "A Pair of Patient Lovers" they refer to their children.

Like all the Basil and Isabel March stories, "A Pair of Patient Lovers" is humorous, told with a light touch, and yet presents serious moral issues. It is a tale of character and psychology, and is set on a small, intimate scale, including only three main characters besides the Marches, who serve primarily as a chorus to the action.

The story is also tied to much of Howells's work by its New England setting and its references to both Ohio (Glendenning is originally the rector of an Ohio church) and Canada. In addition to its treatment by Klinkowitz (315–16), the story is briefly mentioned by Edward Wagenknecht (40, 232) and Oscar Firkins (208).

1899   "The Magic of a Voice." *Lippincott's* 64 (Dec. 1899): 901–28. (C&C) (VB) (*A Pair of Patient Lovers*)

See p. 45.

1900   "The Pursuit of the Piano." *Harper's Monthly* 100 (April 1900): 725–46. (C&C) (VB) (*A Pair of Patient Lovers*)

"The Pursuit of the Piano" is justifiably referred to as "a light story" by Cady (*Realist* 259) and it is interesting primarily because of its similarity to other stories of Howells's, particularly "The Magic of a Voice." (See above pp. 46–48 for a full comparison of these two stories.) The eponymous piano belongs to Miss Phyllis Desmond, whose name on the side of the piano's packing case enchants Hamilton Gaites and lures him to Lower Merritt, New Hampshire. There, the detailed romantic fantasy that he has spun from the name is destroyed and he must modify his imaginative creation in order to make it agree with the reality that he finds. Thus the story, like many others in the Howells canon, uses the device of "fictionalizing" (see above pp. 45–46) to explore both the benefits and the hazards of the romantic imagination.

"A Difficult Case." *Atlantic Monthly* 86 (July, Aug. 1900): 24–36, 205–17. (C&C) (VB) (*A Pair of Patient Lovers*)

See p. 79.

1901   "The Angel of the Lord." First printed as "At Third Hand, a Psychological Inquiry." *Century* 61 (Feb. 1901): 496–506. (C&C) (VB) (TR) (*Questionable Shapes*)

See p. 122.

1902   "His Apparition." *Harper's Monthly* 104 (March 1902): 621–48. (C&C) (VB) (*Questionable Shapes*)

"His Apparition" is a ghost story and a romance. It is also a psychological exploration of the dangers of vanity and the demands of honesty. Arthur Hewson, a bachelor and a New York socialite, is briefly visited by an apparition one morning at the St. Johnswort Hotel. His attempts to discover the meaning of his experience, and to decide whether, and how, to speak of it, are aided by his acquaintance with Rosalie Hernshaw, another guest at the hotel. The story focuses on the effects of a psychic experience, rather than on the experience itself. In many ways, it is a comedic version of Henry James's "The

Beast in the Jungle" (1901) and the two stories are briefly compared in Charles Crowley's *The Mask of Fiction* (146). "His Apparition" is also discussed by Charles Feigenoff, who examines its psychological and "spiritual" realism. The story includes brief references to the practice of spiritualism, to the Society for Psychical Research, and to Ibsen's "Ghosts." Wanhope, the psychologist of the Turkish Room stories, appears as a minor character.

1903   "Though One Rose from the Dead." *Harper's Monthly* 106 (April 1903): 724–38. (C&C) (VB) (TR) (*Questionable Shapes*)

"Though One Rose from the Dead" is the story of Marion and Rupert Alderling, a couple whose extreme intimacy is enhanced by their apparent psychic abilities. Even when parted, they seem able to communicate by thought transference and visual manifestations. The couple, both religious agnostics, debate the possibility of a life after death, and Marion wonders whether their psychic union could survive if one of them were to die. Wanhope, the psychologist of the Turkish Room stories, is a witness to their unusual relationship, to Marion's death, and to Rupert's inconclusive account of Marion's apparent return from death. The story takes the form of a letter written by Wanhope to Acton, the usual narrator of the Turkish Room stories. Wanhope, unsurprisingly, implies that psychological explanations can be found for the events of the story, but he refrains from forming any definite conclusions. In the course of his letter, Wanhope meditates on fiction, marriage, the differences between men and women, the limitations of agnosticism, and the theories of William James. "Though One Rose from the Dead" is insightfully discussed in Charles Crowley's *The Mask of Fiction* (152–55).

1905   "Editha." *Harper's Monthly* 110 (Jan. 1905): 214–24. (C&C) (VB) (*Between the Dark and the Daylight*)

See p. 150.

"A Case of Metaphantasmia." *Harper's Weekly* 49 (16 Dec. 1905): 20–22, 40–41. (C&C) (VB) (TR) (*Between the Dark and the Daylight*)

"A Case of Metaphantasmia," a fascinating if initially mystifying story, has been clearly and convincingly illuminated by Charles L. Crow in "Howells and William James: 'A Case of Metaphantasmia' Solved." The story is told by a Bostonian named Newton to the habitués of the Turkish Room, and it concerns his train trip from Boston to New

York one Christmas Eve. Newton closely recounts his thoughts on that evening, particularly his worries about his fearful wife and his memories of the recurring nightmare of his old college roommate, whom he has just reencountered in the smoking car. He then tells of waking to find the sleeper car in pandemonium, as all the passengers apparently share, by some "species of dream-transference," the same nightmare of burglars. (Metaphantasmia, according to Crow, is "the term for shared phantasmic experience used in psychic research"— 173.) The story offers three explanations for the bizarre events of the night, but, typically, embraces none.

Crow's thesis is that the events in the sleeping car, which are so ludicrous that they "will recall silent screen comedy to today's readers" (172), are dreamt by Newton, and that they are suggested by the stream of associations that precede them in Newton's waking hours. The story is thus a demonstration of concepts that William James proposed in *The Principles of Psychology* (1891), namely "The Stream of Thought" and "Association" (Crow 177). (Of course this story does not represent Howells's only use of these concepts; see, for example, "An Experience" [1915].) Howells's innovation lies not in including stream of consciousness and association in his story, but in making them both "the subject of the tale" and "the structural principle of it" (Crow 177). His achievement is heightened by the fact that the story is both believable and funny.

Crow suggests that "A Case of Metaphantasmia" can be compared to Mark Twain's "Which Was the Dream?" (Twain's "The McWilliamses and the Burglar Alarm" also comes to mind.) Crow also notes that Newton's dream is "based on Howells' own nightmares of burglars and of perilous train rides" (176).

1906 "Braybridge's Offer." *Harper's Monthly* 112 (Jan. 1906): 229–36. (C&C) (VB) (TR) (*Between the Dark and the Daylight*)

"Braybridge's Offer" is a neat example of what Howells's Wanhope calls the "inventive habit of mind" (166) and what I refer to as "fictionalizing" (see above pp. 45–46). The usual occupants of the Turkish Room discuss the recent engagement of Braybridge, a member of their club, and wonder how it came about. Halson, a new acquaintance, offers his guess, which is accepted as the true story by his listeners, but which is finally understood to be pure conjecture. A second reading of the story reveals Halson's pleasure in his fictional creation, and his careful avoidance of claims of actual fact. "Braybridge's Offer" is the story *of* a story, and joins "The Magic of a

Voice," "The Pursuit of the Piano," and the Basil and Isabel March stories in its emphasis on the pleasures and pitfalls of the creative imagination. ("Braybridge's Offer" was reprinted in 1906 in *Quaint Courtships*, which Howells edited with Henry Mills Alden.)

"The Chick of the Easter Egg." *Harper's Weekly* 50 (14 April 1906): 509–12. (C&C) (VB) (TR) (*Between the Dark and the Daylight*)

"The Chick of the Easter Egg" is a sentimental story told by Newton, who also narrates the story in "A Case of Metaphantasmia." Although told in the cloistered setting of the Turkish Room, it is a domestic tale, concerning a family's Easter trip to Bethlehem, Pennsylvania, and the pleasure that their children take in pretending to believe that their colored egg will actually hatch and yield them a surprise. This otherwise slight piece gains added interest from its fairly exotic setting, its descriptions of German-speaking Moravians and their observance of Easter, and Newton's childhood memories of coloring and fighting with Easter eggs—then unknown to New England—in a "soft Southwestern latitude" (presumably southern Ohio). The story is loosely linked to a number of works by Howells; its references to apartment hunting recall *A Hazard of New Fortunes*; the use of the term "goose" ("We were young people in those days, and goose meant everything") connect it to Howells's juvenile sketch "A Perfect Goose" (1859); its treatment of Easter is paralleled by Howells's use of Christmas in many stories; and its comparisons of Boston, New York, and "the West" recall much of Howells's work, especially the Basil and Isabel March tales.

"The Eidolons of Brooks Alford." *Harper's Monthly* 113 (Aug. 1906): 387–97. (VB) (TR) (*Between the Dark and the Daylight*)

See p. 169.

"A Sleep and a Forgetting." *Harper's Weekly* 50–51 (15, 22, and 29 Dec. 1906; 5 Jan. 1907):1781–84, 1862–65, 1899–1901; 24–27. (C&C) (VB) (*Between the Dark and the Daylight*)

"A Sleep and a Forgetting," a long and fascinating story, sheds substantial light both on Howells's theories of psychology and, if autobiography can be inferred from fiction, on Howells's reactions to the illness and death of his daughter Winny. The most thorough discussion of this tale is "Psychic and Psychological Themes in Howells' 'A Sleep and a Forgetting'" by John Crowley and Charles Crow. Crowley and Crow trace the influence of a number of psychologists (S. Weir Mitchell, Pierre Janet, Maurice Maeterlinck, and William James) on

Howells, and show how their various theories (such as Janet's theory of psychic trauma) are explored in the story, which Howells himself called "very subjective, almost psychopathic" (Letter of 11 March 1906). They also note that the piece, like many of Howells's later stories, "does not foreclose psychic possibilities" (47), particularly the phenomenon of mental telepathy. This observation is echoed by Allan Gardner Lloyd-Smith, who calls Nannie Gerald, the heroine of the story, "the vehicle for [Howells's] speculative observations about extra-sensory perception and the intimations of a possible afterlife" (79). Falling as it does into a "crevice between the rational and the mystical" (Crowley and Crow 48), "A Sleep and a Forgetting" is essential reading for those interested in the later, psychological, Howells, and its emphases on memory and perception tie it to earlier work as well. For many readers, however, the autobiographical implications of the story are even more compelling.

"A Sleep and a Forgetting" concerns Abner Gerald and his daughter Nannie, who, after the shock of witnessing her mother's sudden death, loses not only her memory of past events, but practically all faculty of memory. As soon as an event ends, she forgets it, and she remembers people only when in their presence. She becomes, as Crowley and Crow put it, "a perpetually unfallen Eve" (46)—innocent, pure, and childlike. Because the story is set in Europe, Nannie can be seen as an extreme version of Daisy Miller, unwittingly creating social disorder by her ignorance of convention (Crowley and Crow 45). Her relationship with Dr. Matthew Lanfear, an American psychologist who becomes her physician and admirer, is, as Crowley and Crow note, "new fictional territory" (45) for its time, although it has since become a cliché of literature. (An obvious parallel, of course, is *Tender Is the Night*.) Nannie is eventually cured, by another violent shock, and, as expected, she marries Lanfear. The situation of a devoted father caring for his invalid daughter is obviously drawn from Howells's own experience.

What is noteworthy autobiographically, however, is the father's ambiguous desires for his daughter, as he simultaneously hopes for and dreads her possible recovery. Gerald, Crowley and Crow posit, has an unrecognized wish to keep Nannie "in a state of incestuous, infantile attachment to him, to prevent her . . . from waking into psychological and sexual maturity" (49). Crowley and Crow convincingly suggest that Gerald's abrupt death at the end of the story may be simply Howells's fantasy of reviving Winny by sacrificing his own life for her, or more disturbingly, a "symbolic act of suicide, inspired by guilt for whatever unconscious wishes he may have harbored that Winifred would never recover" (49). While they are quick to deemphasize this reading, noting that "Gerald's unconscious selfishness is balanced by his conscious devotion to his daughter" (49), Crowley and Crow have nevertheless added fuel to the fire of speculation surrounding Winny's illness. (For more of Crowley's theories about the relationship between Howells and Winifred, see *Mask* 83–114.)

1907   "A Memory That Worked Overtime." *Harper's Monthly* 115 (Aug. 1907): 415–18. (C&C) (VB) (TR) (*Between the Dark and the Daylight*)
See p. 189.

"A Presentiment." (first printed as "Talking of Presentiments") *Harper's Monthly* 116 (Dec. 1907): 76–81. (C&C) (VB) (TR) (*The Daughter of the Storage*)

This story first appeared as "Talking of Presentiments," in *Harper's Monthly* in December of 1907. It was reprinted as "A Presentiment" in *The Daughter of the Storage* (1916). "A Presentiment" is the eighth of Howells's Turkish Room stories (see above pp. 122–24), and like the others, it is cast as a conversation between four friends. The story within the story is based on a childhood experience of Minver, who tells of an uncle who traveled from Ohio to New York and back, accompanied by a vague foreboding of tragedy. His presentiment, which became clearer and more definite as the trip progressed, was finally realized, although not as he had expected. Minver's childhood resembles Howells's in a number of ways: his home, like Howells's, was just north of Cincinnati, and his childhood friends and relations shared the keen interest in the occult and in psychic phenomena that Howells witnessed in Hamilton. More significantly, Minver's uncle's experience recalls Howells's early presentiments of death, especially his well-documented conviction that he would die at the age of sixteen. Although the Turkish Room frame is not as amusing here as in some of Howells's other stories, Minver's narrative is believable and compelling, and the story's conclusion is chilling.

1911   "The Daughter of the Storage." *Harper's Monthly* 123 (Sept. 1911): 572–83. (C&C) (VB) (*The Daughter of the Storage*)

"The Daughter of the Storage" is a charming but slight romance set mostly in the Constitutional Storage Safe-Deposit Warehouse of New

York. Peter Bream and Charlotte Forsyth meet as toddlers in the warehouse, and their reacquaintance many years later leads to courtship and marriage, both also in the warehouse. Although the plot is conventional, the characters are not, and the insights into the transient life of those who store their goods are fresh. The story can be profitably compared with "Storage," an essay on the philosophical and emotional consequences of storing and then unpacking one's material goods, which appeared in *Harper's Weekly* in 1901 and was reprinted in *Literature and Life* (1902). The subject was obviously of personal interest to the Howellses, who moved from home to home "without ever settling anywhere—until they became nomads whose only reliable address was their summer home" (Cady, *Road* 162). "The Daughter of the Storage" is mentioned briefly by Edward Wagenknecht, who calls it "inconsequential," but adds that it "shows [an] emphasis on moral struggles" (230).

(The story was republished as a separate volume in 1918, apparently as a promotional item for the David Fireproof Storage Warehouses of Chicago. Another edition "was reprinted from the same plates in 1928" for the Security Storage Company of Washington, D.C.—Gibson and Arms 71.)

1912   "The Fulfillment of the Pact." *Harper's Weekly* 56 (14 Dec. 1912): 9–10. (C&C) (VB) (TR)

"The Fulfillment of the Pact" is the sequel to "The Angel of the Lord." Like "Angel," it is a Turkish Room story, and as in "Angel," the narrator Acton repeats a conversation dominated by Wanhope the psychologist, who again meditates on a story told him by Mrs. Ormond. The Ormonds made an agreement to "come back after death and tell the survivor what it's like" and Ormond has apparently fulfilled his pact. Howells includes a short discussion of Platonic and Swedenborgian ideas about the afterlife, and briefly discusses the phenomenon of mental telepathy. The optimism of the story (Ormond's discovery, after death, that "life . . . on earth is not a trick of the Giver" but a pledge of eternal life) is mitigated by the question of Mrs. Ormond's credibility.

1913   "The Critical Bookstore." *Harper's Monthly* 127 (Aug. 1913): 431–42. (C&C) (VB) (*The Daughter of the Storage*)

See p. 198.

1915 "The Return to Favor." *Harper's Monthly* 131 (July 1915): 278–80. (C&C) (VB) (*The Daughter of the Storage*)

"The Return to Favor" seems at first like an odd story for Howells, primarily because of its main character, the ethnically ill-defined tailor. ("Sufferance was the badge of all his tribe" is a paraphrase of Shylock in *The Merchant of Venice* [I, iii] but Morrison is hardly a Jewish name, and the tailor's accent is not easily labeled.) The scope of the story is quite limited; it is as much a character sketch as a story; and the depiction of the battle of the sexes is uncharacteristically pointed. But a closer examination of this slight work reveals that once more Howells is exploring the conflict between romance and realism, between the customers' longing for the ideal and unattainable and their practical knowledge of the way life works. The tailor's promises, though unbelievable, are preferable to the cold assurances of his realistic colleague, and eventually all of the characters realize that what he offers, along with dresses and suits, is an ideal of service.

The story, too, demonstrates Howells's unfailing interests in psychology, particularly the psychology of women; in the world of business and commerce; and in the urban scene. It also reveals his continued skill as a humorist—from the tailor's "airy courage" in pretending that lightly basted garments are in fact finished, to the male customer's simple method of avoiding disappointment.

"Somebody's Mother." *Harper's Monthly* 131 (Sept. 1915): 523–26. (C&C) (VB) (*The Daughter of the Storage*)

"Somebody's Mother" is the odd and largely unsuccessful account of a meeting between a father, son and daughter, a young black woman, and a stranger whom the young woman—in Howells's parlance, "the colored girl"—calls "somebody's mother." It takes place on New York's West Side on a December evening. The story, although weak and meandering, can be included among those that explore the "ethic/aesthetic split," as the father joins "the contributor" (see above "A Romance of Real Life") and Basil and Isabel March in their characteristic bent toward aesthetic considerations. Upon hearing the young black woman's phrase, the father first considers that it sounds "like something out of some cheap story-paper story" (95) and then that it sounds "like a catch from one of those New York songs . . . where the mother represents what is best and holiest." Similarly, upon seeing the old woman being supported by his son and "the colored girl," his first thought is that "the composition was agreeably droll." But Howells makes little of this reaction; instead, he focuses on the honor apparently conferred by the status of motherhood. The story is also interesting in its use of an outdoor urban setting and in its depiction of a small segment of black society.

"An Experience." *Harper's Monthly* 131 (Nov. 1915): 940–42. (C&C) (VB) (*The Daughter of the Storage*)

"An Experience" is a brief account of the sudden death of a stranger. The narrator, an editor like Howells, is moved by the sight of an insurance agent and by the manuscript of a contributor to begin a rambling meditation on human tragedy, language, dreams, and death. His interior monologue is revealed to be a presentiment when the stranger suddenly collapses and dies. The form of "An Experience" is interesting as a Howellsian example of stream-of-consciousness; Howells, of course, through his familiarity with the writings of William James, understood this concept. The story also demonstrates Howells's interest in dying and death; and it is the last story in which he hints at the existence of psychic phenomena—in this case, the narrator's premonition of death.

"A Feast of Reason." (first printed as "Editor's Easy Chair") *Harper's Monthly* 131 (Oct. 1915): 796–99. (*The Daughter of the Storage*)

"A Feast of Reason" is the very odd account of Florindo and Lindora, who, after a thorough discussion of "the grotesqueness of feeding in common," host an afternoon gathering at which no food is served. The bulk of this story consists of their complaints about the ugliness of society dinners, country lunches, afternoon teas, and catered evening parties; and while they bemoan the lost art of conversation, their primary gripe is with the distastefulness of watching people eat. Lindora's social experiment of a menuless entertainment is a failure, but it is hard to tell what conclusion, if any, the story reaches. The piece is, at best, a curiosity, interesting mainly in its depiction of former social customs (and its use of the word "kodaking" to mean photographing).

"A Feast of Reason" was first published as an "Editor's Easy Chair" column in the October 1915 edition of *Harper's Monthly* and was reprinted the following year in *The Daughter of the Storage.*

1916 "The Boarders." *Harper's Monthly* 132 (March 1916): 540–43. (C&C) (VB) (*The Daughter of the Storage*)

Although written late in Howells's career, "The Boarders" hearkens back to Howells's youth, both in its subject matter and in its somewhat overwrought tone. It concerns four roommates (a law student, a divinity student, a medical student and a journalist) living in a poorly run boarding house. Their frustrations over the inadequate accommodations and the bad food culminate in the decision of one to leave; his plan is to sneak away so as to spare the feelings of his poor landlady. But once confronted by the misery of the widow's situation, the remaining three boarders decide to stay as long as they can. They are left, as is typical of Howells, in limbo, wondering if their situation will change.

The story is reminiscent of Howells's early days in Columbus as a boarder sharing a house with fellow journalists, law students, writers, and artists. (It is interesting, but probably not significant, that Howells's story was published the same year as James Joyce's "The Boarding House," with which it shares some common elements.)

"The Pearl." *Harper's Monthly* 133 (Aug. 1916): 409–13. (C&C) (VB)
See p. 219.

"The Rotational Tenants, a Hallowe'en Mystery." *Harper's Monthly* 133 (Oct. 1916): 770–77. (C&C) (VB)

"The Rotational Tenants" is an odd and largely unsuccessful amalgam of a number of genres that Howells used, successfully, in other works. It concerns Fred and Margaret Erlcort, the main characters of "The Critical Bookstore," and begins by continuing in the vein of that story with an emphasis on the domestic dynamics of a realistically presented relationship. It quickly departs from Howellsian realism, however, and becomes a dream vision along the lines of "Turkeys Turning the Table," "A Case of Metaphantasmia" and many of Howells's essays (his Christmas allegories come immediately to mind). Within the dream vision, moreover, is another genre—the utopian, or for Howells, Altrurian, vision. (And because it is set on Halloween, "The Rotational Tenants" can be linked to Howells's other "holiday stories.")

The utopian seed of "The Rotational Tenants" is found, notably, in *The Rise of Silas Lapham* and, still earlier, in Howells's 10 August 1884 letter to his father (*SL* 3: 105). His wonder in that letter at the patience of the miserably housed poor, confronted all summer long by the beautiful empty homes of vacationing wealthy Bostonians, found its way into *Silas Lapham* in the voice of Bromfield Corey. [Howells's sympathy was so deep, in fact, that his original plan was to have Corey wonder why the poor didn't simply blow up the mansions of the rich with dynamite—but the mere mention of dynamite, which was both terrifically destructive and readily available, and so was terrifying to the American public at this time of labor unrest, was enough, as both Kenneth Lynn (279–80) and Edwin Cady (*Road* 68–69) note, to cause "pandemonium" (Cady, *Road* 280) at Howells's publishers. Howells, responding to their immediate and urgent pleas, quickly toned down Corey's comment.] In "The Rotational Tenants," Howells further indulges his speculations about the consequences of correcting the grossly uneven distribution of wealth by renting homes out of season to the needy, as he considers both the practical and the moral problems that this radical housing arrangement would pose. He comes to the conclusion that charity is no panacea and that equality, although theoretically attractive, is practically repulsive. On the other hand, he berates a spokesman of similar ideas, calling him "a mere parasite of pecuniary prosperity" and, damningly, "a capitalist." The story ends with a typically Howellsian lack of certainty.

1917   "A Tale Untold." *Atlantic Monthly* 120 (Aug. 1917): 236–42. (C&C) (VB)

See p. 219.

Works Cited

Primary

April Hopes. New York: Harper & Brothers,1888. *A Selected Edition of W. D. Howells.* Vol. 15, with introduction and notes to the text by Kermit Vanderbilt. Bloomington: Indiana University Press, 1974.

"The Art of the Adsmith." In "Life and Letters." *Harper's Weekly* 40 (9 May 1896). Reprinted in *Literature and Life: Studies,* 265–72. New York: Harper & Brothers, 1902.

"The Bag of Gold." *Ashtabula Sentinel* 32 (22 April 1863).

Between the Dark and the Daylight, Romances. New York: Harper & Brothers, 1907.

A Boy's Town, Described for "Harper's Young People." New York: Harper & Brothers, 1890.

A Chance Acquaintance. Boston: J. R. Osgood, 1873. *A Selected Edition of W. D. Howells.* Vol. 6, with introduction and notes to the text by Jonathan Thomas and David J. Nordloh. Bloomington: Indiana University Press, 1971.

Christmas Every Day and Other Stories Told for Children. New York: Harper & Brothers, 1893. The title story was reprinted as *Christmas Every Day: A Story Told a Child,* with an introduction by Richard Paul Evans. New York: Pocket, 1996.

Criticism and Fiction. 1891. Reprinted in *Criticism and Fiction, and Other Essays,* edited by Clara M. Kirk and Rudolf Kirk. New York: New York University Press, 1959. Reprinted in *Selected Literary Criticism.* Vol. 2, *1886–1897.* Bloomington: Indiana University Press, 1993. (References are to 1959 edition.)

The Daughter of the Storage and Other Things in Prose and Verse. New York: Harper & Brothers, 1916.

The Day of their Wedding. New York: Harper & Brothers, 1896.

A Day's Pleasure. Boston: J. R. Osgood, 1876. (Reprinted from *Suburban Sketches.*)

A Day's Pleasure and Other Sketches. Boston: Houghton, Mifflin, 1881.

Different Girls. Harper's Novelettes. Edited by William Dean Howells and Henry Mills Alden. New York: Harper & Brothers, 1906.

"Editor's Easy Chair." *Harper's Monthly* 107 (June 1903): 146–50.

"Editor's Easy Chair." *Harper's Monthly* 117 (Oct. 1908): 795–98.

"Editor's Easy Chair." *Harper's Monthly* 120 (March 1910): 633–36.

"Editor's Easy Chair." *Harper's Monthly* 125 (Oct. 1912): 796–99.

"The Emigrant of 1802." *Ashtabula Sentinel* 23 (9 Feb., 9 March, 30 March, 20 April 1854).

"Fast and Firm—A Romance at Marseilles." *Ashtabula Sentinel* 35 (24, 31 Jan. 1866).

"A Fearful Responsibility." *Scribner's* 22 (June, July 1881): 276–93, 390–414.

A Fearful Responsibility and Other Stories. Boston: J. R. Osgood, 1881.

The Flight of Pony Baker: A Boy's Town Story. New York: Harper & Brothers, 1902.

"Floating Down the River on the O-hi-o." (First printed as "Editor's Easy Chair.") *Harper's Monthly* 105 (June 1902): 146–51. Reprinted in *Literature and Life: Studies*, 309–23. New York: Harper & Brothers, 1902.

A Hazard of New Fortunes. 2 vols. New York: Harper & Brothers, 1890. *A Selected Edition of W. D. Howells.* Vol. 16, with introduction by Everett Carter; notes to the text by David J. Nordloh et al. Bloomington: Indiana University Press, 1976.

Hither and Thither in Germany. New York: Harper & Brothers, 1920.

"The Independent Candidate, a Story of Today." *Ashtabula Sentinel* 23–24 (23, 30 Nov., 7, 21, 28 Dec. 1854; 4, 11, 18 Jan. 1855).

Indian Summer. Boston: Ticknor, 1886. *A Selected Edition of W. D. Howells.* Vol. 11, with introduction and notes to the text by Scott Bennett. Bloomington: Indiana University Press, 1971.

Indian Summer notebook. William Dean Howells Papers. Houghton Library, Harvard University.

"The Innocents Abroad." *Atlantic Monthly* 24 (Dec. 1869): 764–66. Reprinted in *My Mark Twain: Reminiscences and Criticisms.* New York: Harper & Brothers, 1910. Reprinted in *Selected Literary Criticism.* Vol. 1, *1859–1885.* Bloomington: Indiana University Press, 1993.

Italian Journeys. New York: Hurd and Houghton, 1867.

The Landlord at Lion's Head. New York: Harper & Brothers, 1897.

The Leatherwood God. New York: The Century Co., 1916. *A Selected Edition of W. D. Howells.* Vol. 27, with introduction and notes to the text by Eugene Pattison. Bloomington: Indiana University Press, 1976.

Letter of 11 March 1906. Houghton Library, Harvard University.

"Letters from a Village." *Ohio Farmer* (30 March, 13 April 1854).

Life in Letters of William Dean Howells. Vol. 1. Edited by Mildred Howells. Garden City, N.Y.: Doubleday, Doran & Co., 1928.

Literary Friends and Acquaintance: A Personal Retrospect of American Authorship. New York: Harper & Brothers, 1900. *A Selected Edition of W. D. Howells.* Vol.

32, edited by David F. Hiatt and Edwin H. Cady. Bloomington: Indiana University Press, 1968.

Literature and Life: Studies. New York: Harper & Brothers, 1902.

"Luke Beazeley." MS at Harvard.

"The Man of Letters as a Man of Business." *Scribner's* 14 (Oct. 1893): 429–45. Reprinted in *Literature and Life: Studies,* 1–35. New York: Harper & Brothers, 1902.

"Materials of a Story." *Harper's Monthly* 84 (May 1892): 942. Reprinted in *Stops of Various Quills.* New York: Harper & Brothers, 1895.

The Minister's Charge, or: The Apprenticeship of Lemuel Barker. Boston: Houghton Mifflin and Co., 1887. *A Selected Edition of W. D. Howells.* Vol. 14, with introduction and notes to the text by Howard M. Munford. Bloomington: Indiana University Press, 1978.

A Modern Instance. Boston: J. R. Osgood, 1882. *A Selected Edition of W. D. Howells.* Vol. 10, with introduction and notes to the text by George N. Bennett. Bloomington: Indiana University Press, 1977.

"My Favorite Novelist and His Best Book." *Munsey's* 17 (April 1897): 18–25. Reprinted in *Selected Literary Criticism: Vol 2, 1886–1897.* Bloomington: Indiana University Press, 1993.

My Literary Passions. New York: Harper & Brothers, 1895.

"A New Year's Glimpse of Memory Land." *Ohio Farmer* (5 Jan. 1854).

"Niagara Revisited, Twelve Years after Their Wedding Journey." *Atlantic Monthly* 51 (May 1883): 598–610. Reprinted as *Niagara Revisited.* Chicago: Dalziell, 1884.

The Night before Christmas, a Morality. Harper's Monthly 120 (Jan. 1910): 207–16. Reprinted in *The Daughter of the Storage and Other Things in Prose and Verse.* New York: Harper & Brothers, 1916.

"An Old-Time Love Affair." *Ashtabula Sentinel* 23 (14 Sept. 1854).

An Open-Eyed Conspiracy: An Idyll of Saratoga. New York: Harper & Brothers, 1897.

"Overland to Venice." *Harper's Monthly* 137 (Nov. 1918): 837–45. Reprinted in *Years of My Youth, and Three Essays. A Selected Edition of W. D. Howells.* Vol. 29, with introduction and notes to the text by David J. Nordloh. Bloomington: Indiana University Press, 1975.

A Pair of Patient Lovers. New York: Harper & Brothers, 1901.

"A Parting and a Meeting, Story." *Cosmopolitan* 18 (Dec. 1894, Jan., Feb. 1895): 183–88, 307–16, 469–74. Reprinted as *A Parting and a Meeting, Story.* New York: Harper & Brothers, 1896.

"A Perfect Goose." *Odd-Fellows Casket* 1 (April 1859): 379–80. Signed Chispa.

"The Pilot's Story." *Atlantic Monthly* 6 (Sept. 1860): 323–25. Reprinted in *Poems.* Boston: J. R. Osgood, 1873.

Quaint Courtships. Harper's Novelettes. Edited by William Dean Howells and Henry Mills Alden. New York: Harper & Brothers, 1906.

The Quality of Mercy. New York: Harper & Brothers, 1892. *A Selected Edition of W. D. Howells.* Vol. 18, with introduction and notes to the text by James P. Elliott. Bloomington: Indiana University Press, 1979.

Questionable Shapes. New York: Harper & Brothers, 1903.

"Recent Literature." *Atlantic Monthly* 40 (Dec. 1877): 753.

The Rise of Silas Lapham. Boston: Ticknor and Co., 1885. *A Selected Edition of W. D. Howells.* Vol. 11, with introduction and notes to the text by Walter J. Meserve. Bloomington: Indiana University Press, 1971.

A Selected Edition of W. D. Howells. Edited by E. H. Cady, Ronald Gottesman, Don L. Cook, and David J. Nordloh. Bloomington: Indiana University Press/ Boston: Twayne, 1968–.

Selected Letters of W. D. Howells. Vol. 1, *1852–1872*. Edited by George Arms et al. Boston: Twayne, 1979.

Selected Letters of W. D. Howells. Vol. 2, *1873–1881*. Edited by George Arms and Christof K. Lohmann. Boston: Twayne, 1979.

Selected Letters of W. D. Howells. Vol. 3, *1882–1891*. Edited by Robert C. Leitz III. Boston: Twayne, 1980.

Selected Letters of W. D. Howells. Vol. 4, *1892–1901*. Edited by Thomas Wortham. Boston: Twayne, 1981.

The Shadow of a Dream. New York: Harper & Brothers, 1890. Reprinted in *The Shadow of a Dream, and An Imperative Duty. A Selected Edition of W. D. Howells.* Vol. 17, with introduction and notes to the text by Martha Banta. Bloomington: Indiana University Press, 1970.

"Some Anomalies of the Short Story." *North American Review* 173 (Sept. 1901): 422–32. Reprinted in *Literature and Life, Studies.* New York: Harper & Brothers, 1902.

The Son of Royal Langbrith. New York: Harper & Brothers, 1904. *A Selected Edition of W. D. Howells.* Vol. 26, with introduction and notes to the text by David Burrows. Bloomington: Indiana University Press, 1969.

Stops of Various Quills. New York: Harper & Brothers, 1895.

"Storage." (First printed as "Editor's Easy Chair.") *Harper's Monthly* 104 (Dec. 1901). Reprinted in *Literature and Life: Studies.* New York: Harper & Brothers, 1902.

Suburban Sketches. New York: Hurd and Houghton, 1871. New and enlarged ed., Boston: J. R. Osgood, 1872.

"A Sunny Day In Winter." *Ohio Farmer* (26 Jan. 1854).

Their Silver Wedding Journey. 2 vols. New York: Harper & Brothers, 1899.

Their Wedding Journey. 1872. *A Selected Edition of W. D. Howells.* Vol. 5, edited by John K. Reeves. Bloomington: Indiana University Press, 1968.

Through the Eye of the Needle, a Romance. New York: Harper & Brothers, 1907. Reprinted in *The Altrurian Romances. A Selected Edition of W. D. Howells.* Vol. 26, with introduction and notes to the text by Clara M. Kirk and Rudolf Kirk. Bloomington: Indiana University Press, 1968.

A Traveler from Altruria, Romance. New York: Harper & Brothers, 1894. Reprinted in *The Altrurian Romances. A Selected Edition of W. D. Howells.* Vol. 26, with introduction and notes to the text by Clara M. Kirk and Rudolf Kirk. Bloomington: Indiana University Press, 1968.

"True, I Talk of Dreams." *Harper's Monthly* 90 (May 1895): 836–45. Reprinted as "I Talk of Dreams" in *Impressions and Experiences.* New York: Harper & Brothers, 1896.

The Undiscovered Country. Boston: Houghton Mifflin, 1880.

Venetian Life. New York: Hurd and Houghton, 1866.

"A Word for the Dead." Anarchist File. William Dean Howells Papers. Houghton Library, Harvard University.

"Worries of a Winter Walk." (First printed as "Life and Letters.") *Harper's Weekly* 41 (3 April 1897): 338–39. Reprinted in *Literature and Life: Studies.* New York: Harper & Brothers, 1902. Reprinted in *Selected Literary Criticism:* Vol. 4. Bloomington: Indiana University Press, 1993.

"Ye Childe and ye angell." *Ashtabula Sentinel* 23 (31 Aug. 1854).

Years of My Youth. New York: Harper & Brothers, 1916. Reprinted in *Years of My Youth, and Three Essays. A Selected Edition of W. D. Howells.* Vol. 29, with introduction and notes to the text by David J. Nordloh. Bloomington: Indiana University Press, 1975.

Howells, William Dean, Henry James, John Bigelow, Thomas Wentworth Higginson, et al. *In After Days: Thoughts on the Future Life.* New York: Harper & Brothers, 1910.

Secondary

Abrams, M. H. *A Glossary of Literary Terms.* 4th ed. New York: Holt, 1981.

Anderson, Sherwood. *Winesburg, Ohio: A Group of Tales of Ohio Small Town Life.* New York: Huebsch, 1919.

Baym, Nina et al. *The Norton Anthology of American Literature.* 4th ed. New York: W. W. Norton, 1994.

Bellamy, Michael O. "Eros and Thanatos in William Dean Howells's 'Editha.'" *American Literary Realism* 12 (Autumn 1979): 283–87.

Bennett, George N. *The Realism of William Dean Howells, 1889–1920.* Nashville: Vanderbilt University Press, 1973.

———. *William Dean Howells: The Development of a Novelist.* Norman: University of Oklahoma Press, 1959.

Berkove, Lawrence. "'A Difficult Case': W. D. Howells's Impression of Mark Twain." *Studies in Short Fiction* 31 (Fall 1994): 607–15.

Blackstock, Graham Belcher. "Howells's Opinions on the Religious Conflicts of His Age as Exhibited in Magazine Articles." In *Howells: A Century of Criticism,* edited by Kenneth Eble, 203–18. Dallas: Southern Methodist University Press, 1962. 203–218.

Brenni, Vito J. *William Dean Howells: A Bibliography.* Metuchen, N.J.: Scarecrow, 1973.

Brodhead, Richard H. "Hawthorne Among the Realists: The Case of Howells." In *American Realism: New Essays,* edited by Eric Sundquist, 25–41. Baltimore: Johns Hopkins University Press, 1982.

Brooks, Cleanth et al. *American Literature: The Makers and the Making.* Vol. 2. New York: St. Martin's, 1973.

Brooks, Van Wyck. *Howells: His Life and World.* New York: Dutton, 1959.

Brown, Norman O. *Life against Death: The Psychoanalytical Meaning of History.* Middletown, Ct.: Wesleyan University Press, 1959.

Budd, Louis J. "W. D. Howells' Defense of the Romance." *Publications of the Modern Language Association* 67 (March 1952): 32–42.

Cady, Edwin. "Howells on the River." *American Literary Realism* 25 (Spring 1993): 27–41.

———. *The Light of Common Day: Realism in American Fiction.* Bloomington: Indiana University Press, 1971.

———. *The Realist at War: The Mature Years, 1885–1920, of William Dean Howells.* Syracuse: Syracuse University Press, 1958.

———. *The Road to Realism: The Early Years, 1837–1885, of William Dean Howells.* Syracuse: Syracuse University Press, 1956.

———. "William Dean Howells and the Ashtabula Sentinel." *Ohio State Archaeological and Historical Quarterly* 53 (Jan.–March 1944): 39–51.

Campbell, Charles L. "Realism and the Romance of Real Life: Multiple Fictional Worlds in Howells' Novels." *Modern Fiction Studies* 16 (Autumn 1970): 289–302.

Carrington, George C., Jr. "Howells' Christmas Sketches: The Uses of Allegory." *American Literary Realism* 10 (Summer 1977): 242–53.

———. "Howells and the Dramatic Essay." *American Literary Realism* 17 (Spring 1984): 44–66.

———. *The Immense Complex Drama: The World and Art of the Howells Novel.* Columbus: Ohio State University Press, 1966.

Carrington, George C., Jr. and Ildikó de Papp Carrington. *Plots and Characters in the Fiction of William Dean Howells.* Hamden, CT: Archon, 1976.

Carter, Everett. *Howells and the Age of Realism.* Philadelphia: Lippincott, 1954.

Cook, Don L. "Realism and the Dangers of Parody in W. D. Howells' Fiction." *The Old Northwest* 8 (Spring 1982): 69–80.

Crawford, E. A., and Teresa Kennedy, eds. *The Christmas Sampler: Classic Stories of the Season, from Twain to Cheever.* New York: Hyperion, 1992.

Cronkhite, G. Ferris. "Howells Turns to the Inner Life." *New England Quarterly* 30 (Dec. 1957): 474–85.

Crow, Charles. "Howells and William James: 'A Case of Metaphantasmia' Solved." *American Quarterly* 27 (May 1975): 169–77.

Crowley, John W. *The Black Heart's Truth: The Early Career of W. D. Howells.* Chapel Hill: University of North Carolina Press, 1985.

————. "Howells in the Eighties: A Review of Criticism, Part I." *ESQ* 32 (4th Quarter, 1986): 253–77.

————. "Howells's Obscure Hurt." *Journal of American Studies* 9 (Aug. 1975): 199–211.

————. *The Mask of Fiction: Essays on W. D. Howells.* Amherst, Mass.: University of Massachusetts Press, 1989.

————. "Winifred Howells and the Economy of Pain." *The Old Northwest* 10 (Spring 1984): 41–75.

Crowley, John W. and Charles Crow. "Psychic and Psychological Themes in Howells' 'A Sleep and a Forgetting.'" *ESQ* 23 (1st Quarter, 1977): 41–51.

Dana, Richard Henry. *Two Years before the Mast.* New York: Harper, 1840.

Daugherty, Sarah B. "Howells Reviews James: The Transcendence of Realism." *American Literary Realism* 18 (Spring 1985): 147–67.

Eble, Kenneth. *William Dean Howells.* 2d ed. TUSAS. Boston: Twayne, 1982.

Eichelberger, Clayton. *Published Comment on William Dean Howells through 1920: A Research Bibliography.* Boston: Hall, 1976.

Elliot, Emory, gen. ed. *American Literature: A Prentice Hall Anthology.* Englewood Cliffs, N.J.: Prentice Hall, 1991.

Evans, Richard Paul. *The Christmas Box.* New York: Simon & Schuster, 1993.

Ferlazzo, Paul J. "William Dean Howells." *Dictionary of Literary Biography:* Vol. 74, *American Short-Story Writers Before 1880*, edited by Bobby Ellen Kimbel with the assistance of William E. Grant. Detroit: Gale, 1988.

Feigenoff, Charles. "'His Apparition': The Howells No One Believes In." *American Literary Realism* 13 (Spring 1980): 85–89.

Firkins, Oscar W. *William Dean Howells: A Study.* Cambridge: Harvard University Press, 1924. Reprint, New York: Russell & Russell, 1963.

Fischer, William C., Jr. "William Dean Howells: Reverie and the Nonsymbolic Aesthetic." *Nineteenth Century Fiction* 25 (June 1970): 1–30.

Fitzgerald, F. Scott. "Babylon Revisited." *Saturday Evening Post* (21 Feb. 1931). Reprinted in *Taps at Reveille.* New York: Scribner, 1935.

Fox, Arnold B. "Howells' Doctrine of Complicity." In *Howells: A Century of Criti-*

cism, edited by Kenneth Eble. Dallas: Southern Methodist University Press, 1962: 196–202.

————. "Spiritualism and the 'Supernatural' in William Dean Howells." *The Journal of the American Society for Psychical Research* 53 (Oct. 1959): 121–30.

Free, William J. "Howells' 'Editha' and Pragmatic Belief." *Studies in Short Fiction* 3 (Spring 1966): 285–92.

Fryckstedt, Olov W. *In Quest of America: A Study of Howells' Early Development as a Novelist.* Cambridge, Mass: Harvard University Press, 1958.

Furia, Philip. "'Editha': The Feminine View." *American Literary Realism* 12 (Aug. 1979): 278–82.

Gibson, William M. "W. D. Howells and 'The Ridiculous Human Heart.'" *Studies in American Humor* 2 (April 1975): 32–45.

Gibson, William M. and George Arms. *A Bibliography of William Dean Howells.* New York: New York Public Library, 1948.

Gillespie, Robert. "The Fictions of Basil March." *Colby Library Quarterly* 12 (March 1976): 14–28.

Harris, Susan K. "Vicious Binaries: Gender and Authorial Paranoia in Dreiser's 'Second Choice,' Howells' 'Editha,' and Hemingway's 'The Short Happy Life of Francis Macomber.'" *College Literature* 20 (June 1993): 70–82.

Humma, John B. "Howells' 'Editha': An American Allegory." *Markham Review* 8 (Summer 1979): 77–80.

Ibsen, Henrik. *Ghosts.* 1881. Reprinted in *The Oxford Ibsen* Vol. 5. Trans. and ed. by James Walter McFarlane. London: Oxford University Press, 1961.

James, Henry. "The Beast in the Jungle." In *The Better Sort.* 1903. Reprinted in *The Altar of the Dead.* (New York Edition, Vol. 17) 1909. Also in *Tales of Henry James*, edited by Christof Wegelin. New York: Norton, 1984. 277–312.

James, William. *The Principles of Psychology.* New York: Holt, 1891.

Joyce, James. "The Boarding House." In *Dubliners.* 1914. Reprint, edited by Robert Scholes in consultation with Richard Ellman, New York: Viking, 1967.

Kehler, Harold. "Howells' EDITHA." *Explicator* 19 (1961), item 41.

Kerr, Howard. *Mediums, and Spirit-Rappers, and Roaring Radicals: Spiritualism in American Literature, 1850–1900.* Urbana, Ill.: University of Illinois Press,1972.

Kirk, Clara M. and Rudolf Kirk. *William Dean Howells.* New York: Twayne, 1962.

Klinkowitz, Jerome. "Ethic and Aesthetic: The Basil and Isabel March Stories of William Dean Howells." *Modern Fiction Studies* 16 (Autumn 1970): 303–22.

Lauter, Paul, gen. ed. *The Heath Anthology of American Literature.* Lexington, Mass.: D. C. Heath, 1994.

Leahey, Thomas H. "William James, Heroic Metaphysician." Rev. of *William James: His Life and Thought* by Gerald E. Myers and *William James: Selected*

Unpublished Correspondence 1885–1910, edited by Frederick J. Down Scott. *Contemporary Psychology* 33: 3 (1988): 199–202.

Lloyd-Smith, Allan Gardner. *Uncanny American Fiction: Medusa's Face*. New York: St. Martin's Press, 1989.

Lubbock, Percy, ed. *The Letters of Henry James*. Vol. 1. New York: Scribner, 1920.

Lynn, Kenneth. *William Dean Howells: An American Life*. New York: Harcourt, 1971.

Marler, Robert F., Jr. "'A Dream': Howells' Early Contribution to the American Short Story." *The Journal of Narrative Technique* 4 (Jan. 1974): 75–85.

McQuade, Donald, gen. ed. *The Harper American Literature*. New York: Harper, 1987.

Meserve, Walter J., ed. *The Complete Plays of W. D. Howells*. New York: New York University Press, 1960.

Mitchell, Donald Grant [Ik Marvel, pseud.]. *The Reveries of a Bachelor, or, A Book of the Heart*. New York: Burt, 1850.

———. *Dream Life: A Fable of the Seasons*. New York: Scribner, 1852.

Moore, Clement C. "A Visit from St. Nicholas." New York: Spalding and Shepard, 1849.

Mordell, Albert. *Discovery of a Genius, William Dean Howells and Henry James*. New York: Twayne, 1961.

Murphy, Brenda. "Laughing Society to Scorn: The Domestic Farces of William Dean Howells." *Studies in American Humor* N.S. 1 (Oct. 1982): 119–29.

Myers, F. W. H. *Human Personality and Its Survival of Bodily Death*. New York and London: Longmans, Green, 1903.

Nettels, Elsa. "Howells's 'A Circle in the Water' and Fitzgerald's 'Babylon Revisited.'" *Studies in Short Fiction* 19 (Summer 1982): 261–67.

Norris, Frank. "A Plea for Romantic Fiction." *The Responsibilities of the Novelist*. 1903. Reprint, Garden City, New York: Doubleday, Doran & Co., 1928.

Olsen, Rodney. *Dancing in Chains: The Youth of William Dean Howells*. New York: New York University Press, 1991.

Perkins, George and Barbara Perkins. *The American Tradition in Literature*. 8th ed. New York: McGraw Hill, 1994.

Piacentino, Edward J. "Arms in Love and War in Howells' 'Editha.'" *Studies in Short Fiction* 24 (Fall 1987): 425–32.

Prioleau, Elizabeth Stevens. *The Circle of Eros: Sexuality in the Work of William Dean Howells*. Durham, N.C.: Duke University Press, 1983.

Reeves, John K. "Literary Manuscripts of William Dean Howells." *Bulletin, New York Public Library* (June and July 1958): 267–78, 350–63.

Sandburg, Carl. *Rootabaga Stories*. New York: Harcourt, Brace, 1922.

Simon, Myron. "Howells on Romantic Fiction." *Studies in Short Fiction* 2 (Spring 1965): 241–46.

Simpson, Lewis P. "The Treason of William Dean Howells." In *The Man of Letters in New England and the South*, 85–128. Baton Rouge: Louisiana State University Press, 1973.

Smith, Henry Nash, William M. Gibson, and Frederick Anderson. *Mark Twain–Howells Letters: The Correspondence of Samuel L. Clemens and William D. Howells, 1872–1910.* 2 vols. Cambridge: Harvard University Press, 1960.

Tarkington, Booth. "Mr. Howells." *Harper's Monthly* 141 (Aug. 1920): 346–50.

Twain, Mark. *The Innocents Abroad.* Hartford, Ct.: American Publishing Co., 1869.

———."The McWilliamses and the Burglar Alarm." In *The Complete Short Stories of Mark Twain*, edited by Charles Neider. New York: Doubleday, 1957.

———. "To the Person Sitting in Darkness." In *A Pen Warmed-up in Hell: Mark Twain in Protest*, edited by Frederick Anderson. New York: Harper and Row, 1972.

———. *Which Was the Dream?* In *Which Was the Dream? and Other Symbolic Writings of the Later Years*, edited by John S. Tuckey. Berkeley: University of California Press, 1968.

Vanderbilt, Kermit. *The Achievement of William Dean Howells: A Reinterpretation.* Princeton: Princeton University Press, 1968.

Wagenknecht, Edward. *William Dean Howells: The Friendly Eye.* New York: Oxford University Press, 1969.

Webster's Third New International Dictionary of the English Language. Unabridged. Springfield, Mass.: Merriam-Webster, 1986.

Wheeler, Edward J., ed. Preface to "The Return to Favor" by William Dean Howells. *Current Opinion* 61 (July 1916): 57–58.

Woodress, James. *Howells and Italy.* Durham, N.C.: Duke University Press, 1952.

Wortham, Thomas, ed. *The Early Prose Writings of William Dean Howells: 1853–1861.* Athens, Ohio: Ohio University Press, 1990.

———. Personal letter. 5 February 1991.